# The
# African Boy Legend

### and

# The
# American Girl Superstar

## Adventure, Dreams and Sports in the Rip-Roaring 2020s

King Atlas V

*Atlantean V Bookworks*
*Naples, FL*

King Atlas V/Atlantean V Bookworks
P.O. Box 9651
Naples, FL/34101
https://www.amazon.com/author/kingatlasv

Publisher's Note: This is a work of fiction. Names, characters, places, and
incidents are a product of the author's imagination. Locales and public
names are sometimes used for atmospheric purposes. Any resemblance
to actual people, living or dead, or to businesses, companies, events, institutions, or locales is completely coincidental.

Book Layout & Design ©2017 - BookDesignTemplates.com

Image        E-Book        Cover-        Copyright:        <a
href="https://www.123rf.com/profile_ndphoto">ndphoto / 123RF Stock
Photo</a>

The African Boy Legend and The American Girl Superstar/ King Atlas V
-- 1st ed.
ISBN 978-0-9985856-8-0 (paperback)

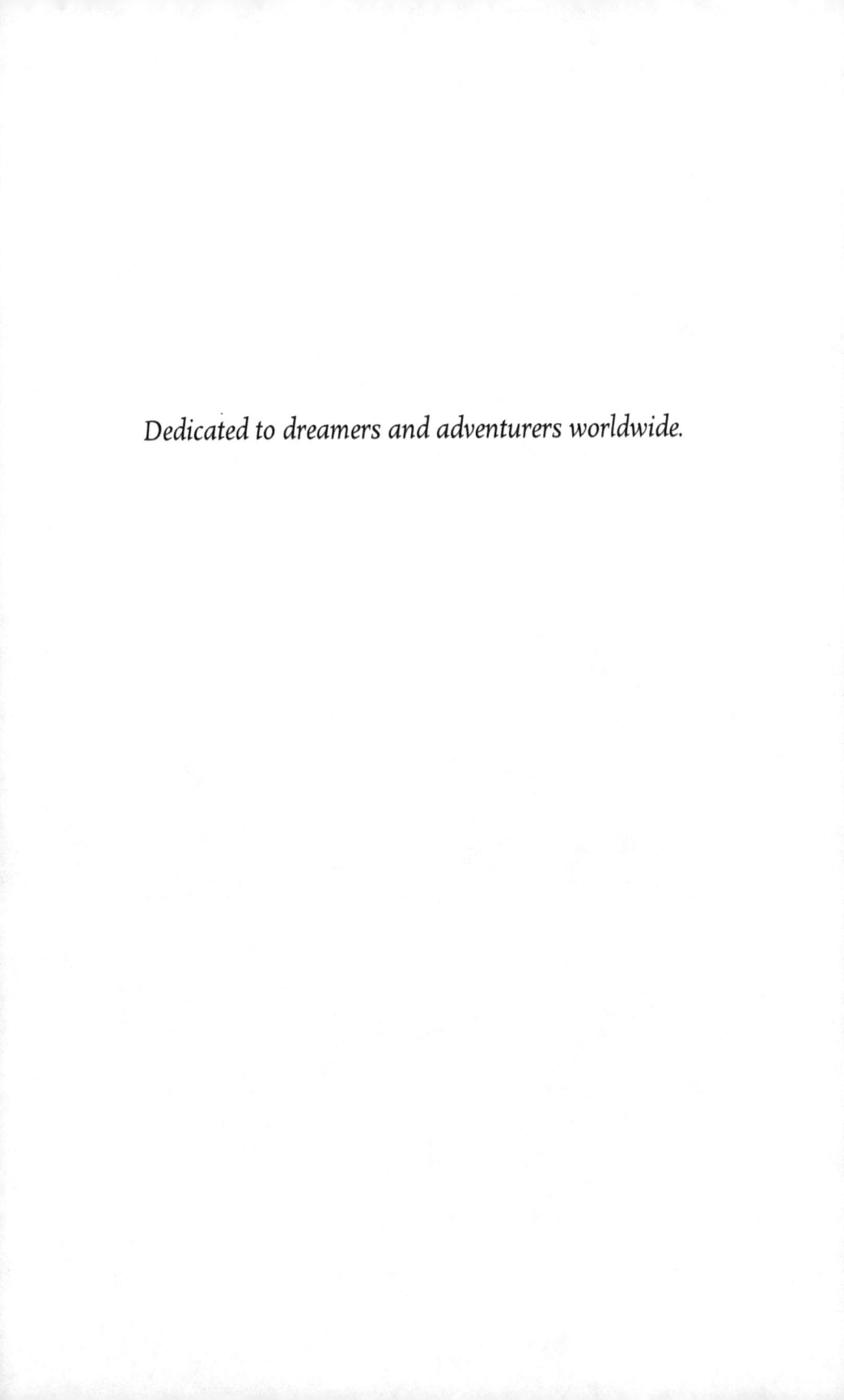

*Dedicated to dreamers and adventurers worldwide.*

*"The Parallel Dream Universe folds into the Real Universe"*

–Africus

# Table of Contents

# 1.

*August 17, 2008*
*Beijing, China*

T HE MAN WITH NO NAME sat next to Francis Stewart. The crowd roared as the women sprinters entered the stadium for the finals of the women's 100-meter sprint at the Beijing National Stadium. In the fifth lane was Great Britain's national sprint champion, Samantha Kensington, from London. She was favored to place fourth or fifth with the American sprinter, behind the three sprinters from Jamaica.

The man with no name spoke to Sir Francis Stewart of Africa.

"And the Crown has been informed?"

"Yes, they are on board."

"And the Nobel prize for physics was awarded to Great Britain's preeminent theoretical physics professor last week."

"All is as planned."

# 2.

HALEY ANDREWS BREATHLESSLY WHISPERED to her husband through her Bluetooth device, brushing aside her blonde hair from her forehead.

"He is the one."

A former Nebraska State soccer star and club lacrosse star, she had left her home in Nebraska to follow her boyfriend and future husband, a Nebraska State football star, to the Preserve in East Africa.

Haley watched the boy, eleven-years old and bronzed by the African sun, sprint ahead through the tall brown grass of the African savannah. Two large male African lions flanked him. The moonlight glistened off his blonde shoulder length hair. He gripped a steel blade between his teeth. His muscular frame glistened in the light. He heard the lions roar, and he roared with them, as they chased their prey. The boy broke left to follow one of the wildebeests.

He flung his knife in a deadly toss, right into its jugular. Two eagles watched from above.

Haley witnessed the successful hunt- six fallen adult wildebeest. The lions began to feast on their conquests.

Haley watched her husband, Mika, the lead ranger in the West Kenya National Wildlife Preserve, put his smart device away in its case. She knew he had snapped some photos of the African Boy Legend. *Likely the first photo of the legendary boy! And now it is safely stored away!*

After years of life together in the savannah of East Africa, she still marveled as her husband's frame- the broad shoulders, long legs and thin waist, the jet-black hair and low hairline, and a square powerful jaw. But mostly she loved is ocean blue eyes. She loved his native American heritage, too.

Mika turned to his wife, trembling. "The legend is true! The one the local tribes call the lion boy, and the African Boy Legend. He is the one I see in my dreams."

The leader of the lion pride, one of the lions running with the African Boy Legend, saw Mika and his wife. He roared loudly and stepped towards them, staring at Mika. Mika snapped some more photos.

"Let's go now, before the lion charges us. We don't want to shoot any lions," Mika quietly whispered to Haley.

"I will call him Africus. I saw him often in my dreams. I was told to call him Africus in my dreams. The male name for Africa. The Roman god of the wind. The boy is the prince of Africa. He communicates with the birds and the animals. We have watched the birds follow him. Look at the two eagles in the sky now. He flies like the wind and runs with the lions," he added.

"Now!" he raised his voice, as the lion leader walked closer towards them and the rest of the pride watched. They jumped in their land vehicle and sped off.

# 3.

S AVANNAH PROVIDENCE STEWART sat in her seat looking out at the sparse trees on the savannah of western Kenya. Golden grass swayed for miles with the wind. She daydreamed about her close encounter the year the before. She knew the safari would stop soon to take photographs of the lions. She remembered this exact spot from the year before. There was the very large male lion, likely the king of the lion pride. And a number of female lions. She remembered a cheetah sprinting to no particular place, and the two soaring eagles. It all seemed so surreal. It was early afternoon, just like the year before, when lions did not hunt.

The stop was near. A cheetah, *maybe the same cheetah*, sprinted along her vehicle, as if it knew her. She heard a ferocious roar, and then saw the same large male lion. Her adrenaline fired through her body. The lead car of the safari stopped. Soon tourists were snapping pictures of the male lion and two female lions. The lions looked on in disinterest, much to the delight of the frightened tourists. And then she saw the *tree*, surrounded by some brush.

She daydreamed about her moment by the *tree* twelve months ago. She had approached the *tree*. She had felt *his* presence. But before the magical moment, her father, Daddy to her, had called her back. For a full year, she carried the thought of *what if?* And now, she wondered, *is he here again? Was he really here last year?*

Her father called her Providence when in Africa, Savannah everywhere else. She stepped out of the largest of the vehicles. She was wearing khaki shorts and a sleeveless khaki shirt. She was still just a girl, with flowing locks of blonde hair, and eyes that reflected the deep blue of the clear sky. White socks and boots adorned her feet. She was comfortable even in the morning heat, even as the guards were perspiring. Her father, a white-haired man with a white beard, held her hand and led her to another vehicle.

She stepped out of the vehicle after going to the toilet. Providence watched her father. He was barking commands to the tourists to stay close to the vehicles and to not approach the resting lions.

She took that opportunity to drift away towards the *tree*. She was now certain it had been *him* the year before, *the African Boy Legend, the lion boy. It is the same lion pride; his lion pride!*

She approached the *tree*. It was over one hundred feet from the road. She trembled in expectation. She went unnoticed by the tourists and the guards, all of whom focused on the lions. The large male lion gave out roar, as she sauntered over to the tree. *A gratuitous and well-timed roar?* She felt the same presence as the year before, even smelled the same odor, not foul smelling, but an odor of some animal that lives outdoors. She glimpsed back at the vehicle train. Her father was in a heated argument with one of the male tourists, a wealthy athlete from England, who felt entitled to march where he pleased.

She hesitated, *maybe it is an animal behind the tree*. She now hoped a guard did have a ready gun. She almost panicked and screamed. But calmness and tranquility overcame her. A feeling she could not express. She boldly touched the tree with her left palm and circled left around the *tree*. She was now out of sight from the safari vehicles. She knew that to a guard, that would mean she was gone forever. There was no turning back once you joined the savannah. Humans had succeeded in Africa as teams, but rarely as individuals. She knew she was risking her life. But she pressed on. There was no one on the other side of the *tree*, but she still felt *his* presence. The smell was stronger. For her, it was a chance to meet a legend, a myth, a fantasy, not the boring and boorish rich boys at her posh private schools.

A female lion had slithered into the tall grass near the *tree*, unnoticed by the guards. It burst forth through the brush. Fear jolted her. *My life is over; how could I really believe the legend and myth were true!* But her fear was joined by disappointment. *There is no African Boy Legend*. The fear and disappointment overwhelmed her as she fell back in fright.

She saw a billowy white cloud in the sky as she fell backwards. *I am on my way to heaven*. But her senses awoke again, and she felt the small but strong arms of a boy wrapped around her from behind. She smelled him again. She was initially startled. He freed her, and she stood up and turned to face him. His stare calmed her. His blue eyes were as brilliant as hers. He was bronzed from the sun, and his long blonde hair bleached from the daily intense equatorial heat, was as shiny as hers. She saw years of life in his young eyes, more than most men would ever experience. She shivered in awe at the legend before her. *The legend is real, or is this a dream, or maybe both!*

"The African Boy Legend?" She whispered. "Lion Boy?"

The boy thought she was calling him familiar names. He had heard the tribesman call him those names, sometimes when he joined them for a trek. He knew it was about his relationship with the pride. But he did not speak English, only some rudimentary native dialect with the local tribesman. Although sometimes the English words seemed familiar.

He pointed to himself and nodded. Silence gripped the two of them. He pointed to his heart and then to her. She blushed and smiled and did the same. He smiled back. He didn't know what else to do. Their thoughts swirled. *I want her to take my hand and take me to the safari. I want him to take my hand and take me to the savannah.* Their bodies still trembled in young love. She had day dreamed about this moment for as long as she could remember; when she had heard of the legend that a young boy was raised and protected by a lion pride in east Africa, deep into the savannah and the jungle, away from the rangers and most safaris. Occasionally, a tribesman would tell game hunters that the legend was true.

They stepped closer together. Their hands embraced in a tender young moment. Her dream had come true. His visions had come to pass.

"Providence!!" boomed the voice of her father, whose large barrel like chest could belt out a yell heard for miles.

"Boom! Boom!" cracked the sound of rifles in the air.

The large male lion roared fearing the African Boy Legend might be in great danger. He charged in the direction of the *tree* and roared again. The African Boy Legend knew the distress call. He kissed Providence, simply, the Girl to him, softly on the lips, and swiftly ran away from the safari, low among the tall grasses. He remembered her from the year before, too.

The large male lion saw the African Boy Legend was running to safety. He himself hid below the tall grasses. Even the guards would not traverse the grasses knowing a large male lion was about.

Providence was overwhelmed with emotion and fear. She shrieked loudly, calling for her Daddy to save her. The guards focus turned away from the lions and to the *tree*. Running at a full gallop with guns in the air, they reached the tree. Providence had fainted. They thought she was dead, possibly bitten by a snake. Her father picked her up in his powerful bronzed arms, fearing the worst. He should have known. She had gone to this same tree the year before.

But she was breathing. Oh, she was breathing. He hurried her back to the medical vehicle. A doctor examined her. He determined she was fine, but in temporary shock. They kept her there for the next two days of the safari. She thought of the African Boy Legend, the lion boy. *Someday.*

The African Boy Legend watched the safari trek away, and with it his dreams. He was unsure if she would ever be back. But she now had a name, Providence.

*Someday.*

# 4.

Friday, May 16, 2025
Jefferson City, Nebraska

THE HEAD FOOTBALL coach looked at his administrator with glaring eyes.

"We are missing one difference maker for this football team. We are so close!"

Jason Smith sat back in his office, now his second year as head coach of the Nebraska State, the University, football team. It was the only division one football program in the state. He was six feet four, with powerful arms and broad shoulders. He had jet dark hair. He knew it was a new era in college football. Four super conferences, each with twenty teams and two divisions, had been formed and loosely based on geographic location. Nebraska State had joined the Conference of the North. Importantly for Nebraska State, Oklahoma was in their ten team Western Division. The renewed rivalry and new conference format were generating phenomenal interest among the Nebraska State faithful, and the Socialverse was bursting with excitement.

Old mid-west stalwarts and rivals Iowa and Wisconsin were also in their division, as well as Kansas. Texas had joined the Conference of the South, renewing its rivalry with Texas A&M, much to the relief of Nebraska State fans, he thought.

"Well, we won the old conference titles in 2019 and 2020 and 2023, and the big one, the national title, in 2020 and 2023, with help from the California, Florida and Texas kids at the skill positions. Maybe we should focus on those states," offered Shannon Garrison, an administrator from the recruiting group, sitting across from him in his office, breaking a medium smile, and revealing her bright sparkling white front teeth.

"Too late for the Class of 2025!" the coach bellowed.

"Yes, but for next year we have great relationships with high school coaches in Florida and Texas, set up by our former legendary coach," Shannon countered.

"Check out the network of our former players. See what leads we may have. Maybe a diamond in the extreme rough is still out there for 2025," Coach Smith ordered with his deep voice.

"Well, we just landed our manned mission to Mars! Former safety Jock Owens, Class of '22, is one of the astronauts! We can be the first to recruit Mars!" Shannon laughed, flipping back her blonde hair with her well-toned arms. Her loose white blouse ruffled as she held her head high.

"I like your forward thinking. The Rip-Roaring 2020s continue to roar! And Wilderness Ventures of Omaha was a lead investor of that government-private venture to Mars!" Smith smiled bemusedly.

"Yes, they call this decade the Rip-Roaring 2020s, just like the Roaring Twenties in the 1900s! And the roar is louder this time around, so I see why they added the Rip!" Shannon exclaimed.

"Yes, hopefully, 2029 is a better year than 1929! But back to football. It took a few years, but college football has now caught up to the roar of the twenties, with the new super conferences and the post season tourney. We need to keep up as well. I realize 2025 may not be a championship year, but I can still dream about that one magical player! But for 2026 and beyond, seriously, for Nebraska State to compete, we need some more top athletes, particularly a difference maker at quarterback, as our starter is a senior. He is a great passer. But in our conference, that is not enough for a championship. We need a dual threat. Like the quarterbacks of the former coach. Texas and Louisiana have been a pipe-line, but our bread and butter is our five-hundred-mile ra-dius. Keep recruiting to our strength. As you say, we have coaches in Florida and Texas that love our program. And yes, start looking in California again. But if you find one diamond in the rough for this year, on Mars, California or wherever, that would be monumental for you! Get to work!" Smith scratched his chin and nodded his head as he spoke to the attractive administrator.

"Don't forget to turn in your cash currency for digital currency by May 15!" Shannon admonished. "Imagine our kids growing up today with no credit cards and no cash currency! Two more ways of life dumped into the Great Dumpster of obsolescence. Things are happening so quickly in the Rip-Roaring 2020s!"

"Yeah, the Currency Act of 2023 D-Day has arrived. Cash will no longer be legal tender. The government is assessing an excise tax on all cash conversions in excess of $10,000 in exchange for tax amnesty. The government is going to use the expected bump in tax revenue from the cash conversion to help pay off the debt used to finance the Great Infrastructure Act of 2020, and, if our President has her way, for space exploration!" she continued.

"Our whole financial life is now so digital and transparent and incorruptible! And use of the digital Z currency and other cryptocurrencies is a new way of life. Blockchain technology, and the new great distributable decentralized database built up on the blockchains and nodes, or the Internet III, really took off this decade. So many life activities are shared and peer to peer. Identity theft is almost gone, too! I get paid some cryptos every month for my data on purchasing decisions! So cool. What will the thirties bring?" She added in awe.

"More science fiction will become non-fiction! Space! That is my bet!" The coach drifted off into the deep caverns of his mind.

"Or internal or inner space! Maybe they are one in the same!" she laughed.

"Enough, find me some recruits!"

# 5.

MIKA WATCHED AFRICUS, now eighteen, chase the wildebeest to the west. He had been with Africus for seven years now. Storm season had ended, and the rangers had to shepherd the Preserve animals to the ground in the west, where there was ample vegetation. The animals always seemed to follow Africus's commands. A special relationship existed between Africus and the animal kingdom that was not discernible to the common eye, but one that Mika saw every day. One that Mika himself possessed. The wildebeest dutifully marched westward toward the highlands. Lions lazily watched in the hot humid weather, waiting for the sun to fall below the horizon. Every few hours they would walk with the herd.

Mika wiped the sweat from his brow. He looked over to Africus, who was at his side. Both were wearing their ranger khaki shorts and short sleeve shirts, but modern and made of wicking material. Mika was wearing a wide brimmed hat over his short cropped black hair. Africus simply wore a headband to hold his shoulder length blonde hair in place. Both were broad shouldered and deeply bronzed. Mika wore boots, while Africus was barefoot.

Africus walked away from Mika and turned to look at him. "Look at the lions, they watch me and listen. I told them NO hunting today. The herds must move forward," Africus said with pride.

"I understand. I have been connected to the animal kingdom since my days on the Native American reservation as a child. It is one of the reasons I came to this Preserve in Africa," Mika reminded the young Africus.

"We both have a special bond with the animal world. And the spiritual and dream worlds of the Parallel Dream Universe!" Africus winked at Mika.

"And your magical places that you visit in the Parallel Dream Universe!"

"When I was young in the jungle, I could do more than dream of them. I went to those magical places, with my friends. They were in real places!"

"Yes, someday, I would like to go to those places with you. But, I thought you only saw them in your dreams. I don't understand how you saw them in reality. You have not told me this before."

"Later. I will show you. Someday."

"Yes, someday."

"Well, African Boy Legend, lion boy."

"Yeah?"

Mika looked away to the western horizon and spoke.

"Haley and I have been thinking. We believe Nebraska State, the University, is a special place, and one that may be special for you, too."

"Nebraska State, the University. Both of your alma maters. Why, did you talk to them?"

Mika took the opening to promote his alma mater. "We have not talked to them. Not yet! But I shall! But, I think it is a fantastic University, and it is in the heart of America, both geographically and economically. We can help you gain admittance. I am sure once they knew more about you, the coaches would be thrilled to have you play football there!"

"Football. You and I have always had that in the back of our minds. I have played many games in my dream worlds."

"Yes, I know. And the Girl! Just maybe she is more than a girl in your Parallel Dream Universe!"

"Yes, contact them. Let's see what they say."

Africus headed back to the savannah that he knew so well and loved so much. *Nebraska State, the University. So, Mika and Haley want me to go to their alma mater to play football and maybe lacrosse. Mika and Haley often talk about Nebraska State, but until now have never asked that I go there. I thought they wanted me to stay in the Preserve. Then again, I know that is not true. America! Football! The Girl. Is she in America?*

But for now, he had work to do with his animal kingdom.

# 6.

COACH SMITH PONDERED the new football world, safe in his office, high up in the administrative facilities inside the football stadium. His high school summer football camps had started at Nebraska State. Some of the nation's best athletes were in attendance, excited for the opportunity to play in a super conference atmosphere. An eleven-game tourney, consisting of four conference championship games, and then an eight-team bracket with the four conference winners and four at large teams, was in their minds and imagination. The second-round games were hosted by the conference champions. The semi-final games and title game were held at designated venues. They dreamed of leading their teams to the tourney, and the national title game. But first they had to establish themselves at the various summer camps. No signings were permitted until December 1 of their senior seasons, the early national signing day. The second national signing day was the first Wednesday in February. Shannon knocked on his door to break his thoughts.

"Shannon, come in. Have a seat in one of our posture perfect modern chairs. Good for your posture and back.

"I see we have twelve young men from Florida, California and Texas at the camps, and twenty-five from the five-hundred-mile radius. You work quickly!" Coach Smith chuckled with Shannon Garrison.

"Yes, so many players like the idea of Nebraska State. A number of key and exciting games, a huge rivalry game, the tradition, the facilities, the fans, the state, and the new agri-tech district that rivals the tech districts of Silicon Valley, Austin and Boston. Our agri-tech research and development, patents, products and resulting booming commercial complex have helped change society. The SuperENZ products manufactured here have transformed the weight loss industry. The FoodBarCodes 3D copy machines produce amazing food products. The machines and the related food inputs are all produced here in the heartland and are gathering enormous popularity for the kitchen fearing generations. Our SUPERSNACKS are so loaded with all the required nutrients and energy producers, we can't produce enough of them. And the new sugar substitutes, all organic and fat based, have eliminated the evils of sugar and last decade's artificial sweeteners. Soda drinks are still a passion for us all. We saved that industry. We are big contributors to these Rip-Roaring 2020s. We have a lot to offer. A safe, family oriented and fun culture. We got it! We are front and center for these Rip-Roaring 2020s!" Shannon replied.

"Ok! But any leads for one final magical player for 2025? Any players from Mars!" The coached searched her eyes.

"Interestingly, I did receive a text last Friday, from the legend, Mika Williams, a graduate and player from 2010. He read online that I was recruiting on Mars. So, he thought

Africa was in play! He is now a ranger at a Preserve in West Kenya. He may have been joking, but he said he has a very special protégé, a young boy that he has taken under his care as a foster parent. Says the kid has not played organized sports, is undecided about going to a 'University', and loves the jungle. But, that he has intangibles that he cannot explain. And he is tall and can fly with the wind. I have not responded to him yet. I was going to text him today. Want me to fly to Africa!!" Shannon continued, now searching the head coach's eyes for a reaction.

"I remember the legend. An All-American safety. He was Native American. A member of the Omaha Tribe of Nebraska. He was so gifted. They say he had a sixth sense. He was always there for the tackle or the pass breakup. As if he knew the play. They say he tapped into his spiritual world during the games. He was amazing. He would have played professionally if he had not destroyed his shoulder on that tackle in a New Year's Day Bowl game. Follow-up. But, honestly, I see this as a ruse. A superhero from the jungle, come on! It certainly is not his son. He is not old enough."

"I said foster son. But, yeah, it's not his son with his legendary genes. I will see what I can do, and yeah, it seems far-fetched," Shannon shrugged, looking down as she left.

Shannon retreated to her office. She ran the idea by her assistant AD. She wanted to make sure that this purported player from overseas would be eligible to play. The assistant AD told her that Mika had married Haley Andrews, a Nebraska State soccer star, and that they did not have any children when they left for Africa. *Clearly, not his son, but he did say foster son.*

The assistant AD informed her that the recruit would be eligible to play if his school was accredited by the Kenyan national government. She searched the internet and found the Kent School as the school for kids from the Preserve in

West Kenya. She was pleased to see that the school was accredited. It was an excellent school. It was where the kids of ambassadors went. She suddenly fantasized seeing herself interviewed by the local and national media for *the one that found the world class athlete that no one else could find.* Awards and accolades, maybe even promotions and endorsements, could come her way. Maybe a job as a national sports commentator at a national sports media conglomerate. Maybe a super new boyfriend, as her heart still burned from her break-up with another Nebraska assistant who went on to manage a *Euro football-soccer-whatever!* team and dumped her for a Parisian model. But Coach Smith would be so proud of her. *AH, just a dream. Maybe I could manage a Euro football team. Hmmm!*

Shannon searched her texts for the text from Mika to respond to him. *Albeit a bit late.* She sent out a quick text to thank him. It bounced. The number was no longer in service. *Was it really a ruse? Or did he have second thoughts?* Maybe she would have to go to Africa anyway, maybe on her own dime. She had some savings for her Master's degree in Business Administration. One that she had yet to start. *I am not getting an MBA, who am I kidding.* A one-year online degree in sports management was way more appropriate. Her undergraduate degree in biochemistry would not help her here. She had once thought of joining the burgeoning agri-tech industry now bustling in Jefferson City and nearby Omaha.

Shannon marched excitedly yet with apprehension to the records department at the alumni office. An older woman met her and searched the records for her on the school's massive database, secured with private passkeys.

"Shannon, Mika Williams recently requested that his contact information be removed on our system. We do permit alums to remove their contacts for privacy. The smart device number you have was his number though. Maybe do a message in the Socialverse for him to reach out to you. Why do you need to find him? He is too old to play now!" the elderly white-haired women at records frowned at her, with some curiosity.

"Not sure yet."

Shannon later that day reported back to Coach Smith. He told her to let it go. Must have been a ruse, he told her, as he had predicted. After all, the Socialverse had been abuzz about Martians playing for Nebraska State. Shannon felt disheartened but mischievous. And why would the legendary Mika pull a ruse? Her conspiratorial mind still churned.

# 7.

SHANNON LOOKED at her upcoming vacation schedule. She swished her Nordic blonde hair away from her forehead. As a former lacrosse standout at Nebraska State, she was fast and athletic. She joined the team in her first year in 2017, the year before the team jumped from a club team to a varsity team in women's lacrosse. She still trained for and ran marathons but had not played lacrosse since she graduated in 2020. She had gone to work for the athletic department right away after graduating, focusing on recruiting for football and women's lacrosse. Nebraska State women's lacrosse had finished as high as second in the conference her senior year, behind eventual national champion, Maryland.

She was scheduled to take off the next two weeks on vacation starting after work on Friday, June 13. It was a slow period in recruiting. She worked furiously on the internet. With changes in regulations and improved worldwide peace, a hallmark of the Rip-Roaring 2020s, she was able to secure the requisite paperwork, in addition to her passport, for travel and vacation to Kenya. Next stop, the clinic for the requisite shots.

That night she purchased her plane tickets, using a considerable chunk of her savings. She could not wait for her journey to begin.

# 8.

MIKA WATCHED AFRICUS return to the ranger station from the savannah, where he had been for a week. When he had freshened up and sat down to eat at the picnic table outside of the shelter, Mika sat down and joined him.

"I sent a text to an administrator at Nebraska State telling her about you. It was perfect timing. I had read online that she was searching Mars for recruits! Why not Africa, I told her. I did not tell her your name or about your past but did tell her how great an athlete you are. I did not hear back from her yet, probably because she thinks it is a ruse, and I felt badly that I did not tell you first. And then I panicked that a world-wide obsession with the African Boy Legend, the lion boy, might ensue! Therefore, I changed my smart device access number and removed my contacts from the University alumni site," Mika explained sheepishly, but eager to see the reaction of his young protégé.

"Interesting," Africus cocked his head to the right and gazed at Mika with a breaking smile. "Maybe you should have waited to see if there was a response? And you did not mention my past, so there would be no world-wide attention on me!"

"You know, Africus, I see what you are saying, but the world does not know about you, at least not yet! Maybe a few broken hearts from some of the safaris that have gone through! But your past as the African Boy Legend is a legend, a myth, a figment of imagination. A legend, that if true, would rock and shock the world. It would be a fantasy that rivaled reality and virtual reality. This could have broken into a huge international story. Honestly, I did not think this through. I don't know what I was thinking. I think I was right to remove my contacts."

"Mika, don't worry about it. That is ok. I am disappointed they did not respond to you. I have dreams, you know. Football in America is a dream! You and Haley were great athletes! Maybe I could be one, too. And because you two went to Nebraska State, then that would be my University, too! Maybe in 2026! I am interested in that!"

Africus looked out across the safari at some antelope grazing. Some vultures were circling endlessly in the blue sky. His mind churned.

"Did they not have an interest in me? Is it because I have no experience in organized sports? Or is it that my story is a fantasy or a dream? Or maybe she did not get your text," Africus panicked and then queried, his eyes eagerly attached to Mika face.

"I can easily renew this conversation, you know."

"Yes, do that."

Africus looked at the sky again. The vultures had landed. He looked back at Mika.

"But Mika, there is the Girl. I want to find her" Africus leaned forward as he hopefully looked Mika for a positive development.

"I know. That is Haley's department. It doesn't look promising though."

Africus looked at him with despondence.

"Yeah. OK. I am out of here for now. But before I go. What of the Preserve plant, Exotica. I know that you have consumed it, and thought it was a mind enhancer. I am surprised that the big pharmas in Nairobi have not discovered it, yet," Africus contemplated the magnitude of this new potential pharmaceutical.

"Maybe we should obtain a patent on its powers?" Mika schemed.

"No, it's for the lions, only! And it is not abundant," Africus was suddenly protective of the lion's special plant.

"Does that account for their superior intelligence and communication abilities?" Mika carefully asked.

"Perhaps, but it mostly just helps them in their day to day acute awareness of their surroundings. They only eat it once or twice a year. I have consumed it as well. It does increase awareness. Maybe it permits access to the dream world of the Parallel Dream Universe? But I have not eaten it since I was in the jungle, as a member of the pride. So, likely not. But maybe. Someday, we can learn to harvest it. It might help on neuro-degeneration. It may make people smarter. Maybe I can bring it to Nebraska State for testing," Africus looked pensive, and unsure.

"Fine, let it be. But we could profit and help people," Mika countered.

"Ok, let me see where I can grow it. It is of the coffee family."

Mika stared at Africus. *Coffee, interesting.*

Africus left Mika to return to the savannah. He walked with the herds. The dry wind blew from the east. Dust filled the air as migrating herds of zebra, wildebeest, and elephants marched forward. The dry grass provided some nourishment, and the river tributary ample water for now. He walked barefoot with hardened callouses from years in the bush. He thought pensively. *Maximilion, the leader of my former lion pride and my friend, the one who brought me to the Girl, is out there. I have not seen him in some time. I will find him on this trek. I will confer with him on my future. Mika and his wife Haley love Nebraska State. Mika was a football star. Haley was a soccer star and part time cheer leader her senior year just for home games. She played club lacrosse, too. I can be a star, too. Maybe fall 2026.*

He knew football. He and Mika often threw the ball around. He would run routes through the gazelles, and with the prides he would run and dodge and jump around the lion cubs, who chased him until he stopped in his tracks, then waited for him to run again. He watched games online with Mika, including college and professional football, and played the virtual games online.

He was so fast. Mika had timed him on a school track for the 100-meter hurdles. It was an unofficial time. But Mika swore it was possibly a world class time, maybe even the world record. The Kenyan Olympic committee had asked to watch him run. Mika had denied that request and did not tell them his time in the hurdles. They backed off. *I should compete with humans, for competition, not survival and his next meal, as I had as a boy in the jungle and savannahs of Africa.* He started to run, with his backpack loaded with water and SUPERSNACKS delivered from Nebraska, and his smart device. The SUPERSNACKS would last him until he found the plants that he enjoyed eating. Soon he would be into the jungle, and he would see the lion pride.

# 9.

*Monday, June 16, 2025*
*Nairobi, Kenya*

S HANNON'S LONG TREK finally came to its final destination. Her jet landed in the Jomo Kenyatta International Airport in Nairobi, the capital of Kenya. *The airport is so busy.* On her trip, Shannon had researched and studied Kenya. Kenya had flourished in the Rip-Roaring 2020s as an economy, especially as pharma companies from Europe had set up production and research and development facilities in Kenya to exploit its natural plant farms. Kenya was the ideal location for a number of plants that produced natural chemicals and proteins that had help win most of the war against cancer and other diseases. The drug companies needed to process the plants immediately after harvesting, so the production facilities were built in the outskirts of Nairobi. More success was had with the anaerobes found deep within Africa's largest volcano, Mt. Kilimanjaro. The pharma companies had developed anti-viral medications that were proving enormously successful. A bird-flu epidemic had been crushed just in time in 2023. The common cold was no longer common. Billions of Z currency, the now favored world digital currency, was spent on infrastructure and new residential areas for the facilities and its workers. Many Kenyans held lucrative jobs at the farms and the facilities. Nairobi was now one of the wealthiest cities in all of Africa. The dark continent was thriving elsewhere as well, as new mineral discoveries and techniques to extract the minerals were made and developed. The new African Stock Exchange and its related exchange traded funds and index funds had exploded. Its returns lead the world in the Rip-Roaring 2020s, even greater than the U.S. Dow Jones, which had just topped 100,000, and other U.S. indexes.

But there was one subject that particularly intrigued her. *Treasures!* The fabled legend of a lost cavern of gold and treasures, known as the Cavern of Lost Treasures, had garnered the public's fancy. Stories with purported pictures of elven-like monkeys, the legendary guardians of the Cavern of Lost Treasures, had surfaced on the internet, sparking a furious curiosity for a world satiated with both peace and prosperity. *King Arthur's sword in the stone and his sword Excalibur, made by Merlin the magician, may be hidden in the Cavern of Lost Treasures. Even the new King of England has spent time searching for the Cavern of Lost Treasures. A find of such royal heritage would provide authority for the throne of England for the ages. Excalibur and the other treasures would jolt the English economy and enliven the English people.*

She read further how Africa itself was close to forming its own union and trading block to trade and deal with the powerful economies of the world. Africa was not only an emerging economy, but a highly-energized economy. Kenya and South Africa were the leaders. Egypt and the northern African countries had abandoned the African trading block and joined the European Union as ad hoc secondary members.

Africa still had kept its natural wonders and national parks. Tremendous environmental efforts had been successful to preserve the animal kingdom in its natural state in the Preserves. *Mika is in the West Kenya National Wildlife Preserve.* Safaris were as popular as ever. The farms were large but were designed carefully to preserve natural habitats. African leaders did not want to repeat the failure in Brazil to protect the Amazon from excessive development. Brazilian leaders had asked the President of Kenya for assistance in designing strategies to rebuild the Amazon, on the hope that the pharma industry would find special plants for even more medicinal drugs in the Amazon jungle.

Brazil still had its snake farms. Certain poisons were found effective, when molecularly altered, to be effective in reversing dementia and other brain deteriorating diseases. But Brazil had fallen behind Kenya and Africa as a trading block.

Other parts of Africa had become profligate in the organ donation business. African baboons had proven effective in matches for human transplants for many organs. Baboon farms were booming. The organ business had survived the onslaught of animal rights activists to stop the farming of organs.

Shannon was overwhelmed at the transformation of Africa. The public transportation, built from scratch, was state of the art. She quickly boarded a super speed train headed to the Preserve that ran on anti-gravity rails at great speeds. After a few local stops, she found herself whisking through the countryside, through the hills and jungle areas, and off to the western savannahs.

But the technology and high state of the art modern transportation suddenly stopped. It was part of the preserve

Africa movement. She stepped off the train at its last stop. Few people had ventured out as far as she had. There were no jobs out this far, no farms and no manufacturing or research and development centers. Just land.

There was a small hut, where bathroom facilities were located, as well as a water fountain supplied by a well. *How good could that water be?* The water in Nairobi was fine, with the vastly improved water treatment and sewage plants. But out here? She took a chance and drank the water. *It was fine.* And then she saw the bus stop. There was a sign for the Preserve.

"Hmmm," she pondered. "When will the next bus depart?"

She wandered over to the bus stop. Yes, there was a schedule. Another three hours. That did not seem such a long time. She checked her smart device. It worked. She had equipped it with satellite service for Africa. Her email inbox was only moderately full, as it was night time in Nebraska.

One email from Coach Smith.

"I hope you are enjoying your trip. Don't know where you are located. I have some great prospects for you to recruit when you return. Oh, by the way, our starting quarterback tore his ACL in summer workouts, and will miss most if not all of the season. So, title hopes, to the extent we had any, may have to wait until 2026! I will coach up the 2s now in earnest."

Shannon did not reply. She had gone radio silent.

The bus showed up on time. A few locals walked off the bus towards the train station. They were hot from the long bumpy ride. It was a two-hour ride to the entrance to the Preserve. She had read all that she could about the Preserve. There were rangers and guards, but also veterinarians. They cared for sick animals and managed infections and diseases among the animals. Others were scientists who studied both the animals and the plants. The balance of life was front and center for this world. So much bio-diversity had benefitted the world recently. New discoveries by the day were all the rage. The thought of the next great substance from a far-off distant place was scintillating to the public and the scientists.

Shannon was thrilled by the excitement of the Kenyans for their importance in the world. She heard her ancient calling to be a biochemist. *Ample jobs are here on the other side of the world if recruiting and sports management doesn't work out!*

She watched the countryside from the old bus window. The modern buses in Nairobi were not available in the country. It was still third world out here. Not even third world, but the world without humans. The world in a pre-civilized state. It was both eerie and enervating.

At last the bus approached the entrance to the Preserve. Shannon jumped off of the bus with her bag. A guard came to her, heavily armed.

"May I help you?" he inquired, but not in a menacing way, as Shannon looked innocent.

"I am here to see Mika Williams. I am from Nebraska, in America," Shannon replied with a big smile, trying to sound nice and not threatening to the heavily armed guard.

"Ah, Nebraska. Yes, follow me. I am sure he will be happy to see you!

"There are dangerous animals out here. They know Africus; so, he is safe. The rangers and guards they respect. The scientists and vets, they leave alone. But strangers, other than those on the safaris, are not welcome. They assume you are a poacher, after their horns, or tusks, or skin," warned the guard.

"I will respect the animals and the plants. Hopefully, they will sense my kindness and admiration for them. I am a scientist by training. Maybe they will know that. Who is Africus?"

"He is a boy. He is a ranger. He is from the jungle.

*I wonder if that is him.*

Together they walked through the gate. A hundred yards more and they reached the shelters. A nice hammock looked so inviting. The guard took her to a clean room. Very few of the scientists or veterinarians ever stayed overnight, particularly with so much to do in Nairobi. They also had their labs and research centers outside of Nairobi.

Shannon placed her bag on the bureau. She unpacked it for now. She did not know how long she would be in the Preserve. It might be one night if this were a lark or wild goose chase.

*But who is this Africus. Maybe he is the speedster-the next great American-world athlete. But why would the animals like him so much. What is all of this? Why am I here. So many bugs outside, so many birds, so much humidity.* She fussed and pondered.

The guard told her she could retire for the night. The shelter was safe. He brought her water and a small meal. He brought her a bug proof sheet, developed by the scientists for their overnight stays in the Preserve. *So much technology is here in Africa.*

"Anyone else live here?" she asked hopefully.

"Yes, the rangers live in the next three shelters. Mika and Haley live in the first one. They are married. They raised Africus from the jungle. The single rangers live in the other two houses. Four guys and two gals. The guards, all four of us, live in the shelter here where you are. You can trust us. The scientists and veterinarians mostly work during the day, and travel back to their homes on the bus and train. But they stay here with the guards, when they do overnight it."

"Where is Mika?"

"He and Haley and Africus are all in the field tonight. They may not be back for a week. I cannot bring you out there. You will have to wait to see him. Sometimes Haley comes home early."

"I can wait. I will take it as a vacation week! What is your name?"

"I am Jorge'. I am from Spain."

"Nice to meet you, Jorge'. My name is Shannon."

"Yes, and you are from Nebraska! Good American football, right?"

"The best is yet to come! Good night!"

"Good night!"

Shannon rested her head on a make shift pillow. *I do feel safe.* She was exhausted. Daydreams about Africus would have to wait until tomorrow. Let her night dreams take over, when they may, of course. She loved to remember her dreams. She studied them and felt they were informative and visionary, not just mental apparitions with no meaning.

Jorge' stayed up on watch. Another guard would take over in four hours.

*The sun has dipped over the horizon. The hunters are on the hunt. The prey is on the defense. Some are both hunters and the prey. It is the endless circle of life in the jungle. Hmmm, a lot like football.* Her mind whirled, but it was exciting.

Later she heard from Jorge', that Africus was out in the fields with the pride, and that Mika and Haley were ensconced together inside their tent, with an eight-hour fire nearby. They now brought synthetic logs that stayed lit throughout the night to scare away the animals. *More technology in Africa. Of course. But I have a week to wait!*

# 10.

Tuesday, June 17, 2025
Jefferson City, Nebraska

COACH SMITH LOOKED at the roster of recruits attending his Friday night summer camp, on June 20th, at the football stadium. Great recruits, but no quarterbacks of note. He would bring in his own back-up quarterbacks, as well as his quarterback's coach, to throw the pigskin around to the bevy of highly ranked receivers, tight ends and running backs that were attending. His quarterbacks coach was young and dynamic, a veteran of professional football, and a former Nebraska State star. But his recruiting skills needed a step-up in intensity. His coaching skills were impressive though.

*He can coach up my back-ups to a respectable level. Maybe we can compete in the new Western division of the new super conference. Maybe I can keep my job for another year. This new conference set up is so daunting!*

Coach Smith called in Tamaric Jones, his quarterbacks coach.

"Jones, we lost quarterback Sampson to the ACL injury. Not like your days, when an ACL injury kept you out for a year, or forever, in my day. But he is out likely for the regular season. He is a fifth-year senior and ready for the Association. He won't take a medical redshirt. We may have him back for the post season, or a bowl game, if we are not in the tourney, but likely, he is done with college ball," the head coach lamented, dropping his head. Jones was attentive, but respectfully silent.

"Jones, I am not sure we can win the Western division without Sampson. Sampson is prototypical pro-style quarterback. The prior staff took Sampson in, even though he didn't fit their run-pass spread offense, because he was a legacy, he loved Nebraska State so much, and he was a five-star recruit from rural Nebraska. He never started under the prior staff, as he was a back-up to a two-time all-conference run-pass quarterback in 2022 and 2023. The plan was to start Sampson in 2024, his redshirt junior season, and tweak the offense for him. But the prior coach and most of his staff left for the Association, after the National title in 2023. We came in and kept to the plan to start Sampson. But, we more than tweaked the offense. We changed it to a pro-style offense. Sampson was that good. Sampson was a Phenom at passing and had great movability in the pocket. But now he is out! But, really, a pro-style offense, maybe is not the best for this conference.

"Jones! Wake-up! What do you think of the back-ups, Pierce and Rodriguez? Both are young, rising juniors, and both athletic. They are not well suited for a pro-style passing offense. They don't throw well out of the pocket, and don't progress through their reads, and seldom check down to the backs or tight ends. They can't throw a screen pass at all. Both were recruited for the run-pass spread offense of the prior staff. They were not the best run-pass recruits in the country, because the better recruits were intimated at the prospect of competing with Sampson. They can run, but pass, not so much. What do you think, Jones?" the head coach glowered at Jones, as he waited for Jones to respond. Jones remained silent. The head coach could not help himself and schemed some more.

"I don't think the backups pass well enough to reintroduce the run-pass spread offense, even though they were recruited for that offense. You know, we still have the power running game that complemented our pro-style offense. Joseph is a devastating back-240 pounds of solid man-child with soft feet. He is punishing. He is patient. He waits for the hole, almost suspended in space and time! Maybe he is our horse. Maybe its Joseph and our D! But who is our quarterback, and what offensive scheme do we run for him? Now is your chance at innovation or maybe just clairvoyance! What do you think, Jones?" Coach Smith asked Jones again, with a steely stare.

"Coach! A lot of questions there. I do like Rodriguez better, now that Sampson is out. Pierce is the better passer of the two, and likely would be the back-up to Sampson, if he were not hurt. But neither is gifted enough to run our pro-style offense. So, we need a new offense. And I agree that we not revert to the run-pass spread offense of our prior coach, the third legendary coach of our great program, because our quarterbacks don't throw well enough even for that offense. So, yeah, I agree, we win with Joseph. We base our offense on Joseph and our pipeline of O-lineman. We rely on our D. D and running. Running and D. That is our plan this year. And, I chose Rod. He is a much better runner than Pierce. Rod can run the rock. He is shifty and strong in his core. He can do some zone read with Joseph. Maybe we put in a few option plays, too. And, we can have some passing. I think Rod can execute the passing game with rollouts and play action. Hey, if we are down, Pierce can throw some homerun balls! But, yeah, we win with Joseph and the D. If the D is solid, we got a shot at the Western. But the Eastern winner will be top five nationally, so likely no conference title or tourney this year. Probably, we get a nice non-tourney bowl game. And we have the benefit of low expectations without Sampson. He was second team all-conference quarterback last year. So, let's shoot for gold in 2026!" Jones replied, rocking back and forth as he spoke.

"For 2025, I like your plan, or was it my plan? Ha! But for 2026! Yes, let us think of the future. I have a plan for that, too. I want you to recruit a top shelf signal caller. Can you get down to New Orleans for the famed quarterback camp run by Spiritis, the great new apparel company of the Rip-Roaring 2020s. They have endorsements from ten Professional Football Association quarterbacks. They want to sponsor our women's lacrosse program. Shannon wants them to sponsor football, too. But that will have to wait until our apparel sponsorship contract expires in August. I like a passing offense, but I want a quarterback with speed, charisma and intangibles, too. A mobile quarterback is the still the most effective weapon. I think next year we revert back to the run-pass spread offense of the prior staff. Maybe, maybe I can someday be the fourth great coaching legend of Nebraska State!" Smith ruminated, smiling at the wall and the three portraits of the three great legendary coaches, hanging on his wall, like portraits of past Presidents, in the White House.

"I have tickets to New Orleans. Shannon got me a job at the Spiritis camp. They really want Nebraska State Women's lacrosse, you know, WLAX. Women's apparel is where they started. They want to dominate that market. Nebraska State WLAX will be a top contender in the Conference in 2026. Helping Shannon get me a job there was part of their romancing of Nebraska State. I fly out Wednesday and will be back on Saturday."

"Ah, ok. I had wanted you here for the Friday camp. No quarterback recruits are coming. I needed another arm to throw the ball!"

"There are some local non-scholarship candidates coming. They would be thrilled to toss balls to the star recruits! And we may find a diamond in the rough!" Jones replied, smiling with a big grin as he left the office.

Smith called in Ray Person, his defensive coordinator. RIP, as he was called, as his devastating tackles caused players to rest in peace, figuratively, was a standout defensive lineman for years in the Professional Football Association, or the Association, as it was known for its dominance in popularity and media ratings. He had been retained from the prior staff with a promotion to coordinator. RIP swung by after finishing a video call with a top defensive end recruit.

"RIP, we will be relying heavily on the defense this year with Sampson out. We are leaning towards Rod at this point, and more of a running game. This way we can keep your D off the field as much as possible. I want to give you the opportunity to tweak or even revamp the defense. This may be a rebuilding year, so we have some patience and time. The landscape is different with the super conference structure. The Conference season will be a marathon. Our divisional winner will have one or two losses, I believe, so we may have some margin for era. Oklahoma is a must win, and it is on the road. Next year it is home. Rod will be in his second full season, so next year we may be in position to compete to win the division and even the conference, especially with all of the marvelous defensive recruits that you continue to roll in. Those brothers from Omaha are going to terrorize running backs this year and next. My own suggestion is to think outside the box. You are a great teacher of technique, and a great leader. Your Xs and Os are top shelf. But a new defense is fine with me, like the New York coach in the Association came up with two years ago, that stymied passing, and led to rule changes because it was so impactful," Smith encouraged.

RIP sat reflective. He had long harbored thoughts of new defensive schemes but had stayed inside the box of his head coaches and coordinators and prevailing football theories. He always adapted well to new rule changes, particularly the heavy restrictions on tackling mechanics that came in 2020, that may have saved the game. New technology in helmet design and functionality had possibly muted the need to keep the restrictions, but the players in the Association liked the new rules, which had reduced injuries significantly. The helmets only added to the security felt by the players.

"I have some thoughts. I will work on it immediately. I will look at an overhaul, tweaks and even a novel system design. We will want intellectual property protection, a patent, on my new design!" RIP laughed.

"Amazing that the Arizona coach wanted a patent on his offense. The Arizona court gave a temporary injunction prohibiting the use of the offense in Arizona by other Arizona teams and visiting teams. The administrative state at its extreme! Thankfully, the appeals court shot it down. It wasn't that great anyway!" Smith laughed, too.

RIP left the office with renewed vigor and excitement. He was thrilled by this opportunity. He was loyal to Smith, but his eye was on the prize. A head coaching job in college, or a coordinator job in the Association. This could be a stepping stone, a cathartic opportunity.

"Where is Shannon? Why is she on vacation now?" Smith uttered impatiently to no one.

# 11.

GAVIN BLOCKER SAT AT HIS DESK in deep thought. He was a seasoned veteran E-reporter for the Nebraska State football team. He also covered women's lacrosse, or WLAX, as it had become the premier women's sport at Nebraska State along with volleyball with its multiple national titles. WLAX was on the verge of its first national title run.

Blocker found the new super conference football format exhilarating. The passion for college football was still powerful in most of the country, particularly the perennial hot beds, in the south and Midwest and Pacific coast.

Blocker loved real football. Virtual reality had taken over the world entertainment scene, including sports. But real football with its links to the human roots as hunters-gatherers, war and intense competition, still was religion to many fans across the country. Other real sports were viable, but heavily relied on their virtual reality side businesses to survive. Baseball was the first to have a sister virtual baseball league, or VBL. Baseball also had a unique 360 degree viewing platform. A drone hovered over the pitcher. For a fee, fans could watch the game from the field. The drone was guided to follow the action and to stay out of the way of the baseball. Fans could view the whole field. Some teams had multiple drones. Fans could choose their preferred vantage point. Most sports still had their fantasy leagues, that were increasingly becoming their own virtual leagues. Fans could watch their fantasy teams compete online against their opponent's fantasy teams with fantastic graphics. But professional football had the best attraction of all-VPR, short for virtual physical reality.

VPR had taken off. Fans were obsessed with VPR. Every player in the Association was outfitted with multiple touch sensors, and visual and audio transponders. The information for each play was instantly downloaded to a computer complex at the Association's center for technology in Omaha, Nebraska. For a fee, fans could hook up to a player during the game and see and hear the ferocity of the game. A super package was available at a higher fee to feel the hits of the game as well. The Association sold the sensor-based uniform that was needed for the touch senses. The fan could suit up in the uniform and feel the pounding, blocking and tackling, but with less force than the real event. Fans could switch players every play or stay with one the whole game. The visual views were 360 degrees. Fans could turn their heads and see even more than the actual player.

VPR had not yet been adopted by college football. The Association was hesitant to share its technology with others. Its patents were zealously guarded. Survival against the new virtual world of sports and entertainment was at a critical point. Professional football was still at the zenith.

But Blocker had pushed for VPR in college football. He had headed a U.S. College Sports Council committee to negotiate with the Association. At this juncture, the Association had considered offering its services for one player on offense, the quarterback most likely, and one on defense. Its command center in Omaha, Nebraska, would be used to collect the signals from each college stadium. Its computers would reroute the signals to a computer at each school, which in turn would be accessed via a school designated website by the fans. The Association and the school would share in the fees. Revenue for the colleges was a driving force. Using the Association E infrastructure could launch VPR for college football as early as the upcoming season. Blocker was confident he could pull off the deal.

Blocker opened his laptop. All laptops had touch screens and artificial intelligence. He could talk to his computer or tap and touch. Smart devices were the same. He touched his personal app for articles; he had sub apps for articles on VPR, articles on Nebraska State football and WLAX, articles on the Association, and articles on his own database of recruits for college football and WLAX. He was a voracious consumer of facts, and easily sorted through opinions, inflated stories, and embellishments and fabrications. His steel trap mind never forgot a play, a name, a comment. He had created a cognitive software program for a database of the information he gathered each day. His use of keyword retrieval for each category of data, was specially designed for his own use. No need to copyright and sell it now. His world of M Followers, short for followers in electronic media, social media and the Socialverse, web-based media, and virtual based media, was tops in Nebraska. He earned a handsome income from his subscribing followers, and his ad revenue was quite profitable. He was paid by local print and electronic media for columns as well.

Blocker was quick to grasp and utilize new technology. The thinking machines, or mini-buddies, they were called, were now the rage. Pure artificial intelligence. He used his mini-buddie to perform most of his perfunctory research. He would drop a recruit's name and wait for the report that his mini-buddy would download on all of his devices. He had a stationary mini-buddy. Most people had mini-buddies that were shaped liked balls and could follow their connected owners around the house or yard.

He also liked to use his Third Eye. Sensodes, as they were nicknamed, were placed above your eyes in the center of your forehead. The leading OEM for the Sensodes used the registered tradename, the "Third Eye", as the Sensode device looked like a third eye above your eyebrows. It is all-knowing and all seeing, its ads would announce. Each Third Eye had circuitry that was unique to each user based upon the unique wavelength signature of each person's brain-waves, a discovery not made until 2023. Fingerprint touch technology was required to activate the corresponding electronic chips on a laptop or smart device. Complex algorithms were used for each Third Eye to block hackers from accessing your thoughts as you thought with the Third Eye in operation. For now, the technology allowed its owner to think thoughts into his or her computer or smart device, as well as give commands. Technology for thought transfer between or among Third Eyes was said to be around by the Thirties, if not by the end of the decade.

Blocker digested the day's articles quickly. He accessed some follow up leads. He then began to spin his magic. Thinking thoughts directly into his machine, a beautiful prose spilled out into his blog. He proofed and made some light edits. A push of the button and his legions of M followers would see his work.

He had one lead on the nation's fastest girl lax player out of Maryland. She had expressed some interest in the lady Nebraskans, much to the surprise of the Maryland faithful. Maryland, like Nebraska State, would compete in the new Conference of the North in women's lacrosse. She would be a pivotal player in swinging the power back to the center of the country. The head lacrosse coach for women at Nebraska State proclaimed that the heart of America beat loudly beneath Jefferson City, Nebraska. You could hear it if you placed your ear on the ground! Nebraska State was also completing state of the art facilities for women's lacrosse. A similar build-up for their volleyball team in the prior decade had led to multiple national titles. WLAX was simply the hottest women's college sport. And it was very competitive, with Maryland bucking that trend from time to time with home spun players.

Blocker delivered his blog.

*Savannah Stewart is taking an official visit to Jefferson City, Nebraska this weekend. She is the top recruit in the country for the nation's fastest growing women's sport and fastest sport for players, too. She hails from the private school in Maryland, The College Preparatory, the top prep school in the country for girl's lacrosse. Savannah was national high school player of the year her senior year. She is a real superstar. She is taking a PG year at Oxford prep, in England, to be near her father for one year. She had promised him one year in England. She has long been considered a lock for Maryland WLAX, but apparently has had a new intriguing interest in the lady Nebraskans WLAX. Nebraska State coach Lindsay Andrews was thrilled to take the call from Savannah the other day that Savannah and her mother would be taking the trip. Stay tuned. Savannah is so good; she could tilt the balance of power to the Nebraskans. She has blinding speed and quickness, and an accurate laser like shot. She is almost unstoppable.*

How much longer until virtual leagues are adopted by the other professional leagues other than baseball, and its Virtual Baseball League, the VBL? I have enjoyed the new VBL. The virtual baseball players with their dramatic physiques and unique names are captivating. Their personalities, spiked with artificial intelligence, are spellbinding and often hilarious, and certainly entertaining. Each team has a sister team in the VBL, assigned to a sister city, with revenue sharing. Kansas City has adopted Omaha as its sister city. The Omaha team is a contender! I think such virtual leagues will work. But I wonder if the Professional Football Association is concerned that a virtual football league might replace real football. The injuries and violence of the sport would never hurt a virtual football player. Ha! What if they jumped out of the virtual world into the real world? Now there is some real fantasy. Or is that an oxymoron. The Association and its VPR sports domination are not likely in trouble. Nothing like real live blocking and tackling. The hunters and the hunted, really, both on offense and defense, all game long. Our deep genetic memories yearn for football. I think football is safe. Thanks to the convention of 2020 and the Wonder Helmet.

The convention of 2020 saved the game, you know, it did. Oh, the Convention of 2020. I covered the convention as a freelancer. The rules changes were dramatic, but the debate and behind the scenes battles were as good as any football game. It was really more than a game. Billions of dollars were at stake. A whole industry. The world's most successful entertainment franchise. Ultimately, reason prevailed and dramatic rule changes were adopted both professionally and in college and high school. The convention really set the stage for football in this decade of the Rip-Roaring 2020s.

Then in 2021, a young scientist, Michaela Roberts, at Cal Berkeley, discovered an application of particulate motion dynamics to materials science, to create the prototype Wonder Helmet. A few venture and crowdfunding dollars later, and the Association held hostage, she was a wealthy young Gen Z kid. The Wonder Helmet now absorbs all the shock and rattling that used to throttle the brains of our football heroes. Her Wonder Company, LLC, made a fortune. Their patented design is a monopoly. But kids can play football again. And lacrosse. The helmets for lacrosse are just as safe. Concussions are virtually gone in football and lacrosse. The Wonder Company is currently working on a modified helmet for all other sports, that is lightweight, sweat wicking, and comfortable. It is expected to be released this August. So, soccer moms, you will be winners, too!

It took a while for coaches, players and fans to adapt to the new rules. But now the game of football is as fast and dynamic as ever and still rugged. The Association coaches who adapted the quickest rose to the top. But copycats are part of life, and the head start that some teams had early on has largely diminished.

But in college ball, it seems coaching is even more critical, so vital. In his prior stop in his coaching journey, Coach Smith, our second-year head coach at Nebraska State, was innovative and inspiring as the head coach of a team that is now not part of the super conference structure. The Nebraska State AD snapped him up quickly for 2024 on the departure of Nebraska State's prior legendary head coach to the Association, after his second National title in 2023. But Smith is going to have to match wits with the Oklahoma coach. Big game this November 28, 2025. Oklahoma deploys four athletes in the backfield. All quarterbacks, running backs and/or receivers, depending on the play. It is very hard to defend. Who even will receive the snap. But Smith was creative for his old team. His first year here, 2024, was vanilla. There were many injuries and a lot of student athletes who left when the former coach left for the Association. He was a great coach, a legend. He inspired our whole state. After he finishes coaching in the Association, he is a lock to be a U.S. Senator! Enough on the legend. Spring ball looked promising this year, but then Sampson was hurt and lost for at least the regular season. It would have been fun to see him, a gifted passer, in a second year of the new pro-style offense that Smith designed just for him. We shall see what happens now, who *is the quarterback, and what is the new offense. Certainly, they will drop the pro-style offense. Looks like another rebuilding year. But Smith really needs a top quarterback recruit. My vote is for a speedy, mobile one, with a terrific arm. Tamaric Jones is in New Orleans at the Spiritis camp to find that recruit! Updates will be yours if I hear anything.*

"In any event, let's hope Savannah likes Jefferson City!

*Friday, I hope to have some updates on VPR for college football. And hail to Nebraska after the completion of the national grid super rail system-The NGSRS. Jefferson City is the center of the NGSRS! It is now the focal point of the United States! Great for recruiting in all sports! Thanks to the Great Infrastructure Act of 2020!*

*Signoff.*"

Blocker looked up and removed his Third Eye. He wondered where Shannon Garrison was. He knew all about her, but still had not met her in person. *Maybe she doesn't know I exist? Surely, she had read my blog. I do talk of WLAX!* He heard she was on vacation. He asked his mini-buddie, but it did not know. Flight records were not publicly available. It was a slow period for football recruiting, and he speculated that she was unaware that Savannah Stewart was taking an official visit when she had left. *But is she really on a stealth recruiting visit. Maybe Africa,* he wondered, laughing at the recent propaganda. More Mythopoeia. More Fantasy. College football needed some of that, maybe, to hold onto the Generation Z and now Generation Alpha kids. Doubtful she is recruiting. She works seventy hours per week.

He liked her, too. He was 35, stood up at the altar once, and engaged a second time, only to be jettisoned again. Always, his passion was for his blog. *It really messed up my personal life.* He still golfed for fun and exercise, the former captain of the Nebraska State golf team. He graduated summa cum laude from Nebraska State with a media and entertainment major.

He thought he would be married by now. Society was changing regarding marriage. More couples raised families without the bond of marriage, and some urban areas were utilizing community family services, where parents and children shared each other in one bigger communal family. *Far out.* Churches and conservatives were appalled. But the administrative state, or the U.S. government, as he thought of it, thought it gave city kids more nurturing and guidance and love. *Violence is down considerably from the prior decade, so who knows. But still, society blesses the traditional family, and genes want to protect and nurture their own offspring, so families are not going anywhere soon, and I want to start a family!*

Blocker grabbed his golf hat and applied his sunscreen for the week. There were permanent sunscreen applications, but he thought they made your skin look a little glossy. Once a week was fine. Skin cancer was curable now but aging and wrinkling still were an issue for most people, and future old people like him. He pulled out his smart device. He checked for the next electric smart car sharing pickup at the end of his block. It was 10:30 AM. He then punched in a tee time at the Jefferson City Country Club. *University coaches likely will be there for a game and more news and gossip and updates.*

# 12.

B LOCKER THOUGHT ABOUT how quickly the transportation industry had evolved in his short lifetime. The self-driving autonomous automobile system, ride sharing system and electronic and solar powered vehicles, known as E-Vehicles, had transformed the auto industry. The auto companies had survived declines in car, van and truck production through diversification into larger transportation companies taking on the new trends as they evolved. The success stories were some of the best-case studies yet for the nation's elite business schools. Gavin, like many Americans, had abandoned the dream of car ownership and the materialistic markings and pleasures of car ownership. No longer were cars a marker of your lot or status in life. The decade before had seen pioneers in the ride sharing business. But just like the radio industry in the 1920s and internet in the 1990s, the new transportation boom was rife with competition. Soon ride sharing services were offered by many companies. The auto industry gobbled up the new ride sharing companies. The drivers needed vehicles. But with more vehicles operating full time, fewer were needed. It had been estimated that automobiles in the early two decades of the century were idle over 95% of the time. The sharing vehicles, were idle only 25% of the time. And then self-driving autonomous vehicles, called smart vehicles, started to work without mistakes. And E-Vehicles were now more efficient, with batteries lasting up to one thousand miles. The smart vehicle, E-Vehicle and the ride sharing industries were a natural marriage. Over 90 percent of the smart vehicles used for ride sharing were E-Vehicles. The government had decided to make it a joint public-private venture. The government with the transport companies, as they were called, set up a nationwide, statewide, countywide, citywide, and town wide ride sharing systems with smart EVs, including cars, vans, trucks and mini-buses. The system was extensive. It was called the Transportation Grid. The transport companies made the cars, vans, trucks and mini-buses, and collected the ride sharing fees, all prepaid electronically in advance by the riders. The apps on their smart devices gained riders access to the ride sharing system. Some people, particularly those in suburban areas, owned their own vehicles. Most of those vehicles were smart E-Cars, that integrated into the Transportation Grid with special apps. Those private owners would ride their own car in the Grid. It was more expensive, but gave the owner a degree of privacy and the ability to store items in their car. The Grid accommodated vehicles that were not self-driven, including commercial vehicles and trucks, and public transportation, like city buses. The relevant government collected a share of the fees through a transportation tariff. The system worked well enough. The change to the transportation industry was one of the great hallmarks of the Rip-Roaring 2020s. *It really shot the Rip-Roaring 2020s forward like a rocket launch!* And the oil companies survived by growing into full service energy companies. The natural gas business flourished as the number one producer of electricity to power the massive automobile transportation complex.

As Blocker waited for his ride sharing vehicle, probably a van today, he thought about how energy reform and advances were a key component of the roar of the Twenties, too. New start-ups were gobbled up by the new energy conglomerates. These start-ups were making substantial headway into wireless energy. Some technologies used the ionosphere, some the rotational forces of the earth, and some the deep thermal heat beneath the earth's crust. *Wireless energy is on its way, and here by the Thirties!*

Blocker boarded his smart sharing van, called an SSV, with three others. The SSV took them to a central station. He then boarded the smart sharing car heading to the west of Jefferson City to the golf course.

As he arrived, he was met by the marshal. He still preferred to walk, but took the smart walking golf cart, "Golf Walker", that synced with an app on his smart device. The Golf Walker carried your bag, went forward on voice command, told you distances, wind conditions, what club to hit, and where the best place to put your next shot. Smart auto-driven golf carts were dubbed "Golf Riders". He preferred to walk, so did not use the Golf Rider.

The "Green Golf Shades" were the rage. He put his on. The sunglasses were terrific at eliminating glare and protecting your eyes. And the gps fined tuned contours of the greens were brilliantly displayed. Reading greens was now a viable part of most amateur golfer's games. The rules were changed in 2024 to permit the Green Golf Shades in amateur competitions. The professional golfers were still required to read greens with their feet and eyes. Blocker knew the story of the former golfer, who played at the bottom of the professional tours, who had developed the glasses with Stanford engineers he had attended college with. He had felt if he could have read greens better, with his ball striking ability, he could have been a contender and a champion. His frustration turned to profit, as his patented technology and trademark took off. The golf industry welcomed his invention in the end, as golf, like other entertainment and sports industries, constantly battled the virtual world for dollars, followers and participants. Playing a miniature video game on the greens, with a real putter and golf balls, had spurred interest in the game by the new generation Alpha youth, the generation Z and the millennials, who now had family days playing golf, as well as golf games for business and competition. Aging Baby Boomers were still the most loyal golf followers. Generation X was close behind.

Blocker then put his special mark on his balls with his Find Me ball marker. He further marveled at the innovative advances in the golf industry as he marked his ball. "Find Me", founded in 2021, was a microchip applied with a ball marker. It blended with the ink, and bonded so well with the ball, that even the professional swings could not knock it off. Each golfer had his own "Find Me" app that was downloaded on his smart device. The lost ball was instantly found.

The newest technology, dubbed "My Golf RVR", for real to virtual reality, founded in March, 2024, combined all of the golf technologies into a virtual reality with yourself as the protagonist. It was founded by three 'hackers' who wanted to play real golf, but then wanted to be virtual champions with their own bodies and swings. They were MIT students at the time. They had received grants from the Stay Real Foundation, a foundation dedicated to keeping the human race from falling totally into the virtual world, with no touch points in reality. The new My Golf RVR required real golf swings, so the touchpoints to reality were there, even though ultimately, the virtual aspect was quite dominant. *Not sure that was a good expenditure for the Stay Real Foundation.* The professional golf organizations likewise made investments. The software program, usable on computers and smart devices, combined all of the information from your round of golf on your swing and ball movement, took your image from videos of your swing from the smart golf carts, and created a virtual reality with the downloaded views of your golf course, or any other golf course. You could take your game that day and play it on the world's greatest links. Your 81 on the local municipal, would translate to a 91 at Pebble Beach. Then the tweaking, tinkering and swing changes by you, the puppet master, could lower your virtual score on your course and the master courses.

Blocker loved real golf, but had spent considerable effort employing all the new technology. He had dropped his score average from 85 to 82 since buying his own My Golf RVR.

Blocker showed up on the first tee. He had played the course the night before on his My Golf RVR. He had shot a 70. His best since college was 74. In college, he could break 70. He thought that maybe today was the day. But thoughts of Shannon, Savannah, the new college football world, even the baseball VPL, still swirled in his mind. He was already putting together his evening blog, usually an extension of his morning blog, as developed throughout the day by his subconscious mind, a mind still uncaptured by technology and the smart world. He often wondered what words would come for his evening edition. His M-Followers were actually larger in number for his evening edition.

His mind silenced as he watched Coach Smith show up on the first tee. He had not interviewed Coach Smith in the past. Blocker was an E guy-operating behind the protection of the E-world and his blog. Coach Smith evidently had planned this foursome. Two students, not particularly athletic, were in tow.

"Mr. Blocker, I see you are well T outfitted for the game today with the Green Golf Shades and Golf Walker," Smith noted, referring to the colloquial use of "T" to refer to technology-based apparel or gear.

"I am a slave to my T apparatus and virtual self!" Blocker laughed in response, pondering the meaning of this extemporaneous meeting.

"My two graduate assistants, my GAs, would like to join us as well. They are 10 handicaps in the virtual world of My Golf RVR, but 24s in the real world! I hope you don't mind them joining us. I am an 18 handicap myself, with a matching virtual 18 handicap. As you might expect, I don't have the time that you do, to practice my golf in the virtual world, let alone the real world. Now since I became head coach, I climbed from a 12 to an 18!" Smith stated.

"Let's play. I can give you some good reads on the greens. You should invest in these glasses! What do the GAs specialize in for you?" Blocker asked in curiosity.

"They are my virtual reality experts. We want to talk to you today about virtual reality. You are quite the expert on the VBL in baseball. You know the VPR football of the Association. You are adept at the golf technology," Smith responded.

Blocker's ever creative and working mind began to spin. *Is he offering me a job? I don't like employment; I am a freelancer. What can I add? What is the tie to college football, to Nebraska State football? But I am one big receptive ear right now.*

Blocker took out his Driver. He recalled his adjusted swing from the night before on his My Golf RVR. He mentally pictured the swing and ball flight. He assured his ball had the Find Me ink mark. All set. Boom. It worked. He striped it down the middle. In a slight trance, he instantly viewed the ball flight information on his smart device. The numbers lined up his visual assessment. The merger of virtual reality with real reality. He loved it.

Smith gawked at the lengthy well struck ball. Even the swing looked fluid and athletic.

"I think Shannon would even find that shot amazing," Smith chuckled, enticing Blocker in the process.

*Even better, this could be about Shannon. He must read my blogs. Only a veiled reference to her last week, and he picked up on it.*

"Yes, Ms. Garrison. The Blog world is in great wonderment at her current affairs and location!" Gavin nodded.

"Just on vacation, to my knowledge," the coach responded honestly.

The coach was very athletic. A former professional football player, he excelled in basketball and lacrosse at the prep level. His athleticism would make up a lot on the golf course that his lack of both real and virtual practice would hinder. He swung his club back slowly, almost too slowly for the eyes to watch, but then furiously attacked the ball with a super whish that sent it sailing into the sky down the fairway where it rested after its lashing, waiting for another beating and chance to find the hole in par.

"I see. Little practice, virtual or real, and you pound your driver down the middle," Blocker admired. "So, I suspect this foursome is not accidental, is it, Coach?"

"You are indeed an astute observer! Yes, we have a proposal for you. We have followed your blogs on the VBL in baseball, and the use of VPR technology in the Association, and all the golf technology you so ably use. We would like to start a new venture in college football. We want to be part of these Rip-Roaring 2020s, too. Let's make some big money before the markets come back to earth. Hopefully, history will not repeat itself in 1929! We would like to utilize virtual reality technology and have a virtual game after the game that the coaches and players could play, based on performances in the game. Plays could be tweaked, techniques altered, coverages changed or disguised, clock management revisited and a host of other changes identified, developed, tested and implemented. We would not sell the program to the public- too many property right issues for the players. We could sell the software to the hundreds of colleges and high schools around the country. I believe we could eventually adapt the technology to lacrosse and other sports. Bink and Bonk, here, are software engineering gurus. They have already obtained patents for the base code and algorithms we will need. We need you for a holistic and practical review, for user friendliness. My role is to review it from a coach's perspective. The University will be the majority owner of venture, as the patents were designed by its students on its facilities. But the four of us will receive profits interests. We will offer you a 5% profits interest in the enterprise. Let me know. The LLC has already been organized. We are reserving another 5% for marketing. We are going to offer Shannon that position. She of course will stay on as our recruiting expert!" The coach offered.

"That is very exciting. Honestly, I am in. Let me review the documents and technology. I will sign the non-disclosure agreement, of course, prior to my review. I have some ideas, including on how to take this to the next level. I would like to work with Shannon on the lacrosse division of the business?!" He jested in search of a positive response.

"Ha! We shall look into that for you. But football is our first priority. Nebraska State football will be our beta testing site. We hope to launch this to market in 2026," the coach concluded.

The four of them played their eighteen holes. Bink and Bonk were thrilled to test the Green Golf Shades, and smart golf cart technology. They improved their score on the back nine by four shots each, due to their quick assimilation of the technology and its application to their swings. Coach Smith was wondering where Shannon was. He had a lot to discuss with her.

# 13.

Friday, June 20, 2025
Jefferson City, Nebraska

SAVANNAH STEWART AND HER MUM landed in the airport in Jefferson City, Nebraska. Mrs. Stewart succumbed to her daughter's wishes to visit Nebraska State for lacrosse. She knew Nebraska State had taken off as a lacrosse program, and that her daughter had never really wanted to play at Maryland, even with its pedigree and championships. Savannah wanted to leave her home state, where she had lived for seven years since her parents had divorced. Her Daddy was a media mogul and had left her Mum quite well off. Savannah for now was not that interested in wealth and splendor. She loved animals, sports and technology. Her Daddy was good to her, but she seldom saw him.

Her Mum would bide her time, before they left for a resort in Vail, Colorado, for hiking, horseback riding and some golf and tennis. The spa, of course, was the real treat. Even Savannah was thrilled about the spa.

Coach Lindsay Andrews was there to greet them at the airport, along with her assistant coaches. They and the coaches boarded an SSV, off to the new and splendid lacrosse facilities near the football stadium.

"Is that the football stadium?" Savannah marveled.

"Yes, that is it, sellouts forever it seems. And last year we sold out all of the WLAX games, too!" one of the assistants bragged.

"Yes, football still drives the engine of the athletic department here and the passion and souls of all Nebraskans, but women's lacrosse has captured fire and brimstone, too! Last year's quarter-final appearance in the national tournament was bedazzling and spectacular for us, and we return nine of our twelve starters for 2026, and only two starters are seniors. When you come for the 2027 season, and I am sure you would compete to start, there could be ten returning starters, including a senior goalie. And we have the number two ranked goalie in the country coming in this fall 2025 as a first year, from a private school in Massachusetts and top club team, as well as the top attacker from her school and club team," Lindsay said as she described her team.

"Coach Lindsay, what is it like to live out here in the middle of the country, and how are your academics?" Mrs. Stewart queried as they disembarked from the smart van, her medium length blonde hair blowing across her face from the breeze.

The five of them walked in awe of the football stadium-so many conference championships, too numerous to count, and the multiple national championships, including the 2020 and 2023 national championships. Savannah seemed lost in thought as she gazed at the stadium. Just then two American eagles swooshed by them. Mrs. Stewart was startled. The coaches looked on in trepidation and awe. Savannah smiled as they flew away.

"Eagles out here! I am amazed. Are we safe, they were so close," Mrs. Stewart retorted.

"Not sure there have ever been any attacks. But those two eagles just recently have come to our campus. They are quite spectacular. They likely came from the hills of South Dakota. But, yes, Jefferson City is a fun city to live in. It is plenty urban, and there is plenty of country all around us. And we now have the top agri-academic-industrial-tech complex in the nation! Hundreds of new jobs are created every year. The health and nutrition strides are so enormous. The blend of technology and agriculture has benefited the world, and certainly has benefited Nebraska economically. We are good people out here. Everyone cares about you. We are the heart and soul of these Rip-Roaring 2020s. We have more academic All-Americans than any school in the country this century, and the most ever all time in football. I know you are an all-American in high school, Savannah, and I think you can reach that potential here at Nebraska State. We have the nicest facilities in the nation, and the largest crowds, and like I said, always a sell-out now in WLAX, too. Plus, all of your games are broadcast and streamed live," Coach Lindsay explained.

"What are your plans for virtual lacrosse. I think you could gain a lot on your competitors by using real to virtual technology, similar to the golf industry," Savannah astutely noted.

"Interesting, that is a good idea. I love technology myself. You can work on that with us when you get here. I will ask the AD about that. We have these two geniuses who came here instead of MIT or Cal because they liked the potential of the agri-tech complex and Nebraska State football. We call them Bink and Bonk! I heard they are working on a secret project on virtual technology. Hmm. That may be a secret," Lindsay replied.

"Maybe before I leave, I could meet them," Savannah noted.

A few students started to congregate nearby as Savannah and her entourage toured the lacrosse facilities. Her stunning beauty and elite athletic form bedazzled the onlookers. The two, mother and daughter, walked wearing their jeans and designer boots. Both sported designer sunglasses. Soon more summer students migrated to the field. Some football players attending summer school and summer conditioning workouts stopped in their tracks, literally, in the middle of pass routes in their 7 v 7s on a nearby practice field. Word soon spread throughout campus in the Socialverse that SHE, the American girl superstar, as some were calling her, was on campus. The students knew not to gawk and continued on with their daily tasks. But most said hello to her by name, a Nebraska State tradition for recruiting. She smiled back and returned the greetings. Her Mum was impressed by the knowledge and niceness of the Nebraska State students. Mrs. Stewart was starting to see the true Nebraska State colors through her very big sunglasses.

Savannah watched the 7 v 7 drills. She was a fan of college football and the Association. Her Daddy cared little for American football, as he was not an American like his ex-wife. Mrs. Stewart liked the Association Championship game, and the college bowl games and tourney, but generally preferred tennis and golf, when it came to sports, and of course girl's and now women's lacrosse.

The football players started to drop balls as Savannah watched. And some showboated more than usual. Finally, some lax players showed up to greet Savannah. She liked them instantly. This was going well she thought to herself. Her checks on her punch list were marked off one by one.

*I like Lindsay. She is awesome. She knows her lacrosse, she has the respect of her players, assistant coaches, the administration, and the financiers of the WLAX program. The upperclassmen are nice, and I know they can sling it on the field. The facilities are far and away the best I have seen. You know Nebraska State has the greatest fans in the nation. Just one large check mark to go.*

Mrs. Stewart and Savannah returned to their hotel in Jefferson City that night.

"Honey, this has gone better than I expected. The students, the coaches, your teammates, the facilities are all quite stunning. I am surprised that I am saying all of this, but it is quite a University. And the agri-academic-industrial-tech connection is impressive," Mrs. Stewart surmised.

"Mum, I was thinking the same as you. I do like it. I may not commit to Maryland on July 1. I may wait. I technically have until April 15 of next year to choose a school. If they don't hold a scholarship for me, well, that is their loss. Right! And it's not as if we can't afford tuition. Daddy has agreed to pay my secondary education and University costs and expenses, did he not? We are just saving him money with the scholarships. Do you think he cares where I go to school? He never went to one lacrosse game at my school, and only went to one club tournament, when he had a convention in Annapolis for the world's media moguls. I don't know, he seldom communicates with me in the Socialverse. I feel like I am just another liability on his balance sheet and expense on his income statement," Savannah hung her head as she spoke to her Mum.

"He loves you my dear. He is driven by business and competition and success. The world waits for no one now, and billions today are easily gone tomorrow. Great inventions are forgotten quickly. Even the great global companies have shorter lifespans. There is no rest anymore. It is like the jungle and savannahs of Africa. Every day you have to survive to live another day. Complacency is disappearing. You are competitive and driven like your Daddy. Look how hard you have worked in lacrosse, your academics and your side technology forays. He talks to me about you. He knows who you are. He follows you online. He knows your wins and losses and statistics. I know love in person is far more important, but he still loves my daughter," Mrs. Stewart's voice trailed off.

"Yes, I know that. Ever since that safari we had. He thought he lost me. He never seemed to trust me again. And then you and he divorced and sent me to the states to boarding schools. You both left me!"

"Darling, I was there for you. I was devastated when your Daddy left me. He left and did not give me a reason. I know I am financially stable, for the rest of my life, as he cashed me out, and I have no interest in his media empire. If it fails, I still survive. And if he succeeds, you will share in that bounty someday as his only current heir. I moved to the states, back home to Annapolis, not far from your school when the divorce was finalized. I have gone to all of your games, and parent teacher conferences. We text and talk and share photos every day! How can you say I abandoned you!"

"I know, Mum. I am sorry. The old family institution is so rare, it seems. I see the kids with happy moms and dads and wonder what it would be like to go home to a family. But you and I are close."

"But you still have not told me your secret!!"

"I will," Savannah said slyly, as she slapped her hands on her front thighs.

"Somehow Nebraska State ties into this secret, I think?"

"My secret may not be a dream!" Savannah insisted. "And you shall know my secret soon. It may dissipate, or it may come true! I honestly don't know!"

"Ah, you live in a Parallel Dream Universe, the fantasy and mythopoeia in your own mind! Your blend of fantasy and reality sometimes blurs! Magical friends, and animals and birds that speak to you. You are quite entertaining, yet mesmerizing, too," Mrs. Stewart gazed at her daughter adoringly.

"I was like that as a young girl, too," Mrs. Stewart continued. "But rigid and structured schooling at boarding schools dampened my creativity and fancy. So much so that I became a young financier and then went to Harvard Business School. I met your Daddy as a young investment banker. We did a number of acquisitions together and fell in love on our long diligence trips across the world. He was soon the head of mergers & acquisitions for the media giants of the day. We got married and had you, our precious daughter. He then joined forces with a private equity firm and started his own platform for acquiring media companies in the digital and social media world, focusing on Africa. His company is now the top media company in Africa. His firm valuation now is in the billions. He may take his company public on the Africa Stock Exchange. The Rip-Roaring 2020s have been great for Africa and his company. I still review his acquisitions from afar. I should have kept working, but I enjoyed being a mother and socialite. And later, I worked with charities while I watched you grow up and mature into the wonderful young woman that you are," Mrs. Stewart reflected.

"I know about your successful past as a financier. I think it is time you strap the helmet back on. You should start your own platform company. You still have contacts in the investment community, and crowdfunding is always available. I can work with you, too. I think the virtual sports industry is still fragmented and can be built up with economies of scale and market power! Nebraska State appears ready to launch into this area. They have the soon to be legendary Bink and Bonk!"

"Maybe. Didn't Lindsay say the Coach Smith was involved. I saw his picture online. He is my age, and also divorced."

"Mum! You have not dated since the divorce!"

"Just saying!"

"And you still speak to Daddy?"

"Oh, something like that."

Savannah was perplexed, but let it go. She and Mrs. Stewart then retired for the night.

# 14.

MIKA JUMPED OUT of the range vehicle back at the entrance to the ranger station and shelters. He saw Jorge' talking to an attractive blonde woman resting in a hammock drinking cold lemon water. Haley saw her, too, and saw the young woman watching Mika as he walked towards her. Haley's guard was up, and she too saw the athletic form and beauty of this person lounging in her hammock.

Haley reached the women before Mika could address her. She checked her out from head to toe and scoffed at her poor attempt to dress for the savannah.

"I don't think you are wearing the right gear for this hot, drenching weather? And who are you and why are you hear? We don't like unexpected guests at the ranger station. Safaris and visitors have their own entrances into the Preserve," Haley scolded the new guest.

Mika piped in unexpectedly, "I see the red NS on your backpack. What is that?"

Shannon recognized Mika and determined that this other woman must be his wife, Haley Andrews. She saw that Haley was indeed rugged, yet pretty, and definitely fit and experienced for the tough life in the jungle and savannah.

"Are you Mika Williams?"

"What? You know Mika? Why are you here again?" Haley complained.

"I am Mika Williams. I have a suspicion on who you may be and why you are here. But you better be quick, or my wife Haley may run you out to the jungle to fend for yourself!" Mika jested in amusement at the tension between his wife and this stranger.

"I am unofficially here. I am from Nebraska State, the University."

"Nebraska State!" Mika exclaimed.

"OK, keep talking," Haley acquiesced.

"Well, we received your message, Mika, about a possible landmark recruit at your Preserve here in Africa. And we certainly know of your legendary past at Nebraska State! But you went radio silent, and the department thought it was a hoax or fantastic fiction. There is so much virtual reality these days, and no one believes fantastic things are real anymore, or do not care if it is real, and fiction sells as well as reality, so following superheroes in any setting is often viewed as more entertaining than the real thing. In any event, your message was dismissed as nonsense, and fortunately never got any traction in the media or Socialverse.

"But I thought it was real. When your contact information was dropped, I suspected you had changed your mind, or that your star recruit wanted to stay home in the Preserve.

"It has been a long journey for me to get here. But, I am here unofficially, to see if the recruit is legend and myth or real. I hear he is very real from Jorge' and that his name is Africus! I am here to unofficially recruit Africus. We would love to have him join the Nebraska State family and football program! I am an administrative assistant in charge of recruiting. I can assist in all of the paperwork, visas, international clearances, academic clearances and other administrative matters.

"But where is Africus? I would like to meet him," Shannon finished.

Mika and Haley stared and each other. They communicated well without spoken words. Haley spoke first.

"We will discuss this with him when he returns. He will be back tomorrow morning. He is out in the savannah. He is with his animals. He is leading them to the grounds in the western part of the Preserve. Meanwhile, tell us about Nebraska State. I went to Nebraska State, too, you know. I played soccer. I was a cheerleader for some home football games my senior year. Mika was a safety on the team. He started and was quite good. He was seriously injured in the bowl game, probably knocked him out of a professional career. When we realized that football was no longer in the cards for Mika, we decided to go on a safari. Mika became friends with some of the rangers here at the Preserve. One thing led to another. Mika took a job as a ranger, and we were married here in a destination wedding, although not many people came, not even our very disappointed parents. Later our parents visited. Well, we don't have children. I did not want to raise a child in the jungle. But we have a foster child! He is heaven on earth," Haley opened up, now relaxed and smiling.

Shannon studied Haley, and then opened up herself.

"I played lacrosse. We were part of the first varsity teams. When I arrived, we were a club team, but became a varsity team my sophomore year. An anonymous donor financed our new lacrosse stadium and facilities and scholarships! Later we heard it was the founding partner of Wilderness Ventures of Omaha. He had made a fortune in the global E-goods delivery business, which he funneled into an even more lucrative space launch and "S-goods" delivery business. The Rip-Roaring 2020s are the gift that keeps on giving," Shannon added in a friendly, soothing manner.

"Lacrosse is such an amazing and fast sport. I played some as a little girl with my New England cousins who played division 3 lacrosse in the NESCAC in college. Great sport. They loved it. One won the division 3 national title! Nebraska State did not have varsity lacrosse when I was there. Later there was a club team. I certainly would have loved to play. With its speed and elegance, it certainly rivals football as the sport of the Rip-Roaring 2020s. Anything else?" Haley asked.

"I stayed at Nebraska State, chasing a dream, well, my dream guy. That did not work out. He left me for a Euro chick from Paris! He took a great job managing a Euro soccer team in the English Soccer League. He had his choice of Euro ladies, and I was quickly forgotten! He is engaged now. Yes, I still keep track of him!"

Mika listened as the two women began to bond. He texted Africus in the field on their special radio frequency that was satellite based and encrypted. They did not want poachers to know the travel lanes or plans of the African herds. But this text was social and personal.

"A young attractive lady from the Nebraska State, the University, is here to see you. She is on an unofficial recruiting trip. She is fairly high up. I think if you want to pull the trigger, this might be an opportunity. We will keep her busy for today and tomorrow. If you don't want to see her, we will escort her back to the train to Nairobi tomorrow!"

Africus did not pick up the text when it was sent. He was busy refereeing a dogfight among two rival African wild dog gangs.

Mika joined the conversation. "Yes, Haley was a soccer star. I had a crush on her my first three years at Nebraska State, before I finally captured her attention and her heart senior year. She was love struck on her prep school boyfriend from Massachusetts."

Haley interrupted Mika. "Yes, Shannon, just like you, I was unceremoniously dumped by my old boyfriend. He was one year ahead of me, and he fell for a female associate wall street investment banker that he worked with. The girl was from Princeton, like he was, and they had known each other a little bit at school. They worked on a deal team and spent weeks together on a diligence trip the summer after he graduated. They fell in love, and I was history. Oh, well. But then I went out with Mika senior year! And look how I ended up! In Africa, at a wildlife preserve, living without the luxuries of the modern world and the Rip-Roaring 2020s!"

"Oh dear, but you have me, the love of your life, and the animal kingdom at your feet!" Mika assured her. "And Africus, the lion boy, the former African Boy Legend, and future real-life superhero!"

"Tell me more about Africus! Why did you call him the African Boy Legend?" Shannon eagerly asked.

"Shannon, we have kept the story of Africus secret and safe. His story would likely be an international sensation. He would be like an animal in a zoo. Safari's would advertise the chance to see the African Boy Legend, as the local tribespeople called him. I am still amazed that his story has stayed quiet. With the boom in Nairobi from the Pharmaceutical-African plant farm marriage, with its multinational investors, managers, their families and friends, and thousands of tourists and hundreds of safaris, how he stayed under the radar I don't know. He certainly had caught the eye of many a female safari participant, and photos of him were certainly taken, but for the most part, he was ignored beyond his status as a ranger to ooh and ah over, by the non-African world. He is legend to the native tribes, and the legend of the African Boy Legend still persists throughout East Africa. But no one has linked the ranger and the legend," Haley explained.

"But there have been some interrogating minds that have asked about his past and his heritage. We usually lie and say he is our son. That sends them sniffing on another trail," Mika added.

"A safari trekker asked a lot of questions a few years back. He did not ask about Africus in particular. We don't know if he had seen or known of Africus. But he asked many questions about the legend of the African Boy Legend. We denied the stories as legend. He never came back again, though. And the world is still silent regarding the story of Africus," Mika continued.

"We can keep his past secret. We can keep him listed as your son. The school he attended is qualified internationally, and he is qualified academically in the U.S. by attending that school, assuming he had adequate grades. He will have to take a standardized test, however, if he has not already done so," Shannon contended.

"Oh, his school. How do you know what school he attended?" Haley asked in surprise.

"I read that students of rangers were offered free tuition and enrollment at the Kent School, outside of Nairobi. I assumed he attended that school! How were his grades! Test scores!"

"Shannon, he did not attend the Kent School in person. He went to my home school here in the Preserve, along with four other students from the local tribes. My school was affiliated with and supported by the Kent School, but it was a separate school. The degree was from here. I home schooled them based on the curriculum and study materials provided from the Kent School, mostly online. We had full access to the Kent School e-lectures. But I administered his tests and gave him his grades. He did quite well, I would say, as he did pass the high school equivalency test at the Kent School, mandatory for home schooled children, and he performed in the top 99% on the standardized test offered to Kent School students, similar to the ACT and SAT, and the same test for all children of diplomats in Africa, Asia, and some of the Euro countries. The Kent School guidance counselor assigned to Africus said he thinks he could enroll Africus in a prestigious University in London. Nairobi University would certainly offer him a full scholarship. There is an endowed scholarship for children of rangers in the Preserve at the University. But Africus has recently expressed an interest in Nebraska State. Your timing is impeccable! But I don't know how the U.S. College Sports Council would view his qualifications," Haley confessed, twirling her shoulder length sun-splashed sandy blonde hair.

"That is likely an issue that needs to be determined. I would have to petition the U.S. College Sports Council about his situation to offer him a scholarship. I am certain he can attend Nebraska State academically. It's just that scholarship offers are subject to rigid requirements. I can work quickly on this. Does he have a legal name?" Shannon asked.

"No, he does not. He has no birth certificate and does not know his parents or origins or heritage. We believe he was from an English-speaking family because he picked up the English language very quickly. He had a slight accent, maybe English, or Australian or even South African, but not enough to pin it down. He sporadically would recall a character from an old children's movie. So, he wasn't an alien, or superman from Krypton, or messenger from the heavens! He had a past. But it was likely sometime before he was three is our best guess. And there may have been a traumatic event that caused amnesia. Maybe he saw his parents killed. We have checked the records in Africa for deaths of foreign visitors at the time of his apparent arrival into the jungle and have not connected any dots. We have searched the internet for stories of kidnapped or missing children of his age back at that time as well. Nothing. Frankly, I was obsessed with his past for years, but have now given up," Haley welled up in tears as she spoke.

"Do you think that trekker may have been his father or a relative?" Shannon sheepishly asked, afraid of pushing the subject further.

"We did. But he had no resemblance whatsoever to Africus, and his interest did not seem paternal in any way. Maybe we should have pursued it further. At the time, we were more concerned he was a reporter or sensationalist, looking for a quick Z coin," Mika replied.

"We had heard of the legend of the African Boy Legend for years. The tribesman freely spoke of him. His legendary ability to communicate with all animals in the animal kingdom, including the birds of prey, was paramount to his legend. He was raised by the king of the lions, and his best friend was a lion cub that became the next king of the lions. He and his lion friend, it was said, ruled the jungles and savannahs of our Preserve and maybe even all of East Africa. He restored order in the chaos of the jungle. He also ran with the tribesmen from time to time and learned the ways of the man hunter and gatherer. He learned some of the local dialect from them. We used that dialect to refine his study of the English language," Mika unfolded the story further.

"Africus eventually, over time, in bits and pieces, retold his story to us, often as stories, fables, poems, and narratives. He often spoke of the surreal and supernatural, of myths and legends, of secret caves, maybe the Cavern of Lost Treasures, waterfalls, secret gardens and splendid wonders. Maybe all of this is just in his Parallel Dream Universe, or, Ha, maybe in a Parallel Real Universe! His attunement to nature, the animal kingdom, the birds, it is all amazing and breathtaking. To this day, he has full communication with the lions, particularly, his lion pride. He maintains an intense loyalty to the head of the lions, his friend. He calls him Maximilion!

"His first memory is as a young boy, maybe three years old, we speculate. He was alone in the high grass near some trees. A large male lion stood over him, ready for the kill. Lions generally don't like to eat people, but they do sometimes kill them if threatened or bothered by them. Before the fatal blow with his paw, a young lion cub stood between Africus and the male lion. It was the son of the male lion, who was leader of the pride, and we later found out really the leader, or king, of all the jungle and savannah in the Preserve. The lion cub nuzzled up to Africus and licked his face. He mewed and was playful. The lion pride king stepped back and roared. The lion cub roared. Africus roared, and together the three of them trotted back to the pride. Africus learned the way of the pride. He learned to hunt. He learned to protect himself and the pride from natural dangers and other aggressive, competing carnivores, particularly, the hyenas.

"We first spotted him a year or so before he finally joined us in human civilization. You know, we wonder to this day if we should have left him in the savannah and jungle. But sooner or later, someone else would have captured him. And poachers likely would have killed him, as he constantly warned the animals of their approach and whereabouts. He even set traps for them, although they thought it was the tribesmen.

"The first day we saw him was special. We knew at that moment he was more than a legend. We watched him help Maximilion chase down the hyena leaders. We have pictures of him that day of him running with the lions, with the dagger in his mouth. We have pictures of him resting on the back of Maximilion, lazily resting in the sun. We have pictures of him playing with the lion cubs, frolicking and wrestling and freely enjoying himself and their attention. The lion leader, Maximilion, let us know it was time to leave. He seemed anxious that day. Almost like he knew the future. That we were the ones to finally take Africus back into the fold of humanity.

"Over the next year, we watched him in great awe. His communion with nature was almost supernatural at times. He would leave for western Kenya, deep into the jungle with Maximilion. It is known as the Deep Jungle. That part of the jungle is so deep, that no man has ever entered that area of the jungle. He will not tell us what is back there. More legends and myths! He had an ability to watch and apparently see through the eyes of the birds of prey, particularly the African eagle. The tribesmen respected him and gave him his space and peace. He brought them gifts from the jungle that pleased them to no end. He would see us from time to time. He was not afraid. He seemed mostly not interested in us but let us watch him. The lions knew we were there as well. They left us alone, probably at his request, unless it appeared we were trying to capture or shoot him, in which case they would charge at us to back us away.

They never attacked or hurt us though. Just a warning. He seemed more interested in watching Haley at times. She would smile in that maternal way, I think. Then, one day, he simply walked over to our range vehicle and jumped into the back seat. He became our responsibility. Unofficially, we became his guardians, or foster parents," Mika concluded.

"Amazing story. I will keep it to myself. Maybe I will become a ranger and stay here, too! It is not poverty. This is heaven on earth! Why is he named Africus?" Shannon longingly responded.

"Mika had a dream. He was Africus in the dream. And he communicates with the animals and the birds. You know, we could use another woman ranger, for sure! We have three now, counting me. This is the smaller Preserve in Kenya. The larger one, which garners more safaris and world-wide attention, has many more rangers and employees. They are good at paying us. Our Z coins just keep accumulating. They send us food and uniforms and give us new vehicles every two years. Guns and ammunitions are in good supply. Kenya is a wealthy country now. They take great pride in the Preserves and animal heritage. We don't spend any money. And our income is under the U.S. threshold for income tax, and we are exempt from income tax in Kenya, as we work for the Preserve.

"Once a month an administrator visits the Preserve to check on us, and I give her my daily blog. The animals are healthy, and there is a good balance among the species. So, we have done well. I think, as does the administrator, that Africus is of great assistance in keeping the balance. She keeps our secret about him, although she only has suspicions, not actual knowledge of his past. She has received some handsome bonuses for the management of the Preserve. She wants all the accolades. That is fine with us. We have received bonuses every year since Africus has been here. He is paid, too. He has enough currency to pay for a couple of years of University, at least, a public University.

"So, in reality, this is Paradise!" Haley laughed.

They all laughed heartily. A couple of the rangers stopped by to meet Shannon. Two of the male rangers seemingly competed for her attention and affection. Mika scolded them for now but knew in the long days and nights in the savannah, these men yearned for the affection of someone like Shannon. Shannon loved the attention. One of the woman rangers had already paired up with one of the guards. The other was careful not to be profligate, but she was human, and had her indulgences, too.

*Who needs the stress of America! I want to be like Haley! Burned and spurned in the USA! Time for Paradise. I could handle this lifestyle. Nature. Super Nature. Legends and myths. Omigod!*

Shannon's smart device buzzed. Another text from Jason Smith. He wanted her back for an exciting new tech based, virtual reality-based project. Super recruit Savannah was in, and apparently was wowed by the visit. More importantly, her high society Mum, seemed overwhelmed as well.

*Omigod. Savannah! What a boon for WLAX at Nebraska. I love technology and virtual based applications. What to do! Paradise or virtual reality?* she thought to herself again.

"I am hungry," Shannon blurted out unexpectedly.

Mika laughed and watched the two rangers rush to pre-pare a grilled wild water buffalo plate for her, just like in the wild west in America. Some roasted native vegetables, packed with super nutrients that were fueling the Pharma-African farm boom, were served as well. Fresh milk from the antelopes was served chilled. It had a nice aftertaste and was loaded with anti-oxidants and vital nutrients.

After the meal, Shannon was replete, her famishment dissipated. Her mind drifted as it so often did. She was a dreamer to the nth degree. A booming tech company, a national championship in Nebraska State WLAX, or even two or three. A legend for the ages to lead the Nebraskans in football. National athletic assistant administrator of the year-but wait, there is no such award. A retired life in the savannah with a ranger and many children, all frolicking in Paradise. *Which life do I want?* She fell into a deep slumber on the hammock, happy and peaceful.

"She appears to be a remarkable young woman," Mika told Haley.

"I don't think her AD or head coach know that she is here with us. I don't think that they know about Africus specifically, or that generally, he is anything but a myth. We talked to him about going to the University in 2026. Recently, he confided to us he would try to go in 2026, if all worked out. We supported his decision. But, now, with Shannon here, and his voyage to Nebraska so real now, I don't know. Selfishly, I want him to bring Nebraska State to greatness on the gridiron. But who knows if he ever will be a football player, let alone a great leader on the field. He has not played organized football. And what will happen to the balance in the Preserve without his leadership with Maximilion. Plus, I will miss him so much!" Haley softly spoke, as she wiped the moisture from her eyes.

"I have played football with him. He is the fastest person I have ever seen. He can cut and turn better than anyone. I think right now he could be an Olympic gold medalist in the one-hundred-meter hurdles! Maybe even the one-hundred-meter sprint, too! No one could run past him or around him. He can run with the ball, catch the ball, and pass the ball with tremendous skill and accuracy. He could be special. He could be a legend in the real world, and a superhero in the virtual world. Limitless potential. But he might leave here and come home right away. This is his life. The dual life with us, and the life in the animal kingdom. I know he has decided to go to Nebraska State, but think he still has some uncertainty. I think the choice of 2026, instead of this fall 2025, helped him decide to try to go the University, as deep down he knows he has time to change his mind and stay in his home here. But I think he truly wants to go to Nebraska. But the pull of home is strong. Very difficult decision, possibly, for him. When he returns, we can all talk with Shannon. Who knows, she may stay here, too!" Mika responded.

"I am mixed on this. I want him to go and stay! Surely, he would come home for the U.S. summer months," Haley questioned, her eyebrows now raised in contemplation and confusion.

Mika and Haley retired to their shelter. The rangers lifted the limp Shannon from the hammock and put her inside on an extra bed. All of them slept for the night. But one ranger gathered up his bag loaded with cash and took off back to Nairobi under the cover of the night.

\*\*\*

The night sky over the western part of the Preserve was clear. Thousands of stars twinkled. The moon was hidden this night in its monthly progression from full moon to new moon. It was fairly dark outside. But game time was on. Africus walked with the lion pride. The hyenas cackled and the wild dogs howled. The prey nervously kept together in groups for greater protection.

Africus found his friend, a female cheetah. He called her Citra. Citra was with him when he first saw the Girl. Citra was a long-time friend, just like Maximilion. But she was on her last legs. Any night now, could be her last. He guided her to an old antelope waiting to join her ancestors and away from the hyenas. Citra found the antelope and managed to take it down. She pulled the antelope into a tree, to avoid vultures and other scavengers, who were now her match in strength. Soon young Africus climbed the tree. It was the tree where they first had met. Africus stroked the forehead of Citra as she ate her last supper and drank blood for the last time.

"Citra, you are my friend in this life and beyond. Soon you will dance with the twinkling stars above. I may leave to the north and west soon. You have mothered many young cheetahs. Your legend continues through them. The cheetah is protected in this Preserve. Not many people visit the western Preserve. That is good for now. Kenya is now a great country. It will support this Preserve from development and human advanced civilization. I will see to that. Mika and Haley will see to that. Your offspring will be safe, other than from nature itself. Citra, you are a special animal and spirit. Someday, if you return as another cheetah, let me know. So long my dear friend."

Africus stared at the stars along with Citra. Citra enjoyed her last supper and drink. She gazed into Africus's eyes, as if holding a special secret. She took one last look at the stars in the horizon. She was ready to return to the afterlife, and spiritual realms. She steadily released her last breath and rested her head on her front paws. She died in peace and tranquility with her dear friend at her side. But unknown to Africus, she knew she had not really died.

Africus was happy for his friend but saddened by his loss. Africus had suffered many losses in the jungle and savannah. It was never easy. He shed a tear, and gazed at the horizon, waiting for a new twinkle. He thought he saw one but was not sure. A shooting star crossed the sky. Surely, that was Citra! But shooting stars were not uncommon in June.

Africus took Citra to the grassy field nearby. He called out to the heavens and to the scavengers. Vultures and other scavengers gave Citra her proper African burial. Africus climbed back into his favorite tree. He saw that Maximilion and his pride, on this very dark of nights, had successfully hunted their next meal. The Pride was eating its prey and preparing for a lazy few days of full nourishment before the next hunt. Mating season was approaching. Maximilion nervously looked over his foes. He was still the head of the pride but was aging quickly with the rigors of his reign and was seriously injured in a fight with the hyenas a few weeks ago.

Africus checked his smart device. One message from Mika. Someone from Nebraska State was here. This was coming quickly. It was supposed to be another year-2026. And he wanted to stay and see if Maximilion kept his throne. But still, the opportunity seemed to be blossoming, like the flowers in early summer after the rainy season. He saw America in his mind. Was it truly such a grand country? A chance at a University education seemed promising. Football seemed like a good sport, like the night time in the jungle and savannah. Mika said he had the skills and instincts to be great. Maybe the safari Girl was in America and would recognize him.

He had used Haley's computer to research American football. He studied Nebraska State football, the offensive and defensive plays, the formations, the tackling techniques, the hunting and the fleeing. He saw things that maybe ordinary humans raised in civilization would not. He saw pursuit angles and signals from runners and tacklers as to their future motions and actions that others would not observe. He puzzled over certain plays and formations. He envisioned different plays, formations, and tackling techniques. The movie reel worked in his subconscious mind as he worked his job in the field. He was ready, he knew it. He lay his head on the tree limb to sleep. Morning approached, another halftime in the savannah for all to prepare for the game the next nightfall.

Maximilion heard his thoughts. He was preparing himself for the departure of Africus, his life-long friend. He recalled the first time he had seen Africus, a small boy, helpless in the jungle, his father ready to kill him. But he recalled his eyes. His friendly, inviting, familiar eyes. He saved Africus, not to save a human, but to save a friend in this life and likely others. He would miss Africus, but knew it was time. And his time was not far in ending either. One last season, he thought. One more season. *Farewell, my friend.*

# 15.

Tuesday, June 24, 2025
*West Kenya National Wildlife Preserve*

AFRICUS FELT THE INTENSE HEAT on his back, as he drove his range vehicle back to the ranger station. It had air conditioning, which he never used. The eagles soared above him, watching for lurking dangers before him. He still thought of Citra. All their time together, although they were together in mind more than in person. He often felt the presence of other animals that had passed. Not this time. Maybe Citra was reborn right into the jungle. Or a puppy in North America; no, more likely, a kitten. He felt the pressure on Maximilion to uphold his throne. He knew he could not interfere in that annual ritual. But Maximilion was his lifelong best friend. He rooted for Maximilion to hang on for one more season, and then another.

Suddenly, up ahead there was trouble. The eagles swooped down in front of his vehicle. Poachers, heavily armed. *They want me. I have disrupted most of their ventures. They have conspired and convened. I am their enemy, their prey. They do not see my future in America that Shannon, Mika and Haley see. I messed with their profits. But they are evil. They have taken so much. The ivory and paws and livers. The heads and toes. The hides. The rugs made of male lion manes. The cheetah faces. The eagle feathers and talons. The crushed bones, thought to have immense spiritual healing powers. It is time for battle. And just maybe they want more. The Cavern! Of course, they have never attempted to harm or kill me. Maybe they know.*

The eagles relayed the alarm. Africus stopped his vehicle. The poachers were over the hills. *This is my battle.* He thought someday it would come. He had never killed a poacher. Some were injured by some of his traps. But he had prevented them from capturing innocent animals. They had left for the larger preserves, out of frustration. But now the larger preserves had veritable armies of guards. They had tried to infiltrate the guard ranks but were flushed out and killed on the spot. So back to the West Kenya National Wildlife Preserve. Few guards, few weapons, lots of game.

They were two hills away. The eagles again sounded the alarm. The animal kingdom was on high alert. Nearby elephants fled for the cover of the jungle. Rhinos went to the rivers. Vultures circled the skies, anticipating a free meal. Monkeys and chimpanzees screeched and fled for cover. The poachers saw the excitement in the skies and heard the noise level raise from its normal high levels.

"He must be near. The ranger, that traitor, said he would come. He earned his pay. I am sure he has vamoosed back to Nairobi by now. We need to capture the African Boy Legend. Once we do, we will torture him and find out what he knows about the Cavern. Once he tells us where it is, we will kill him! My prosthetic leg is here because of that trap he set for us. Our vehicle plummeted into the river. The crocodile, probably on his command, ate my leg. I am lucky to be alive. Maybe we feed him to the crocs in the river!" the lead poacher cranked out with his burly voice.

"He seems to be one with the jungle. If we kill him, maybe the whole jungle turns on us. The boss man wants him alive," another speculated.

"Yeah, I know we should not kill him. But we can kill his lion friend. A hefty price will be paid for that mane. The mane of the king of the animal kingdom in the Preserve could fetch hundreds of thousands of K currency in Russia and China. A bidding wars!" He roared.

Africus could hear the roar of the poacher. He was Russian. His name was Igor. Africus remembered his hideous voice, and hideous smell. He had not tried to kill Igor five years ago. But the vehicle had veered into the river. The crocodiles were hungry and did not listen to Africus's request to spare the poachers. Unknown to Igor, it was Africus who pulled him from the river. Africus had put a tourniquet on Igor's leg to stop the hemorrhaging. Igor's mates had run scared, except the local tribesman and deputy of Igor's local troops, Adar, who came back for Igor and brought him back to the tribal huts. Eventually, Igor, with only a stump left for his leg, made it back to Russia, where he obtained a prosthetic limb.

*I am the hunted now, again. I am the prey. It is survival or death. I am trained by the best hunters in the world, the lions. I survived as the hunted many times. Now is the time to live, to outclass the hunter.*

Africus put his range vehicle in reverse. He did not know the extent of the weaponry of the poachers. He did not know if they had grenade launchers, or automatic guns. He feared the worse. He knew the fields, the trees, the shrubs, the roots, the creeks, and the holes of every square foot of the savannah. He veered his vehicle off the road onto the paths. He sped quickly, weaving around potholes, rocks and fallen trees. He had a head start. The eagles soared ahead of him. Igor saw the eagles. He had seen them before. He suspected they somehow worked with Africus.

"Let's go!"

Igor and his fellow poachers piled into their four range vehicles and burned rubber screeching up the road. They could see the eagles and the dust trail created by Africus's vehicle. They had powerful vehicles. They were well financed by a billionaire collector of African relics and animal artifacts back in Russia. Someone very tied into the top level of government. Someone who wanted the biggest prize of all. The Treasures in the Cavern. But Igor would keep many of the artifacts for himself for the bidding websites.

Igor ordered one of his comrades to launch a grenade near Africus's range vehicle to knock it over.

The grenade was launched, but Africus, tipped off by the eagles, dodged the crater. He dodged three more craters created by grenade launches. He then saw the four vehicles had panned out in horizontal formation. Two of the vehicles picked up their speed and were soon even with him. They slowly pinched closer to him in a pincer move. The other two stayed behind him. He was surrounded, but still was not captured. They could easily shoot him. But their rifles were not raised. *They want me alive. They want the location of the Cavern.*

He downshifted and pressed the engine as fast as it would go. He knew ahead was a shallow recently dried out creek bed. He knew where to launch his vehicle to clear the creek bed. But did he have enough power? If he crashed in the bed, he was doomed. He reached the launch pad, a dirt pad he had built as a makeshift way to get over the creek when it was flowing, instead of building a bridge. He pressed the pedal down fully to the floor and downshifted one more time for added power.

His range vehicle jettisoned into the air. It landed on the other side of the creek. The two flanking vehicles saw the creek bed at the last second. One vaulted headlong into its center, thrusting its passengers, other than the driver, airborne, with rifles and provisions spewing everywhere into the dry creek bed. None were killed or maimed. The driver mashed his head and chest into the steering wheel and windshield and was in critical condition. The vehicle was still in workable condition despite the crash. The other vehicle managed to stop, doing a 180 degree turn just short of the creek bed. The men in the second vehicle went to the aid of their fallen comrades from the vehicle that had crashed. They cared immediately for the injured driver, who appeared in critical condition. Chaos reigned among the poachers in the creek bed. Chasing humans was not in the contract.

Igor was in one of the two remaining vehicles pursuing Africus from behind. He saw the launch pad in time and formed a single file with the other pursuing vehicle. Both vehicles launched successfully over the creek bed.

Africus needed some more tricks and immediate help. He pushed the distress button on the driver dashboard. It notified the Kenya national guard of an urgent crisis at the Preserve, and also notified the guards and rangers back at the ranger station. But they would not arrive in time to save him. The distress signal was two blasts, which meant imminent danger from poachers.

Africus banked hard to the west. A mile away was the river. He floored the pedal one more time. He knew where the potholes and fallen logs were. He zig-zagged his way for the mile. He could hear the swearing of the poachers. He closed in on the river of crocodiles. There was no bridge. He would need a head start. The river was too deep to drive the range vehicle through it. His hope was to swim to safety.

Africus reached the river. He leapt from the vehicle and lunged towards the river. Africus grabbed a vine hanging from a tree hanging over the river. He swung far into the river and dove deep into the water. He held his breath and swam downstream as fast as he could. Igor stopped his vehicle at the bank. His companion vehicle stopped as well. He would not get out of the range vehicle with his fear of crocodiles. A few crocodile heads popped up.

The poachers suddenly panicked and fired repeatedly at the crocodiles. The crocodiles had left Africus alone. He was their leader, too. Africus warned them of the bullet dangers. They dove deep into the stream as well. Africus finally surfaced more than two hundred yards downstream. The swift current and his powerful stroke brought him that far. He dove down again and swam to the other side. He ducked into the high grasses. Lions came to his aid. The poachers backed away from the river, in total fear of the crocodiles. Africus bellowed a loud chilling call to the wild. The savannah was quiet for an eerie second. He then saw the two other vehicles that had stayed behind in the spring bed speeding away towards Uganda. Igor had a partial mutiny on his hands.

Igor was incensed. His anger overcame his fear. He drove his range vehicle down the riverbed side with his companion vehicle in tow. He determined Africus must have swum to the other side. He parked his vehicle after traveling a few hundred yards. He opened wild fire at the tall grasses across the bank to flush out Africus, suddenly not caring about the Cavern or the boss man. Hundreds of bullets. Africus hid in a creek bed, safe from the onslaught.

The shooting stopped. But then a loud noise arose from the distance. Dust billowed in the air. The noise became a roar. The crocodiles lay in wait at the river bottom.

"What is that? Igor bellowed.

"Let's get out of here!" a comrade screamed.

"I told you not to kill him!" another cried out.

Soon hundreds of wildebeest swarmed towards the vehicles. The two vehicles were tipped over and bodies and wildebeest fell into the river. The strong current carried the bodies downstream. The poachers shot their rifles incessantly. The poachers, other than Igor, could not swim and soon drowned or were eaten by the crocodiles. Igor floated downstream, expecting a crocodile to take his other leg at any moment. He saw a crocodile's eyes. He raised his rifle and fired. The crocodile rolled over in death. He wondered if it was the one that took his leg. One down, he thought, now the African Boy Legend.

The river floated him down a few miles. He dragged himself out. He radioed the other two vehicles that had fled. They found him and picked him up. His prosthetic limb had washed away. He wept in sadness and relief. Defeated again, he headed back to Uganda.

Mika heard the radio calls from the poachers over his radio devices and received the distress call from Africus. He recognized the voice of Igor-one of the most feared and successful poachers in Africa. He, Haley, Jorge' and one other guard took their rifles and headed out in a range vehicle as fast as they could drive. They expected Africus was in trouble. There was total silence and total determination. They could track the poachers' vehicles, too. They called the Kenyan military. Helicopters would be there soon. They had picked up the distress signal from Africus earlier as well. Mika expected the poachers were headed to the Ugandan border.

"They have a head start. Let's try to contact Africus. Let's save him, first. The national guard with its helicopters will track down the poachers," Jorge' belted out a desperate cry. His father had been killed by poachers, defending some elephants. He wanted revenge. But he knew they were outgunned and would stand little chance in a shootout.

"Ranger First Class Mika, this is Scorpion 1 of the Kenyan National Guard, elite special forces helicopter unit. We have locked onto the two vehicles of the target poachers. Please confirm that these are poacher vehicles."

"Ranger First Class Mika, here, one of the vehicles may be friendly. We are searching for the ranger vehicle as we speak. Will return asap, Out."

"Will stand by. Twenty minutes to targets."

"Africus will not answer. The satellite tracking system is now up on my computer. Here it is. His vehicle is disabled in the croc river. Hopefully, he is ok!" Haley cried out.

"Scorpion 1, ranger vehicle down and not one of the targets. Permission granted for you to proceed to the target vehicles."

"Scorpion 1 on route. Do you know if they have grenade launchers, or earth to air missiles?"

"Not sure. Suspect the worse."

"We will keep our distance and follow them out of the country. We will notify our embassy in Uganda to seek arrests at the border."

Scorpion 1 picked up the scent of the trail. Igor bellowed orders to fire at the helicopter. He risked an international incident. His days as the lead poacher could be ending soon. He resented the ranger boy with extreme hatred. He ordered the grenades launched. But the grenades were launched too far away to strike the helicopter. Anti-missile ballistics knocked out the firings that were close. One of the vehicles crashed, as the launcher jolted the vehicle into another dry creek bed. The vehicle exploded and all of the passengers perished.

Igor's vehicle crashed through a border fence. Adar was the driver. He shot his passengers to death, other than Igor. No loose ends. Adar and Igor traveled through a jungle path, and eventually found a road. They turned on their radio. A national alert was out for their arrest. Shoot to kill was the mantra. They feared for their lives. Would a helicopter from their boss man rescue them?"

Africus swam back across the river. The two eagles saw him and flew to the rescue vehicles. Mika saw the eagles. Africus had told him about the eagles, but no one else, except Haley. Mika followed them down some beaten animal paths to the river. There they spotted an exhausted Africus.

Haley ran over to him and hugged him. He hugged her back.

"I am safe. I escaped my enemy, but I did not defeat him. The battle is on. We must track down the enemy."

The group headed back to the ranger station in silence. Haley feared for her foster son's life. Jorge' wanted to personally track down Igor. Mika thought about Nebraska State. The future was turning course again. Time to regroup. Time to work with the national guard. Time to be the hunter.

"Take me back to the river. I need to be in the kingdom," Africus exhorted.

"Yes, Africus, we trust your judgment. Do you want to wait a day? Get a good meal, fresh clothes and arms?" Haley pleaded.

"I can feed myself. I do not need clothes where I am going."

Mika acquiesced and took Africus back to the river. The rest of them returned to the ranger station.

Shannon was freaked out. She saw them return without Africus. She presumed he was dead. Her dreams were dead. She fainted.

"Take her to her room. Best she is rested before we send her home," Mika ordered.

Jorge' took her to her room and rested her comfortably on her back. He put a pitcher of ice lemon water by her bedside. She rested soundly, her subconscious mind dreaming wildly about the day's events, secrets and people.

The next morning, she awoke. Soon her mind reeled. She raced to the shelter where Jorge' resided and barged into his room. She shook him violently.

"Tell me what happened. Is Africus gone?" she cried, almost hysterically, fearing the worse, but hoping for good news.

Jorge' broke from his exhausted slumber. He wiped his eyes as consciousness drifted back into his mind.

"Shannon, he is alive. But he is gone again, likely deep into the western forest, in the Deep Jungle, the deepest jungle in Kenya. He was hunted by poachers. The lead poacher killed my father. They tried to kill Africus. He escaped in the crocodile river. The Kenyan national guard chased the poachers into Uganda. The Ugandan government is searching for them. Igor is his name. He is the number one on the most wanted list for crimes against the animal kingdom throughout Africa. He has heavy armaments. The helicopter had to keep its distance. Someday we will capture and execute him."

"Will Africus return?"

"Not for a while. When human events unravel, he still reverts back to the jungle and savannah. He may not be back for a few weeks or even months. I don't know."

Haley arrived into the shelter.

"Shannon, I often dreamed of Africus attending Nebraska State and playing football or another sport. I am not sure on timing. Originally, we were thinking 2026. But we need to see how this latest event impacts his decision. Will he still want to go? Will he want to go earlier? But let's still prepare as if he is still going. With this event, 2025 and 2026 are both in play. Or maybe nether. I will give you his academic records, test scores, high school equivalency report, curriculum, grades, and all that I have. I was his teacher, coach, and principal. You can determine his eligibility for a scholarship, and whether he can be accepted to the University for matriculation. He is very smart. He could pay for the first year of tuition. You can let me know the timing of his acceptance, when he can play sports, his eligibility for a scholarship, and logistics. You need to determine his international travel status. He has no birth certificate. We are not legally his guardians or foster parents, either. I know the envoys at the U.S. embassy in Kenya. I can introduce you to them. But do your homework first, before we expose our boy to the world!"

"All right. I will pursue this with full vigor. I will keep it discreet. Any sniff of a football recruit from Africa will light up the scoreboards of the Socialverse. Other coaches will descend upon this Preserve, looking for his commitment. This could be a squeamish tightrope walk. If you prefer, I could wait."

"No, it is what he wants. Fall of 2025 or 2026. Maybe never. Let us see," Haley concluded.

Haley and Shannon exchanged contact information. Jorge' took Shannon to the bus station. It was on time. She hugged him good-bye.

# 16.

*Wednesday, June 25, 2025*
*Western Kenya*

AFRICUS ARRIVED AT THE EDGE of the Deep Jungle in the western part of Kenya. Few humans ever entered the Deep Jungle. The umbrage was so thick it was dark on the ground. The jungle floor was slick with moisture, and thick with vegetation. Insects were thick in the air; birds sang loudly and often. Snakes had left this portion of the jungle years ago.

He looked for the opening. He could not find it. He waited patiently. He could hear distant musings-telepathy from Maximilion. Suddenly, the Great Ape swung through the trees and with one swift motion swept up Africus under his arms. Africus smelled a familiar scent and was soon unconscious. He was glad to see the Great Ape from his childhood again.

*Finally, I am going back to the Waterfall and Paradise in person in the Parallel Real Universe! My first time back since Mika and Haley took me to the Preserve. Since then I have only visited* there in my dreams in the Parallel Dream Universe. I have read enough science books and science fiction books to confirm what my friends said- that the openings are a portal into another universe, a parallel universe, or world. My friends call it the Parallel Real Universe, to mirror the name of my dream world-the Parallel Dream Universe. The openings are Portals, and access through the Portals is called a Passage. Each Parallel Dream Universe and its corresponding Parallel Real Universe are the same Universe, just accessed in different ways. One by dreams, and the other in person by Passage through the Portals. But there are multiple Universes. But my special places all appear to be in one Parallel Universe.

"And my friends, who are my guides or guardian angels, are known as Special Beings. One is the white zebra. There are others like the Great Ape and the elven-like monkeys and the two eagles. And Maximilion- my friend and king of the lions. He is a Special Being, but one that now lives in our mortal world. When he dies, he will be like the others. And maybe Citra is a Special Being.

The Great Ape swung him through the trees. He heard the distant Waterfall. It became louder and louder. The mist of the Waterfall was soon upon him. The thoughts of the great lion leader were roaring in his ears as loudly as the Waterfall. The Great Ape dropped him from the giant tree that overhung the small lake at the bottom of the Waterfall. He plummeted into the water headlong but managed to somersault underneath the surface to avoid hitting the rocks on the bottom of the lake.

Africus kicked his legs hard like a frog towards the surface. He inhaled a huge bale of air and mist. He coughed as the mist tickled his throat and lungs. He wiped the mist from his eyes. The noise from the Waterfall was thunderous. Two large African eagles soared above the sky and dove straight for the lake. They splashed the water with their giant talons and each grabbed a large fish. They flew up into the air and landed on the twin rocks that oversaw the lake from behind the Waterfall. Africus swam to the bank of the lake and climbed up the slippery surface to the land. Heavy, lush plants populated the bank. Flowers abounded. He pushed through the thick leaves to an open path to the Waterfall. He walked behind the curtain of the falling water. The eagles screeched. He grabbed some of their fish from the shredded fish carcasses. The eagles seemed pleased he had shared their conquest. He acknowledged their gift with a loud coo.

Africus had returned to the Waterfall, his favorite spot in the world. He was exhausted from the prior day's battles. But today it was the white zebra who beckoned him to the Waterfall, in the Parallel Real Universe, not in a dream. He enjoyed the mystery and supernatural aura of this hidden Paradise, away from the civilized world. Myths and legends of mysterious creatures kept the locals away. Thick bush, swarming insects, predators and crocodiles kept the tourists away. Africus knew the plant oils to bathe his skin in to avoid the predatory insects. The crocodiles felt his presence and left him alone. They would heed his admonitions and orders, as well.

He called the white zebra with no stripes Essence. Essence was of the purest spirit. He soaked in her energy and divinity. He was not sure why she was here today. Maybe it was his brush with mortality. Together they had shaped history in the region, yet their role in participation in the historic event was not known to the civilized world, even with all of its technology.

Africus grabbed Essence around her face and gazed into her blue eyes. Together they flashed back to that fateful day- the Great Defeat.

*The fog was thick at the eastern ridge of the deep jungle in the western part of Kenya. The section of jungle was simply known as the Deep Jungle. Hundreds of tanks and thousands of heavily* armed soldiers were marching towards Nairobi on foot and in trucks, skirting next to and under the umbrage of the Deep Jungle. The attack was to be a surprise attack, well schemed and planned. The heavy fog hid the marching troops from satellite reconnaissance.

A white zebra, with a young boy riding on top of her, emerged from the Deep Jungle onto the road in front of the lead vehicles. The boy's shoulder length blonde hair glistened as if the hair of a deity. At his side was a sheathed sword. The driver, awestruck, stopped, causing a serious back-up and numerous fender benders. The General was in the lead vehicle. He stepped out of his vehicle with his assault rifle. It appeared he knew the boy was the African Boy Legend. Ground troops slowly caught up and were a hundred wide and hundreds deep. More troops rode in the trucks.

The boy was neither political, nor civilized. He only saw this army as danger to the animal kingdom and natural wildlife in the Preserves in Kenya. It was a war against him and his kingdom. Soon two large male lions flanked the African Boy Legend and the white zebra. The four stared at the General. The soldiers were restless and nervous. They feared the supernatural. They feared the legends and myths of the Deep Jungle they were skirting on the way to their conquest.

"Give yourself up! And lead us to the Cavern of Lost Treasures!" The General shouted, partly in fear.

The boy was silent. He did not know their language, other than in parts. He and his stalwart companions knew the devastation of the guns. Their ruse was one of intimidation and superstition. They had seen locals and soldiers flee before at their presence. He was the legend of the African Boy Legend, the supernatural deity from the sky and the jungles. A myth and legend that traveled by word of mouth but was never sanctioned or proven. But here he stood, towering over the foot soldiers on an angelic zebra.

Two eagles descended from the sky and screeched as they zoomed by the General and his lead soldiers and officers at the

*front of the battalions. The eerie fog played heavily into the super-*
*natural ambience of the moment. A thunderous roar arose from the*
*distance. The sky darkened further. The soldiers felt panic. Sudden-*
*ly, a dozen more lions appeared out of the fog from the Deep Jungle.*
*They collectively roared. The roar reverberated for miles, as the fog*
*held the crucibles for longer echoes. The darkness of the sky soon*
*descended upon the troops in the form of thousands of birds of*
*prey and vultures. It was a scene of madness and utter catastrophe*
*to the soldiers. The roar in the distance turned into violent tremors.*
*Thousands of wildebeest and other grazing animals, now foot sol-*
*diers, stormed towards the troops. The boy called to the wild in a*
*bone chilling scream. He unsheathed his sword, a medieval blade*
*bejeweled with dazzling gems. Ancient inscriptions adorned the*
*blade. It was magical and historic. The soldiers saw the glistening*
*and shimmering of the ancient steel and cowered back in fear and*
*awe. The lions roared louder. The General's eyes suddenly were*
*plucked by the two eagles, and he lost his sight. Two lions tore him*
*to shreds. The troops retreated in total terror, many into the Deep*
*Jungle they feared so heavily. The trucks retreated but were soon*
*toppled by the thundering herds. Many of the soldiers perished.*
*They were consumed by the scavengers. It was a total annihilation.*
*The animal kingdom had won. So too had Kenya. But little did it*
*know. It was to be known as the Great Defeat.*

Africus's mind drifted into a trance like state back in
time. There he was, riding bareback on Essence. Only elev-
en years old, he had not yet joined the rangers, nor been
taken in by Mika and Haley. He was free and wild-part of
the spiritual bond of the animal kingdom. It was shortly after the day he had met Providence at the magical tree.

Africus flashed back to the present. He knew from talking to Haley in home school, that the slaughter was a great
mystery. It was thought by insiders that the General may
have set out to conquer Kenya, with its vast wealth in plants
and pharmaceutical substances and ties to the pharma com-

panies. The Kenyan army was no match for his forces, and it was suspected he was backed by a silent major power, seeking to indirectly control the pharmaceutical pipeline from Africa. Plans were underway for billions in infrastructure spending in Kenya. But Africus knew they were also after something bigger. *The Treasures.*

Haley had taught him that the government in Uganda dismissed the incident as a training exercise gone awry, where insubordinate troops mutinied, and killed their general gone awry The Kenyan government denied that there was a planned attack, particularly one they would not have been prepared to defend, and one where total defeat was certain. The world press was not terribly concerned. The pharma industry was full bore on the new frontier, oblivious to the dangers in the jungle and local political instability. The Kenyan national guard quickly cleaned up the battlefield. The tanks and trucks were confiscated by eminent domain. The tanks and trucks were disassembled and the parts were sold. The dead were returned to Uganda for proper burial. And Kenya and Uganda signed an economic treaty, where they agreed to work together in the new African Pharma-industrial-agricultural complex. Uganda offered up many special plants for research and development, too.

The legend of the African Boy Legend had exploded locally. It was word of mouth. Government suppression of the press prevented it from international sensationalism, and his existence and a coordinated attack by animals was anathema to the government spin on the disaster. The African Boy Legend lived on in obscurity in the real world. His myth was legendary.

Others thought he was a spirit from the heavens, along with his spiritual horse, all mystical and powerful. It was divine intervention, that the General should fail and be defeated. Peace had taken over the region ever since. Fear and

apprehension and superstition of the return of the two spirits was rampant and promoted the peace. The sword held
the most sway. It was believed to be the sword of the archangel of God himself. Its power could stop an entire army.
Others speculated it was Excalibur, the very sword of King
Arthur of England, as made by Merlin. Rumors of the Cavern of Lost Treasures with vast Treasures and historic English artifacts had abounded for centuries. The rumors were
heightened by the wielding of the sword by the African Boy
Legend, or boy deity. Rumors exploded that the General
was really after the Treasures in the Cavern more than the
pharma business. Africus had never told Haley or anyone of
his role in the Great Defeat.

Africus hugged Essence. "We rode together with an army
at our side. It was momentous!" Africus recalled with chills
and tears.

"I have not seen you since we were together at the Great
Defeat! Where have you been?

"I have been around. I am always watching over you and
watching over the Cavern of Lost Treasures!"

"I know that you are a Special Being, with powers to take
me to magical places, like this Waterfall and the Cavern. But
now that I have lived in the world of mankind, my curiosity
is greater! What are you, Essence? What is a Special Being?
Are you a spirit, as the locals believe?" Africus guardedly
asked.

"I am from the same Great Realm as the elven-like monkeys and the Great Ape. I am a being from a superconscious
state with access to multiple Universes, both real and
dream. Think of the Great Realm as a place in a different
time and space dimension, but one in a higher realm. Your
friends on earth might think of it as heaven. I am real in my
dimensions of the Great Realm. I cross often into your
realm and dimension, or your Real Universe, as you would

deem it, as do the monkeys. I cross over into your dreams, but also into your world, mostly now as an animal-taking over their mind. More importantly, I have the Knowledge to gain Passage through the Portals to the Parallel Real Universe where the Waterfall and Cavern exist. My Knowledge is how I bring you to the Cavern of Lost Treasures and your Paradise with the Waterfall in the Parallel Real Universe. Those places are not accessible by mortals on the earth plane, except with one of the Special Beings. Those special places are accessible for those with the super mental abilities, like you, Africus, and the Girl, though their dreams, in the Parallel Dream Universe. Maybe someday the technology of mankind will develop and acquire the Knowledge to gain Passage to the Parallel Real Universe where the Cavern and Paradise are located. That may be some centuries into the future! And someday I will impart the Knowledge to you, but not now.

"Africus, it is time for you to return to the Cavern by Passage through the Portal into the Parallel Real Universe with both me and a phalanx of elven-like monkeys. The elven-like monkeys are your friends and allies. They await you in the Cavern of Lost Treasures. Ride me again. We shall return to the Cavern with the monkeys. You will not see the Portal to the Cavern. We pass through a field of poppies. You will pass out until we are in the depths of the Cavern. You shall see the Treasures again," Essence soothingly explained yet with a tone of excitement.

"I am ready. I am ready for my mission. I am ready to go to America as well, if that is the plan."

# 17.

AFRICUS JUMPED ON THE BACK of Essence. She jumped through the Waterfall, and they dove together into the small lake below. He held on to her mane as she scaled up the side of the lake onto the grassy banks. She was sure footed. The birds hooted and sang in a cacophony of music and song. The crocodiles opened their mouths in a sendoff. The Great Ape swung on vines with them as she galloped deeper into the jungled forest. The forested jungle became darker as the trees grew in length. The mist in the air was thick, while the air gradually became cooler. She had headed east into the Rift Valley towards the mountains. Soon the field of poppies was upon them. Africus did his best to note his itinerary and location. Soon elven-like monkeys were screaming and jumping all around him. The poppies were thick and tall enough to shield his vision as Essence galloped through the field. He saw the snowcapped mountain before his view was cut off completely by fog. His eyes became heavier and heavier. He became sleepy and peaceful. The sounds of the monkeys dimmed in the gradual darkness. Soon he was in an unconscious state, only physically aware of his surroundings, and his subconscious mind had taken over, as well as his inner spiritual self.

The elven-like monkeys led Essence with Africus slumped on her back high up the mountain to the Cavern entrance. A mist billowed out of the Cavern entrance. The elven-like monkeys and Essence made Passage through Portal entrance. They then traversed a thin trail down into the center of the Cavern.

Africus awoke and was stunned again by the beauty of the Cavern and its majestic Treasures. He had not been there since he was a boy.

"Tell me the story and history of this Cavern of Lost Treasures! I need to know! The elven-like monkeys never told me the history," Africus feverishly begged Essence.

"Indeed. The Cavern of Lost Treasures was originally found by an ancient people. They were the last refugees from the sinking continent of Atlantis. They managed and exploited its bountiful treasures. It is their ten-foot-long skeletons that remain inside. The Cavern had contained rich veins of gold, which the Atlanteans had mined and processed. Buried in here, too, are Treasures from Atlantis, including books and tablets containing many of the technological secrets of their great society. There is also the Great Book of Wisdom from a Great Society, written by King Atlas V, who died as the last emperor of Atlantis on its final plunge into the sea. It is preserved in a decay proof plastic bin. I am afraid that even if the Great Book is discovered, its language may not be decipherable today. It not only contains messages for later civilizations on earth about technology, society and government, but also on the dangers of supreme technology not properly harnessed and controlled. There are also fragments of the base components of the great crystalloid engines from Poseidon, the capital of Atlantis, that powered the city and the country with wireless power waves. The technology to use the engines is certainly contained in the Great Book written by King Atlas V. The crystals utilized quantum physical properties and generated energy from the thermal heat of the earth's crust and energy from the ionosphere. There was also the technology for anti-gravity forces, used for transportation and construction. They had hover crafts. I knew King Atlas V!

"The Cavern of Lost Treasures was later populated by hundreds of small white elven-like monkeys who protected it and its priceless gifts.

"Later, in the fourteenth century, explorers from England discovered the Cavern. The elven-like monkeys had permitted their leader to access the Cavern. The explorers were financed and governed by a secret society in London, more secret, and more inside the framework of the world order behind all of the world kingdoms and empires, than even the mighty Templar Knights. The secret society, known simply as the Society, whose mark was the African Lion with large angelic blue eyes, and large white wings, commandeered the Cavern of Lost Treasures and kept it secret among its highest inner circle. In time, only the leader knew its location. The original explorers mysteriously vanished, other than their leader, under the ruse of sunken ships in an Atlantic hurricane. The Society thus avoided risk of disclosure with the ultimate price. The lead explorer was the head of the Society. The families of the victims were well compensated and did not even challenge the story of the sunken ships. The Society kept the existing Treasures untouched. The local natives stayed away from and did not search for the Cavern. Fear and treachery wrapped its fabled legend into a place of sacred untouchable space. Fear overwhelmed the natives when asked about the legend of the Cavern of Lost Treasures. No words were ever spoken of its existence or location. Only the incumbent leader of the Society knew the location.

"A hundred years later, in the fifteenth century, the head of the Society was Marcus Aurelius VIII, of Roman heritage. The King of England, the only person, not a member of the Society, to know of the Society and its leader, was pressuring the Society to reveal England's most cherished Treasures, the artifacts from the kingdom of King Arthur, to his subjects. The King wanted to solidify and confirm his right to the throne. It was a tumultuous time, where rival groups lay claim to the throne. But Marcus did not succumb to the pressure. He felt compelled to hide and shield those most cherished, fabled and legendary Treasures. He conspired to bring them on a secret trip to the secret Cavern of Lost Treasures.

"Marcus with a band of elite guards went to the hills deep in the English country side and unlocked the hidden iron doors to a secret underground museum, founded and built by King Arthur's son prior to his death. The Society had guarded the museum for hundreds of years. But the legend of the museum had reached the ears of the King, and his rival groups. Dozens of treasure hunters, knights and soldiers scoured the country. Only the King knew of the Society. He knew they were the guardians of the museum. Prior Kings left the Society and its secrets alone, both out of fear of reprisal, but also in need of finance and support. The new King was embattled. His claim to the throne was challenged. The tale of King Arthur, his alleged ancestor, was questioned, as was his lineage from King Arthur. If he had the original crown and the sword inscribed by Merlin, as Excalibur, his kingdom would be secure, and his opponents silenced.

"Marcus brought the most revered and sacred Treasures of England to the Cavern of Lost Treasures. The elite guard carefully removed the sword of King Arthur, Excalibur, King Arthur's crown and crown jewels, Guinevere's crown and crown jewels, and the sword pulled from the stone and the stone by a young Arthur, as well as other artifacts, jewels and treasures. By cover of night and covered wagons, they safely brought the Treasures to the London harbor and boarded the cargo on their ship. The ship appeared to be an ordinary ship of commerce, but it was laden with cannons and weapons. Marcus immediately set sail. The ship sailed from the port of London around Cape Horn into the Indian Ocean. The crew did not know of the Treasures that their ship carried. Later a solo pirate ship had attempted to seize the Society's ship, but a mysterious fog had enveloped the ship on most of its voyage, hiding the ship from the pirates' canons, in a thousand-mile mission of stealth and hide and seek. Captain Marcus engaged in a few brief skirmishes with the pirate ship while sailing along the coast of Africa in the Atlantic Ocean. It was clear the pirate ship did not want to sink the Society's ship. Marcus determined the adversary was likely more than just pirates-likely, an enemy of the Society itself. Capture of the English Treasures could either be held for enormous ransom or used to sway the balance of power to another secret group conspiring to rule the earth at a supra-governmental level. The swordsmen on the English ship in the brief skirmishes quickly dispatched their counterparts with skilled swordsmanship. But Marcus determined that the pirate ship was there to follow their ship and steal its Treasures and to find the Cavern of Lost Treasures. Marcus decided to be the hunter when the ships sailed up the coast of Africa in the Indian Ocean. The English ship went broadside with the pirate ship. The pirate captain did not know the commercial vessel was loaded with armaments. Marcus unveiled and unleashed the fury of his hidden cannons in a complete surprise in what was the last and final skirmish, sinking the pirate ship at last in the Indian Ocean. The captain of the pirate ship screamed in his dying breath that he would haunt the Captain and his Treasures in the afterworld. It was a terrifying scream, one that the English Captain Marcus forever remembered.

"Upon reaching the shores of East Africa, the elite guard unloaded the crates of Treasures. Golden artifacts, jewels, chalices, ancient coins, and other riches were stored in the many crates, too. After the crates were unloaded, the elite guard carried the crates for miles on a beaten animal path heading to the mountains. They came upon an extensive poppy field. Soon the elite guards were asleep. The real guardians of the Treasures of the Cavern of Lost Treasures came forth in the hundreds. The elven-like monkeys garnered and carried the crates up the mountain to its entrance, hidden from our world, by space and time dimensional disparities. The crates were brought below and safely and securely stowed away. The commander Marcus was allowed Passage to the Cavern of Lost Treasures. The monkeys communicated spiritually with the great leader of the secret English society. They cautioned him against betrayal and against public disclosure of the location and existence of the Cavern of Lost Treasures.

"Marcus held Excalibur in his hands and lifted the ancient and powerful sword above his head. He sheathed the sword and wept. The great King of England, King Arthur, was real and not a legend. He held the crown but did not adorn it on his head. He kissed the crown, made of jewels and lace, of the queen. He could not pull the sword from the stone. Ah, he was not to be King. The monkeys sprayed a special incense on him, and he soon swooned. When he awoke, he and his crew of elite guards were on their dories, sitting idly in the bay. As they awoke, Marcus ordered them to return to the ship. Four more pirate ships appeared over the horizon. Marcus knew the Treasures were safe and secretly secure. He was the only living person to know the location of the Cavern of Lost Treasures. The great leader died in the ensuing battle, taking the knowledge of the location of the Treasures and the Cavern of Lost Treasures to his grave. The pirates searched for years for the Treasures, exploring all the cave systems and mountains and riverbeds and ancient burial sites to no avail. Soon the Treasures and imaginary Cavern of Lost Treasures became legend and myth. Trekkers and spelunkers alike could not find it. The supernatural, transcendent cave remained just out of reach of the material world, in a dimension of a parallel world, milliseconds and millimeters away in the space-time continuum," Essence shrugged and looked away as she finished her tale.

"So, to this day, neither the King, nor the Society, know the location of the Cavern? No descendants of the pirates and no local tribesmen know of the location either?" Africus inquired, still in awe of the story and the Cavern.

"Come with me. That is true. And you are the only person who has been here since Marcus," Essence beckoned.

Essence led Africus deep into the Cavern. The elven-like monkeys were excited to have Africus back in the Cavern. They brought him a gold chalice filled with chilled water from the stream that flowed through one of the mined veins that was once filled with solid gold. Africus looked at the beautiful eyes of Essence. He wondered if her spirit were somehow a spirit he knew somewhere else. He believed there were other realms of existence and that dimensions of time and space were maybe part of the science and mystery of the other realms.

"Essence, why I am here. It is certainly one of the wonders of the world. There is Excalibur. Its power is monumental. We defeated a powerful army with the magic and wonder of that sword. The elven-like monkeys brought me that sword prior to the Great Defeat. There is the sword in the stone. What if I pull the sword from the stone? Shall I be the heir to a kingdom? The kingdom of England! Or the Kingdom of Africa? The birds hear my thoughts, and the crocodiles leave me alone. I run with the lions, the wild dogs obey me, and the snakes slither away from me. The elven-like monkeys treat me like royalty. They had taken me here dozens of times when I was a boy and before I went to the Preserve with Mika and Haley. I wonder why all of this is the case. I don't recall any life before the jungle and before Maximilion and his father took me into the pride. I did have an easy recollection of the English language. I have seen some movie clips that look so familiar. But Haley researched endlessly for my ancestry and lineage and parents. Nothing has arisen. I fell in love with the Girl on the safari. She never returned. Haley could find nothing on her. Did I really ever meet her? Was she an illusion or hallucination? But her eyes. I saw her soul. I saw true love! What is my life all about? Am I just a member of the animal kingdom? Should I go to America?"

Essence listened to Africus. The elven-like monkeys brought him more of the refreshing and ice-cold water. Africus drank it slowly and sumptuously. The water invigorated him. It felt like the blood of the Gods was coursing through his veins. *The Cavern is certainly mystical and supernatural, yet so real.*

"Africus, the elven-like monkeys view you as their King. You have been summoned by them to the Cavern of Lost

Treasures. They are going to crown you the King! You shall be the trustee and keeper of the Treasures. The Treasures are yours to keep and dispose of as you determine. The English Treasures you shall hold for the Crown. The other Treasures are yours. You are the prodigal son they have waited for hundreds of years. Your presence was foretold by Marcus Aurelius VIII. The Society secretly once ran the world from behind the scenes. They once ruled the kings and queens and dictators. He foretold the monkeys of a boy who would be their King, who would grow up in the jungle and savannah with the lions. You are that boy. So today is the day.

"The Girl is real. It is her destiny to meet you again. She yearns deeply for you and has searched relentlessly for you. She moved away from Africa after you met her. She has not been back to Africa at all. That has hindered her mission and quest to find you. She does not know that you are a ranger in the Preserve. She does not know of Africus. But recently, she has discovered clues. She is a young Sherlock Holmes. Small clues are not lost on her. She seeks you in a determined yet desperate way. You are still a figment in her past. Her father tells her she was one with an active imagination, with imaginary friends. Some of those imaginary friends are real. I once showed up in her backyard, in her father's mansion in the south of Africa. She gazed at me for an hour. She thought I was a unicorn. Soon she ventured out to the backyard. I knelt down and she climbed aboard my back. We pranced through her magnificent estate, and then into the jungle. A pride of lions idly watched as we strode by them. Snakes slithered out of the way. Chimpanzees cheered and clapped! She giggled and laughed and tickled my mane. I returned her to her estate. It was a glorious day. I knew she was destined to be a princess and a queen.

"She said goodbye. This was before the last safari with her father when she met you. She had heard of your legend, like most school girls in Africa. But she dreamed of you as well. She left the safari camp, in an earnest attempt to meet you. She strongly sensed your presence. She felt your being. Then she saw you. You locked eyes. It was true love. It was destiny. It was serendipity. Your fates are interlocked in the spiritual and material world. She has studied the legends and fables. But she has discovered nothing in the present world. She awaits you, yet has doubts about her dreams and mystical insights," Essence finished in her soothing and calm voice.

"I remember when I first met you. It was the same. I gazed into your eyes for so long. I trusted you. You rode me through the Deep Jungle to the Waterfall for the first time. It was magical. Who rode you first?"

"You were first. Then the Girl. Then you again when we defeated the imperial army."

The monkeys soon descended upon the two. The Cavern suddenly glowed in a luxuriating luminescence. They sang loudly, hailing the new King of the Cavern. Essence lead him down very deep into the Cavern. The Cavern opened up in a large cylindrical opening. The ceiling was at least one hundred feet in height. The walls were circular above the Cavern entrance, with a diameter of three hundred feet, the size of a football field. The walls glowed with bioluminescence. The small river of water that flowed through the Cavern swept through the opening at a quickened pace, as the descent angle was larger. A throne lay in the middle of the opening. *It must have been put there by Marcus. Or maybe the Atlanteans.* Africus sat on the throne. Once seated he smelled its mustiness. It was ancient, at least hundreds of years old. It must have been from medieval times as well, and not from Atlantis, he speculated.

"Africus, this was the chair of King Arthur. It was brought here by Marcus on his expedition from England. You are now seated in the throne of the first King of England. He was a real person, of great importance in uniting the people of England under one flag. You are now the symbolic King of this Cavern. Your powers and communication skills with the animals, and birds, will magnify and multiply exponentially. Your mind and spirit will be as one with them. Your skills and senses and instincts are already well developed to survive and thrive in the jungles and savannahs of Africa. Humans will not understand your role in your kingdom, or your powers and instincts, so you will need to work through human channels and administration," Essence explained.

The monkeys continued their chanting and excitement. Soon they brought King Arthur's crown to the opening. Essence dematerialized as an albino zebra, and for a moment took the form of an angelic creature of extreme beauty. A woman with the wings of an angel.

"I am a Special Being, as I have told you, from the Great Realm. I can take many forms, at different times. I am Essence, a state of being with the oneness of the Great Realm. And now I place upon thee, but wait," she stopped.

The Giant Ape soon appeared. He carried with him Excalibur. He placed it upon each shoulder of Africus. He was first made a knight of the now royal Cavern.

"Now that you are Sir Africus of the Society of Knights, you are now eligible to be King. I place upon thee head the crown of King Arthur, the first King of England!" Essence raised her hands to the ceiling enclosing the opening.

The monkeys shrieked in approval. Africus raised the heavy sword in his right hand to the ceiling as well. Everything is well. Africus, the King of the Cavern, held his head high.

Africus sat on the throne for an hour. The monkeys continued to keep him hydrated with the cold, refreshing holy water from the stream. Soon they brought nuts and berries that they had brought with them from the valley and mountainside. Africus ate in peace. Essence sat on a carved stone bench at his side. He was amazed at her sheer beauty.

"Essence, may you not enter this material world and become my queen?"

"I am your guide. I am now forbidden from entering the material world, as other than as a beast, unless I stay until death of my human body. I am here to guard the Treasures and to guide you and the Girl in specific missions and duties. I will be there for both of you when needed. SHE is your destiny."

"I see. I think your beauty radiates to and is reflected in the face of the Girl. I am anxious to see her. How do I ever find her?"

"Follow your heart and your urges and desires. It is all right to excel in the material world, the world of humans. Athletics is a form of excellence and perseverance. It reflects the animal kingdom, where the hunter and the hunted play for survival. It is a game that reflects the battles of life. Much can be learned, and much taught through sports and athletic games. The sports are rooted in early human ancestry, when humans lived and hunted and competed with the animal kingdom, as if merely another species. Now man is locked into the world of his cerebrum, increasingly disconnected from his physical self, real world and the kingdom of earth itself with its bounty of species of life."

"What must I do. I shall find the Girl first."

"No, follow your dreams first. The Girl will come to you naturally. Your union cannot be forced. Give it time. Pursue your worldly dreams. You were placed with Mika and Haley. Why is that! Think of why they were your foster parents."

Africus was overwhelmed with thoughts of his impending duties and roles, and with the admiration of the monkeys. He was exhausted. Soon he tired and fell into a deep sleep on the throne.

# 18.

*Thursday, June 26, 2025*
*The Waterfall*

THE NEXT MORNING AFRICUS awoke in a sea of poppy plants. The wind was blowing hard, so the aroma was not overcoming his senses. He slowly stood and looked for miles. No sign of life anywhere. Where was Essence! Where were all the elven-like monkeys. He wondered if he had died, and this was a waiting spot for the spiritual realms, and heaven itself. He gathered himself and noticed a white butterfly. He thought of Essence. She could take any form as needed to help and guide and save and protect him. *It must be her.* He followed the fluttering butterfly as fog soon encapsulated the mountain. Soon he could ascertain a trail. He even thought he could hear the footsteps of the elite guard as they carried the crates full of Treasures. *Did they know the magnitude of importance and the immense value of the Treasures? How did they resist mutiny, with a chance at unparalleled wealth and possibly power for the ages?*

He reached to unsheathe his sword, but it was not there. He felt his head, there was no crown, but he thought his hair felt as if he had worn a headpiece, or hat, of some weight. He thought he smelled the musk of an old artifact. *Ah, the poppy plants. I must have passed out. And the elven-like monkeys must have taken me to the Cavern. Where was the Portal? And is the Cavern real or a dream? No, it is real. I was there again in the Parallel Real Universe.*

Soon he was below the cloud line. There was his giant friend, the Great Ape. The Great Ape grabbed him and swung on the vines. It seemed like an endless swing from tree to tree for hundreds of trees. He fell asleep again. When he awoke, he was back at the Waterfall, deep in the jungled forest. And there was Maximilion, next to him.

"Maximilion, you are here. How is your annual battle with the young princes going?"

"Africus, I am leader of the lion pride and thus the animal kingdom here in the Preserve. But I am growing older and tired. I had a setback recently with injuries to my back in my continual fight with the hyenas. And, yes, I will have more lion cubs, and I hope for more years as head of the lions. If I perish, you will know. I will come to say good-bye. We will meet again in the afterlife, in the dimension not far from here, as you speculated, in the space time continuum."

"Maximilion, do not die so soon. I would miss you terribly. You are my lifelong best friend!"

"I will always be your friend. Time is endless and marches on forever. We just enjoy our brief relationship with time on our short visits to the material realm. Boundless is time, yet it is all relative. Time is so slow in the other realms. You can miss much on earth in a blink of an eye," Maximilion hypothesized.

"Speculation is running rampant. I am now just a boy in the Deep Forest, in the magnificent Waterfall of the jungle. I sometimes wonder if this is all a hallucination, an illusion. Do I really talk to lions and eagles? Mika and Haley don't do that and can't do that. NO humans do! There are so many wonderful drug compounds in Africa, billions of dollars' worth. Is my sanity and reality altered by my rich African diet of native plants? What of Exotica? Does that cause delusions or hallucinations, or entry into the Parallel Dream Universe? Are the elven-like monkeys real or apparitions? Is the Cavern of Lost Treasures real or fable? I never concerned myself with these issues when I was pre-teen and pre-civilization. The life I sensed, felt, smelled, saw and heard, was reality. My communication with the animals was real. But now I have doubts.

"It is as if once I joined human civilization, I began to gradually doubt my prior existence, but I never abandoned it. My work as a ranger kept my relationships with you, and the animal kingdom fresh and active. But still, as I lay in a bed at the ranger station, I would struggle with my dual reality. I told some things to Mika and Haley, but no one else. Certainly, Jorge' and the guards and other rangers saw my behavior, and my odd schedule, and week-long adventures and sojourns into the field.

"I just wonder if I go to America, will I forget. Will I forget my roots, my relationship with the animal kingdom, my sense of the spiritual realms and Parallel Dream Universe, my ability to enter the Parallel Real Universe with a Special Being to see the sword and the crown and elven-like monkeys. Almost like the biblical story of Eve biting the apple, and finding the tree of knowledge, when she lost Paradise. She lost her connection to her God.

"Will I lose my connections? Every day, I grow a little further away. Maximilion, if you die, I feel that if I am in

America, my connection to the world I knew will be lost. I will revert to the full human world, separated from the animal kingdom and the realms of the Parallel Dream Universe, and time-space dimensions of the Parallel Real Universe, that are so near to us. They say I may be a link between the human world and these other worlds. But, how can that be, if I figuratively take a bite of the apple?"

"Africus, I do not believe that will happen to you. You are not living in an apparition or a dream. Your dual worlds are both real. You passed the test of duality. You have lived in both worlds now for many years. You still are here in the Waterfall with me. The plant, Exotica, does not bear on any of this, yet it may have medicinal value for humans with mind illnesses. The Deep Jungle is protected from mankind by its density and by superstition. The Waterfall and Paradise are only accessible by Special Beings and their guests, and by ones like you through the Parallel Dream Universe.

"But there will be tests. You must succeed in the realm of games and sports. It will be new to you in form, but you have always succeeded in survival and in hunting. You must succeed in finding your true love. Yes, it is the Girl. Together, you and she can start the link between the dual worlds. But later, after you have met and both succeeded in the games, the games of survival."

# 19.

S AVANNAH PUT ON HER HIKING BOOTS to finish her hiking wardrobe. She and her Mum, had been here for a few days after their visit to Nebraska State. Two of her friends from the College Preparatory school had joined her the day before. Early next week, they would compete in the annual Vail lacrosse tourney for college kids and recent alums. But for now, it was time for some fun. Mrs. Stewart was the chaperone for her friends, at the request of their parents, whom she had befriended on the sidelines at so many prep school girls' lacrosse games. She knew her two friends quite well. Both were stars like Savannah. Bethany was committed to North Carolina for lacrosse and Becca was committed to Stanford for lacrosse. Both teams were perennial national title contenders, with North Carolina winning a few titles. Everyone still competed with Maryland. The Maryland coach wanted Savannah, Bethany and Becca as a package, but Becca and Bethany saw it as a ruse, and opted to go their own ways.

"Savannah, I will drop you and the girls off at the trail head. It is 7 am. I will be back at 4 pm. Keep your smart device active and send me updates every hour. I have my tracking software on, so I will know where you are on the mountain trails. Let's do live streaming at noon! I think you will be fairly elevated by then. I look forward to some spectacular views. Bring the mace in case any wild beasts look at you as prey!" Mrs. Stewart said, with a levity in her voice.

"Mum, we are well prepared. And I am an experienced hiker, you know. Daddy used to take me on safaris, until the time I was threatened by lions. He never took me again. I still think of Africa. It was years ago that you and I left for the U.S. You and Daddy were divorced right after that safari. He told me at the end of the safari that you were taking me away from South Africa to the states. Back to your home in Maryland, where you were the local legend in lacrosse. Back to your roots. I was born in Baltimore, so I am a U.S. citizen, too. Daddy has not been to the U.S., for so long now. He barely speaks to me, but I should see him often in England next year. But I remember my safari training and skills, and I am not afraid of big cats! The lions were friendly to me," Savannah mused.

"Ha! That is ridiculous! Didn't you tell us that the African Boy Legend saved you! That you would have been another meal for the big cats if he had not rescued you!" Becca teased, testing Mrs. Stewart's patience.

"That is our secret, Becca and Bethany! To the grave secret!" Savannah warned. "But Mum believes it was my imagination!"

"Savannah, you know we told you that was a figment of your very active young imagination! There was no boy. Your Daddy's guards rescued you and shooed away the lions without killing any of them. Killing a lion in Kenya would fetch a nasty fine and rebuke and maybe even some prison. So, the situation ended well. You should not have left the vehicles!"

"Yes, Mum, it was a dream!"

Bethany and Becca laughed. The dreams and stories by Savannah of her early days in Africa amazed them and piqued their interest at the highest level. They lived vicariously through those stories and dreams. They wanted to believe that Lion boy existed, as much as Savannah wanted her vivid memories to be true. Whether a dream or reality, the three agreed to keep that as a sacred secret.

Savannah's Mum had sat her down with the family phycologist many times during her childhood, including one final time after the safari and before she left for America. Her ruminations about communication with animals and her story about the African Boy Legend were put to rest. She was persuaded it was her active imagination, created by her subconscious mind to create fancy and fun in her life, as she had no siblings, and went to a strict private school, where she attended as a day student, while most students boarded. She had lost two of her best friends at a young age, killed in riots. Her loss was severe, enough so, said the psychologist, that she invented beings, and invented spirits for the animals. She bought into the hype of her psychologist at the time. But deep down, she held on to her dream. She vividly recalled her connection to the animal kingdom. Ah, the birds would sing and fill her heart with love. The ride on the albino zebra!

"Ok, you girls, we shall leave. Maybe I will commandeer a helicopter and join you for lunch and tea on the mountain!"

"No, Mum! You shall not!" Savannah laughed.

Mrs. Stewart dropped off the three girls at the trailhead. They had their backpacks loaded with water and dehydrated fruits and protein. They had bug repellent and climbing gear. They did not intend to go too vertical. They mapped a trail on their smart devices that traversed the mountain. They wrapped around the mountain gradually achieving higher altitudes. They had trained for the hike in the two weeks after their conference lacrosse tournament had ended, in a championship of course. The thin air was difficult to prepare for, but this was not a marathon or a triathlon. Those maybe would come after college, when lacrosse ended, other than for those on the U.S. National team. Savannah did not want to compete for the national team. She aspired to work in her Daddy's media empire.

The girls quickly disappeared deep into the western paradise of trees and nature. They kept well hydrated and marched quickly at first. They all had the trail map sketched in 3D before their eyes in a hologram, emanating from their smart devices, through the chip on their sunglasses. It was easy to keep on the trail. Trail markers still existed to back-up the hologram markings. They were always in synchronization.

Savannah thought about how the hologram industry had boomed in 2022, after some significant breakthroughs in technology. The trail holograms were used for trails in the western forests and mountains. The chambers of commerce had spent the infrastructure dollars to totally map the west, well ahead of their eastern counterparts. GPS technology was useful, and there were interactive trail maps linked to gps. But seeing the trail in in a hologram was the preferred methodology of the hikers. Spelunkers used the holograms because GPS still was not usable in subsurface conditions.

"Holograms are amazing, Bethany, are they not?" Becca asked Bethany, as she was glued to the trail markings in her smart sunglasses.

"Yes, I use hologram technology now to read my books. The words appear in front and above my eyes, emanating from chips placed in my eyeglasses from signals sent from my smart device. Multi-tasking is so easy. I can practice lacrosse shots or do chores and read at the same time. I hear companies are competing furiously to bring hologram movies to the front vision of human eyes, too. I read that prototypes are beginning their beta testing," Bethany ruminated out loud, touching branches along the trail.

Savannah chimed in, too. "I think the most exciting hologram technology was introduced in 2024. Now, when you talk on your smart devices, you can choose to see the other person in a video display, as was always the case, or a full hologram of the person, with their current movements presented in right in front of you. You cannot touch them, but it seems like you can. I know our pets initially went crazy over holograms. But holograms have no scent. So soon our holograms were dismissed as nonsense by our pets. But they still barked and mewed over the sounds of our voices that came out of midair. What is cool is that the smart devices refract sound waves to make the voices sound like they were coming directly from the mouths of the holograms," Savannah mused while watching the sunlight glisten through the branches of the tall trees.

"I love to use the holograms for my calculator. I can do calculations and math homework while watching video streaming in the background on our wall video display or walking across campus. I know we can read texts and emails in front of our eyes, too, but reading it on the smart device is so easy, I usually don't do it," Becca added, amused by her conversation with her best friends.

"I know a lot of kids like the Gaming holograms. Oh, the Rip-Roaring 2020s have spawned so many new technologies and made life so much easier and fun! Holograms of creatures appear in homes and playgrounds, upon finding them based on clues and algorithms. Virtual games mostly are on screens and televisions, but miniature holograms are making their mark. My little brother has small armies battle on our living room floor, similar to the miniature plastic armies of the twentieth century. The best is the fake fish in our fish tanks!" Bethany laughed, looking closely at the trail ahead and her hologram markings.

Becca and Bethany were tiring from the thin Colorado mountain air. The temperature was warm. Savannah streamed her journey to her Mum, with live commentary. Becca and Bethany tried to comment as well but struggled to keep their breath. Savannah paced vigorously up and around the trail. Becca and Bethany implored her to stop.

Savannah soon drifted off the trail up the mountainside. There were openings to traverse and animal paths to walk on. The trail became steeper. She had turned off her smart device. She hiked on instinct. She went deeper into the woods and had to push away brush and branches to continue. She felt a powerful presence. She felt drawn to it. She started to revert to her childhood where she opened her mind to nature and heard its calls and sounds. It was peaceful. The presence did not scare her. Soon she was so high, she saw exposed rock formations. She could see the valley below and other mountains. The air was cooler, and the sky perfectly blue. Only a few white clouds would drift by.

Then it appeared. It had stalked her for the hike up the hidden trail. It was a female mountain lion. It snarled at first. She did not fear it even upon seeing it. The lion crouched down as if to pounce on her. Her Taser was in her backpack, as well as some pepper spray. She did not reach for either of them. She sat down on the large boulder before her. She took off her backpack. She glanced at the mountain lion. It locked eyes with her. She saw its spirit. It sat on its haunches, as if with another lion.

Savannah reached for her smart device and turned it on. Numerous frantic calls from Becca and Bethany were highlighted. A mountain lion had been spotted on the trail, where was she? Her Mum was anxious to hear from her, not yet knowing of her detour.

Savannah looked back up at the mountain lion, beckoning it to sit next to her. The lion obliged and sauntered over to the big boulder. They sat in quiescence for a seemingly long moment. Savannah stroked its back. The lion purred softly. The lion soon walked away and looked back at Savannah. She saw the signal and followed it. They walked for a few hundred yards. They arrived at the den of the lion. Inside the den were two lion cubs. They playfully looked at their mother and then at Savannah.

She reached in and held one them. It was friendly to her, as if it knew she was not an enemy or predator. Soon two bald eagles flew over and dropped the carcass of a freshly killed small animal. The mother lion brought it to the cubs. They heartily enjoyed their late breakfast.

Savannah drifted deeper into her trance like state. She had the vision of the eagles in her mind. She saw the lower mountain. Men with rifles were walking up the mountain. She knew the mountain lion was not safe.

"There are patrols coming up the mountain for you. You should stay hidden in your den until nightfall. At night, you should take your cubs to the north away from the ski mountains and housing developments of the people like me," Savannah warned, hoping the lion would understand her message, even though spoken in a language not known to the lion.

The lion understood her vision and thoughts. The lion communicated with her in their minds.

"I am Essence. I am from the animal kingdom. Remember me? You once rode on my back in Africa when I was a white zebra! Thank you for your warning. I will protect my cubs and march them to safety," Essence soothingly spoke to Savannah.

"I remember vividly! But was it not a dream, a vision, a walk in the Parallel Dream Universe?" Savannah excitedly responded.

"Savannah, it was not a dream! It was real. I was in your world, not in the Parallel Dream Universe. You are a special young woman. You have a destiny. You will understand more as you proceed through time and space.

"And you are to meet a special boy. You and he are destined to be together. You are important to the world. You share innate abilities that only a few can attain. You have access to the communication network among animals, and access to their inner spirits. Your journey and voyage through life will be challenging and exciting. Together you will accomplish great things, and find immeasurable love for each other," the lion finished.

"It is the African Boy Legend! I know it is! He is not a figment of my imagination. He is not an imaginary friend! How do I find him?" She cried out in joy and anxiety.

"Follow your heart and your instincts. You are quite the detective! Use your skills in tracking to follow your leads. You shall find him. He has tried to find you, as well, to no avail. He believes you exist, but that you have forgotten him."

"How do you know about him?"

"I have followed him for years. I am a guide of sorts for him. We have battled together, discovered Treasures together, and laughed and cried together. I was once a white zebra, a cheetah, then an angel. Now a mountain lion in America. Next, you may see me as a white zebra again, or a bear! I freely enter and leave the bodies of the animals and take over their minds and spirit. You must go. I think if they find you they will stop their pursuit of me. There is another lion here, who will take the fall for me, if necessary. Now go!" Essence pleaded.

"I hope to see you again! At least in my dreams!"

Savannah scurried away from the den. She made it back to her backpack on the boulder. There perched on the boulder were the two bald eagles. They stared at her with intensity. Soon their thoughts reached her. The African Boy Legend was real. They had flown with him in Africa, but in different bodies. Now they reincarnated in America, just like Essence described that she could do, to guide him and her, until she reunited with him.

"Thank you so much!" She cried again. She stroked their heads, and they seemed to smile. Soon she was overwhelmed and passed out. The eagles flew away. The lion and her cubs escaped quickly to the other side of the mountain and beyond. Moments passed.

"Over there," a patrol yelled out.

"Is she dead?" another screamed in panic.

The two patrolmen hurried to her side. She was flat out gone to the world in exhaustion, but very much alive.

"I believe she is passed out. Probably from exhaustion. Look there is some lion scat. Oh, some eagle scat, too. The eagles maybe scared the lion away. Maybe saved her life. She probably fainted in fear on seeing the lion. I am surprised the lion did not attack her from behind. They like stealth and to stalk from behind. You never know they attacked you, until it is too late."

"Certainly, the eagles scared away the lion. Don't know why. Maybe the eagle's nest is nearby, and they were attacking her and the lion."

"We need to awaken her. The trail is too steep. Her smart device is buzzing."

"Hello, Vail patrol here," the first patrol said.

"Where is my daughter! Is she all right!" Mrs. Stewart shrieked on hearing the voice of a patrolman instead of her daughter. Horrific thoughts flashed through her mind. *Why would a patrolman answer her smart device? Had she fallen? Been attacked by a wild beast! We moved from Africa to protect her from wild beasts, who she thought were her friends. Oh, she probably tried to play and befriend a wolf or a lion!* she thought to herself in morbid fear.

"She is fine. Just exhausted. We think she had a run in with a lion, or maybe eagles, or both. But she is unmarked, and untouched. She survived the encounter. We will bring her down soon."

"Use a helicopter! I will pay for it!"

"We cannot do that. She is safe and secure. Oh, she is waking now. She will be able to ambulate freely on her own," he said as he hung up Savannah's smart device.

Savannah gazed at the patrolman's eyes. Quite a handsome young dude, she thought. *Hmmm. Maybe he was the African Boy Legend!*

"Are you from Africa? Have you ever ridden a white zebra?" She sang out, still a bit dazed and in her trance.

"I don't believe so, but if that would make you like me, I can go to Africa and ride the zebras!" He laughed.

Slowly, she recovered her faculties. *The African Boy Legend is not real. Maybe another dream. Another figment of my imagination. Just like Dorothy in the Wizard of Oz! I still need help! But, no that was real! It must be!*

"Are my friends here, Becca and Bethany?"

"They are safe below. They returned to the trail head. They are waiting for your rescue! Did you see a mountain lion or eagles? There is scat here that suggests both were here."

"I may have. I do not recall. I need to go to the trail head."

The patrolmen followed her down the path back to the trail. They barely kept up with her, amazed at her athleticism, and ability to follow the trail back down.

"I appreciate you finding me! I was not rescued! I am fine. I was just napping!"

Off she went, somewhat skipping down the trail.

*Follow the yellow-brick road! Maybe dreams are true and may come true, just as Dorothy sang about.*

She soon reached the trail head where her friends awaited her in anticipation. Becca and Bethany shouted out to their lost friend and ran to hug her. They half laughed and half cried.

"Where were you? Why didn't you answer our calls or texts? Why didn't you wait for us? We were so afraid. You Mum told us once about how she feared for your life in Africa, because you thought you were friends with all the animals. We thought you were planning to run off with a pack of wolves or wild horses! Omigod!" Becca screamed again.

"Girls, I am fine. Pack of wolves. Wild horses. Really!" Savannah laughed back.

"But why did you run off?"

"I felt a calling. A call to the wild. A presence. Maybe it was a dream, maybe it was an apparition or a ghost, or even a hologram! I may have talked a lion, or even two eagles, I don't know or care to speculate, my dear girls!" Savannah stated as her eyes gazed at two soaring eagles.

Becca and Bethany saw the eagles. They shivered in excitement and apprehension. Their thoughts were in unison. *We long doubted yet are suspicious of our friend's extraordinary powers with animals. The dogs and cats always gravitate to her, and howl when she scores. Is it coincidence as the crowd roars simultaneously, or truly a connection, a gift from nature. We notice things other players and coaches do not. Birds seem to flock to the nearest power line to watch her play. Never go to the zoo with Savannah, Omigod! And then there is the secret they would take to the grave, unless he came to America! The legend of the African Boy Legend.*

Savannah saw her friends gazing at the majestic eagles.

"Coincidence, my dears!"

"We hope so!" Becca agreed.

"I hope it is real, Savannah. Someday, maybe your dream will come true!" Bethany blurted, not knowing why she did so.

"Dreams! I love to dream, and they love me, I suppose!

Soon Mrs. Stewart was there to pick them up. The calmness and giddiness of the three girls soothed her frayed nerves. *They are all right. She is fine. Whoa. I will let this one pass, for now.*

# 20.

SHANNON SAT NEAR THE LAKE with a picnic blanket and a picnic basket. She thought she had gone back in time to the early twentieth century. Girls were wearing sundresses, and women were wearing sunhats of various shapes and sizes. It reminded her of the Kentucky Derby, or Saratoga Springs, during racing season. She rested her head on her blanket and gazed at the wonderfully blue sky. The temperature was a warm 86 degrees, but there was a light breeze and humidity was low. Usually, July fourth was a steamy affair, but not this glorious day. Fireworks would start near sundown at about 9:00 P.M. She loved fireworks. She thought of her long-lost love, somewhere, probably in the French Riviera, with a beautiful, Parisian woman, well dressed and well-spoken and likely so attractive. She still pined for his love, but knew it was a lost cause.

So much had happened in Africa that she was still star-struck. She had not seen Africus herself. She had some lingering doubt that he existed.

*How could anyone meet the expectations and descriptions of his prowess, looks, athleticism, history and connection to the animal and spiritual worlds! He must be a figment of Mika' imagination, a ruse to bait me to Africa all the way from Nebraska. Everyone was on board for the ruse. I could be a laughing stock if I pursue this. I don't know what to do.*

*But I believe! Even if he is not the African Boy Legend, and only the 'ranger boy'. Basics, first. Does his record qualify. Does his home schooling qualify? Certainly, there are many charter schools now, that rely heavily on online classes and virtual classrooms. Old fashioned home schooling has been accepted in the U.S. for academic qualification. I will check it out on Monday. I have not heard anything from Mika or Haley. Africus must still be in the jungle. Still with Maximilion.*

*Of course, not. That is simply not possible in this modern world. Too many chances he would have already made world news. Come on, Shannon!*

*But they were so believable, especially, Haley and Jorge'. Monday, for sure.*

Shannon fell into a half state of consciousness as her mind did somersaults. She was quickly in a dream state. Her eyes were closed. She saw two beautiful eagles soar through the sky. They were not indigenous to Nebraska, but occasionally flew to Jefferson City from South Dakota or even Colorado. *Awe the majesty of their wings.* Soon she drifted away and followed their minds eye. The lake looked smaller, then disappeared. Soon she saw a football stadium. The eagles landed on the cross bars of the field goalposts-one on top of each upright. She saw the field. Her eyes closed. Her mind now entered the full dream state. There she saw Africus on the field. The crowd was on fire. The bright stadium lights. The roar of thunder. A big game. Fourth quarter. So much excitement. More to come! Africus was running-so much blazing speed! Touchdown! Someone hugged her as he scored. He was familiar, but not someone she knew well.

She finally awoke at the snap of a firecracker near her blanket. A pesky blonde boy giggled as he saw his prank worked to awake the sleeping beauty. She sternly looked at him, enough to cause him to scamper away. *Oh, what a dream! Who was that that hugged me! Omigod! Maybe I have hope!*

Soon a booming voice echoed near her from across the lake. She knew the voice. It was the head coach, Jason Smith. You could always hear his voice. Shortly, he was up-on her location.

"Hi Shannon. We have missed you. Vacation and then a week of sick leave? I hope you are back to work on Monday. We have a few special projects for you, you know," Smith teased and tested her interest.

"I am quite rested and well. I am prepared to work hard, efficiently and thoroughly. I will achieve maximum performance, with maximum results," she blurted out.

"Whoa, slow down, my dear friend. We value your performance at the highest level! But I need to give you a heads-up. And I need you to tell me what is up! I am very curious and suspicious. As you note, you are very efficient. I suspect there was more than a vacation or getaway on your trip to Africa?" He raised is right eyebrow, dark and thick, as he spoke.

"Coach, I have a cleansed and refreshed mind. I am ready for your projects. Africa is an amazing continent. It is a burgeoning region filled with promise and grandeur. Possibly, it can become a recruiting ground someday. But, as you know, they do not play organized American sports, especially, American football!" she stated, staring directly into his eyes without flinching.

"All right. You can do some grass roots work there later. Although it is creative and forward thinking, I believe there are better recruiting avenues out there for us. Let me tell you about some projects.

"We have some of the top students in the country in technology here in Jefferson City at the University. We have some top-level consultants available to us as well. In particular, Gavin Blocker, the noted columnist and blogger has agreed to work with us on a new virtual reality technology. We have followed his blogs on the VPL in baseball. We would like to start a new venture in college football and women's lacrosse. We would create a virtual game based on performances in the real game. Plays could be altered, and changes in game plans tested. There is no limit to the variations that could be tested. We could sell the software to colleges and high schools. The University will be the majority owner of the venture, as the patents were designed by its students on its facilities. We raised funds in a crowdfunding over the Internet III. The University and the investors hold the capital interests in the venture. Others who provide services to the venture will have profits interests. We will offer you a position as chief marketing officer, and a 5% profits interest in the venture. Let me know. The LLC has already been organized as the entity for the venture," the coach finished.

"Gavin Blocker? I thought he was a lone wolf. I know of him but have not met him in person. Do you really trust him? Who are the engineers? Has legal blessed this! There is competing technology in the marketplace already. Doesn't the Association dominate this space?"

"Legal is reviewing it, but their preliminary conclusion with the help of an IP firm in Omaha, is that the patents will be granted. Bink and Bonk are the students involved. Two of the professors will likely demand interests as well. Your 5% likely will be diluted at some point, particularly if outside investors are needed. But it is a fascinating opportunity. You likely will be put in charge of lacrosse!"

"I will review it with you on Monday," Shannon agreed, cautiously.

"Great, Gavin Blocker is coming in Monday as well. We will send the legal documents for you and your counsel to review. There will be an LLC operating agreement, a grant agreement for your profits interest, and of course, there will be some restrictions in a Non-Disclosure Agreement. There will be a vesting schedule for your profits interests. You can't just quit and keep it. It is favorable, though, only two years. If this is not up and running in two years, it will be too late," Coach Smith finished.

"Coach, the Nebraska State fans want wins, division winners, conference champions, all-conference players, all-American players, playoff contenders and national championships! How can you coach and still run this megalithic organization, and work on a new technology venture? Does not it violate your contract?" Shannon admonished the coach.

"It does not violate my contract. I specifically negotiated this clause. The venture is permitted so long as the University is the majority owner, receives all of its investment back first as a priority, and retains all the intellectual property rights. Also, the University would stand to profit the most by far. My role would be as an advisor, focusing on the global view and what coaches would want to manipulate and review. Coverages, substitutions, officiating, play changes, scheme changes, player changes, formation changes, protection changes, techniques and so much more. I would be limited to working on this in the offseason as well, and not in recruiting periods, other than using it in a beta test at our University this fall. So, I think that should address your concerns. You would be subject to similar restrictions but based on football not lacrosse seasons."

"I see. Well, this sounds exciting. I am looking forward to Monday! Let us share in the dream of the Rip-Roaring 2020s!"

Coach Smith walked away. Shannon daydreamed again about her impending fortune. She sucked in the succulent air and breathed out many of her fears. But soon a new suitor presented himself.

"Hi, are you Shannon Garrison?"

A tall man of six foot four inches, broad shoulders and dark black hair and blue eyes, approached her. He was thirty-two years old. He looked like a runner and was in good shape. Her eyes twinkled at her first glance at him.

"I may be. And who are you that asks?"

"I am Gavin Blocker. My guess is that Coach Smith just told you about me and the new start-up technology company we may be partners in," Blocker said, with demanding eyes.

*So, that is Gavin Blocker! You have got to be kidding! Why have I not heard he was so gallant!*

"Oh yes, I will review all of that in the next few days. Seems a bit bold to me. I am glad I am only putting in time, not invested dollars. I think there are better investments elsewhere, like African pharmaceutical companies," she casually proffered some investment advice, slyly hiding her exuberance for the project.

"Oh, Africa! Yes, some of us are in quite a state of wonderment over your trip to Africa. It seems unlike you. I hope you were able to join a safari or see a Preserve," he retorted, frowning in anticipation of her answer.

"And how and what would a stranger like you know any-thing about me!" Shannon stated emphatically, feeling awkward.

"Shannon, I am a beat writer for Nebraska State football. I know you are a recruiting director. I read and hear about your reports and activities. I am paid to keep track of re-cruiting and scoops on recruiting. I know that Savannah Stewart was here recently for a lacrosse visit and you were not here. As a head administrator for women's lacrosse re-cruiting, I found that quite odd. So, I suspect there was something very important for you in Africa. I know that a former Nebraska State football player is located in Kenya. Does that have a bearing on any of this?" Blocker fished for information.

"I suspect it is not your business what I do on my per-sonal time. I was on vacation. I was not working. It was a notable trip. I was exposed to the majestic beauty of Africa, and its booming economy. Its roots are still present in the Preserve system. I did visit a Preserve and did see some Af-rican animals!" She defended herself, with her lips puck-ered.

"I see. Whatever it is, you are keeping it close to the vest. I will leave you alone for now," Blocker answered in frustra-tion.

"Sounds to me, you are more interested in a scoop from me than this new venture!"

"Well, I am always looking for a scoop. But, I am sorry. I did not mean for this meeting to be so formal. I am locked up in my blog and web worlds, so much so, that I some-times am a little awkward."

Blocker looked at her sheepishly. She sized him up. She heard this about him. *He was awfully good looking for a web worm. Maybe a second chance?*

"Well, no more business or football talk? Except maybe about Savannah Stewart, the American Girl Superstar and the future darling of the athletic world. Her future agent will be quite rewarded," Shannon replied brushing her blonde hair, back away from the right side of her face.

"Ok! I love the fireworks here. And I would love to hear more about Savannah. Wait. I have a picnic lunch, too. Even a picnic bag, a bit modern for I suppose for this venue," Gavin offered, with puerile innocence.

"Well, go get it!"

Blocker retrieved his picnic bag. A poor example for a picnic lunch, she thought, as he unpacked processed packages of food. He did have some bottled water, and no alcoholic drinks or other mind enhancing drugs. *Apparently, he is a straight and narrow type of guy. His shoes are very expensive. Good taste, I see. Preppy shirt for Jefferson City, Nebraska, too. I suppose that is ok!*

They spent the afternoon enjoying the crowd, the frolicking of the children, the kite flying, and the assorted fireworks. They talked about Savannah, and the possibility of her attending the University. Why Nebraska State, was the prevailing theme. But that was for another day. The night time fireworks were wonderful, they both thought, not like the Boston fireworks over the Charles River on the Esplanade with the Boston Symphony Orchestra, or the New York fireworks over the Hudson river in front of Manhattan with the latest music stars officiating the event, but nonetheless, a remarkable Midwestern affair.

# 21.

COACH SMITH SAT DOWN with his coaches. He summoned RIP.

"RIP, I know it has been only a few weeks, but do you have any ideas on innovative schemes or play designs? Any out of the box ideas? Any way to take advantage of the new rules? We have fall camp opening in four weeks. It now may be too late for major changes, but we need to plan for years from now, as well as this season."

"I have some keen ideas, coach. I think we can implement some of the ideas this season. On technique, I have some innovative ways to group tackle better within the new parameters of tackling above the knees and below the neck and head. Rugby tackling combined with impact tackling is the current trend, and we follow that well. This combines rugby and impact tackling with group dynamics. I have some software that will demonstrate strategic angles that increase the effective speed of our team. I have studied pack animals and their hunting strategies. As you know I was a major in animal studies at A&M. I did my major in African animals, both lions, hyenas and wild dogs. There are many similarities in their hunting tactics. The group model is excellent and has launched these hunters to the top of the food chain. The angles and feigns and deceptions, the closures, the red herrings, are fascinating.

"I have some new schemes that promote the team rugby style tackling and angular approach to accelerate effective speed. The schemes promote teamwork, and bonding and communication are implicit in the schemes, as well as trust and instinct among the players. Offenses have long invoked deception in their pre-snap routines and formation shifts. I believe defense should respond with effective decoys and ruses. Certain formations can be designed that are malleable on demand, and unpredictable to an offense. We can dodge and duck blocks, and maneuver into open areas for tackling machinations. I think I will call it the Amoeba Defense!" RIP excitedly rolled on.

"RIP, I knew there was some light on in there. You are truly a coach for the Rip-Roaring 2020s. Maybe we should recruit some young players from Africa to take advantage of your hunting philosophies!"

RIP pondered that last comment, but let it go.

Coach Smith was a genius in his own right, but one of his strengths was delegation. He also was a skilled manager of managers, as well as a leader of players. His high forehead and dark hair gave him a distinguished appearance, and his broad shoulders and deep voice gave him an imposing presence. He was always the first one noticed in any room. Leaders gravitated to him. Subordinates saluted him, marched to his commands and were inspired by his words and deeds. He was an enabler and an enforcer. His first year in 2024, was respectable, yet unremarkable. He was 9-3, and won his secondary bowl game, to finish with ten wins. But key road losses to top twenty-five conference teams, left a sour taste in the minds of some fans. This was his second head coaching position. His first was a stint at a non-major program. He won 75% of his games and was undefeated in bowl games. In ten years, he had four conference championships. At age 50, he was considered reasonably young. He was focused, yet realistic. He was charming with the media yet did not suffer fools lightly. He was open with the media, and often entertaining. The media respected him and gave him leeway. He had a five-year contract, and to the media, a five-year leash. He knew what his leash was, so he fiercely looked to 2026, 2027 and 2028 for a run at some championships. But he knew the quarterback position was key. In the back of his mind, he feared 2029. Ominously, it was 1929 that lead to the Great Depression after the Roaring Twenties of the Twentieth century. Would history repeat itself. He wanted his finances secure by then.

Smith nodded at RIP. He was impressed with the clarity and quickness of RIP's report.

"RIP, send me your diagrams and notes. Let me study them. Let's meet with the position coaches next Monday when they return from vacation. I am impressed with this. We are planning on using Nebraska State as a beta test for some new technology in the virtual reality space, with video from the live games. We likely can overlay your concepts here on film from last year. I think we will even be able to change angular momentum on film, with moving players virtually on the screens. This is fantastic."

"I heard about the new technology. Other schools may try to beat us to the punch here. We should conduct the beta testing now with last year's game film. And maybe I should be part of the team," RIP implored aggressively.

"Ah, I see. Well, it is not up to me."

Coach Smith sat back pensively. He knew RIP was going to be an awesome defensive coordinator. His new schemes would be innovative and revolutionary, at least until they were replicated and adopted by other schools. Smith was decisive.

"They are giving me 5%. And that will be diluted by future investors, if Nebraska State does not foot the whole bill. I will set aside 2% for the staff. You will get at least 25% of that, or .5%. Final offer."

RIP knew Smith was decisive. He knew that he did not negotiate either. But Smith hired him as defensive coordinator after serving as the line coach at Nebraska State for a number of years. He paid top dollar. He would be in the upper quartile of assistant coaches who were coordinators, even as a young coordinator.

"Done. I may be willing to go lower, depending on the value of the contribution of the other coaches. We are one here. A team. Hey, it's the Rip-Roaring 2020s, let's make a go of this."

"Done. A lot of paperwork will be done this week. Some ancillary agreements, too. Shannon Garrison is part of the team as the marketing director. Maybe she will have some marketing to do sooner than she expected. We can't work on this during the season, other than beta testing. They want our full attention addressed to coaching the players and recruiting."

"All is good. I have some recruiting calls to make. A giant defensive end just decided to transfer for his fifth year. He passed on the Association draft, but then his coach was fired. Not a happy camper. He is out of the Conference of the South. Six-foot-eight with a giant wingspan."

"I loved that guy. Absolutely, try and get him here for a visit! Speaking of recruiting, where is Tamaric?"

"I am here coach." Tamaric was in the hallway, thinking of how he might be even half as impressive as RIP.

"Tell me about the Spiritis camp. Are you on their payroll now?"

"Yes, they indeed love Nebraska State and love Shannon. I think they will offer her a position she cannot refuse. I think the VP of marketing has the likings for her big time. He was a star lacrosse player at Penn."

"That is not legal. It can't work that way. You cannot hire someone to date them."

"Maybe so. But the President of the company is a woman from Stanford, a lacrosse star from way back. Shannon is hot in the industry. I just think we may lose her."

"Maybe not. We have some hot projects here going on as well."

"I know. We will see. But the camp was awesome. I made some inroads with a rising junior out of Kansas City. Super arm, great field vision, high intangibles. Already six feet four inches. He wants to stay in our conference, and preferably our division. A real homerun."

"Does he play baseball. We have lost too many star quarterbacks to professional baseball."

"Yes, he is a star pitcher. Heavily recruited. I told him he could play both sports here."

"Let's bring him in. We can offer, but baseball will definitely be an issue. Any rising seniors for 2026?" Smith asked.

"You are right. A rising senior is imperative. Rod and Pierce will both be graduated when a rising junior arrives in 2027. It would be difficult to start a true freshman."

"I know. I would like a season of maturation and learning the speed of the game. Any JUCOs we could bring in next season, 2026 to compete with Rod and Pierce? I do want a quarterback in the 2026 class," Smith concluded.

"I am on it. I will have a report next week for you and the OC on innovative offenses, as well. Coach Parsons, the OC wants to participate in my creativity!"

"Fine, I like teamwork. Carry on."

Tamaric Jones left the coaches office. Recruiting a quarterback just became priority number one. The innovation would have to wait. Without a horse at quarterback innovation would likely fail miserably.

# 22.

HALEY CHECKED her smart device. A message popped up from Shannon Garrison.

"Haley, I have cleared Africus for admission at Nebraska State, the University. I did not use his name, of course, but the "charter home school" that you provided him and your other four students, was approved, when combined with his test scores and equivalency tests. The bad news is that he is not eligible for an athletic scholarship under new conference rules and U.S. National Sports Council rules. He can play sports at Nebraska State, and eventually earn a scholarship after his first year. I know there is so much going on out there for him, and for you and Mika. If you would like to submit a formal application, let me know. We have a rolling admission, so he could still apply for fall 2025 or spring 2026. I have kept this discreet. I have not told Coach Smith or others in the athletic department. If he does matriculate here in the fall of 2025, I am sure he could walk on and join the scout team. As you know, he could redshirt, so playing on the scout team would not hurt his eligibility Or, because he has not played football, he may be better off joining the team in the spring.

"The next steps are to formally submit his application for admission and to obtain a student visa. You would need to start working on that quickly. I am not sure how it works for his situation, where he does not have a birth certificate or known parents. Is he a citizen of Kenya? Let me know if I can help."

Haley read the email with intense interest. She was so fond of Africus, almost as much as if he were her own child. He was likely eighteen years old. She was thirty-six, and old enough to be his mother. She wondered who his parents were, and how he ended up in the jungle. He was English speaking and white. The universe of his beginnings was quite large-America, England, Australia, and Africa. She had searched endlessly on the internet for reports of lost boys, particularly, in Africa, and in Kenya. Nothing. She had contacted all of the safari organizations for reports of lost children on safaris. She had looked into records of deaths in Africa, to see if any persons had died unexpectedly in Kenya or in nearby states, who may have left a young child behind. Studying American reports was voluminous. She matched searches with safaris and Africa and missing children. She thoroughly searched missing children reports and records. No photographs looked promising. And then there was his athleticism. His parents were certainly of athletic stock. But no reports of great athletes who were missing children. Maybe he was a son of a great athlete born from an indiscreet moment. The mother may have given him up for adoption. The new parents may have been the ones who lost him or died themselves. Such a mystery. Maybe if Africus achieved success in American sports, his parents would step forth. Maybe he was an alien from a planet of super humans! Her mind, as it often did, continued to operate at breathtaking speed.

She checked her news feeds. She saw a headline that piqued her interest. A man of Igor's description had been detained in Uganda. He had killed some locals, while attempting to hijack a boat on Lake Victoria. He was captured and now in local jail. She knew it was him.

At least in was incarcerated for now. Would his benefactors buy his freedom? Even if not, new poachers would return, whether supported by Igor's benefactors or others. It was a constant threat. Her team were few in number. The Kenyan national guard had as one of its missions, the protection of Kenyan wildlife. But they were only on call. Often a rescue was too late. Their own guards were good, including the chief guard, Jorge', but they could only do so much. The Preserve was large with many natural borders, one national border with Uganda, and many uninhabitable areas. Access points were difficult to constantly monitor. She and Mika had established a somewhat reliable reconnaissance system with cameras in various parts of the Preserve. They were constantly in need of repair and maintenance, as nature, both storms, and predators, and sometimes poachers, would destroy or break apart the apparatuses.

A satellite monitoring service would be most ideal. Haley recalled her considerable effort meeting with Kenyan officials to link up with some private satellite companies to provide the service. The cost was exorbitant. The Kenya government offered her the national guard support as an appeasement, while she and they continued to explore satellite and other forms of advance security. She knew the some of the borders did contain a fence system to contain the wild animals. It was in reasonable shape, as the government allocated funds annually for its upkeep, as well as the upkeep of other Preserves.

Haley heard a range vehicle pull in from the savannah side of their home. She knew it was someone from the savannah, likely a guard or ranger. But she saw Mika jump out of the range vehicle, wipe his brow and head for the door. She felt excitement when he entered the room, but usually feigned indifference at his arrival.

"You look lost in thought as usual! But you are bothered by something. What's going on?" He asked.

"Igor has been incarcerated in Uganda. It looks serious. They caught him murdering some locals. I am not sure his benefactors will bail him out this time. The Kenyan government will want to extradite him. Poaching is subject to the death sentence. I will be happy when he is gone. He went after Africus directly. There must be a history here. Africus certainly has thwarted many a poacher.

"And, some good news, my dear, on the home front. Africus will be accepted at Nebraska State for admission, if he applies. But no scholarship offers for sports. I know he has savings to cover a year or two of school. And Nebraska State is not as expensive as the private universities around the world and America.

"The bigger hurdle may be immigration. Africus is unknown. He is not a citizen of any country. He has no birth certificate," Haley expressed her concern raising her eyebrows looking for an answer.

"Maybe he should stay here at the Preserve. He is very happy here. The limelight of his story and background could be intense. And then if he fails, the world would scoff and mock him and us," Mika expressed doubts as well, his shoulders slumping a bit.

"He has not returned yet, either. We have not heard from him since the poacher event. I know he must be fine, but I sometimes wish he would let us know where he is. Or if we could place a monitor on him!" She looked up at Mika hoping he would agree, as she let her hair down and then put it back into a tighter pony tail.

"No, he won't wear a monitor. He has some secrets, and some secret places. I think there is some exotic stuff going on sometimes with him, bordering on the mystical or spiritual, or an alternative reality or zone! He probably has found the Cavern of Lost Treasures! At least in his Parallel Dream Universe! And he sometimes mumbles about his secret Waterfall and Paradise," Mika laughed with some edge to his voice, as he knew what he said was actually true. He put his hands on his hips and held his head high.

"Yes, all right, no monitor. I know he has his special places in his dream worlds, or Parallel Dream Universe, and who knows, maybe they are real, too," she responded, believing but always puzzled by the dream worlds of her husband and foster son.

Haley looked away and walked to sit on her chair next to her desk. The desk was a standard office desk, very plain and metal, and felt cold on her arms as she rested them next to her computer. The chair, with its leather covering, felt comfortable and comforting to her. She was an active person, but still loved academics, and even paper work. She loved research. She gazed up and saw Mika sit on the couch in the same room. One room contained her kitchen, dining area and living area, as well as her office. She streamed in the local news. She did not need a television. All the video she needed could be streamed on her computer and her smart device. The broadband infrastructure had made it out to the Preserve. She was thankful for the tall cell towers every time she saw them on the train ride in from Nairobi.

She smelled some fresh meat cooking on the grill. Ah, Mika could grill the best antelope steaks! He was grilling some fresh vegetables from the field, as well. Fresh and organic food every night, she thought. But she fondly remembered her stops at the local ice cream parlor in Jefferson City, Nebraska, particularly after soccer home games. Her favorite had been almond joy ice cream, with fresh pecans.

Haley felt the evening breeze blow through the windows. She got up from the desk and turned off the two fans. She took a towel and dried her face and neck of perspiration. She washed her hands in the metal sink, with lavender soap. She sauntered into the second room in the house. She grabbed a fresh blouse from the open closet and put it on after throwing her day's safari shirt in the basket. A small sink stared at her. She felt the urge to wash her face with the water, even though it was warm. But she walked out to the outside. The steaks sizzled. She was hungry for a good meal.

Mika served her first with a juicy steak, and heaps of grilled fresh African vegetables. Haley wolfed down the vegetables. A long swig of iced lemon water washed it down drenching her thirst. She let out a sigh of relief. The steak was the dessert. She slowly cut off pieces and chewed them methodically as she spoke to Mika about his latest venture.

She heard his words, and they were the same words he had spoken on his many returns. Her listening was acute, and she waited for nuances or differences, but as usual none appeared. Her stock answers seem to appease Mika once again. She had often joined him on the trips into the Preserve. She loved adventure and even danger. But now she was less interested. She felt a deep yearning to return home to Nebraska.

"Mika, I need to talk to you. I have been thinking. After the five students from my school graduated last spring, my teaching is now complete. We have not taken in any more kids from the local tribes. And there are no more lion boys or girls. I am thinking that I may want to go home," she shyly looked into the grill fire that was still flaming from the fat of the steak. Her chin filled her hands. Her eyes moistened.

"You know, I love this job and this Preserve. I don't think I can leave, Haley. You know you go through this once a year. You will get over it again," Mika gruffly replied, staring at her intently, his jaw firm, but not clenched.

"Maybe. I don't know. But I could take Africus to Nebraska and stay with him to make sure America and the University are right for him. And I could come back here for the holidays and the start of the next season. Then I would know, too. Plus, what if he plays. I would want to be there!" Haley said more enthusiastically, her shoulders now back and square.

Mika loosened his jaws. He opened his mouth to talk but fell silent.

"I can get all of the immigration papers ready for Africus. We can be his guardians. Kenya will give him a birth certificate with an estimated birthday. I am sure. I asked the embassy about it a few years ago," Haley continued, building confidence.

"Yeah, I think Africus will go," Mika added, glumly, knowing the two closest people in the world to him might be leaving his favorite place in the world.

Haley sat silently. She stared at the unfinished steak on her plate, twirling her fork. She took a tooth pick and picked at some meat stuck in her teeth. Mika got up and shut down the grill. He cleaned the table and dishes and disposed of the trash. Haley finally put her plate in the sink. She sat on the couch, and downloaded one of her television series, Season 5, Episode 4. Her trance like viewing calmed her and took her away from the present day.

She heard Mika retire to bed. She knew he was tired, as he exhaled deeply on plopping heavily on the bed. No covers tonight. It was very warm. No intimacy either. "I guess that is my fault," she whispered to herself.

Haley sat at her desk. She started up her computer. She prepared his college application for him to sign. He still had to prepare a few essays to submit. She retrieved her recommendation from the archives on her computer, one she had written a while ago. She emailed the U.S. embassy for information and forms for his student visa and emailed the bureau of records in Nairobi to set up an appointment to obtain a birth certificate and some record of citizenship. Next Monday would work for her. But would Africus be back by then, she wondered.

Haley's eyes were now heavy from exhaustion. She barely stood up from her chair without falling. She fell onto the bed in her clothes and fell into a deep slumber. That the bed was so comfortable was her last thought, as she drifted totally out of consciousness. Together she and her husband lay fast asleep in the same bed. Her final thought was *I am ready to go home.*

Mika lay there quietly. *Maybe I should go to.*

# 23.

AFRICUS LOOKED into the eyes of the dying lion, bloodied in battle with another young male lion. Africus knew the dying lion, it was a young male lion, one of the sons of Maximilion.

"I was attacked," the young lion whispered to him.

The moonlight shone on Africus's face, chiseled jaw, and sun-bleached blonde hair. He glared at the lion that had attacked Maximilion's son. Their eyes met in a stalemate. The lion, weary from battle, roared and lifted up on his haunches. Africus crouched on his feet, ready to fight or to flee, unsure of the lion's next move. It had already attacked Maximilion's son. Africus saw three other young male lions watching him nearby. The lions must have sensed Maximilion's weakness from his injuries and long years leading the pride and ruling the animal kingdom in the Preserve. The battle was on now. Maximilion would have to fight dearly to grab another year at the helm. It was a constant battle to stay on top.

Africus grabbed his dagger. Maximilion's son roared one last roar and then perished. His spirit lifted toward the moonlight. Africus felt the heavy heart of Maximilion.

The three lions launched their attack. They first pounced on the exhausted lion that had attacked Maximilion's son, and quickly slashed him with their powerful paws. One lion crushed his throat. He let out his last breath. They now turned to Africus.

Kill Africus, they thought, and then they could kill Maximilion and rule the Preserve. They would divide up the Preserve into three new prides and kingdoms, one for each of them. The birds of prey screeched. The vultures flew in great circles waiting for the carnage. The hyenas laughed in glee.

Africus knew he could not outrun all three lions, skilled at group hunting. He did not think his chances were great in a direct battle. He saw a tree that might provide him safety, as the branches would not hold the weight of the lions, but the lions could hold out longer than him. He did not have his smart device or radio to call for help. It was back at the range vehicle. This was a rebellion and mutiny. The battle to be the head honcho.

The lions hesitated, pondering their next move. Maximilion would be a formidable and angry foe if they killed Africus, even in his weakened state.

They roared again and launched forward toward Africus.

Africus jumped and accelerated to full speed in a split second. He ran to the left of the charging lions towards an open field and foot long grass. Rocks and trees studded the field. Two of the lions flanked him to his left and right in a pincer move. The third lion was in direct pursuit behind him.

Africus stopped suddenly. The pursuing lion leapt into the air for the kill. Africus dove underneath the five hundred pounds of heaving flesh and flipped onto his back, diving his dagger deep into the lion's heart. He rolled out from underneath the flopping lion in time to avoid its crushing weight. The other lions closed in formation.

Suddenly, another roar louder than any other roars filled the night. The two lions stopped in their tracks. Maximilion pounded onto the field at full speed at the two lions. Fear struck their hearts. They bolted away into the higher grass. Africus stayed with Maximilion as they hunted the two lions. Maximilion soon tired. The two lions escaped.

"One of my sons is dead. He was the one I chose to take over the pride when I pass, which may be soon. We must find a new successor," Maximilion huffed, holding his head high as a show of strength to the remaining members of the pride.

Meanwhile, a large horde of hyenas had gathered nearby. They had witnessed two powerful male lions perish, and two more take off. The odds now looked promising to them. The hyenas howled, trying to intimidate the reduced lion pride. They started to circle the lions. Africus knew another war was brewing. The heckling of the hyenas grew louder. The vultures impatiently waited for the battle to start. The hyenas had far greater numbers. Soon monkeys filled the trees to witness the war. The lions were ferocious fighters, and the female lions would defend their cubs at all costs. The hyenas did not care about individual casualties. A victory over the lion pride would be historic and give them control of the hunting grounds.

Maximilion looked into Africus's eyes.

"The hyenas have never accepted the lions as the kings of the jungles and savannahs. They will attack. You must go. There is no reason for you to perish today. You should go find your love. She awaits you. I may win this war today, but it is in the fates now. GO, Africus!"

Africus was stunned. He cared for Maximilion more than anyone. He would not abandon him. He watched Maximilion return to the inner circle of the pride. He stood outside the circle, still with room and time to run. The hyenas were not watching him. There focus was on the lions.

He watched as the hyenas circled closer and closer to the lions. A cub ran in fear. Two female lions left the pride to rescue the cub. They were surrounded by more hyenas. A ferocious battle ensued. Five hyenas perished from the battle, but the two female lions and cub died of mortal wounds.

The hyenas' strategy was to attack single lions with overwhelming odds. Three more lions perished. Africus had entered the fray from afar. He had flung his dagger deep in into the heart of the lead hyena. It did not matter, two young hyenas stepped up into a leadership role. He fired rocks at the hyenas, knocking a few unconscious. He took a large stick and pounded the skulls of nearby hyenas. But the odds were too great. Oddly, they did not attack him.

Maximilion roared to the sky and led the remaining lions into a frontal assault. Hyenas were shred and killed in droves. But the greatly outnumbered lions were slaughtered one by one. The vultures were already on the ground. Africus looked on in horror, as he swung his stick like a knight wielding his sword.

Africus looked to the skies. He saw the milky way on a clear night. He saw seven shooting stars. He then drew in the deepest breath of his life and belted out the loudest call to the wild he had ever yelled. The jungle went quiet. The battle stalled. Maximilion looked over at Africus. Their eyes locked in hope. Maximilion bowed his head and roared just as loudly. Two female lions, one with serious wounds, were left with Maximilion. Maximilion was losing blood and strength. But the hyenas' frenzy abated at the moment of silence following the call to the wild.

Then the earth rumbled. Hundreds of wildebeest burst over the horizon. There was an all-out stampede. Dozens of elephants pounded the turf from the other horizon. Eagles flew over the sky and prepared to dive.

The twenty hyenas still left, a third of the original pack, looked to the horizon at the wildebeest and ran. They ran right into the onslaught of elephants. Africus watched as those not crushed reversed course and ran into the thundering herd of wildebeest. The wildebeest instinctively veered around the three remaining lions and Africus. The pack of hyenas all perished.

The stampede stopped. Africus went to the leader of the elephants and wildebeest and thanked them for their help. The leaders each bowed before him. Africus walked over to Maximilion. He saw that Maximilion was dying. A lion cub popped out from behind the rocks. It was the last cub. It nuzzled Maximilion and licked his wounds. One of the female lions growled and passed on into the spirit world. Africus held Maximilion's head close to his chest. He wept and caressed his head. Maximilion's eyes met his eyes for the last time. A lifetime of friendship passed before both of their eyes. And then the spirit of Maximilion left the earth.

Africus walked a few miles with the remaining female lion and lion cub into a denser jungle. There he took the leaves of an African plant, he called Healica, and squeezed the juices onto the non-mortal wounds of the female lion. The lion cub playfully tugged at him. Soon the wounds healed. Africus had not told Mika of the power of Healica. The leaves, it appeared, contained a substance that was capable of turning on the genetic alterations necessary to regenerate other cells, in different forms. *It must contain the proteins that trigger the regeneration response. Organs, limbs, who knows the potential! It must be similar to the early development of stem cells into all the different cells of the body.*

He turned to the lion cub and picked him up into the air.

"You shall be the new lion leader. You shall be named Minimilion!"

The lion cub understood and licked Africus's face. He placed the cub down next to the female lion, who was not his mother. His mother had been killed in the battle.

"The young Minimilion shall become the new king of the jungle in the Preserve when he grows up. The poachers are defeated and gone. The hyenas are defeated and gone. It should be safe for you to raise the cub," Africus said solemnly. His broad shoulders drooped in exhaustion and sadness. He said farewell to the two remaining lions.

He trekked back to his range vehicle a few miles away. The sun would peek over the eastern horizon in another hour.

Africus sat in his range vehicle. He was pensive and stunned. He had trouble breathing. He pounded the dashboard over and over again. He pulled his hair and just cried.

"Maximilion!" He screamed.

Visions of their first meeting overcame him. The little lion cub that saved his life and spared him from the paw of Maximilion's father. The many days of frolicking in the high grass, running and tackling. The hunting expeditions and feasts. The communication in their minds and the higher realms of consciousness. Together they ruled the jungle and animal kingdom in mind and spirit. Now Maximilion was gone.

Africus fell into a trance like state of light sleep. His dream state was active. More memories jumbled together. Soon Maximilion was in his dreams. He was staring at Africus. He was speaking to him again. Maybe one last time.

"Africus, you have been a great friend and brother. You have accomplished much and brought order to the savannahs and jungles. Minimilion shall be a great leader. He could use your guidance and training, but you must consider your own destiny and fate. It is your choice. I will guide Minimilion until he is fully grown. We are in the bonds. Essence is here and says hello! Watch for her in the future, she says. So long! I am well up here. May you make the right choices," Maximilion winked and left Africus's dream state.

Africus awoke. He had vivid recall. He was alarmed and relieved. But he was confused. He looked down the road back home. He looked at the jungle. He dropped his head into his open hands and drooped over the steering wheel. He heard the monkeys screeching and vultures chomping.

"I will stay."

# 24.

SAVANNAH WALKED out to her backyard overlooking the western shore of Chesapeake Bay. It was a hot sultry day, with a temperature at 92 degrees. She was at her summer cottage. She sat on a pool chair in her bathing suit and watched the sailboats. The seagulls were active in the bright sun, chasing crab boats and fishing boats for tossed fish parts. She pulled out her laptop.

She searched again on the internet for stories or mentions of a lion boy from Africa. It had been a few weeks ago that she had discovered a post mentioning a football player from Kenya possibly looking at Nebraska State. Her internal alarms had sounded loudly. She had been so enthralled that she scheduled a visit to Jefferson City.

*I liked Jefferson City. And the school thinks it is just a ruse. Like a man from Mars! Little do they know that there really is a lion boy. And he is not a figment of my imagination?!*

She crossed her legs and tied her hair into a bun. She grabbed a swig of ice tea sitting on the table beside her. She then dove back into the e-world. Countless searches later, she found an odd article on an arrest in Uganda. A poacher had been detained and faced imprisonment. There was a quote about a ranger boy that would pay for his losses. *He had poached in a preserve in Kenya. Her safari had been in Kenya. Could it be?*

She did more research and found that Igor was one of the most wanted poachers in the world. Scary person. She kept researching.

Another article popped up on the West Kenya National Wildlife Preserve. It was about a former Nebraska State football player, Mika Williams, and his wife, Haley Andrews, a former Nebraska State women's soccer star. *This is getting eerie.*

Little else appeared when she ran their names, other than old reports on their athletic success in Jefferson City. *Why Africa.*

Her eyes grew heavier and soon she fell into a deep summer nap. The soothing sound of gentle waves lapping at the shoreline cast her deeper into her slumber. Unfiltered dreams danced in her mind. Images of the African Boy Legend, staring at her, so long ago, were cast in stunning detail. *The eyes of the lions, were they laughing? The mountain lion from Colorado, did I really communicate with it? Was that real! The lion cubs! I saved them! Or was that a figment of my imagination as Mum says? The eagles! Did they have a message for me? Oh!*

Savannah awoke from her dream. She felt confused. Her blur of imagination and reality befuddled her. Then there was virtual reality. All three sometimes blended.

"I am not sure there is an African Boy Legend. But I see his face so vividly. I can't believe I went to Nebraska State on such a lark! No one from Africa is matriculating this fall. There are no potential recruits on any website for any team from Africa, let alone Kenya or the Preserve! If the African

Boy Legend exists, he would be an international sensation! But Essence told me there is a boy!" she quietly talked out loud to herself.

Then her mind retrieved more data she had found or heard in the past. There was the story of the Ugandan general and his troops defeated in the Kenya Preserve. Mystery and cover-up prevailed. Only glimpses of information were available. Her Daddy had dropped some information once, but quickly covered it up with another lame story. *Could the African Boy Legend have been responsible for the defeat of the Ugandan army? Was the army even on the attack! Does the story have any truth or merit? Both governments covered it up, called it a training exercise gone awry, with a mutiny of insubordinate troops. No official pronouncements were made, just a new treaty with Kenya and Uganda. A thesis for me at Oxford Prep!*

Savannah walked onto her back lawn overlooking the bay. She picked up her lacrosse stick and methodically and rhythmically rattled shot after shot into the net. It was effortless for her, and now even mindless, as her mind ever drifted away. Again, she was overwhelmed with thoughts. She hurried back to her computer and did more research on the Uganda uprising. *Why was there an exercise in the Preserve in Kenya? Why did the troops mutiny? It doesn't add up.* Then she found some blogs. There were references to a great spirit and his spiritual horse, the sword of an archangel or Excalibur. She knew the locals loved to speculate, particularly about mysticism.

One blog jolted her with a story from a local tribesman.

*A young angelic like boy rode atop a white zebra carrying a large medieval like sword, heavily adorned with jewels. He bellowed an ear-piercing call to the wild, and animals came from land and air, including regal looking lions.*

The blog was blaspheming a local man for making up this story. But the words rang loudly in Savannah's mind.

She was numb. It had to be the African Boy Legend. Her imagination was disappearing into a blistering assault of reality. She felt in her heart it was him. It had to be.

"He must be in the Preserve! He must be with Mika Williams and Haley Andrews!"

"I must call Shannon!"

She hurried to the cabana on the opposite side of the pool. She had Shannon's number. Shannon was not there when she visited campus. *Oh! I later found out she was in Africa! This is all getting so surreal!* She made the call.

"This is Shannon. I recognize this number! Hello, Savannah! Or is this Mrs. Stewart?"

"This is Savannah. Do you have a moment?"

"Of course, I do."

Savannah drew in a heavy breath. The breeze swept her bangs to the side. One more sip of ice tea.

"I heard you have gone to Africa. It must have been a special trip! I wanted to hear about it."

Shannon was suddenly unnerved and defensive. She had not told anyone at the University about what she had done on her trip, other than generalities about 'her vacation'. Not even Gavin Blocker had garnered anything worth blogging about, other than possible idle speculations. She had not mentioned Africus, or Mika or Haley. She had surreptitiously researched his eligibility issues.

"It was a nice trip, nothing romantic!" She skillfully diverted attention from her secret.

"Shannon, let me tell you a story. Only my family and a few friends have heard this story. It may be a childhood dream, but I think it is real. And I know Mika and Haley are in the West Kenya National Wildlife Preserve."

Shannon flushed in anticipation of the story. Her heartbeat raced. *How did Savannah know she was with Mika? What was on the internet? Had Blocker published his idle speculations?*

She quickly opened all of his social media accounts and blogs. Nothing. She quickly updated her search on the Mika and Haley. Nothing. She panicked.

"I have to go Savannah!"

"Let me tell you about the African Boy Legend!"

Shannon's breath stopped. She got up and closed the door to her office. She sat down on the couch and nervously drank the rest of her energy drink bottle on the table. Beads of perspiration dripped from her forehead.

Savannah sensed the emotion of the moment. She had struck gold. She was ready for the attack. But Shannon needed to be an ally. And Shannon was covering this up. *Everyone is covering up the African Boy Legend!*

"Shannon, maybe you should come on a recruiting visit to Annapolis. The all-star tournament is next weekend for all the club teams. You can recruit the rising juniors and the rising seniors who are still diamonds in the rough. I will be there. I think we need to talk in person."

"Savannah. I did not meet him in person. He was always in the savannah. He may have been hurt by poachers. I am sure he is real, but do not know for sure. I doubt Mika and Haley would lie to me. I have independently determined he is eligible to come to America and to attend a university. He is not eligible for an athletic scholarship, but he could play. I don't know what he is going to do. I last heard he will apply. But he is still not back home since the poacher incident. I am sure he is alive, but they have not heard from him, last I checked."

"Alive! You are scaring me!"

"I know! Savannah, I believe you. I know you lived in Africa, and likely went on safaris. Omigod! Savannah!" Shannon shrieked.

"What? Omigod! What!" Savannah shrieked back.

"Let me catch the next plane to Baltimore. Lindsay Andrews is already out there watching the eighth graders and first years. We have a lot to talk about!"

"You can't leave me hanging!"

"Nothing bad! No new news on the African Boy Legend! They call him Africus now!"

"Africus Williams?"

"No, just Africus."

"Call me anytime. I will look forward to seeing you. I help coach one the youth squads."

"Sounds good."

Shannon hung up and nearly passed out. Too many thoughts crashed through her mind. It was all happening so fast. She had to focus on some football recruiting before she left. She had to call Spiritis. Too much to do.

Savannah picked up her computer and furiously searched for the African Boy Legend, or any human named Africus. Nothing relevant came up. Small doubts still flickered in her mind. Shannon had not seen him. Mika may be continuing the ruse he started a few weeks ago, preying on the unquenchable thirst of recruitniks for diamonds in the recruiting rough.

*Maybe I will just daydream! Daydreams always have a happy ending!*

Savannah started daydreaming about Nebraska State lacrosse. She envisioned Africus watching her from the new stadium stands. But what did he look like. He was only eleven or so when she met him. Or did she meet him? And then, of course, after they both had championship rings, she dreamed he gave her a special ring from Africa. *A very special ring, maybe one worn by an English queen! Maybe the very first queen!*

She knew the rumors and stories about the hidden Treasures in the legendary Cavern of Lost Treasures. Was it real? Would Africus have discovered it? Where else would he have found a medieval sword? *So much to fantasize about! And we live happily ever after!*

"Savannah! Wake up! Are you daydreaming again? You need to focus on reality! You need to select your courses at Oxford Prep. You may meet the Prince of Denmark! He will be a senior there this fall, just one year younger than you. He plays English football. I hear he has talked of you on his social media pages!"

"A prince! Well, that will do! Ha! But I doubt he talked of me?" Savannah let her hair down and brushed her hands underneath it to fluff it up. She cocked her head and eyed her Mum.

"Well, maybe he did! But just kidding, you know. But I am sure he will notice you!"

"I will need a sport to play. Maybe I can play English football, as well. But I may find my own prince. One with a sword!" Savannah mused.

"You are so dramatic Savannah and such a dreamer! Ah! But when you are young you should dream. Create your own Parallel Dream Universe. If you don't dream, how can it become true? Dreams are the sparks of the future. The means to your ends. Visions must come first," Mrs. Stewart spoke and was amused by her own narration. She flipped her hair into the breeze and held her chin up. She flattened her belly and admired her svelte figure for a 50-year-old.

"Mum! You are so vain! And you are so fair! The fairest of them all! Ha! We should go for a sail, maybe a sailor boy will notice you!"

"Only an admiral, my dear!"

"So, Nebraska State is attending the lacrosse festival in Annapolis. They want to speak to me. It is that Shannon Garrison. She was not there on our trip. She was in Africa.

But she is the one who has recruited me for some time," Savannah dropped her voice, while raising her eyebrows.

"Africa! What is with that? They don't play lacrosse or football in Africa! Was it just a vacation? I don't know much about her. I would like to meet her myself. Do you really have an interest in Nebraska State? I thought it paid for our Colorado trip, and gave Maryland some nervous moments. Or do you want to pursue the Ivy League. Princeton will still be interested, especially, after a year in Oxford! What prompted Nebraska State anyway, my young dear? I know you, there must be some reason only known and understood by you!" Mrs. Stewart probed, rubbing her chin.

"Mum! You think you know me so well! But I am interested in the competition in the conference. They may have one of the top teams in the country when I am in college. Maybe a little espionage on my part?" Savannah floated a believable concept.

"I will find out. You inherited your insatiable curiosity from me! And your extraordinary detective skills from me as well! And I can smell a shark a mile away!" Mrs. Stewart smirked, raising her palms in the air.

"Maybe there is a reason. Maybe you will discover it. We shall see! But let's shop for London!" Savannah tossed the towel to the chair. She put her shawl over her shoulders and headed to the outdoor shower for a very cold and refreshing summer shower.

Mrs. Stewart smiled, determined to get to the bottom of this charade.

# 25.

IT WAS ANOTHER HOT DAY in the savannah. Africus ran and tussled with the young lion cub. It growled and frolicked in the tall savannah grass. Africus ran and it chased him. It was quick and agile. It kept up with the light-footed Africus and matched his speed. The cub was eighteen months old, and half grown. The female lion watched in amusement. Its mother had been killed by the hyenas. But another three female lions had joined the guardian and cub. Two eagles had guided the three female lions from another pride in the northwestern part of the Preserve. Together they formed an adequate hunting team.

Africus saw the range vehicle hiding in the tall grass behind some trees. He saw Mika. Mika was silent and stern. Africus ignored him. He played relentlessly with the lion cub. Hunting practice was next. Minimilion was his mission now. The jungle was his home.

Africus watched as Mika crawled out of the range vehicle. Mika openly walked toward the field where Africus and Minimilion played.

"Africus, I am so glad you to see you! We did not know where you were. You did tell us about the war between the lions and hyenas. And the death of Maximilion. I am so sorry!"

"Thanks. The hyenas are gone. Minimilion shall be the new king of the jungle in the Preserve. He is the son of Maximilion. I will help train him with the female lions."

"All right. But there is more news. Everything is happening at once. Haley left Africa last night and is returning to Nebraska. I wanted to tell you in person. She wanted to tell you herself but was just flat out desperate to leave. She loves you dearly, and you can text her anytime," Mika spoke directly from his heart.

"She has been hired just this week by Shannon Garrison in the athletic department to help in marketing and recruiting. Shannon is the one who was here to recruit you."

Africus just listened.

"Haley was saddened by the recent events, the poacher attack, the death of Maximilion. She is convinced that you will now stay in Africa, the savannah and your secret places. She knows that you need to train the new lion leader."

Africus continued his silence, waiting for more.

"She was tired of the minimalist existence. She had fulfilled her dreams of helping animals and young African children like you. The home school is closed-there are no more students. You are grown and affixed to your environment. She felt her purpose here was gone.

"She wanted me to return with her last night. But I wanted to catch up with you, and to set up an orderly transition of the management of the ranger station. She understood. I told her I would go to Nebraska in a month or two. She fears that I will stay," he said as a tear trickled down his face.

"But I realize my love for Haley is stronger than my love for the savannah and the Preserve. I have been gone long enough. Haley did not want to have children in the jungle. If I go back with her, we can start a family. Africus, I am going to leave, too."

"But I am family?" Africus retorted, eyeing Mika sternly.

"Yes, you are. And you can come with us to Nebraska. That has been your plan. Maximilion blessed your plan. I hope you still want to go," Mika hesitantly stated, looking down at the ground.

"I think you should go with Haley now. I will train your replacement. We will be fine. I will train Minimilion!" Africus said looking to the sky and throwing a rock at a tree.

"It must have been quite a battle. The lions won," Mika said solemnly.

"Maximilion fought like the warrior king that he was. He saved the life of Minimilion But many lions perished, too.

"But enough of that! GO! Leave with Haley! Jorge' can take your spot for now. He can be an effective ranger. GO! GO!' Africus yelled while looking away, hiding his saddened face, and grief-stricken feelings.

"Africus, we want you to come with us to Nebraska. You are family!"

"NO! I am home now. This is my family. This is my home! GO!"

The female lions sensed the distress in Africus's face and voice. They rose and approached Mika. Mika was without a weapon. "GO!" Africus shouted.

Africus raised his right hand. The lions stopped. Mika took one last look at Africus. He turned, kicked some stones, and walked slowly back to his range vehicle. His head hung low. He hopped in and rode back to camp.

"Jorge', it shall be. Good luck, my friend and son!" Mika whispered to himself under the roar of the range vehicle.

*But I understand. Maximilion has died. Africus views himself as a co-leader of the Preserve. His loyalty to Maximilion extends back further in time than his time with us.*

Africus watched Mika leave. He picked up a stick and flung it as far as he could. He held back his desire to scream at the top of his lungs. He flung another stick into a tree. The lion cub stared at him, befuddled. The cub ran and retrieved one of the sticks. Africus was taken aback. Cats were not retrievers. This was personal. The cat has empathy, he thought.

Soon the afternoon drifted past evening into the early night. The female lions were restless. So much had happened. So many members of the pride had perished. Africus watched as they paced across the field. He knew hunger had set in. It was time to hunt, soon. The cub would have to join in the hunt, even at a young age. The cub would be prey as well. The African dogs were still around.

The pacing lions were anxious. There was no lion leader. Africus was now the pride leader. He felt awkward. He had participated in many hunts as a young boy, but was always in the background, using sticks and stones at first, and then his dagger. Now he was an animal. One of the pride. He stared at the lion cub. Minimilion would have to grow up quickly to lead the pride. He had an idea.

"Minimilion You are young, but even as a young cub, with no hyenas around, you can lead the pride. I will guide you. Listen to your instincts. Your father may guide you, too. The female lions can go for the kill. But you must lead them to the prey. It is bright tonight. A mile from here, a herd of wildebeest are grazing. Lead the lions to the herd. I will distract the herd, and you can attack the rear and take down the old and tired," Africus instructed the lion cub, cradling his face in his hands.

The lion cub licked his face. He knew he was ready to lead the remnants of his father's pride and the newcomers. He roared. The female lions responded well. They lined up on his flanks. Off they trotted toward the herd. The four lions softly tread through the high grass with Minimilion No hyenas screamed out their location. They were soon upon the wildebeest. Africus hooted to the leaders in the front of the herd. The herd rumbled forward. Soon the old and tired were exposed in the rear. The female lions attacked and quickly took down two of the wildebeests.

The wildebeests suddenly broke into a gallop. Minimilion took down a healthy young adult wildebeest on his own. Africus pounded his chest in acknowledgment of the take down. Africus flung his dagger and another beast fell. It was a successful hunt. The female lions were in full trust of Minimilion, even at such a young age. He was now the king of the pride.

Together the lions feasted on the fallen prey. Their appetite was satiated. Africus made a fire and cooked some of the leftover meat. African dogs licked their chops and finished off the carcasses. The vultures were not hungry. The war had given them ample food for the week. Hundreds of vultures had partaken of the bountiful sight for them.

The lions slept. Africus could not sleep. He lay on his back and stared at the stars. He thought of Maximilion mostly. He thought of Mika and Haley. All of those so close to him were dead or leaving. He felt sadness.

Africus fell into a deep slumber. By early morning just before the sunrise, he entered his dream state, his Parallel Dream Universe. Soon visions of his encounter with the Girl swamped his subconscious mind. She suddenly danced around him and the lions. Flowers were everywhere. It was like the poppy field he had traveled to with Essence. White clouds filled the skies. The air was cool like the mountain breezes. She wore a white dress, not the khakis she was in years earlier. She sang to him in the sweetest voice.

"Follow me! To the land of magic and enchantment! It will be fun! We shall play and frolic," she sang and let her hair down from its pony tail.

But she was no longer a little girl. She had grown. She disappeared behind a tree. He gazed in anticipation. He saw the white paw of a zebra. Soon she appeared again in a regal white gown riding a beautiful white zebra. He saw the eyes. It was Essence. They galloped by him, giggling and smiling in a soft peacefulness. They circled and came back. The zebra raised on its haunches, and then knelt down. The Girl slid off the back of the zebra in front of Africus.

"Come with me to the land of opportunity and excitement. Follow me!" She purred.

He was dazed by the vision.

"No!" he said. "Come with me to my home here in Paradise! I will show you the secret jungle Waterfall, the hidden Cavern of Lost Treasures! Essence will join us together in the earthly and spiritual realms. We can rule the Cavern together!"

"Maybe in the future! But follow me! To America!"

She jumped back on Essence, and they rode away. He saw the flowered crown of England on her head. She had been to the Cavern of Lost Treasures. She was wearing the crown of Queen Guinevere!

The sun rose over the horizon. Africus felt the nuzzle of a cold wet nose. He awoke in perspiration. It was Citra.

"I thought you died?" Wait, how are you here?" A stunned and confused Africus asked.

"Did you see her?" Citra asked.

"It was in a dream!"

"Yes, it was! And it was a message. Just follow your dreams and follow the trail. You will see clues and messages."

"AH, Citra! Are you telling me to follow the Girl to America? How do I know she is there? How do I know who she is? Must I not stay here for a while with Minimilion? But he is nearing his time. I think he will be ready shortly to run the pride and all the prides. We shall see? But I thought you had died!"

"It is me! Just in the body of another cheetah! I told you I may return! I will leave this body, too, even before it dies. Next time you see me, I may be the white zebra again! Or a bear!"

Africus brushed his hand across the forehead of Citra. They locked eyes for a long moment. Africus smiled and walked away. Citra growled in recognition.

Africus stared out at the trees. He saw a herd of antelope grazing. Heat radiated from the grass even in the early morning. He watched Citra spring from the higher grass and take down one of the older antelopes. Citra dragged it patiently and slowly back up her favorite tree. The tree she and Africus often spent time together in. His mind swung back to his dream.

*What is real? What is fantasy? Do I only imagine my relationship with Maximilion? With Citra? Is the Girl imaginary? Just a fulfillment of my need for female human companionship? There is no trace of her on the Internet or social media. Should I go to Nebraska State? Join civilization? Reality? Use my jungle instincts to play the American game of survival?*

Africus returned to his nearby range vehicle. He leaned his head on the steering wheel. It was terribly hot. It shocked him back to the present. His current reality. He turned the key. Citra turned and watched. The hawks above circled. Minimilion poked his head above the tall grass and furtively growled. His home. His friends.

He drove the vehicle down the road back to the ranger station. Dust billowed behind his range vehicle. Minimilion followed for a while. Soon he stopped and was herded back by one of the female lions. One of his future brides.

Africus arrived at the ranger station. A couple of guards approached him.

"Haley left for the United State. It was sudden! But we saw it coming. She has been aloof and despondent since the last kids graduated from her home school. And you are almost always in the Preserve," one guard said solemnly, shoulders hanging to the side.

"Mika left for Nairobi this morning. He is trying to go back home, too. Haley will work in the athletic department at Nebraska State. That may work out, you know. It may take a while for Mika to get the paperwork done. He needs a new passport. But the embassy may help. It is like an emergency. I don't think he is going to tell Haley when he his returning until he is set to go," the other guard added, feeling knowledgeable.

"Thanks. So, who runs the Preserve now? I presume it is Jorge'?"

"No, Mika called authorities in Nairobi this morning before he left. The Kenyan government is sending a ranger from the Big Preserve. He was number two there. They don't really know about you. We think you should be the commander. What happened in the jungle? Reports are that the hyenas are gone and many lions are gone as well."

"It was a lion thing. A civil war. The hyenas took advantage but were defeated. We lost Maximilion."

"We heard. We are so sorry."

Africus went to his room. He crashed in his bed and fell into a deep sleep.

# 26.

Saturday, July 26, 2025
*Annapolis, Maryland*

SAVANNAH SPOTTED the two women on the sideline wearing their scarlet t-shirts with the crimson NS. They were watching the top rising juniors. One girl from the College Preparatory school was playing, too. She recognized Lindsay Andrews, the head coach. She assumed the tall blonde next to her was Shannon. Her heart raced.

The game ended and the two furiously dictated notes into their smart devices. Shannon caught Savannah's eye, and immediately waved with a big smile. She had seen many films and pictures of Savannah and recognized her right away. She waved Savannah over. Because Savannah was already graduated from high school and was to attend a foreign institution in the fall, there was no ban on the coach and recruiter on talking to her.

Savannah gave a thumbs-up to the College Preparatory girl as she traversed the field. Two seventh graders giggled and asked for her autograph. She laughed with surprise, but graciously obliged. It was early morning, but still a hot summer day on the eastern shore of the Chesapeake. She finally approached the two women.

"Hi Coach Lindsay! And I assume you are Ms. Garrison?" she nervously smiled.

Coach Lindsay Andrews hugged her recruit in a professional manner.

"Yes, this is Shannon Garrison, head of WLAX recruiting at Nebraska State."

"It is nice to meet you Savannah Stewart!" Shannon said with a warm smile extending her hand in greeting.

Savannah and the two recruiters talked about lacrosse, recruiting and the hot weather. Soon Coach Lindsay left to speak with some of the club coaches. The head of the northeast team from Massachusetts was always loaded with the top recruits from New England. She walked over to him.

"Savannah, I am so anxious to hear your story. I have so much to tell you, too. Haley Andrews left Africa a couple of days ago. She is returning to Jefferson City to work in marketing and recruiting with me. It was bang-bang. I was looking for help, and she called me out of the blue. I hired her on the spot. Eventually, she will get back to coaching, probably soccer. She should arrive soon."

"What of Mika? And..." Savannah asked hopefully.

"Mika was staying temporarily, last I heard, but was planning on coming back, too. But Africus is incognito. But you and I are going to do something about that! But what is your story?!"

"Oh, the short or long version?"

"Let's go over to the tent and grab a coffee. I want the long version!"

The two walked to the tent and grabbed a pastry and coffee. They found a small table away from the parents who ambled around the tent. Everyone was wearing the latest fabric that wicked away perspiration and protected against mosquitos and sunlight. The sunglasses were huge, as were the hats that had reverted in style back to the roaring twenties of the twentieth century. The earth's temperature had gradually risen every year but one since 2014. It was hot and the styles and apparel industry reflected the heat.

"Global warming may be here to stay. I am so concerned about the future," Shannon stated as she turned toward an outdoor air-cooling fan.

"It seems so random and episodic. Torrential rain and storms in one continent and drought in others. Thank God for the latest advancements in water desalinization. It saved California! The southeast now looks like the rain forest! New England finally broke its drought. There are so many dikes in Florida now. My mon won't go to Florida anymore. I think the Midwest is the safest place for now, maybe. Its rainfall has increased. Farming is booming. It is not as hot as the northeast!" Savannah added.

"There is a world conference on this subject every month now. Maybe our new President will be strong on this issue, as she promised in her campaign. It's hot in Africa, I know that," Shannon added.

"So, you never saw him? Are you sure he is not legend? There is so much legend in Africa. Here we have virtual reality, there they have old fashion legend!" Savannah exclaimed, relaxing as they changed the subject. She wiped her brow. She gazed deeply into Shannon's eyes waiting for her response.

"I believe there is an Africus. I believe he is a ranger. I did not see him. But I spent time with Haley. There is true maternal like love there. So, I believe her. But I don't know if he is the African Boy Legend, or if he has mystical or interdimensional powers! So, what is your story. You seem quite obsessed with this boy!" Shannon smirked while she teased Savannah, forgetting for now the usual obsequious behavior of recruiters on the recruiting trail.

"I am not obsessed, just in love with a dream! A dream I even had recently, about a white zebra, and waterfalls and treasure filled caves and a boy!

"When I was nine, my Daddy and Mum were still together. We lived in South Africa. He was a successful businessman, but not as successful as he became later. He was the first to promote and offer full social media, digital tech, digital banking, and wireless access to the all of sub-equatorial Africa. He combined that with a burgeoning African media empire to become a legendary businessman in Africa, philanthropist and author."

"I know he is one of the richest men in the world," Shannon acknowledged.

"When I was still ten, he took me on a safari. We were in East Africa. I heard the legend of the African Boy Legend, who was raised by and lived with lions. I had heard he was the cutest boy that ever lived, with beaming blue eyes and blonde sun-bleached hair and sun bronzed skin.

"On the safari, we stopped for a bathroom break. My Daddy was leading the safari. I snuck out to the brush near a tree. I felt and sensed a strong presence. I never saw him, just sensed him. I even smelled him! My Daddy had found me, and I returned to the safari. For a whole year, I thought of him every day. I could not wait for the safari at the same time the next year.

"The time came; we went to East Africa again. We stopped like clockwork near the same tree for a bathroom break. My Daddy was in an argument with an English athlete, one who later won a gold medal in the decathlon in the Tokyo Olympics!

"I went to the same tree. Surely enough, I felt the same overwhelming presence. Even the same smell! I had the courage if not stupidity to wrap around the tree. A female lion burst through the brush. I thought my life was over. How foolish was I to believe in a myth! But then the African Boy Legend appeared. We did not talk. We locked eyes in what seemed like eternity. Suddenly, there were gunshots and my Daddy was screaming. The African Boy Legend gently kissed me. MY FIRST KISS! He took off. I screamed. My scream was feigned, of course! I diverted attention away from the African Boy Legend, and the large male lion charging toward the safari. I then swooned," Savannah paused in exhaustion.

"The lion was Maximilion, the lion leader. He is Africus's best friend. The one that saved him as a toddler," Shannon briefly added, her focused eyes wide in excitement and thrill.

"Omigod! Really!

"Yes!" Shannon exclaimed.

"After that my Daddy lectured me never to leave a safari again. He seemed to know what I was doing. Later he told me that legends were simply legends. Let them be. But my Daddy divorced my Mum that autumn. She immediately moved me to the United States where she was from. Right here in Maryland. I have not been back to Africa since.

"I told my Mum the story of the African Boy Legend. Over the years, she had me convinced it was my imagination. I spent time with psychologists and was tested repeatedly. I have abilities, I know now, like communicating with animals, that were deemed hallucinations, and day dreams. I was told I lived in my Parallel Dream Universe! Fortunately, my Mum never let them put me on drugs. I never found anything concrete on the internet, media, social media or news outlets on the African Boy Legend. I let it go and became a lacrosse star. I even had a boyfriend my junior and senior year. I broke up with him last May.

"I still had my devices all wired for any stories on the African Boy Legend. I had creative word choices to capture what I could. It was one story that really caught me. It was about a football recruit in Africa that Nebraska State was targeting. The story quickly was doused as a ruse and tied to recruiting on Mars. I was very suspicious.

"Nebraska State is an up and coming lacrosse power. My Mum and I were going to spend time in Colorado, so why not set up a trip to Nebraska! Yes, it was convenient. But I had to check out Nebraska State, just in case.

"I later found that a real Nebraska State football player and his wife lived in Kenya. It was too close to ignore. And you were not there when I visited! But on a mysterious vacation in Africa! It was all too suspicious! I then found articles about a poacher and his statements about a boy. And blogs about an event years ago, where a mystical boy may have led the defeat of the Ugandan army. It was too much. That is when I called you," Savannah continued, breathless in excitement.

"I was startled when you called and then why you called. But what an amazing story. I did not know about Uganda. I knew about the poaching incident. I did read the poacher was captured and incarcerated.

"But what an amazing story! It appears that the African Boy Legend and Africus are one in the same. It is amazing that the world media has not latched on to this story. And your father is in media. He did not run with the story. Savannah, we need to come up with a plan to bring the African Boy Legend to Nebraska State, or at least the United States. To be with you!" Shannon shared her excitement.

"Or maybe to London! They would love him there. Maybe there is truth to the Cavern of Lost Treasures! Maybe the British crown would want to know about that! There may be Treasures from long lost English kings and queens!

I wore the English crown in my dreams!" Savannah concluded.

Shannon and Savannah sat in silence for the next few moments, locked in deep visions about the future. Savannah was smiling. Her face shone with happiness. She was not likely crazy after all. Shannon was caught up in the romance of it all, and maybe her own fame for discovering this extraordinary human.

Savannah spoke first.

"How do we extricate him from Africa? I think you said he wants to leave."

"I think we use true love! I think you should commit to Nebraska State for 2026. We will publicize it and make sure Haley let's Mika know. Hopefully, they get in touch with Africus before next year!"

"What if I commit for 2025? I don't think I want to wait that long!"

"Well, we certainly would welcome that!" Shannon stood and jumped for joy.

"Let me talk to my Mum. That may be an issue, but we shall see. I will have to talk to my Daddy as well. But, I am so excited!" Savannah stood and embraced Shannon. They embraced for a long moment.

Savannah went to her car to return home. Shannon talked to Lindsay. She told her of the possible commitment, but not about the African Boy Legend. Coach Lindsay promised to keep quiet until the commitment was official. *But what if Mrs. Stewart or her father says no.*

Shannon tried to call Haley. There was no response. She texted her as well. No response. She thought of reaching Mika but stopped short of calling him.

# 27.

Monday, July 28, 2025
Jefferson City, Nebraska

GAVIN BLOCKER WAS STUNNED at the news. He could not believe it. Shannon had delivered him the good news. Savannah Stewart was committing to Nebraska State. Not only that, she was matriculating as a first-year student the fall of 2025. She would be a full participant in the fall WLAX schedule. He opened his computer to write up his blog. He also heard the story on Haley Andrews return to Nebraska State. He and Shannon still had not gone on a date, even after their friendly encounter on July 4th, but she had just given him the giant scoop. The scoop would not register that much in the national sports networks, but it was huge in the world of women's lacrosse and in Nebraska. But Shannon said bigger news was possible, more to follow. He had racked his mind to discern that further scoop. Nothing. He speculated it was about Africa. But there were no organized sports in Africa that Nebraska State played. Mika and Haley did not have any children that would be old enough yet. He doubted it was a track athlete. Maybe Savannah's father was to make a large donation. He would dig later. Ask her on a date later, to sway her over.

He submitted his daily blog.

*The VBL is hot as ever. It runs parallel with professional base-ball. America is hooked. The virtual leagues are keeping real sports in vogue. Fans still like the real sports, but like the virtual parallels. The fantasy teams of the last decade are still popular, too, for both the virtual leagues and the real leagues. So much to do in the digital world!*

*Back to real sports. Nebraska State, the University, just secured the commitment of the top girl's lacrosse player in the country. Savannah Stewart, always considered a lock for Maryland in 2026 after she returned from England and Oxford Prep, has committed to Nebraska State. Not only did Nebraska State obtain her commitment, but she is foregoing her year at Oxford Prep in England, where her father is located. She is coming to Nebraska State this fall. She will participate in fall games and practices. She is fully eligible to play. She did not accept a scholarship. The scholarship would have reduced scholarships from existing players. Even though she does not qualify for financial assistance, the gesture was noticed by her new teammates. She will likely play midfield. Her blinding speed will serve her well on the midfield, and her quickness and sharpshooting will help on offense as well. The University has a blog on Savannah and lacrosse. See the link below.*

*Nebraska State has reunited with former star athlete Haley Andrews, class of 2010, wife of former Nebraska State football stand-out and legend, Mika Williams, and sister of head WLAX coach Lindsay Andrews. She has spent the last fifteen or so years in East Africa running a home charter virtual school for rural kids and serving as a ranger in one of the Preserves for the African wild animals. She recently closed the school down after all her students graduated. All but one of her students are matriculating in colleges. What a great success. She will serve a marketing and administrative role in the athletic department and will assist in coaching the*

WLAX program. Welcome back. No word on Mika. I presume he will join Haley. That is personal.

Well, the Nebraska State football team starts fall camp a week from Monday. The quarterback battle will be of significance. The winner will not jolt anybody into visions of a division title. But the defense is solid, and RIP should have some brilliant schemes this year, or at least that is what Africus told me. The defensive line will be anchored by twins. The receiver core is solid, as usual. The prior staff left the cupboard full. The offensive line is fast and athletic. The line is small for the new Conference of the North, but they should hold their own with skill and technique. The ancient o-line coach, with thirty years of experience in the Association with multiple titles, is really a great stopgap until the young GA in waiting steps in next year. The running back is a bull. Lots of yards after carry.

But the biggest question is what offense they will run. So many new offenses are out there. Oklahoma shot out the gate the quickest last year with their amorphous offense. Let's see if the Nebraskans can follow suit with some innovation as well. We play them again this year! More on that this November, and it is the day after Thanksgiving Day!

Nebraska State looks to set up virtual reality this year for each game. The virtual reality will initially be used by the coaches to help in their coaching. Nebraska is on the cutting edge of virtual reality for college football. It could be a bold new year for the football program using the new technology. If it works, the University will license it out for substantial royalties. More on that later.

The Association just announced that VPR for college football will be launched in 2025! The command center will be in Omaha, Nebraska, just as it is for professional football. VPR will be limited to the one player on offense and one on defense. My guess is the quarterback and the strong safety. Revenue sharing with the Association will result in revenues to the colleges based on usage. I *would think the profits will be there for the schools, particularly those with versatile super quarterbacks, like Jackson from Clemson.*

*Oh, the weather. It is not so hot in Jefferson City, but the heat wave and drought in the east are taking its toll. Thousands of elder folks have fled to Canada and Alaska for the summer. The east has been slow to build the desalinization plants that California built early in the decade. The water infrastructure is critical for our country and the world. We have no ocean here. So thankfully the river is running full, and we have normal rainfall in this flip flop weather pattern. And hurricane season may be as bad as 2021, the worst season in recorded history. Parts of Florida just stayed under water with the rising sea surface. No Dutch water barriers or dikes could be built. The rest of Florida, with its extensive dike system, more sophisticated than the Netherlands, is bracing for the season. God bless them.*

*"So, a new year, a new super conference, a new President, a healthy bond market for the millions of retirees. THE RIP-ROARING TWENTIES are in full operating mode! Plans to colonize Mars in the Forties and Europa in the Sixties. I wish I was younger! Signing off."*

Gavin stepped away from his computer. His mind still raced.

*What did Shannon have. I have to get the scoop. Maybe even before she does. Maybe Mika has some information. Mika is not in the database anymore. Maybe Shannon has something to do with that. Clearly, she had met with Haley in Africa. Now Haley works for her. Interesting. That old story about a football recruit from Africa. Hmm! Then the Mars angle and everyone laughed. Ah, one student is not attending college. Who is he or she? Is he the phantom recruit? What happened in Africa that sent Haley home, beyond her school closing. Why no new students. New pharma industry, maybe it eliminated the rogue rural student. Maybe.*

Gavin perused the internet and databases for odd stories in East Africa. Nothing much until he read about a notorious animal poacher's incarceration in Uganda. There was a brief reference to a jungle like boy.

BAM! Gavin stood up in fear and excitement. Had he hit the jackpot?

*Should I blow the lid off Shannon's little secret? Who is this boy? Maybe I should go to Africa. A safari in East Africa. Whoa! Savannah was originally from Africa. Is there a connection?*

*Oh, Shannon, you are a superstar! We are made for each other! Don't you know that?*

Gavin was stunned at his revelations and detective work.

*It could be pie in the sky. Fall camp starts in a week. There are no Africans on the roster and no African walk-ons. I will sit on this. I will work on Shannon.*

Gavin called Shannon. She picked up. It was the first she had heard from Gavin since July fourth. He had not even thanked her for her text tipping him off on the Savannah scoop.

"Why haven't you called, Gavin, we had a nice time on the fourth," she teased, as adrenaline rushed through her system.

*OH, I must like him if I feel this rush of excitement. Hold back girl!*

*I did not know she wanted ME to call her! Be cool!* Gavin thought as he stared at his smart device.

"Whoa! OK! Well, how about I meet you right now at Barnaby's bar and grill on Eighth street. I can be there soon. A ride sharing auto-driven car drives by my house every half hour. I will catch it and meet you there in an hour! Good-bye!" Gavin offered.

"Wait! What! Gavin? OK!" Shannon blurted out, pressing her thighs with her hands.

Shannon didn't even change her clothes. But she was dressed nicely with her work attire of pants and a blouse. She brushed her hair and touched up her eye make-up. She briefly thought that at age 26 she was only fifteen years younger than the President of the United States, a Midwestern girl from Wisconsin. She thought more about her President, who she adored.

The President, Jessica Parsons, was very attractive, and unfortunately, a widow. Her older husband had been stricken by heart attack weeks before the election. Some say a sympathy vote help propel her to the electoral college victory, as she eked out state after state by the narrowest of margins. She was even first in the popular vote ahead of the other party candidate. Her popularity among world leaders was unparalleled. She joined the cadre of youthful leaders that were now running the governments and economies of the world and the global economy. Many were women. Her focus on space exploration, education, infrastructure, technology, job growth and training, climactic change and global economic harmony had brought her many votes.

Tax reform had been tackled by prior administrations, with a current Tax Code that was fair and competitive globally. Most of the large multinational companies kept their headquarters in the U.S. A national Value Added Tax closed the deficits and help fund low tax rates on income. Compliance with the fair system was historically high. Entitlement reform had been painfully dealt with over the prior eight years, but the reform was generally working. Technology had reduced both medical costs and healthcare administrative costs significantly, helping reign in the burgeoning costs along with the reform measures. The low hanging fruit had been targeted first. The retirement ages for Social Security and Medicare had been increased to age 70. Income based limits had been installed for Medicare, too. More complex reform had been installed by regulation and executive orders.

So, the new President thought big and thought bold. Her adventurous and audacious plans for the future compelled many to adore her and follow her as a leader as well as an elected official. She was a lead proponent of interplanetary colonization and beyond. She also had been an astrophysicist major in college and was fully on board for all forms of research and development of space travel, worm holes, space colonies, and other once far reaching science fiction topics. She also was interested in the concept of parallel universes, and the multiverse.

Artificial intelligence had taken off and improved productivity of American workers to an astonishing level. Many jobs were displaced, but more technology jobs had been created. A massive job education and redeployment effort had paid dividends by matching displaced workers with higher paying jobs.

She was middle of the road on social issues. As the Rip-Roaring 2020s roared and most Americans were economically comfortable, social issues had receded somewhat from the front row of presidential politics. Women's rights and racial equality had improved substantially over the prior decade. Immigration was still much discussed but had found an equilibrium. Laws on qualified foreign workers had been relaxed, and non-criminal illegal immigrants had been granted resident status. Mexico had turned its economy around and fewer of its citizens attempted to leave, resulting in a net outflow of Mexican citizens back to their country. Unlike, parts of the U.S., Mexico had been spared of any major drought.

Transportation was well taken care for her voters. And energy strides were dramatic. The discovery of viable fusion technology in 2022 had been the start of an energy revolution. It was still not full scale, only accounting for ten percent of energy production. Oil was more plentiful with the technologies of the prior decade, and new technologies that produced oil from deep in the earth's crust. Most of the deep oil was of geologic origin and not biologic. It seemed boundless. Micro grids for electricity had flourished with blockchain technology and the Internet III. And forays into wireless energy were dramatic and exciting. The energy innovations and discoveries were a key ingredient to the insurgent Rip-Roaring 2020s around the globe. *Amazing! What a decade! But I need to stop thinking about the world and focus on Gavin!*

Gavin reached Barnaby's first. Shannon lived in an area of Jefferson City where the automated cars only came every forty-five minutes. She stopped the car at Barnaby's. It was on her Avenue so she did not have to change cars. The cars were set up almost like an above ground subway. Always moving. The number of cars programmed to match the demand for ridership. Very few urban dwellers owned cars. Intercity transportation with the massive federal speed rail system completed was efficient as well. *The U.S. transportation infrastructure is so good!*

She saw Gavin standing at the bar. She knew where he was from her app on her smart device. She toyed with him at first, pretending to be an admirer. But he quickly caught on.

Shannon, you look nice for coming straight from work! Has Haley started working yet?"

Shannon felt a tinge of self-defense as the subject of Haley came up. *Did I say too much-probably as bait for this get together?* She kept her composure.

"Not full time until after Labor Day. She has a lot of transitioning to do, finding a home, dealing with Mika. I will be patient. She will help her sister mostly in coaching this fall. SO, I must have really piqued your interest with my potential other scoop. I am guessing you are on to something, or you would not be here," she suddenly said despondently, not hiding her emotions.

"Well, honestly, yes, but honestly, I did want to see you. Two birds with one stone, they say."

"How romantic, NOT! I think I have to go. If you have a lead you should just blog it. Pick up the pieces later, right? Blame it on unknown source in the athletic department. Well, the AD is a woman, and I think she will believe me over you!"

Gavin grabbed her arm firmly. She flinched but waited for his response.

"Please stay. I will hold the story. I have an idea. It is so wild. But I have no confirmation. My wild guess is that there is a boy in East Africa who was raised in the savannah. He has legendary, extraordinary gifts, but maybe he is just a boy from the jungle. He is the source of the original story about a recruit from Africa, because he is tied to two Nebraska State alums. But something has gone awry. He is still in Africa, Haley is here. And somehow, Savannah, who is originally from Africa ties into all of this. I can only piece it together loosely. But ultimately, if there is no recruit, there is no story. Maybe there are plenty of boys who grow up in the jungle or savannah, and maybe even run with the lions. Sounds awesome, unless you live in the wilderness in Africa, and it is just part of your life. We Americans are so in love with superheroes, that we love to create them when they don't exist. Many of the virtual games, and virtual living pod experiences are tied to superheroes! So, am I close?" Gavin finished, somewhat proud of his sleuthing abilities.

Shannon shifted in her chair. She burst forth with her information. "Well, I found more that you did! You are not the only good one here in forensics!"

"I thought I was close. Did you meet the African Boy Legend?" he responded in anticipation and satisfaction.

"NO, I did not personally meet him. He is a ranger that lives with Mika and Haley in the Preserve in West Kenya. His name is Africus. But, I am still not sure if he is anything more than a normal African boy from the bush. But Mika and Haley speak highly of him. And I can tell the motherly love of a woman! So, I think he is real and possibly extraordinary. They say he is a superhero in the savannah. I don't know if he is an Olympic athlete, or great future collegian. But he is special. There are rumors of mysticism, and Treasures to speculate about. He may be just a ranger boy. You are right. But I think we may never know.

"Haley told me that Africus was once on board to come to America. But now she is concerned that he may retreat to his past. He lost his lifelong friend, a lion leader. Really, the king of the jungle in the Preserve. It crushed him.

"Mika is supposed to return to Nebraska, to join Haley but now is incognito. She is concerned that he may not return. No word from him at all since she left. But her guards said that he had left for Nairobi, so she is optimistic. But Mika may be staying in Africa with Africus, I don't know.

"Then, there is the Savannah connection. You are on to something there. Savannah told me she once met Africus, when he was a boy-the African Boy Legend! When he lived in the wild, the locals dubbed him the African Boy Legend. I think I believe her. She and I thought that if she came to Nebraska State, he would follow his heart and his true love to Nebraska to find his princess bride, just like in the movies. I told Haley about Savannah and her prior connection to the African Boy Legend. She was floored. She cried uncontrollably in relief and exhaustion. She thinks the 'American Superstar girl' could pull Africus from his dual worlds to America and Nebraska!" Shannon looked gleefully into Gavin's eyes.

"SO, this could be one of the biggest stories ever! In our world, a real-life boy superhero with a real-life girl superstar would still trump the virtual universe!" Gavin responded with a laugh.

"But there is no story yet. Haley is trying to contact Africus through her ranger station. She has left him texts about Savannah. The rangers and guards say he returned two days after Haley left, but left the next day. They are not even sure he is in the Preserve. He may have headed back to other parts of East Africa where he was raised," Shannon said, her shoulders drooping as she stirred the ice in her drink.

"Shannon, any idea where he is from, or who his parents were? What a strange story."

"Haley said she researched that matter for years and came up with nothing. The only clues are that he understood English from day one, even with no exposure to it. He also knew some movie characters from some family films produced in the west. So, he may be American or European, or possibly from South Africa," Shannon said deep in thought.

"Shannon, this is so amazing. What do we do. Should we fly to Africa?"

Shannon thought of the adventure of searching the savannah and jungle for the lost African Boy Legend with a swashbuckling Gavin Blocker, and her, the ambitious and gold seeking beauty with extraordinary sleuthing abilities. Running from danger and into the teeth of danger. Just like the films of the 1980s searching for lost Treasures.

"No, not now."

Silence overcame them. They were at a standstill. Romance seemed far away for now. But the base attraction was there. So were their common interests, she thought.

# 28.

MIKA LOOKED IN AMAZEMENT through the curtain of the Waterfall into the waiting lake below. The umbrage of the lush trees cooled the air. The flowers smiled in laughter. The crocodiles rolled in the water. The Great Ape watched them from the canopy. Little Minimilion growled at the crocodiles. Most amazing was the white albino zebra with the brilliant blue eyes that looked like they were from a faraway dimension. *I remember her from my dreams. She foretold me about the boy and to name him Africus. Africus talked of her often. Am I in the Parallel Dream Universe? I must be. Or is it the Parallel Real Universe! Whoa! My ancestors' spirits would love this! I am finally here. Of course, the white zebra is a Special Being. She took me here.* The eagles guarded the air atop their perches on the rocks on the top of the Waterfall.

Africus gazed at the lake as well.

"You finally brought me here. It is what you described but filled with even more wonder than I anticipated! Is this the Parallel Real Universe? I see two Special Beings, the white zebra and the Great Ape, so the Parallel Real Universe at last?!" Mika queried to himself as much as to Africus, his steely eyes melting in awe.

Africus was amused by Mika' intense reaction but wanted to break his trance for more important matters. "So, Haley found the Girl?" Africus stared intently at Mika, raising his forearms with his palms open.

"Yes, indirectly through Shannon Garrison."

"Yes, Haley told me that. But it seems improbable. How would she be connected to Nebraska State?" Africus breathed harder and leaned closer to Mika.

"Serendipity, I suppose?"

"Fate, maybe," Africus stared at the Waterfall recalling his visions. "It seems too surreal. According to Haley's texts, the Girl was originally from South Africa. She could have made up the story about the safari and the kiss. My legend was strong and powerful. It would not be a leap to concoct that story. I want to believe it so much though. And the story is so accurate. After all these years for the Girl to suddenly show up."

Africus climbed up the rocks to the top of the Waterfall. He stared down at the lake. The crocodiles swirled around. The eagles squawked. He raised his arms above his head and jumped up high. He jackknifed and headed headlong with the falling water to the lake below. He dove deep into the lake-deeper than the falling water. He swam downstream underneath the crocodiles. They saw him and ignored him. They knew Africus. He belonged to their Paradise. They were guards. He was the guarded.

Mika looked in awe at the dive, and then in horror at the crocodiles. He contemplated diving. The Great Ape held up his hand.

"NO!" was the message.

Mika brushed his dark black hair back. It was longer now. He pulled it back out of his face, revealing his low hairline, and accentuating his strong jaw. He waited. The white zebra left, with a wink, when Africus left. He had plenty to drink, and the Great Ape brought him bananas and fruit. It was fruit he had never seen or tasted.

*This is Paradise. Paradise and the Cavern of Lost Treasures do exist, but just not directly in our universe or reality. The Parallel Real Universe is real! It appears Africus was right!*

Soon Africus returned up the path next to the lake and back behind the curtain of the Waterfall.

"Africus, I first named you Africus, because the white zebra told me to, in my dreams before I met you! And does the white zebra have a name?" Mika exclaimed while he raised his eyebrows.

"Her name is Essence. She has been my guide for years. She is of another world, the Great Realm. I think you understand the Great Realm from your heritage. But she can appear in our Real Universe or world, too, often as an animal, and she can appear in our dreams in the Parallel Dream Universe.

"But Mika, the Girl. Haley said her name is Savannah. But her father called her Providence, not Savannah. Again, how do I know it is her?" Africus looked away and flung a stone into the lake. The crocodiles looked up and then kept swimming.

Mika turned his gaze from the crocodiles to Africus. "As Haley told you and me in her texts, the Girl was from South Africa. Her parents divorced, and she moved to Maryland. She searched for you as much as you searched for her. She found some mention of you from the poacher event. She plays lacrosse. Nebraska State was recruiting her. Somehow, she found the recruiting news about an African recruit for Nebraska State. She and Shannon had a simultaneous combustible epiphany, I think. Amazing. True Love!"

"True love, that is why you should return to Haley right away," Africus pointed at Mika with a smirk.

"Yes, I will. I have my paperwork. No job, yet, but I am going back. But I have E-tickets. I haven't told Haley yet when I am leaving. It will be hard for me to leave Africa, you know. I would rather persuade her to come back to Africa. But, yes, true love must triumph again!" Mika said as he looked at Africus with a broadening smile. His perfect smile was blemished only by one broken front tooth on the right top side. He refused to fix it. It was part of his identity. It was broken when he was still on the native American reservation in a fist fight with his best friend. They both broke a tooth and swore never to fix them, as a life-long bond and penance for their fight.

"She will be so happy," Africus smiled, with a slight glisten in his eyes. "I want to go with you. But I need more proof it is the Girl. This Shannon is a recruiter, and she is the one that told Haley. Haley has not met Savannah."

"When you do decide, I can help you. I know the American envoys in Nairobi well. I was just with them. They have a visa and passport for you. Haley worked that out for you. You can pick them up anytime. You have enough money to buy plane tickets. Shannon says you have been accepted into the University. You are enrolled. They set up all of your courses online. You are an electronic online student, like over 40% of their students-an E student. All you have to today is confirm your enrollment, and E-transfer the University the tuition and fees. Haley and Shannon took care of everything else, including your application. Shannon has sent you an email with all of the information, including costs and payee instructions. And you are eligible to play sports! But in the meantime, if you stay here, you can start your University education!"

"Shannon and Haley did all of that?" Africus looked surprised and excited. I haven't checked my email in a while. I will do that."

"Yes, they did," Mika confirmed.

"Smell this flower. It will put you under. The Great Ape will take you back to your range vehicle. I will drive you home. When you awake, I will be gone back to the savannah. I will have my computer that Haley left for me, and my smart device. No tracking devices though! I think I will be an E-Student! I have some classes to attend!"

Mika looked at Africus. His eyes moistened.

"That is great Africus. The next step would be to join us in Nebraska. But we won't rush you."

"We shall see. I need to talk to this Savannah. I will know if it is her. If it is her, I will come to America!" he yelled to the Waterfall.

"Africus, brace yourself. I have a picture that Haley got from Shannon. Haley has not met her in person yet and has not shown her or Shannon any of your pictures, including the ones we took when we took you from the jungle. Savannah, like you, still has some doubt that you are the African Boy Legend!" Mika trembled as he spoke to Africus.

Africus shook. Mika fumbled around searching his pocket for his smart device. But it was not there. Africus relaxed. The moment of truth would have to wait.

"Send me the picture when you wake up. And have Haley send me her contact information. I will know!"

"Africus, this place exists just like you told me a few months ago! I am so glad you brought me here!" Mika yelled in glee. He sniffed the flower, and seconds later was passed out. Africus watched him pass out. His mind drifted to the Girl.

*I saw the Girl in my dreams. It was her as a grown Girl. Maybe she is only in my Parallel Dream Universe. Maybe, I only met her originally in the Parallel Dream Universe. My nomadic life was desolate. An imaginary beautiful Girl makes sense. But this Girl. I am now thinking it may really be her! Omigod!*

Mika passed out, as did Africus. The Great Ape took Mika and Africus back to the edge of the Deep Jungle.

When they awoke, Minimilion soon joined them on their march back to the range vehicle. Minimilion let out a soft roar.

# 29.

SAVANNAH SAT IN THE OFFICE with her coach Lindsay Andrews, Haley Andrews and Shannon Garrison. They all were in a festive mood. Good coffee from Africa helped their mood. It was Mika's special brew. He had found a nice plot of land fairly high up one of the mountains in central Kenya earlier in the year. He told Haley he was staying to harvest the coffee, and to her consternation, his departure was still somewhat up in the air. The climate was perfect for coffee bean plants. *It is very refreshing and rejuvenating!* Savannah thought.

"Haley! This is the best coffee! Are you sure you don't want to go back to Africa and build a coffee empire with Mika?" Shannon chortled, leaning towards Haley from her desk.

"Happy to be in the states, darling!" Haley relaxed, laughing.

Savannah loved the African coffee. She watched the three women relax while they smelled and sipped the delicious coffee. It reminded her of her childhood. She was excited for her practice with the team that afternoon for fall ball. A round-robin scrimmage with Conference of the North teams was scheduled for the following week at Maryland. Her Mum would be there, as well as many of her friends and teachers from Maryland. She would headline the scrimmage. She was apprehensive and excited. But her thoughts were still somewhere else. The smell of the coffee sent her back home. The African Boy Legend was there. She had gotten his text number from Haley. She texted him two weeks ago, and simply said, "Hi, I am Providence from Africa." He had texted her back the next day, and she responded immediately. The memory of that day overwhelmed her. But after the initial exchange there was silence. His first text was simple. "I remember our kiss!" She knew it was him at that very moment. Her heart burst in love. She wanted to talk to him. *It is you, the African Boy Legend! I am now Savannah. You rescued me from the lion! Come to Nebraska!*

"Where are you Savannah! In Africa, I suppose!" Haley knew only so well. Shannon saw Savannah's intense stare. She broke the conviviality of the meeting.

"He is taking classes on the internet. He is an E student. The registrar confirmed he has signed up for four classes, confirmed his application and admittance, and paid his tuition. The teacher assistants confirmed he has logged in for every lecture. We don't know if he is in the savannah or at the ranger station. But he is learning. He is also officially able to compete for any sports team," Shannon explained with her pouty lips.

"He loves to learn. I am sure he is devouring the lectures and devoutly reading all that he can online on the subject matters. He has texted me a few times. He is enjoying the learning," Haley added, recalling her days with Africus as studious teenager.

"I need your focus on lacrosse! Be the star, and he will come!" Lindsay blurted out, half in jest.

"When will Coach Smith hear about Africus?" Haley asked.

"I think we need to know if there is any chance Africus will come to the states. No need to distract the team and Nebraska State nation. Africus would be an obsession for the media and Nebraska State nation! Also, he has never played organized sports, so his impact is in the future!" Shannon explained, more serious in her demeanor.

Lindsay smiled at her sister Haley.

"Will Mika return? Africus may come back if he does," Shannon asked.

"He had plane tickets to come back but decided to delay his return. He feels responsible for the Preserve and to Africus and his coffee farm. He has one year to use the refund to buy new tickets. He was going to show Africus Savannah's picture, but that never happened. His smart device is not programmed for international calls, but it does take texts. I have texted him often. He did tell me that he is enrolled as a e-student, which you confirmed. We installed power Portals though out the Preserve for charging smart devices and other electronic gear. So, he can study under the stars, when he is not hunting or going to his magical places. Mika told me he went to one such magical place. It is like a Paradise. Mika thinks there is a Portal to get in! It is other worldly! And Savannah, your parents thought you were off the wall in your imaginary land! There is supposedly the Cavern of Lost Treasures, a well-documented legend, that Africus may have accessed, too. Mika does not know for sure, on that, as Africus did not take him there, but he often talked about it, even to me. That is one of our family secrets. But Mika thinks the coffee plants may be near the opening of that Cavern, even if it is a Portal!"

"I have had dreams. I think I may have seen these places in my dreams!" Savannah excitedly stated.

"This is a little far out for me," Lindsay chided her peers. She raised her hands up to stop the speculation about other parallel worlds.

"OK, sister. For now, we will focus on coaching the real superstar girl who is here via Africa. She will be a real-life hero, the American Superstar Girl, and leader for our program and state! Savannah, focus that intelligent and enormously creative mind of yours on a national championship for the Nebraskans!" Haley responded, tilting her head to the right, and letting her hair down from its pony tail.

"But no word from him on coming here as a boarding student?" Shannon asked hopefully, raising her eyebrows, and changing the subject once again to Africus.

"Only a few weeks ago he was certain he would come to Nebraska State. Now, I don't know. I don't think he will come here before 2026. By then, who knows. It is possible he may never ever leave the Preserve. I told him I would visit him and Mika over the holidays and next June. But, I don't know what I will do if Mika stays. I miss him, but not Africa. But I have hope that he will come home, back to America," Haley pouted in self-pity.

"Well, the Nebraskans are 1-0! Rod is playing all right at the quarterback spot. The defense was swarming all night long. 42-0 is better than we all expected, even with a non-major conference opponent. RIP has really taken off as the D coordinator! Africus, I think would redshirt this year if he were here. What position do you think he would play, Haley?" Shannon asked, raising her eyebrows.

Savannah listened intently to the conversation between the women. She wrapped her hair in a pony-tail to prepare for her first practice. She envisioned Africus coming to the football stadium. *The roar would be historic*, she thought.

"I think middle linebacker with his hunting instincts!" Shannon suggested.

"Quarterback in 2026," insisted Haley.

"Oh, with his height and speed, I think wide receiver," Lindsay laughed.

"No, he will play lacrosse!" Lindsay changed course and scoffed at football.

Savannah was now quiet. She checked her smart devices for messages. None.

Savannah left the coaches room quietly, the ladies laughing at one of Lindsay's stories of her childhood with her sister. *He is not coming to Nebraska State.* The thought struck her hard. She found an empty room and impetuously called her Daddy. She was startled when he answered.

"Savannah, you so seldom call me. I think it has been awhile. You caught me at the airport. I have a few minutes. Honestly, I was expecting another call. But what is on your mind?"

"You are so formal! I am your only daughter!"

"And?"

"Well, what would you think if I transferred to a University in Africa this January, or even now?"

"I am not sure about that. That would be an abrupt decision. Let's talk later. Why not a University in London. I am sure you would be accepted. In fact, I am sure you could still do a PG year in Oxford. Why now?"

"I don't know. Maybe some things are on my mind."

"I say no to Africa. If you want to fly to London this week, I can arrange to have you admitted to the preparatory school. I think you could be admitted to the University as early as January, too. You can play football here. You were always talented at football, as you were in lacrosse," her Daddy finished abruptly.

"Daddy! I have found the African Boy Legend! His name is Africus! He is a ranger in a Preserve in East Africa. He is the one. He grew up in the savannah. I want to go to Africa to see him! Africus is the one that saved me from the lions! He is the African Boy Legend!" Savannah blurted out, wrapping her arms around her stomach.

Her Daddy was silent and breathing heavily. *Has the African Boy Legend really been found? Is he really alive? Did he really survive?*

"Honestly, do you really think your story of the African Boy Legend is true and not imagination! I think it must be a coincidence that this ranger in Kenya grew up in the wild. You had so many dreams as a child. They were indistinguishable for you as a child. You were in both the real world and dream world at the same time, almost all the time. Anyway, I do not want you to see this ranger!"

"Daddy, you do not know me that well. You won't tell me who I can see or not see!"

"I control your future, though, if you ever want to work in my media empire! Or be my beneficiary of my trusts!"

"You are threatening me with power and money. Just like Mum said you did with her. But you did not do so well with her in the divorce!" Savannah shrieked out, trembling in anxiety.

"Look, I just do not want you to base your life on following a boy, who likely is not the African Boy Legend of your dreams, because your dreams are only a dream. I have to board my plane. Let me know if you want to return to London. I am here and can help you. I apologize for my statements. But you need to leave the Parallel Dream Universe, honey, and partake in the Real Universe!"

Savannah hung up and threw her smart device into the chair across from her. She rubbed her eyes hard with her hands. *Is my Daddy correct? Did Africus just know the story and pretend to be the legendary, yet mythical, African Boy Legend? Why is the Real Universe and the Parallel Dream Universe so interchangeable in my world?*

Savannah left the little room. She picked up and held her smart device in her hands. She scrolled to her contacts. She had a text number for Africus. She had not called him, because Haley said his smart device was not in service for international calls. But she did not call him.

*Enough!* She thought. *Time to move on. Balls in your court African Boy Legend! If that is really you!* She slumped forward as she walked.

*Time to grow up. I committed to Nebraska State, so I will stay here for one year. Daddy, was right. My decision was too abrupt. I will apply to a London university next year. I will take that summer internship Daddy has offered me every year of the last four years next summer. Mum will have to know that I am the daughter of two parents!*

Savannah went to the locker room. Her whirlwind changes of direction on Africus were too much. She was so confused. It was time to meet some of her teammates. She drew from their energy. It was the first day of practice. Classes were in their second week. She liked her teammates. The other first years were nationally rated recruits, mostly from the Midwest, with one from Texas and one from Boston.

"Hi, I am Savannah," she introduced herself to the girl from Boston.

"I am Clay, from Cambridge. I played against you in Downingtown, at the national tournament, twice!"

"Oh, yes, I remember. You are so fast and have a lightening quick stick. Now we will play together!"

"There are three spots open for starters. Maybe we can grab two of them. I am an attacker. I guess you will still play midfield?"

"Yes, that is my plan. The soccer coach asked me to play soccer here, but I said no. I want to focus on lacrosse. I will be going back home next week, when we play in the Maryland invitational. My Mum will be in attendance!"

"How sweet. Yes, my parents will be there. They never miss a game. So, I think we may dress a little preppie for the Midwest! I may have to wear my sweatshirt and leggings more often!"

"I think a little preppie won't be minded!"

Lindsay burst into the locker room. She was funny most of the time but had on her game face now.

"One week of tryouts. Play your best. We have five walk-ons. We will take thirty-two players. We have thirty-five trying out. And all starting spots are open for now! Competition breeds success. I want peak performance this week. I hope all of you are already in shape, and this week is not about conditioning!"

The young women lacrosse players took the field. Savannah felt spring in her legs. The air was refreshing at 72 degrees with low humidity, an unusual day for late summer in the Midwest. Her speed easily eclipsed that of all her teammates, while Clay was the second fastest. She and Clay teamed up for a number of assisted goals. Savannah was a cheetah in the midfield, she felt, as she tracked down ball carriers with ease, and stopped them cold, or caused turnovers. She felt exhilarated back on the field and in competition.

Lindsay, and her newly appointed assistant, Haley, were in awe of her play.

"Better than the hype!" Lindsay softly said to her sister, hands on her hips in an authoritarian pose.

"Oh, yes. If Africus could only see her!"

"Well, that ship may not sail. Let's hope she doesn't jump on a plane back to London or Africa!"

Practice ended. Savannah and Clay went to the football practice field to watch the end of the no pads practice. It seemed like the practice halted when they walked up into the stands, clad in white shorts and red Nebraska State tee shirts.

"Ah, do you think they notice us!" Clay observed.

"Ha! Doubtful. We are too Eastern preppie; don't you think?"

Savannah watched the quarterbacks. How good were they. If too good, Africus may not come anyway.

*But wait, he is not the African Boy Legend! I have no interest anymore!*

"I have seen enough. I am going to dinner," Savannah said.

Clay followed her, glancing back at one of the players who watched her as she left.

"I think Rod, the quarterback, just stared at me!"

"Hmm."

The two left for the athletes dining facilities for the best prepared and nutrition packed food an athlete could find.

Across the fields in the new offices for WLAX coaches, Haley looked at Lindsay.

"I know what would ignite the Nebraska State nation. There would be an absolute explosion in the Socialverse. Mika and I took a picture of Africus when he was still in the wild. He had a dagger in his mouth and was running between two large male lions on the hunt under the moonlight in the tall grass fields. He was an eleven-year old with flowing blonde hair, young athletic muscles and golden bronzed skin."

"What picture is this?" Shannon interrupted the sisters.

"It is the first picture we took of the African Boy Legend in the wild. He was just a legend until we found him one day on one of our missions around the outlands of the Preserve. We had always heard the African Boy Legend but seeing is believing and taking a picture memorialized the dream.

"We suspect he let us take that picture. He was ready to return to mankind. He let us find him, I am sure. We suspect he was spying on us while we were searching for his ghost!" Haley finished.

"Let's hold that picture for now. Maybe we can use it as bait. Let me think about this. Who has seen this picture?"

"Just Mika and me. We have not shared it on social media."

"Has Savannah seen it? Or any other pictures of Africus?"

"No, she has not."

"Interesting. She is still relying on blind faith. I wonder still, if this is all too unreal?'

"It is not. But let's play this out."

Mr. Stewart just stared at his smart device. *I can't believe it may be true. Just maybe, my dream will come true, too.*

# 30.

*Monday, September 15, 2025*
*West Kenya National Wildlife Preserve*

AFRICUS RETURNED from the Waterfall, knowing he had been in the Parallel Real Universe, with access by Passage through a Portal with the Great Ape. But he knew he could return there himself in the Parallel Dream Universe with his mind and spirit, in a dream state of unconsciousness. But that was not his focus. He yearned to see the picture of Providence. He feared it was not her. Haley and Shannon could have simply told her the story. Her background from Africa would make her the perfect foil to get him to Nebraska State. It was Haley's alma mater, after all.

*I have had enough!*

He texted Mika. "Send me the picture, now!"

He turned off his smart device. He went to his favorite tree. Citra was there, of course. *Is Citra a mystical character, too?* Night fell again, and the moon shown its silvery light.

"You want to see Essence, don't you?"

"I do. But I need to be with someone right now. My epiphany will come or not come, momentarily. My childhood memory of the Girl may be a dream from the Parallel

Dream Universe, and she may not be real. I will know for sure."

"We shall wait together, then."

"Do you remember when you had the visions with Essence and the Girl? You went to both of your magical places, the Waterfall and the Cavern," Citra asked, slightly purring.

"Vividly. I see her face all the time. It looks like what the Girl would look like when she was older."

"Africus, I am Essence."

Africus howled to the moon. Two eagles swooned in and landed on the tree. Africus hugged Citra and patted the heads of the eagles.

"AH! The eagles. Special Beings, too."

"They are your guardians, too."

The eagles chirped but did not speak.

Africus stared out at the silver splashed landscape.

As he stared, a text came in from Mika. There was an attachment. Africus opened it up. Citra and the eagles eagerly looked on. Africus was stunned. The picture matched his vision and dream. She was dressed in athletic gear instead of a flowing white regal gown, but it was unmistakably her. Even without the dream, she looked like the grown-up version of the Girl he had met seven years before. The eyes were the beautiful eyes that captivated him in that magical moment and for years thereafter. He fell back against the tree trunk, his legs dangling on either side of the heavy branch that supported Citra and him.

"It is time!" the eagles roared, as they took off in flight and soared into the night sky until they were out of sight.

"Citra, what now?"

"Follow your heart and your instincts. Your way has been paved. Follow the yellow brick road!"

"I shall start my journey tomorrow! Hail King Arthur! Ha!"

"Don't laugh!"

"Wait! What?"

"You sound like Shannon! So, long Africus," Citra laughed as she slithered off the tree in complete silence and dashed through the tall grasses. No animal could catch Citra. Soon her trail disappeared into the dark trees across the field. Africus was alone in his thoughts.

He started to fall asleep in his favorite tree again. *Maybe the last time?*

Before he fell asleep, he pulled out his smart device and took a selfie. He sent it to Providence.

"Providence! I saw your picture. It matched my vision of you in the Parallel Dream Universe! I know it is you. THE GIRL! THE AMERICAN SUPERSTAR GIRL! Here is my selfie I just took in the savannah from my favorite tree. Citra just left me. I know you know her!!!! Remember the white zebra! Africus!"

# 31.

Tuesday, September 16, 2025
Jefferson City, Nebraska

GAVIN BLOCKER RETURNED Shannon's call. He knew she was upset by the sound of her voice.

"She unexpectedly took an early plane to Maryland today! She said she likely would be back by next Monday but was not sure. She would not say why, but I think it is because she may have heard from Africus. Haley said that Africus had asked for and received a photo of Savannah from Mika. Maybe that started a chain reaction. Mika has not seen Africus since August. Haley has not heard from him in over a week. He is still signing in online for his courses, or at least someone is on his behalf. So, I don't know what is going on. I don't know if you want to write about her departure. Certainly, the team knows that she has left. She told the team it was personal. I don't know. I think I put too much into those two. It is so hard to bring in the best, and two of the best, even harder! And then they are tied together from the past, and in their so-called Parallel Dream Universe! I wish I could enter the Parallel Dream Universe! Oh, don't write about that!"

Gavin sat back in his chair. He had garnered much attention for his following of the Savannah storyline and recruitment. He owed it to his followers to keep them informed. But he still held out hope for the affection of Shannon. He directed his voice back into his smart device.

"Shannon, I will just say that she is gone for a week for personal reasons and is expected back for next Monday's practice and next Wednesday's game against Michigan. Most people will want to know who is going to replace Rod as the starting quarterback, after he was lost for six weeks with a serious high ankle injury. Too bad, the defense is so solid. Still no touchdowns allowed. Only one non-conference game left."

"I think the women's lacrosse team would have a legitimate shot at a national championship with Savannah. She really is the American Girl Superstar! I hope she stays for the year. I think if Africus does not come here, she will transfer to a London school, or even Maryland, and sit out a year. It is sad," Shannon whined on.

"Yes, they won all three games in the Maryland jamboree. Savannah was the best player on the field. Her speed is breathtaking. I watched the stream of the games. That Massachusetts girl, Clay, was special, too. They teamed up on some nice scoring plays. I sensed a passion for the game. I think she will be back. She showed a genuine fondness for her teammates. Her pride!"

"Ha-ha!"

"Well, I need to write my blog, and talk to Coach Smith about our software for virtual football. I need to know if it is working and if it is adding value for the coaching staff and team. I heard the VPR has taken off for college football. I will write about that. The Clemson quarterback, the dual threat superstar, and the middle linebacker at Illinois were the top hits last weekend. The linebacker had five TFLs and twenty-two tackles! The Clemson quarterback ran for three touchdowns and threw for four more! Tough ones. Illinois may prove a formidable opponent for our division! But Oklahoma is still the top rival!"

"You don't seem too worried about Savannah!" Shannon cried out, and then hung up abruptly.

*Man, what I am I supposed to do! Get on a plane to Maryland and bring her back? Maybe? Na.*

Gavin Blocker thought about Savannah for a moment. *She will be back.*

He then proceeded to called Coach Smith. He was not there. But Tamaric Jones picked up the phone.

"Gavin, I bet you want to know what we are going to do about the quarterback spot! Well, Pierce will start next week. We have a true walk-on freshman that has impressed, but he still has a long way to go on learning the offense. Rod was really developing in the OC's and my new flare offense. With Pierce, we will pound the rock with Joseph. He is tough to bring down. Like those old Bama backs from the last decade. Our defense is one of the best in our division, if not the conference. So, I am sure you have not learned anything! By the way, the virtual football software is great. Too bad it is not approved yet for the actual game. We use it right after the team leaves the locker room after the game on game day and helps us set up the next week schemes. The players like it, too. What if I had cut the other way, or made that block? The tech isn't perfect, though. More data needs to be loaded to cover the enormous variations. But it is really useful and can only get better! That's it. Need to coach up Pierce!" Jones hung up, letting out a sigh of relief.

Gavin Blocker was exasperated. Smith had been ducking him. He went to his refrigerator. He took out his favorite Drink-Garrison's iced tea. The company was founded by Shannon's older sister. The tea leaves were imported from

Africa, of all places. He opened his laptop. What not to cover today.

*Hi folks. A few notes to pass on before we jump into college football. Savannah Stewart, our American Girl Superstar, is taking a leave of absence for personal reasons for a week. The coaches and athletic department personnel have approved the absence. I am concerned about her absence. Her father is a billionaire and based in London. He is a media and social media magnate. He is audacious and brilliant. He dominates the exploding Africa market, and owns five satellites dedicated to Africa, all launched by private space companies. There is a lot there for her. Plus, I hear her heart may still be in Africa. So, success and love. I don't know. I can see her leaving. There are no intercontinental transfer student athletic restrictions. Just saying.*

*College football "preseason" is over. All of the super conference teams have cross games with other super conference teams this weekend. The games are important for the wild card selections for the college football tourney. The Conference of the North teams square off against the Conference of the West. The Conference of the South will square off against the Conference of the East. Every year the conferences will rotate, as will the team's home and away venues. Nebraska State takes on old foe Colorado at Colorado. Should be fun and bring back memories from the last century. How about Alabama and Florida State? Clemson and Georgia. Lots of fun. Two of the Eastern division powerhouses Michigan and Maryland play the two LA schools, both in LA, in a double header at the professional football Association venue. Loads of great football. The new format is so exciting. And four teams make the tourney plus the four champions. The champs grab the top four seeds, and home games for the round of eight. Then the semifinals and finals at set destinations. The finals are back in Dallas again this year. Great venue for college football.*

*Nebraska State will use its second-string quarterback, Brock Pierce. He is a smart game manager with an adequate arm. The fluid offense philosophy, in its nascent state the first two weeks, will likely be shelved for now. So, Oklahoma will still be the pioneers and experts of that offensive system. Expect power running with Joseph and a lot of short passes. The defense with RIP, however, is a championship defense. They swarm to the ball and drape the ball carriers and receivers. The key statistic for me, is that opposing quarterbacks do not have a single positive rushing carry. The containment is splendid.*

*I think Nebraska State is a year or two away. We need a great freshman quarterback next year, and there are many promising recruits. Nebraska, as a state has so much to offer now. The weather here is now better than the south with global warming. We are in economic powerhouse with the agri-tech industry, and Nebraska is the epicenter of the National Grid Super Rail System. The main east-west and north-south lines intersect and stop in Nebraska. The Air Force has consolidated most of its operations in Omaha. And one of the top private space companies is setting up a launching pad in the center of the state. More later on that. The infrastructure and attendant businesses will generate thousands of jobs. SO, recruits, Nebraska State is the place of the present and the future!*

*Well, maybe we should reverse fortunes, and ask Savannah to have her father move some of his businesses to Nebraska. There is a lot of cross-business relationships between the Kenyan and other African nation pharma businesses and the Nebraska Agri-Tech industry that can be cultivated and grown. Hmm.*

*Welcome back Haley Andrews. She will coach with her sister Lindsay on the WLAX team. Haley was a star soccer player here last decade. Her husband Mika Williams, the legendary All-American safety for the Nebraskans, is still in Africa. Good luck with that!"*

*The VPL playoffs for baseball are underway and will have their championship before the real baseball playoffs start. They are a lot of fun and have attracted much interest and betting! The Omaha team is in the semi-finals, but down 3-2 in games. Game 6 tonight! We have the homer hammer going for us, so we have a chance!*

*More on technology and sports. The Association has licensed its VPR technology to the Professional Basketball League. King Alexander the Great of the Boston team will be the first to test the technology. Imagine following his eyes to the rim on one of his free-floating masterful dunks.*

*Exciting news. The unmanned mission to Europa, the promising and storybook moon that orbits Jupiter, has been success. Robots have been on the ground and exploring its surface for two years now. The President has announced that we will be sending a manned mission to Europa. The launch date will be in the Rip-Roaring 2020s. July 4, 2026, is the target launch date! They will land in four years in 2030. The spacecraft will be launched from Nebraska by Wilderness Ventures of the North's subsidiary Space Frontiers, Inc. More good news for the state of Nebraska. With men and women now on Mars, and soon to be on Europa, the President's bold plans are off to a roaring start!*

*That's all. I think I may receive a call or two today!*

Gavin push the submit button. His followers would soon digest his material. But Shannon Garrison was the one he cared about. He knew he went too far. But she was not responding quickly to him, and his followers were very important, too.

# 32.

SAVANNAH OPENED THE DOOR into her home. Her Mum was not startled to see her. Savannah had told her she was coming home but had not told her why.

Savannah had determined not to show her Mum the picture. She would tell her it was a false memory, or an illusion. So, she just needed some time to think.

"Mum, I think I may want to take this semester off. Then return to a University in London. What do you think? I would like to do an internship with one of Daddy's companies in Africa next summer, too. For business reasons!"

Mrs. Stewart smiled slightly. Let's go this weekend to London. We can visit schools, and you can decide next week what you want to do. Talk to your Daddy about an internship. I am fine with that."

"Whoa! No arguments! OK. Let's go. I am going sailing tomorrow and Thursday then."

"Fine, I will get plane tickets for Friday night."

"Great!" Savannah hugged her Mum, looking out at the bay, puzzled by the ease of the transition.

# 33.

Sunday night, September 21, 2025
London, England

M R. STEWART FEIGNED A SMILE. "SAVANNAH, it is great to see you. And you again, Mrs. Stewart. You kept my name all these years."

"Daddy, why are we here at your place. Mum why are we here with Daddy?" Savannah yelled out, shocked at her parents together for the first time in seven years.

"Savannah, I left your Daddy. He worked so hard, he was never home. I was so concerned for you, always in your dream world, or Parallel Dream Universe. No psychologist could crack your case. You were irretrievably locked in the Parallel Dream Universe. We could not get you out of it. The African Boy Legend dream was the spark that lit the fire. You almost were killed by lions when chasing a ghost. I was so mad at your Daddy for not watching you. You said you were going to find the African Boy Legend. You almost did. But in the Parallel Dream Universe, life after death!

"Well, your Daddy never remarried. We have been having a secret affair for the last couple of years. I am sorry I did not tell you," Mrs. Stewart said, her eyes streaming tears.

Mr. Stewart sat next to his daughter.

"Savannah, you, Mum and I are getting back together. And all of her money and assets will stay in her name," her Daddy stated as a matter of fact.

Savannah fell back on the couch. She just stared at the ceiling. She started to kick her feet up and down in a tantrum like drumbeat. She just closed her eyes and started to sing African hymns she learned from her teachers in South Africa.

"She is locked in her safe place. Who knows who is in there with her?" Mrs. Stewart said.

"I can shock her back to the Real Universe," Mr. Stewart said wryly.

"Don't condone her dreams! You are scaring me. I think she got this from you!"

"Let us not go there again!" Mr. Stewart frowned at Mrs. Stewart, brushed his hair back with both hands and then placed his hands on his hips while he was standing.

"Savannah, open up in there. Let us in."

"What! You have totally shocked me about you and Mum, and now you want me to leave my Parallel Dream Universe!"

"You are not dreaming. I know you, even though it has been so long. You are listening keenly to us. And to me. You know there is more, don't you?"

"I suspect that I do! And maybe more than you know! Mr. emperor of Africa."

"That is not my plan! To be emperor. Power, fame, and wealth are important, but rebuilding a continent is legendary, rewarding and fulfilling. Legacy, that is important to me."

"Tell Mum, Savannah, what you know about Africus," Mr. Stewart requested, scratching his goatee.

"Mum, do not think I am in my Parallel Dream Universe!"

"OK, but I am freaking out here, you know," Mrs. Stewart said, folding her arms across her chest.

"Family! Let's hug!" Mr. Stewart grabbed his daughter and former wife in a group hug. Mrs. Stewart cried. Savannah stared at the grandfather clock, listening to its chimes, as the clock struck the hour.

Savannah broke from the embrace first. She sauntered over to a different large couch that was under the window frame. There she stared out at the street pedestrian traffic below. No automobiles were allowed on her Daddy's street in front of his spacious flat. The sky was overcast, but no showers were forecast for the day.

Her parents were silent, too. She knew her Daddy was up to something with Africus.

*Did he die in an apparent accident? Did Daddy threaten him?*

She looked at his eyes. Deep into his eyes. Yet his eyes were not devious or empty. They actually shone with joy.

*What is going on here?*

Savannah tensed. She clenched her fists and started to breathe quickly. She was overwhelmed with feelings.

*Was he in London? Was he here? Daddy is so powerful and well connected. Or is he gone! NO!*

Savannah suddenly lost control. She hyperventilated and ran from the room. She felt enormous fear and anxiety. She headed for the door.

"Savannah! It is OK. Africus is safe! He is fine!" Her Daddy screamed with rare emotion.

"I love you little girl! Come here with us!" He cried out.

Savannah collapsed in exhaustion and relief. Both of her parents picked her up and brought her back to the couch. Her Mum rubbed her back gently and put a light cotton blanket around her. Her Daddy went to the kitchen for iced lemon water, her favorite.

The three of them sat silently for moments longer. Finally, Mr. Stewart opened his smart device. He showed Savannah and Mrs. Stewart an incredible photo. There in the savannah was Africus and Minimilion, the new king of the jungle in the Preserve. And next to Africus was her Daddy.

"Who is that?" Mrs. Stewart asked, expecting the answer, but waiting to hear it.

"He is a ranger in a Preserve in East Africa. His name is Africus."

"Africus is the African Boy Legend, Daddy! He sent me a picture of himself when he was the African Boy Legend! Here is the picture!"

Mrs. Stewart passed out and fell back onto the couch.

"Daddy, I know Africus is the African Boy Legend. I was set to forget about him, but then he sent me a text of this selfie. It is him. The same the African Boy Legend that saved me. There is no deception."

Her Daddy remained silent. Her Mum awoke.

"I came home to tell you, Mum, but then bailed on that idea. I was afraid of your rebuke. But then the trip to London. I have spoken about going to London with Daddy. Now I want to go to Africa!"

"I knew that. That was part of our plan. The timing was right to bring us together. But I did not know about your Daddy's trip to Africa last week. I did not know you were communicating with the African Boy Legend! I am still perplexed by this. Is he a nice boy, Mr. Stewart?" Her mother replied with a frown.

"Indeed, and very much in love and awe of our daughter. He lives in the Parallel Dream Universe more than Savannah does!"

"Daddy, do you believe Africus is the African Boy Legend now? Or do you still think he is fantasy!" Savannah blurted out in confusion. "And why would you have a sudden interest in Africus?"

Mr. Stewart appeared nervous for a moment but gained his composure and remained silent.

"Daddy, my middle name is Providence, and you called me that as a little girl in Africa. But now you call me by my first name. Why is that?"

"I love the savannah, so I named you Savannah. And you spent much time in the savannah, including on safaris. I also named you Providence, because I thought you were an angel from heaven or the Great Realm. For years, I saw you in your dream world and your fantasy world and thought that confirmed my belief. Your Mum believed otherwise, and thought you suffered from delusion or other mental illnesses. And I thought that someday you might help me find the African Boy Legend! And you did!"

"What is he like Daddy? Why did you suddenly have an interest in Africus, in the African Boy Legend?"

"He wants to meet you Savannah! We can take my private jet tomorrow. Mrs. Stewart, you of course are welcome to come. But he wants to take Savannah somewhere in the jungle. Paradise, he calls it. I am sure it is special. Another place in the Parallel Dream Universe, possibly, but if so, you both will certainly see it! We can have our preparations done for a Tuesday departure. Sleep on it if you will," Her Daddy finished, his eyes glazed in excitement, like a little boy.

"No need to decide. I will go for sure? But why now, after all these years?" Savannah asked again with persistence.

"Yes, why?" her Mum piped in, wanting to know more, after years of believing the African Boy Legend was a legend and fantasy.

"I have known of the legend of the African Boy Legend, more so than you would want to know. It was not until two weeks ago when you called me about the ranger at the Preserve, that I thought the legend may be true. So, I took a trip to the Preserve at the end of one of my scheduled business trips to Africa, to find out for myself. I found him. I had told the rangers and guards to tell him the father of Providence was here to see him. It was not long until he returned from the savannah to see me. I saw him. He stared at me, and then said he recalled seeing me at the safari seven years ago. The safari when you ran from the vehicles to the jungle and were almost eaten by the lions! We talked about you. He told me he had seen your picture. I showed him a picture of you both as a little girl and one from your graduation. He was quite emotional."

Savannah looked at her Daddy for more.

"I did not believe you seven years ago that you had seen the African Boy Legend. I had heard it was fable. I thought he had died. Your Mum thought you were crazy! You did spend much time in your dream world!

"I am so happy. What do you mean he died?"

"I didn't mean that," Mr. Stewart hesitated, but then continued unfolding some of his cherished and deeply held secrets.

"I have spent much of my life dreaming of finding the Cavern of Lost Treasures, the most captivating and intriguing legend of Africa. My safaris were really in search of the Cavern! I never found it or any clues about it. The legend of the African Boy Legend often came with allusions to the Cavern. So, I wanted to find him as much as you do. Africus spoke of magical places that you and he had been to in your Parallel Dream Universe. The talk of the Cavern has captivated me. Maybe it is accessible in the Real Universe, too! Maybe Africus is the key to finding it." *Oh, he may be the only key.*

"Would not that be fantastic! Now, who is living in the dream world, Daddy! I think you are still hiding something, though."

"This is too much for me," Mrs. Stewart stated abruptly. *But maybe not!*

The three of them were all lost in thought and day-dreams.

# 34.

*Monday, September 22, 2025*
*Jefferson City, Nebraska*

GAVIN BLOCKER SAT in his chair. His laptop was open with Shannon staring at him through his computer. She was furious with him for his blog last week. But she took his call.

"I did not report anything on the African Boy Legend, you know."

"Yeah, that is to protect yourself from embarrassment when nothing comes of it. Especially, after the loss to Colorado! They will accuse you of living in a Parallel Dream Universe!" Shannon responded, still annoyed at his blog last week.

"She did not return, did she?" Gavin interrogated.

"Of course, you know the answer. Why would I take your call? She went to London. Her social media had photos of her at Buckingham Palace. Her father is in London, and she was originally going to school in London, before we pulled her here to Nebraska State. Her father must be swaying her to London. What I did not understand was that her mother was in the picture. I frankly am baffled. Her parents were divorced seven years ago. I can't see the two of them in the same city. But it does not look promising. And the African Boy Legend is not in London! You know, I never saw him. Probably a big ruse by a girl who lives in the Parallel Dream Universe, just as her mother always said," a resigned Shannon confessed.

"But why would Haley Andrews participate in this ruse?" Gavin pondered out loud.

"Maybe the stress of living in the jungle, I don't know. Just last week we joked about bringing him here next year. Savannah and Haley all played along. I think he is real, but just not anything more special than a good ranger with special skills in dealing with animals. Small stories can easily be magnified into legends and lore. Haley would not talk to me this morning. She was stressed. I don't know."

"Shannon, I will bypass any reporting today on Savannah. It is too personal for you, and frankly for her. She can still enroll in January and play next spring 2026."

"That is true. Clay, her friend, said she was "sure" Savannah would play spring 2026, but admitted, that was likely it."

"Lunch?"

"Why not!"

Shannon hung up. She had to meet with Coach Smith first. He had summoned her.

*I think I know why. Pierce was awful. Four interceptions. So many penalties. He was desperate for a quarterback recruit for fall 2026.*

She marched down to his office, with a kick in her step.

*Wait, why am I suddenly in a good mood? Savannah is AWOL, and Africus is real but likely just a ranger boy, not a star football player in the making. The football team lost, making the tournament bid all but certain to rest on winning the division and the conference. But Gavin Blocker for lunch. Hmm. Maybe. Just Maybe.*

"Shannon!" Coach Smith barked out with his arms folded tightly across his chest.

"The administration demanded that I drop the tech project. It has a lot of bugs, and multiple companies are developing similar projects as we speak. The market will be flooded with this technology next year. At least twenty other schools have developed similar software with their own patents for their teams for use this year. So, we will use the software we have developed this year for our team. But the dream of financial nirvana, I think is gone," Coach Smith reported with despondence and continued.

"You know that Nebraska State nation is not pleased with our loss to Colorado. The Socialverse is blaming our distraction with the tech project. And you, our recruiting liaison, are on the hot seat with me!' Coach Smith glared at her with an edge to his voice.

"Your threats are idle, coach. You may be on the hot seat, not me!" Shannon fired back, her back arched and face reddening.

"You lost your prized lacrosse recruit, 'the American Girl Superstar', too, didn't you?" Coach Smith countered.

"Ouch! But, I think so," Shannon said hanging her head and slumping her shoulders.

"Maybe you are right. Spiritis wants me to work for them. Maybe I will," Shannon said defensively, while thinking it was maybe a good idea.

"All right. Peace. Listen, I need you to find me a quarterback. Work closely with Tamaric Jones. He is pursuing quarterbacks who are juniors in high school. Tell him our need is now more immediate. Here are the names and bios of two junior college quarterbacks. Recruit them hard. Also, I know he is committed to a top ten team, and is a five star, but recruit this high school senior from deep in the heart of Texas. His school has three five-star recruits on the roster already, and the starter is only a junior. So, he can start here, very potentially. And I mean that. It is not an empty promise. Get him here for the Michigan game. He does not have a game that day. Bring his parents and family. But this is your number one project. Savannah is gone. Lindsay and Haley can handle their recruiting. The administration wants you to focus solely on football, now," Coach Smith rattled on, a man deeply scared for the first time since his arrival in Jefferson City.

"So, I have been fired for WLAX recruiting because Savannah went AWOL. That is a bit extreme! Spiritis. Where is your contact information again?"

"That is up to you, I believe in you. I believe you can land me my quarterback! I hope you stay. Your compensation will stay the same," Coach Smith stared at her, with his big hands now palm down on his desk.

"All right. I will find you your quarterback!"

Shannon stepped away. Stunned at her perceived demotion, she walked by players and coaches with no salutations, or eye contact. She stared at the floor in front of each of her next steps to her office. She tossed the sheet of paper with the names of the three quarterbacks on her desk and took off.

*And tomorrow I have my gene procedure. They are going to alter my genetic code with gene therapy and replace my defective gene! I won't die in agony the way my Mom did from that insidious disease. I miss my Mom. I wish they had this technology last decade. But at least I have lunch with Gavin.*

# 35.

MIKA LOOKED UP at the sky and watched the helicopter flying in from the distance. It did not look like a military or national guard helicopter. He rounded up Jorge' and the other rangers with their guns, just in case it was a wealthy poacher with firepower descending on his lightly protected Preserve. They took positions behind their trucks and jeeps and stayed out of sight.

The helicopter hovered near the ranger station and landed. Mika could see two women in the back and no soldiers or men bearing armaments. The rotor blades swished for a while, but slowly the whirl ceased. A tall man with white hair and a goatee stepped off the helicopter first. Mika recognized him. Mr. Francis Stewart, the African media magnate and safari captain in his leisure time. Next, an attractive middle-aged woman, dressed in safari gear stepped off. He supposed it was his significant other, as he had known Mr. Stewart was long divorced.

Mika stepped out from behind his range vehicle with the rest of the rangers and guards. They dropped their weapons into their vehicles. Mika approached Mr. Stewart.

"Good morning. I am Mika Williams, head ranger at this Preserve. You are Mr. Stewart. Your daughter is at Nebraska State. Why do I think this is about one of my rangers!" Mika startled Mr. Stewart, smiling broadly as he extended his hand in greeting.

Savannah then stepped off the helicopter. Mika noticed her athletic physique and striking beauty. She looked more mature than the small smart device photo had revealed.

"You must be Providence!"

"No one has called her that since she left Africa. I see you may know quite a lot," Mr. Stewart responded, not sure how stern to be. Mika ignored Mr. Stewart and continued to speak to Savannah.

"Providence, Africus has been waiting for you for years now! I expect that you are here to see him with your family. I would call him and tell him that you are here, but I cannot get ahold of him. He turns his off his communication devices in the savannah," Mika told her and then switched his attention back to Mrs. Stewart.

"Mr. Stewart, please introduce me to your friend," Mika beckoned, watching Mrs. Stewart staring at him in amazement.

"I am Mrs. Stewart. I am Savannah's mother. We have been divorced for years, legally, anyway. But we are still together. I have been skeptical about the African Boy Legend, forever. But I am here to see and believe!" Mrs. Stewart proclaimed, holding her chin high.

"Pleased to meet you, Mrs. Stewart," Mika shook her hand as well. "Let us talk about Africus at dinner. Come, we will bring you to your quarters."

Mika and Jorge' took them to the new guest cottage, and watched the Stewarts move their bags into the building. They freshened up as Mika prepared an African dinner. Soon they all sat together at the picnic table with Mika and ate grilled antelope steak strips. Mika spoke first.

"I believe the best way to find Africus is for all of you to spend the night here. Providence, you and Africus are connected in many Universes! Tonight, under the wondrous African starlit sky, I think you shall find Africus. You and he will connect, I am sure. Tomorrow, Mr. and Mrs. Stewart, I believe just Providence, a couple of the rangers and I should head out into the Preserve to find Africus, unless he comes back here by morning. I believe this is the best plan," Mika said expecting resistance from the powerful father of Africus's dream Girl.

Mrs. Stewart grabbed Savannah's arm and looked into her eyes. She turned and spoke directly to Mika.

"That is the plan. But a brief tour of the Preserve for Mum and Daddy for the balance of the day would be grand!" She gleefully smiled as Mika agreed.

Mr. Stewart smiled slightly.

"I have been on many safaris. I will stay here and conduct some business," he said as he agreed to the plan.

Savannah was lost in thought. *In Africa, I am Providence.* Her eyes were glazed. She was not going on any tour. Not now.

Two of the rangers took Mrs. Stewart out into the Preserve. Providence rested in the hammock, and Mr. Stewart went to work back in the helicopter that he had piloted. Mika hung out, resisting the temptation to contact Haley.

Nighttime soon came and all retired for the evening. Mrs. Stewart was exhausted and fell quickly to sleep. The African spices that Mika gave Mr. Stewart at his request sent him into a deep slumber. Providence slept in the hammock, covered with an insect repelling cloth. Mika sat in his chair waiting.

Midnight passed and the sounds of hunters and prey could be heard in the distance. The sky was filled with noise, a veritable cavalcade of communications among the animal kingdom. The night was clear. Starlight filled the sky as the moon was hidden behind the earth. Mika was wide awake, his senses on high alert. Providence was asleep.

Mika heard the soft steps of hoofs walking toward the shelters. He strained his eyes to see. A white animal silhouette approached the hammock. It appeared to be the shape of a zebra, but with no stripes. He thought of the Zebra at the Waterfall, and in his dreams. *Of course*, he thought. *It is Essence*. Soon a sleeping beauty, still trancelike, walked over to the zebra and climbed on her back to ride her. Off the zebra trotted, soon invisible over the horizon. Mika was star struck again at the sight of Essence. His eyes grew very heavy as a pleasant aroma overcame him. *Must be from Essence*, he thought, as his heavy eyes closed, and his mind drifted deeply into its unconscious state.

When the darkness of the night slowly slunk away as the sun approached to peek over the horizon, Essence brought Providence to the precipice of the Deep Jungle. Soon the Great Ape appeared. She watched the Great Ape wave some exotic plant beneath her nose, and she drifted back into her unconscious state once again. The Great Ape took her through the vast path of limbs and trees to the center of the Paradise, to the awaiting Waterfall.

Providence lay on a giant leaf, still in her safari clothes. The sound of the pounding Waterfall was loud, yet soothing. The mist was cooling. The air was refreshing. The smells of flowers and plants were imbibing. She was immensely relaxed and calm. As she opened her eyes, she saw rays of sunlight sneak through the tall umbrage of the massive rain forest type trees. A breeze softly brushed her. Slowly, images became clearer. Slowly, her senses awoke. Two eagles appeared to be perched atop the branches of opposite trees. She saw two eyes peering at her through the thick leaves.

She sat upright. Her senses were bathing in the sounds, scents and visions of Paradise. Her conscious mind tried to scream out, but her subconscious state of tranquility restrained it with a large harness. Slowly she stood and walked to the spot of the creature staring at her. She pushed the leaves apart.

"Roar!" a young male lion roared and stared at her just a yard away.

She stepped back in fear at first. But the lion did not attack. It was eerily similar to seven years ago. The lion looked familiar, but different. Soon the lion seemed to beckon her to follow. She followed the lion. The moss was soft on her feet. The Waterfall was getting closer. Soon she was near the backside of the Waterfall.

*I am certainly in the Parallel Dream Universe. Mika was right! I shall meet with Africus in the Parallel Dream Universe, and he shall tell me where to meet him in the morning! This is so filled with love and happiness and wonder!*

A white zebra soon met the lion and the Girl.

"Are you the Lion Girl?" the zebra asked, with a sly smile.

"Are you Essence? Mountain lion girl? Zebra girl? The queen's advisor? Ha-ha!" Providence teased back, standing on her toes to see as far as she could see.

"Follow me."

"But of course. I rode you here, did I not. I love the Parallel Dream Universe! May I fly in the air! Drift upon the air ventilating up from below like a floating flower!" Providence giggled in a silly voice.

"Walking slowly will do. You are really here this time!"

"But, of course!"

*What did she mean by that?*

Providence followed the white zebra to the back cavern behind the Waterfall. She saw the silhouette of the young male, barely dressed, with flowing locks. She knew instantly.

"Providence, it is me!"

Providence walked close to Africus, and smelled his breath, and felt his strength. She slowly looked up his body from his ankles to his stomach, to his chest and to his neck. She trembled in excitement. Soon her eyes looked at his smile, and then thunder struck her as she gazed into his eyes for the first time since her childhood. She wept in joy, and never left his adoring gaze. Slowly, he embraced her. She responded and held him more tightly than she had ever hugged anyone in her life.

She looked up at him again. Slowly their faces got closer. At last, their lips reunited for their second most loving kiss.

Together they spent the morning swimming in the lake beneath the Waterfall, swimming among amazingly friendly crocodiles. Birds whistled and flew around them. Monkeys brought them fruits, and water from the lake was as pure as any water she had ever sipped. Even the sun's rays seemed to dance and frolic with them in the water. No words were spoken. High above the two eagles marveled at them. And peering below through the Waterfall were the blue eyes of the white zebra.

Soon Africus led Providence back up the path to the cavern behind the Waterfall. Providence still felt dreamlike. She waited to hear words, directions for the upcoming day.

"Providence, this is my Paradise. You are really here this time, in the flesh. With the help of Essence, we are really together. Feel the plants, touch the animals, smell the air, see the resplendent beauty, hear the pounding water falling into the lake. All of our senses are active. I do come here, but I don't know how. I arrive at the border of the Deep Jungle, and the Great Ape puts me under. When I awake, I hear the pounding water, and smell the lushness of the deeply forested jungle. We are real here, together, in the flesh. We are not imaginary to each other. I am here with you! Forever, I hope!"

"Forever, Africus! Forever! I will stay here in the Water-fall and Paradise, too, forever! I feel your realness, I do!"

*So, Essence meant what she said. I am here for real. Some sort of alternate reality or parallel universe.*

"I want to stay here, too, but Essence says there are lim-its to the time I spend here. There is another place of beau-ty and splendor, that I am able to visit. Someday, with Essence, maybe soon, I shall take you there!" Africus said lovingly to his new companion.

"I shall love that, but Paradise and the Waterfall are just fine!"

Essence soon appeared with the lion, Minimilion

"And this is Essence. I hear you have met before! And this is Minimilion, the son of Maximilion, the dead king of the jungle in this Preserve."

"Essence, my dear! Nice to meet you your Grace!"

Minimilion purred as Providence brushed his head. He sat down and rested his head on his paws, staring at the three of them.

Essence spoke softly.

"You both are destined not to stay in this purest of worlds. You will leave by morning. Tomorrow, Providence, you will see the Cavern of Lost Treasures. And then deci-sions must be made. It is up to both of you to make the de-cisions. Follow your hearts and listen!"

Essence then drifted out of sight and disappeared through the falling water. Vanished, they thought. Minimilion walked away as well, headed back through the deep and lush jungle brush. The eagles squawked and flew high through the canopy of the trees and out of the jungle retreat. Providence and Africus lay down, now alone, and stared at the glimpses of the sky above. Soon aroma from a flower filled their nostrils, and they fell deep into sleep.

Hours later, Providence awoke. She was alone outside of the Deep Jungle. She smelled ape on her skin. The morning retreat flashed vividly before her eyes. She started to cry.

"Oh, no, it was the Parallel Dream Universe! He is not of this world! The pictures, the ranger boy, it is all just a mixture of dreams, fantasies and real worlds! The ranger boy is just an African boy, with large dreams, but not the African Boy Legend. My mind is so active in the fantasy world. Mum was right. They brought me here to find out for myself! There is no alternate reality or parallel universe! But why did Daddy say he was the African Boy Legend? How did he have a photo of him? What is going on? Oh, he is real, but just a great looking ranger boy," she cried out loud again.

She remained there alone only for a few moments. Soon strong arms were wrapped around her. The sun seared at her skin. The hands were soon rubbing her with oils from African plants, protecting her from the sun. The hot air was real, as was the dirt of the African savannah, and the blowing grasses from the hot breeze. *Wait, is this real? The savannah is real, and I am awake, so, this is no Parallel Dream Universe!*

She slowly turned around. There again were the eyes of the boy she had so long ago met. She fainted in exhaustion and disbelief. Africus carried her to his range vehicle, and gently placed her in the rear seat. He headed to the mountains in the central part of Kenya, to the east of the Preserve. In a few hours, they were high up the mountain, walking through poppy fields and a coffee farm.

Providence awoke in the cooling mountain breeze. Again, she saw Africus. She gasped again. Her senses were so overloaded. He lay her down gently. Soon Essence returned. Providence felt relieved. She calmly exhaled.

*I am back in the Parallel Dream Universe! I least I am happy here, even if it is not real, or if it is real, not of our universe.*

"More aromas for you, my dear!" Essence responded, waving flowers beneath her nose and the nose of Africus. Soon the two of them were in a trance like state. Essence carried them on her back to the entrance of the Cavern of Lost Treasures.

Deep in the Cavern, Africus awoke first. He held Providence closely in his lap to brace her when she awoke.

"Is she too overwhelmed?" Africus asked, raising his eyebrows in concern.

"She is fine. She has been preparing for this her whole life. She knows of this place from the Parallel Dream Universe! She has been here in her dreams," Essence soothingly replied.

At last Providence awoke. Her eyes gazed into the eyes of Africus again.

"Another kiss, my love?"

Africus bent over and together they kissed. Providence looked into his eyes again, and he looked away into the Cavern. She followed his eyes and then gasped at the Treasures before her. She sat up and stood and then walked deeper into the Cavern.

"These are lost Treasures from long ago. Many Treasures are from early England, including Treasures from the first King and Queen of England. The Treasures are real, not myth or fantasy. They have crossed over into our world at least once. I brought the sword of King Arthur himself, Excalibur, into battle. Its power was all I needed to defeat the enemy. I returned it here where it belongs. And the crown of Queen Guinevere is here. You shall wear that crown now!" Africus said to her with a spark of romance.

Africus took her hand and walked her into another room in the Cavern. There he gently took the crown of Queen Guinevere.

"I hereby place this crown upon the new queen of the Cavern of Lost Treasures, Queen Providence! To join me as the new King!"

Providence bowed and then hugged Africus again. They kissed as King and Queen and held each other tightly.

Essence soon reappeared and spoke to Providence.

"It is time. We must now depart to the world that you know as real, what you and Africus and others call the Real Universe. But never forget that this is real as well, just in another parallel universe. Remember this moment! I have taken you here through a Portal from one universe, the one you know, to a parallel universe, close in time and space. It is what we call the Parallel Real Universe. You can also come here, as you have, in your dreams in the Parallel Dream Universe in your mind and spirit, but not your body. You cannot get here without me, or the elven-like monkeys, all Special Beings, that have the Knowledge and power to transcend time and space and walk between different worlds in inter-universal travel. And we put you under with the aroma of special flowers for your Passage through the Portal. Your mind could not handle the Passage and its impact on your body and mind in your conscious state until you acquire the Knowledge. But now, it is time to go."

Essence placed the potent flowers under both of their nostrils again. Soon they fell upon her back, and she carried them back to the coffee farm on the waiting mountainside below.

Providence awoke again to the cool mountain air, and aroma of coffee beans. She was still dreamlike, so was not stunned by yet another change in scenery and reality.

"Africus, where are you, I am no longer surprised by anything anymore! Come to me! I am confused. Was that the Parallel Dream Universe or the Parallel Real Universe? Same with the Waterfall and Paradise? What did Essence tell us again? Something about a Portal?" she asked with her watery eyes gazing deeply into his soul.

"Yes, they are real places. You can visit them in the Parallel Dream Universe in your dream state, but you can visit them in reality, too, like we just did. Essence explained to you that they are in an alternate reality or the Parallel Real Universe, as she and I call it. Once you are there it is real! And it is really just one parallel universe, accessible by different means and in a different form. And we need Essence or the Great Ape or the elven-like monkeys, all Special Beings, to take us to the Parallel Real Universe. The Special Beings are able to bridge the gap between our world and the other parallel worlds!"

Africus took her hand. Now, in the African mountains, they felt each's other's presence with all five senses, and the sixth sense that they both harnessed. Hand in hand, and in silence, they traversed the mountain until they reached an access road. There waiting in his truck, was Mika, with Mrs. Stewart.

"I told Mrs. Stewart that you were showing Providence my coffee farm," Mika winked at Africus.

"Indeed!" Africus responded, with a smile.

"Indeed!" Providence added, smiling at Africus, as they boarded the range vehicle.

*Very exotic coffee*, Africus noted to himself.

# 36.

*Monday, September 29, 2025*
*Jefferson City, Nebraska*

SAVANNAH STEWART WALKED OUT onto the practice field. She was fifteen minutes late. The players dropped their sticks and stood and stared at her.

There was an ambience about her that they could not explain. She looked as if she was angelic and had been to heaven.

Savannah saw her teammates and smiled. They stepped out of their awe and rushed to greet her. Clay was the first to embrace her. Together they jumped in unison and sang the Nebraska State fight song. They laughed and ran back to their sticks. Haley, now assisting the midfielders, approached her.

"I did not hear anything. I did not know if you would come back. I heard you were in England, possibly to return to your original school," Haley said, relieved and shocked to see Savannah.

"So, Mika has not contacted you?"

"He has not," Haley said nervously, her mind racing.

"Well, you and I need to have some Mika African coffee after practice!" Savannah beamed.

"I can't wait that long!" Haley shouted.

Savannah trotted to her position on the field.

"Coach us up, Lindsay and Haley!" she returned the shout.

"OK!!" Haley said, and blew her whistle.

Shannon Garrison sat in the stands, shocked to see the return of Savannah. No one had seen Savannah return. But so much had been made of the two eagles that were flying around the campus all day, routinely landing on perches and window sills and flag posts all over campus. Shannon just watched in delight as Savannah scored effortlessly at will and galloped like a racehorse up and down the field.

Lindsay walked over to Shannon.

"Well, they should give the recruiting position back to you for lacrosse, Shannon. The savior, the American Girl Superstar, is here. And the football team lost again in a defensive squeaker with a division opponent. Pierce is a handoff machine. Not the most exciting game to watch either. But at least the sellout streak is still ongoing! Any luck on quarterbacks for next year?" Lindsay asked.

Shannon was still speechless. She saw Haley on the sideline, speechless as well. Certainly, something was up. She was going crazy not knowing. But the thrill of seeing Savannah slice through a great defense was overwhelming, too. *The lady Nebraskans will be national title contenders for sure next year.* Shannon finally could not wait. She half ran to the field to see Haley.

"Haley, what is going on?" Shannon talked so fast Haley could hardly understand her.

"Say what? I don't know! What did you say! I am so shocked she is here. She asked if I heard from Mika. What is that all about? What have you heard? Did Lindsay say anything to you? I have to coach. Go away!" Haley was fired up as she dismissed her new friend in her frenzy.

Savannah suddenly dropped her stick, raised her arms to the sky, and just screamed. The whole team stopped in their tracks. Savannah screamed again but was smiling. The girls saw she was not in pain. They all dropped their sticks and waited for Savannah to speak or act again. Savannah shrieked again. Soon the two mysterious eagles soared over the field as if beckoned by Savannah. They circled at rapid speeds and suddenly dove for the field. The girls hit the ground as the eagles appeared to be in attack mode. The eagles dropped to ten feet above the field and swooped the length of the field. They slowed to land on the lacrosse net posts. The goalie stood there, stunned. She saw them coming at her at blazing speed. She thought she was dead. But then, there they were, right behind her, protecting her and watching her. Savannah lifted her right hand in jubilation and whooped at a high pitch. The goalie took off her mask and shrieked as loud as she could. The whole team led by Savannah charged the goalie. They jumped up and down for moments that seemed like an eternity. Lindsay, Haley and Shannon charged the field and joined the girls. Nebraska State, Nebraska State they shouted. "Hip-Hip-Hooray," Lindsay shouted. "Woo-Hoo," Haley shouted. "GO-U-Nebraskans," Shannon shouted.

The eagles acknowledged the excited girls with loud squawks and took off away from the stadium. The girls all waved and cheered them as they left.

"It is an omen of good things to come," Savannah finally told her teammates.

"We are One! We are Nebraska State! We are the chosen! I love my pride!" Savannah cried out, now overcome with even more emotion. She cried a fountain of tears. Her teammates gathered around her to protect her from prying eyes, reporters and other students. She finally gathered herself and slapped all the hands of each teammate in a high five. They were so excited by the explosion of emotion, yet so stunned and confused at the reason for the enormous eruption of energy. But it was all good. They all forgot all their worries for a magical few moments, forgot all of their nagging injuries, all of their social mishaps and hurt feelings. Things were suddenly magical and even mystical.

Lindsay was stunned and overcome herself with emotion. It was Monday, a day for drills and technique. But what the heck.

"Let's scrimmage the boys!" She roared.

Shannon watched as the Nebraska State men's lacrosse team ran towards the field. It was a club team, not varsity. Varsity baseball still dominated the Nebraska State spring teams, along with spring football practice. The men had gathered near the field, hearing and feeling the commotion. Soon they were lined up against the women.

"No checking. We play women's rules!" Haley belted out.

Shannon saw Lindsay and Haley suit up for the game, as did the men's coaches. She witnessed the football team and women's soccer players rush to the field to watch the match. She felt the energy level among all the players soar to unfathomed heights. She heard the players from all the teams chanting Nebraska State! Nebraska State! Jumping up and down with fury and fire.

On they played. *The girls' energy level is so high that the men do not stand a chance,* Shannon thought. They achieved athletic performance at levels they had never experienced, let alone even contemplated. Shannon's mind raced even more.

*Is a savior coming for football, as well?!" Omigod!* Shannon screamed inside her own mind in head pounding volume.

News spread across campus. An electricity was spreading like wild fire. Energy bursts seem to erupt around campus. Smart devices were buzzing uncontrollably. The game was called as the men increased their intensity with new found force and energy from their rivals. The football players came in to break up some pushing and shoving. Savannah howled again and all the players calmed down. Shannon was stunned by the power of the energy transfusing through the campus. The players relaxed and gave each other high fives. The football players one by one slapped high fives or pumped fists with Savannah.

"Nebraska State royalty," a back-up linebacker from Gretna, Nebraska said as he hugged her instead.

"If only you knew," Savannah thought, smiling broadly and perspiring profusely from the intense action.

Shannon texted Gavin Blocker.

"The girls just played the boys in an impromptu scrimmage. The girls won 4-3, before it was called for too much intensity. The football team had to separate the players. Savannah had all four goals. YES, she is back. Don't have anything more!"

Shannon and Haley walked over to Savannah.

"Let's have that African coffee now!" Haley ordered, hoping for a positive response.

"I have to be with my teammates! Tomorrow morning? Don't worry! Everything is well!" Savannah hurriedly replied, running to jump with her teammates in celebration of their win.

"I can't wait! I am calling Mika now," Haley exhaled from her perceived rebuke.

"But he has not responded to your texts or calls," Lindsay cautioned, frowning in concern, and holding her hands on her hips, as a big sister often would do.

"I know. I have to try," Haley interjected, her shoulders hunching a bit in despair.

"I just searched all of the Socialverse and the internet. Nothing on Africus or Mika. SO, maybe it is all about Savannah. I think that is all right. Africus won't arrive until

January at the earliest, if at all?" Shannon mused aloud, eyebrows pinched in a pensive glare.

"Let's have coffee anyway!" Lindsay offered with her classic winning smile and broad grin.

Off the three went to the coaches' offices. On the way, Coach Smith admonished the lacrosse coaches for stealing his players for a short time.

"But I like their newfound energy level," he added, as he stared at Shannon, with inquisitive eyes.

"Nothing new," she said with some disappointment.

Coach Smith's grin turned straight lipped, and he walked back to his troops.

*Well, my procedure went well, anyway.* She smiled.

# 37.

Saturday, October 11, 2025
Nairobi, Kenya

MIKA AND AFRICUS SAT in the office of the U.S. embassy in Nairobi. The administrator, Sally Johannsen, was studying all of the paper work and knew that her boss was close with Mr. Francis Stewart. She fidgeted in her seat, feeling the stare of the most handsome, rugged and intriguing young man she had ever seen.

"It looks like all of your paperwork is in order. Your student visa is good to go. When do you fly out?"

"I fly to London next Saturday, to visit Mr. and Mrs. Stewart. I have some final work to do in the Preserve, well, you know, to set up the command structure of the animals in the Preserve," Africus responded, impressed with the flair of the U.S. administrator sitting across from him.

"Of course. I am from Kansas, home of Dorothy and the Wizard of Oz! I know about these matters, dreams, alternate realities, talking lions!"

"I love that movie, too," Africus admitted, smiling now at the articulate and now poised administrator.

"Ms. Johannsen, we must go. Thank you for your efforts," Mika interrupted, cutting off the mutual flirtations.

Africus hesitated, but then got up and left with Mika. A final look, and he was gone.

"There will be many temptations for you in America, Africus. You basically have known only Providence. There will be hundreds of girls seeking your affections in America, and London! You must be careful," Mika lectured.

"A harmless exchange. No one will take me from Providence. But Kansas, that is near Nebraska. Maybe I should go to Kansas. Maybe I am one of Dorothy's long-lost descendants!"

Mika and Africus took the high-speed train and then the bus back to the Preserve. Soon the night fell, and the starlit night was filled with the sounds of the savannah once again. Africus slid out into the night and waited. Soon Essence was there. He climbed on top of her back, and they rode to the Cavern of Lost Treasures.

Africus succumbed to the powerful aroma of the poppy flowers once again, in complete submission to his guide and friend, Essence. Soon they were in the Cavern.

"Africus, I have long been the guardian of the Treasures and the Cavern, with the assistance of my army of elven-like monkeys. You are the trustee and steward of the English Treasures, and the owner of the other Treasures, for as long as you are living in the Real Universe. But I am still your guide.

"Africus, as your guide, I have a plan to propose for you to consider. I believe that it may be time to return some of the English Treasures to the English Crown. I am not sure of that, as the time may be later in time. And, I am not sure how to commence the return process. But my proposed plan is that you should bring a small gift to the King of England on your sojourn," Essence stated in regal fashion.

"And I would like you to choose what to bring as a gift," she added.

Africus gazed at her, wondering what thoughts and memories were in her mind.

*Was Providence once Guinevere? Was I once King Arthur? Was Essence there, too? The sword feels magical, yet so familiar in my hands!* He pondered again to himself.

"Ah, your mind is drifting!" She laughed, her eyes twinkling in the Cavern light.

"Of course, you can hear my thoughts! AND?"

"Well, you and I are here for a reason. And Providence is a special Girl!"

"I thought as much! When shall I bring Providence here again. She looked so regal in her crown! Does she suspect who she may have been?" he asked.

"I think she lives in the Parallel Dream Universe, as much as you.

"And her visions are magnificent! Someday, together, you will have great understanding of many things. But for now, choose a gift!" Essence danced among the many Treasures as she gazed at Africus. Africus thought about his choice of Treasures, with wide open eyes and excitement.

"There is so much to choose from," he exclaimed. Then his emotions changed and he became contemplative.

"I think Excalibur should stay, as I am concerned Mr. Stewart has his eyes on this prize. And there is no way I could take it on a public jet or mail it with any mailing service. Just too much risk," Africus explained, looking suddenly concerned and unsure.

"And, I think if we take anything to the King, this region will be flooded with treasure hunters. The legend of the Cavern of Lost Treasures has been around for hundreds of years, but nothing has been found. Secret expeditions are still funded and run every year by the world's billionaires.

But nothing. I am afraid once I am in the public eye, the story of the African Boy Legend with a medieval sword will spark an avalanche of interest in the Cavern again. I am even sure my life may be in jeopardy. But I do not know how to get here, without you. So, they could interrogate me and even torture me, but I don't know the whereabouts of the Cavern. And even if I admitted to having been here, the Cavern would be safe, as I simply don't know where it is, other than that the entrance is somewhere near the coffee farm on the mountain," Africus said thoughtfully, examining the famous sword, and touching the intact steel alloy. Essence then asserted herself, and her broad powers and influence over Africus and the Cavern.

"Bring this small chalice. It is a chalice that a fourteenth century king used. See the markings. It will cause great intrigue to the Crown and its historians, but not much interest to the public. Don't worry, the Cavern is safe. International treasure hunters cannot find it," she concluded.

"Let me think about your proposed plan. But, yes, I will take the chalice with me. But when and how I deliver it will take some thought and planning. We should meet again to discuss the English Treasures."

Essence grabbed Africus by the hand and took him near the stream inside the Cavern.

"Africus, on a different note, I want to give you the Knowledge to access the Passage through the Portal. The Portal is mystical and supernatural to the untrained and unknowing. But the science is real, just decades or maybe centuries still ahead of today. Knowledge is the key to access the Portal. Without the Knowledge, you can only access the Cavern with the Special Beings, like the elven-like monkeys. You shortly will have a vision on how to achieve

Passage through the Portal. You will find the Knowledge in the Parallel Dream Universe!" Essence explained.

Africus marveled at the Treasures again. The Cavern was lit with a resplendent radiance from the century's old crystals. Essence's white hair appeared radiant. She walked to the mountain stream to drink the cold clean water. Africus followed her and drank as well. He jumped into the water with the chalice and swam downstream. Soon the current quickened its pace. Essence's white radiance grew dimmer, as he floated further away. The river turned suddenly away, and Essence was gone. Soon the current quickened again as the water started its path down the mountain. Africus was now thrashing in the torrid stream as it plunged downwards toward the bottom of the mountain. He turned and dodged sharp rocks and stalagmites. The sound was deafening.

Finally, after what seemed like a long time, he fell over a huge Waterfall deep into a lake below. Crocodiles swam around him. He caught his breath, and realized he still held the chalice. He looked up and saw the Great Ape staring at him. With a powerful hand the Great Ape lifted him out of the water. He saw two eagles perched on the rocks. No Citra or white zebra. But he knew where he was.

*The Waterfall is the back entrance to the Cavern of Lost Treasures. They are connected. I don't think I can swim upstream and up a Waterfall. SO, this is the rear entrance. I will await my vision for the main entrance. Essence? Can you hear my thoughts from afar?* Africus thought as he lay on the moss overlooking the lake and the Waterfall.

Africus regained his strength. He found his smart device. Fully waterproof, it was in good order. He snapped a photo of the chalice.

"It stays here for now," he spoke out loud to no one in particular.

Africus spent the day in the lake and surrounding jungle, eating the fruits and nuts, and bathing in the lake with the leaves of native plants. The oils of the plant leaves had protected his skin from insects and the sun for years.

Soon it was nightfall again. He lay down on a soft mossy area and fell deeply into sleep once again. His mind was active in the dream state. Visions of Providence playing in the jungle oasis darted across his mind. The dreams bounced around his past life, running with the pride, playing with Maximilion as a cub, talking to Citra, having lessons with Haley, and dinner with Mika and the other rangers, and fighting the poachers. His mind then settled. Soon he was floating above the poppy field, past Mika's coffee farm. He saw a faint beaten path, one made by the hooves of one animal, Essence, and small elven like monkeys. He smelled the perfumed aroma of Essence, as he traversed the trail. Soon he was well up the mountainside, enshrouded by clouds. He could here water beneath the earth. And then he saw it. An opening. It was an illusion, he thought, in his dream state. It looked like a normal rock formation, but in the dream state he saw the opening. Tremendous radiant energy and light flowed from the opening. It was an energy and light that could not be sensed in the conscious state. It was the Portal. Maybe the slightest of variation from the present dimension of time and space where his conscious mind resided. *I know where it is. I know how to gain Passage through the Portal. Will I retain this Knowledge in my world to access the Parallel Real Universe? It must be the case. We all have the Knowledge. It is deep in our mind and soul. We just have to open our minds eye!*

Africus awoke in the morning. He hid the chalice behind the Waterfall. He knew it was safe. He now had the Knowledge of the Special Beings. He now knew how to enter the Deep Jungle and the Cavern of Lost Treasures on his own. He was ready. Minimilion soon showed up at the Waterfall.

"So, the lions have access to the other dimensions, and can access the Parallel Real Universe, I see!" Africus exclaimed.

"No, just the king of the Lions. Maximilion had access, and now I do. But lions are extraordinary in their powers of communication and their access to the worlds humans cannot see or feel, except deep in their dreams. I am not a Special Being, like Essence. I simply have the Knowledge to access the Passage through the Portals," Minimilion acknowledged and explained.

"Minimilion, I am going to leave for a while. I hope to be back, in a few weeks or months, but I am not sure. You are now the King of the animal kingdom here. I leave you here to run the kingdom. Essence will surely be around to help you, probably as Citra. Your father, Maximilion, was a great leader, and my best friend in life. Minimilion, I will miss you as well, but I will come back," Africus said, with his right arm around the neck of the large, adolescent lion.

"Africus, GO. We are ready for you to leave. We hope you VISIT, but expect you to thrive in the human world, too. The jungles and savannah will miss you. We will carry on the ways of the animal kingdom as Maximilion and you set forth. I, and the Great Ape, the eagles and the crocodiles, will keep the Waterfall safe in the Parallel Real Universe, and protect the rear entrance to the Cavern of Lost Treasures. Essence and the elven-like monkeys will keep the entrance to the Cavern and the Treasures safe as well.

"Leave the chalice here. Men do not have the power to access the Parallel Real Universe. Even if the chalice ignites a new treasure hunt, the places are sacred and secure. Besides, a photo is just as provocative, as the real artifact," Minimilion speculated, licking his young paws, and thinking about the next mating season coming in the upcoming weeks.

"Yes, I will leave it here for now. The photo is safe in my smart device. I may not go to London. I think Mr. Stewart has bigger plans for me, other than attending a University in America. I do believe he is obsessed with the Cavern of Lost Treasures. He probably has plans for me to visit the Buckingham Palace to meet with English royalty, the King," Africus replied, his right hand now holding up his chin.

"And you should pull the sword from the stone and proclaim yourself the King!" Minimilion laughed.

"AH, that could ruffle some serious feathers, I think!"

"But you did pull the sword from the stone in the Cavern," Minimilion teased, testing Africus.

"That sword, surely the original sword and original stone, were not locked together as they were when Africus pulled the sword. That sword fit snugly but not firmly in its bay in the stone. It was easy to pull free," Africus retorted, eyeing Minimilion with seriousness.

"Just testing you. I agree. The magic of pulling the sword is no longer present. But the perception would be so regal! It would be breathtaking to the subjects of the kingdom," Minimilion said, in an exploratory manner.

"It is Excalibur that would ignite the fire of the subjects. Its power is not only legendary, but it is enormous. It taps into some universal force or energy. It is best to keep it safe in the Cavern, protected in the Parallel Universes," Africus elucidated, hands now on both knees, his eyes looking at the Waterfall.

"You are ready to go. Your head is upon your shoulders. Be wise and vigilant. And enjoy the hunting game," Minimilion said, as he slowly waddled away, the Great Ape walking him out of the jungle Paradise.

"Yes, American football, the hunting game," Africus said, waving good bye, and slapping his thighs as he stood.

The Great Ape returned, and escorted Africus out of the Deep Jungle. Africus awoke quickly and walked a few hundred yards and reached one of the towers, with a satellite hook-up. He called Mika to pick him up. Mika would be there in an hour. Africus opened his smart device again. He accessed the Nebraska State sports website. Nebraska had lost its first conference game, against a staunch team from Wisconsin.

"Two losses and no room for error," he thought.

He then placed the picture of the chalice in the search engine. A few articles written by a professor of Gloucester College in England populated his search results. The pictures were drawings. The drawings were of the chalice used by King Richard II, from 1377 to 1399. The article noted that the legend of the chalice was of its healing powers. Those who drank from the chalice, were healed of their ailments and maladies. The professor suspected the metals comprising the chalice may have emitted ions or other chemicals that were responsible for the healing properties, or that there were bacteria, passed on from the many who drank from the cup, that served as a killer bacterium, like the antibiotics of the current day, or super biotics of the current decade.

Africus wished he had brought the chalice with him now.

*Was it supernatural? Was King Richard II a clairvoyant? Did he have access to the Parallel Dream Universe? The Parallel Real Universe? Had he passed his secrets on through secret societies, through the Society, through Marcus? Had King Richard II ever been to Africa?* Africus questioned as he was absorbed by the magnitude of the simple chalice that Essence had chosen for him to take.

He studied further about King Richard II. There was not too much written about him. He was not thought of as a great king. His healing powers were attributed solely to his chalice. But he found that the chalice had been lost or stolen about 1399. Shortly, thereafter the King abdicated his throne, and later perished. The chalice had evidently kept King Richard II alive and healthy, longer than his foes and comrades. Africus speculated the Society had taken the Chalice from the King. It never surfaced in history again.

Mika soon drove down the path to the tower. Africus clicked his smart device shut.

"Africus, I presume the torch has been passed, and all is well?" Mika addressed him, with a beaming smile.

"I sense you are ready to leave your home in the savannah!" Africus responded.

Mika stopped smiling and waited for Africus to hop on board. They were silent for the whole ride back.

"I want to fly to America. I don't want to stop in London to see Mr. Stewart," Africus demanded.

"I thought that may be the case. Your visas are set, too; Ms. Johansson took care of that. I told Mr. Stewart we did not want to fly in his private jet. If he ever were considered a college booster, that free ride would be an impermissible benefit. He understood. I have a ticket already to America. We will buy you one with your savings. We can skip London. I will let the Stewarts know. He will be upset, I am sure. I suspect this relates to the Cavern, and that you suspect a nefarious purpose in his interest in you in relation to the Cavern?"

"Let's not talk about that. Let's follow your plan."

Mika and Africus left.

"Follow the yellow-brick road! Is not that what Sally said as we departed?" Africus said, laughing lightly, his eyes viewing the savannah on the bus ride to the train.

"Indeed!"

# 38.

Monday, October 27, 2025
Boston, Massachusetts

AFRICUS TYPED IN THE EMAIL of Professor Donovan Lancaster, head of English History at Gloucester College in Gloucester, England. He attached the picture of the chalice with its ancient inscriptions still legible on its side. He pushed the send button on his smart device. Off it went. He had set up a new email account with the fictitious name John Maximilion. He awaited the reply.

Africus enjoyed the crisp autumn air in Boston. He had split up with Mika in Paris. Mika had stayed to see the city. Africus recalled the long two weeks of travel just to get to Boston. He had purchased his air transportation to Nebraska. He was to leave on Tuesday.

Africus walked through the Boston public gardens and watched the ducks march across the park. He watched the ancient duck boats still carry tourists. He walked some of the freedom trail and admired the statues of Paul Revere and other patriots. *So much history in America.* The cityscape was daunting, much bigger than the buildings in Paris. The people were dressed warmly, for the cool, crisp day. He was chilled with only a golf shirt, designed by Spiritis, on his back. He opened his duffel bag, with his limited belongings, and pulled on a sweatshirt, with a large NS on the front. One bystander told him it was a North Shore State sweatshirt. All the clothes in America were made with high technology, with synthetic and natural fibers, that provided sun screen, bug repellent, and odor and perspiration removal. They never needed to be ironed and stretched easily with movement and waistlines.

People barely noticed him, as they were locked into their 3-D virtual screens above their eyes as they walked. They barked orders, took commands, and even did chores and work as they walked. Little communication occurred. The smart devices told them where to walk, and when to stop. There was no traffic. Smart buses and cars were everywhere and linked to people's smart devices. The people moved orderly on and off the buses and cars. He ventured towards the Charles River. There he found many people running and walking. There were even sail boats on the river. The sail boats were still navigated by the people, not the smart devices. *Probably, because they are so small.*

The city seemed diverse. Most cultures on earth seemed to be present. He knew Americans generally called themselves a type of American based on their heritage. He supposed he would be an African only, as he was not an American. The hospitals dotted the skyline down the river bank. *Impressive structures. The best physicians combined with the best medicines from Africa. Everyone looks so healthy.*

He was hungry. He searched for natural food restaurants. There were only a few. Most people were eating bars, apparently, precisely engineered food stuffs, combining synthetic and natural foods, in uniquely designed variations for individual tastes and needs. He had eaten this foodstuff for his entire trip.

He finally found an ancient restaurant, called the Nineties. There they had steaks and eggs and vegetables, cooked to order. He stepped in and grabbed a booth. Again, most of the patrons were alone and engrossed in their smart devices and 3D screens in front of their faces.

The menu was an E-menu. He punched in his order for steak, broccoli and spinach. He declined the French potatoes. He had never eaten a potato. Within seconds, an older woman brought him his meal, with a bottle of spring water. He had already paid for the dinner by an App on the E-menu. The plates were disposable, as were the utensils.

He opened his smart device. He did not read his messages on the device. Most were from Haley and Savannah. He had not responded to them during his long sojourn on so many plane flights, and ferry rides.

He noticed a few young college girls in a neighboring booth, wearing their modern tight fitting, stretch, technological clothes. *But they still wear old-fashion flip flops that Haley wore often.* They had put down their smart devices and now were focused on him, sitting across the way. He heard them snickering about his unusual haircut. *My long locks must not be the style in Boston.* Most of the men had short cropped hair. He knew his clothes were not modern or state of the art either. But his eyes dazzled the girls, as did his powerful physique. He heard them mention North Shore State. Then he saw them taking 3D pictures of him. Nothing was coming up on their searches of his image. He saw them typing frantically to hook up with him on their devices. But he had not downloaded all the latest social apps. He was disconnected from this new social world.

His device buzzed again. He had now signed up for Gavin Blocker's blog. It had just come online. He saw that Nebraska State football had won again in another defensive struggle. Still only one conference loss. Oklahoma was the beast of the Western Division, demolishing opponents with their furious, yet powerful offense, and hunting down opposing offenses with their defense with intense avarice. *Savannah, is dominating the LAX world, too.* A smile crossed his face. He looked up, and the four girls were all staring at him.

Then his device buzzed again. Another blog from Gavin Blocker.

It was short and explosive.

*The African Eagle, yes, the African Boy Legend, has landed! He is in Boston!*

Africus was floored. He was not really sure what would happen when he arrived. Would he come in silently like the jaguar, or with a roar like the lion? He had hoped for something in between.

Soon more messages from Haley and Savannah poured in. He dared not open them. He hesitated, then opened the Nebraska State football site. His heart pounded more than it had ever pounded in Africa, even when faced with certain death, or dealing with the horrid poachers.

"African ranger, thought to be the African Boy Legend, to join Nebraska State football team," was the headline, and there on top of the article was a picture of him when he was eleven. A knife between his mouth, running with Maximilion and another lion, barely clad with a loincloth, and long golden locks, held together with a ragged and dirty cotton cloth headband.

Under the picture was a caption, "Africus, the African Boy Legend, running with the lions as a young boy!"

The article was short, it only mentioned that he was from a Preserve in Kenya, and had been raised by two Nebraska State alums, Mika Williams and Haley Andrews. It noted he was already enrolled as an E-student, that he likely would start football in the spring, and that he once ran with the lions in the wilds of the African savannahs and jungles. No mention of Maximilion, or Savannah. More to follow he thought.

He saw the Socialverse was exploding before his very eyes. The hits on the article were rocketing higher and higher. It seems Nebraska State nation was stunned, and wildly excited about the news.

Africus started to shake. He was sweating heavily. He was no longer hungry but gulped down his water.

He looked at the girls again. They looked concerned, but evidently, his current image still did not pick up the scan of the picture of him as an eleven-year-old, or any other picture identifying him. The girls did not know who he was, not yet, anyway. He smiled at them, and as they collectively said hi, he just picked up his duffel bag and headed back to the park. He noticed they were following him. He picked up his pace. Still no signs they knew who he was.

He texted Mika. "I want to go back to Africa. I am going to book a flight back to Europe right now. On my way to Logan International Airport. I have the funds to pay for it."

He did not hear a response.

They he heard a primal shriek, like he had heard in the savannah, when prey was falling victim to their hunters. He turned and saw the girls all staring at their smart devices.

"Africus!" they yelled over and over. He took a selfie as he started to run towards the underground subway, called the green line. He put it in his search base. Within seconds the article on him on the Nebraska State website appeared. The technology could match faces from a person's youth! He knew they were on to him. He then saw Gavin Blocker's blog light up again. "Africus and African Boy Legend" were in the headline. SO, the girls knew he was in Boston.

Soon he was flying to the green line. He managed to board before the girls could follow him. He then set up his smart device to receive notifications of hits about Africus.

In a few seconds, the hits poured in. Numerous Nebraska news sites were running with a rehash of the reports. Then Socialverse hits started to accumulate. Bang. A Boston news site reported an "AFRICAN BOY LEGEND SIGHTING" in the Boston Commons area.

He felt like the hunted. He was skilled as a hunter, but equally skilled at avoiding his predators. He had never been the subject of much attention in the human world. It was happening too quickly. He knew the fight or flight response of the prey in Africa. He had overcome that with calculated defenses and movements, always outmaneuvering his adversaries, with stealth, wit and speed. *I have outrun the girls.* He looked around the subway car. Many were staring at him. But none were fixated on their devices. He was unusual in his dress and style. He was also tall with a riveting physique. He noticed some young professional women, professionally dressed, with modern fabrics and looser fitting attire, staring actively at him. He saw their smart devices opened, but they had not snapped photos of him.

He read the map of the Boston subway system. He saw he had to get to the Silver Line. He had to switch right away to the redline on Park Street to catch the redline to South Station. The doors opened. He scampered out. No one followed him.

He boarded the redline train to South Station. He was impressed that he had not made a navigational error. No bushes or rocks or trees as trail marks. Just signs and maps. He still felt the weight of many eyes upon him. More he thought, for his looks and foreign appearance.

"Is that Zaazaan?" He heard a young boy say to his mother, while pointing at him with wide and wild eyes.

"Yes, he looks like the actor in the new Zaazaan action hero virtual reality game you just bought, but of course it is not him. This is Boston!"

Africus felt relieved. Still the whole world seemed to be staring at him-like when he was a young boy in the jungle, feeling the stares of predators hidden in the night or in the brush.

His device buzzed constantly now. New hits on his name were too numerous to view. He shut down the alert app for hits with his name. He knew it was likely everywhere now. His email and texts were lighting up.

He decided to read the one from Mika.

"Don't turn back! Your flight to Jefferson City is tomorrow. Spend the day outside of Boston. Go incognito! Store your luggage and go. I looked online. The North Shore looks safe and quiet. Try Ipswich or Gloucester."

He then opened an email from Haley.

"Sorry Africus! I did not know this would happen. I hope you still come tomorrow! Savannah and I will pick you up. We have a place for you to stay, too. Please don't go back to Africa. This will die down, when they know you are just like the rest of us!"

He opened the last text from Savannah.

"I am hopelessly in LOVE! See you soon!"

*She is not watching what is going on.* But his urges and affection for her stoked his internal fire. The onslaught seemed less daunting. He turned his alerts back on.

"The African Boy Legend has landed in Boston! Sighted entering subway system." The alert seemed to scream out. It was on the lead news site for local Boston news. He read a few more alerts. It appeared Haley had not submitted any recent pictures of him. This would give him some cover. He quickly jumped off the redline at Downtown Crossing. He boarded the Orange line to Park Street and took the green line to North Station. The transit car was less crowded. He drew in a huge breath.

Soon he was traversing North Station. He took the first train he could. He was bound for Newburyport. He hopped on, still hanging on to his duffel bag. The stares seemed to have diminished. Not many people were going outbound in the middle of the day.

A new batch of alerts came in. One with a video attachment. He could not believe is eyes. Hundreds of Nebraska State students were in the campus quad area. Africus signs were everywhere. Nebraska State students were singing chants and yelling his name. Some campus pranksters were dressed as a boy raised by lions and hanging from the trees in loin clothes. Some girls dressed with skimpy ragged wraps, and sandals to look like jungle girls. Girls were dressing in early 1960s garb, with sundresses and high white socks because someone said he was the great-grandson of an early sixties rock star. Most students seemed unsure what to do, but to celebrate the arrival of someone magical and foreign and mystical. A legend come true.

One sign read, "He is from the Parallel Dream Universe!!"

He was startled at the sign. It was not Savannah carrying the sign. He searched the video clip for her or Haley. No sightings. The students looked like they were having so much fun. "I want to join in the fun!"

His device buzzed again.

Now his current photo was viral. It was everywhere. The girls at the diner had posted it, and it was quickly downloaded and reposted on most of the news sites. His cover was now gone. Even his sweatshirt was shown. And the world knew it was NS for Nebraska State, not North Shore

State, as the girls said they had thought when first seeing him.

Africus took off the sweatshirt. The people on the train were older and seemed disinterested. He felt some relaxation.

*I am not being hunted.*

He closed his eyes. Soon the conductor yelled out Ipswich. He jumped off the train.

He walked toward a downtown area. He was hungry again, and really thirsty. He found a small sandwich shop. An older woman was at the counter. *Surely, she will not care about Africus.*

Surely enough, she served him with barely a smile. No fuss or inquisition. He ate his sandwich, and drank two bottles of Glisten, a special purpose spring water, loaded with nutrients and protective substances. Finally, he got up to leave.

The older woman smiled.

"I won't tell anyone you are here in our special town, Africus," she startled Africus, with a wink, and an old-fashioned flip of her short hair.

"What?" He said, clearly taken aback.

"I saw you walking down the street. I knew it was you! I was watching the story on the news. It is all over the local news feeds. All over the news stations on my smart device. There is footage of you walking in North Station. The news folks mistakenly had you boarding a train for Gloucester. So, the world is awaiting you in Gloucester! You are safe in Ipswich. I am a good secret carrier!"

The woman, with some unusual gray hair, undid her apron, and looked attractive for what Africus thought was a woman in her early sixties, maybe old enough to be a grandmother. She wore a long skirt with a woolen sweater.

*How nice it would be to have a grandmother.* She seemed so nice. Were all Americans this nice.

"So, Africus, a smart bus will stop by down the street. It goes to Cranes Beach, one of the wonders of the world. You should go there and relax. The news even knows you are flying from Logan tomorrow to Jefferson City Airport. I am now a fan of the Nebraskans! I can't wait to watch you play next year! Ha! I think a lot of people are suddenly going to be Nebraska State fans!"

The elder woman then packed him a basket for dinner. She did not charge him, but he paid her anyway.

"Keep your bag here. The bus returns at sunset. I own a bed and breakfast down the road. The house was built in in the 1600s! You are welcome to stay. And I can see you will pay your fare for the stay! Enjoy!" She seemed so maternal, he thought.

Off Africus went to the bus. It was a cool autumn day, so the bus was empty going to the beach. He had put his Nebraska State sweatshirt back on, turned inside out. The bus traveled by a street with colonial homes built at various historic times.

The bus continued down a long access road. Towards the end of the road he saw what appeared to be a castle. He gazed in awe. It was called a castle. He wondered if the English had built the castle in colonial times. He wondered if there were any Treasures hidden inside. Maybe with his powers he could find them. His mind drifted away from his sudden fame. He thought deeply about the Waterfall and the Cavern. He thought about the Parallel Dream Universe and the Parallel Real Universe. *I firmly believe the Waterfall and the Cavern are real in another parallel dimension. I am thrilled that I have the Knowledge to gain Passage through the Portals to access the Waterfall and the Cavern in person, not just in my dreams in the Parallel Dream Universe. I believe in Essence and*

*Maximilion and Minimilion I missed Maximilion.* The bus came to its automatic stop. He jumped off the bus. He looked out to the sea. Ipswich Bay was quite striking to him. The surf was up somewhat. The sand dunes were high and well built. It had been four years since the mighty hurricane of 2021 had wreaked havoc on the shoreline.

He walked to the water's edge. The seagulls were flying around everywhere, screeching too loudly he thought. He walked east towards Conomo point and the mouth of the Essex river. Soon he broke into a jog, then a run and then an all-out sprint. The seagulls followed him like the pied piper. A few beach walkers watched in awe. As he sprinted down the beach, a pack of coy dogs, a blend of coyote and wolf, and mostly wolf, bounded from the sand dunes, blood dribbling from their mouths after killing and feeding on a deer. The coy dogs ran alongside Africus, as if he was the alpha dog. They howled in support of the sprinting human, larger than most they had seen. He finally slowed and dove into the cold waters. The water was so much colder than the Indian Ocean water he had once jumped into. The coy dogs howled louder. Seagulls circled him. He swam back towards Ipswich a hundred yards out. The coy dogs and seagulls stayed with him. Most of the beach walkers had scurried off the beach, with the sight of a pack of coy dogs. Africus finally returned to shore. The coy dogs circled around him. The seagulls all swooped down and stood on the beach.

Africus did not fear the coy dogs. There were few big cats in America, he knew. The dog family was the dominant species, along with bears, whom he knew little about. He barked out a guttural yell, and the coy dogs all sat down, and licked their paws. Africus sat down with them. It was like his army was with him.

"I am Africus," he said out loud, wondering if the coy dogs would talk to him like the lions.

The coy dogs did not talk to him but howled in response. He understood. They knew who he was, even in America. Even the American dog family, he surmised in surprise, respected him, as it did in Africa.

Africus took out his smart device. The coy dogs left for the sand dunes. The seagulls went out to sea in search of fish. He sat down and opened up the classroom app for his two lectures he had missed earlier in the day. For the next two hours, he listened to the professors.

He listened attentively, interested in the subject matter of American history and American government. But then he jolted upright. The class room suddenly went chaotic. Students were jumping and laughing and slapping each other. He heard a chanting of what sounded like "Africus! Africus!"

*Oh, no,* he thought. *Who do they think I am? How do they even know if I can play ball, or do anything American? I am the mythical king of the Cavern, and sometimes thought of as a parallel king of the animal kingdom in the Preserve along with Minimilion, and Maximilion before him. But the human world is distant and new to me. This is crazy!*

Africus closed the classroom app. He opened his travel app and cancelled his flight to Nebraska.

"Now what?" he thought.

He jumped back in the water. It was so refreshing. He wished Essence would appear. But she did not. No Citra, no Maximilion or Minimilion, nor the Great Ape. No friendly crocodiles. He saw some seals frolicking near the Plum Island beach. They looked playful and friendly. But they were too far away to play with.

He returned to the shore and walked up to the castle. An iron plate recounted the history of the castle. It was not an

English castle. He was disappointed. He returned to the bus stop and waited for the smart bus.

He flipped on his smart device again. More messages from Haley, Mika and Savannah.

*I guess I must call her Savannah now.*

His other inbox had a lonely message. He expected it was from Gloucester. Not Gloucester, Massachusetts. He opened up his inbox for John Maximilion. There it was. A message cited important. It was from Professor Lancaster.

"John Maximilion! I don't know who you are or where you are, but I am stunned by this photo. Only I would know that the inscriptions are real, the old English and the manner of carving. Even the metallic finish and condition of the chalice look age appropriate. I am afraid to ask how you found this, with a certain fear in mind, and hope it was a random finding. But I fear you are on to something much larger. I am steeped in the history of the Society and the legend of Marcus Aurelius VIII. I will keep this photo of utmost secret. I know the Society is still alive and well. Oh, I do believe in conspiracy theory. I soundly believe that the Society does not know the location of the chalice or other artifacts, but they believe they are in Africa in the mythical Cavern of Lost Treasures. Marcus died without reporting the whereabouts of the safe haven. Please keep in touch. I can fly anywhere to meet you.

In the Bonds,

Sir Donovan Lancaster,

Professor of English Antiquities

Gloucester College"

Africus read the text carefully. He pondered it for the remainder of his bus trip.

As he got off the bus, clarity of thought overcame him.

*He is with the Society. They certainly have technology to locate me. They would have my IP address from the message. They can find me. They likely already know I am in Ipswich. Or they will shortly because I opened the message. Time for a new smart device.*

Africus removed the battery from his smart device. He also knew how to disable the tracking devices. Mika had taught him this trick, so he could remain hidden in the savannah as needed to avoid poachers, or just to stay incognito. He did not know if it was too late. He did not believe the world or the Society would associate John Maximilion with him. Then another thought occurred to him. Mr. Stewart was so high up in world, and he had so much control over Africa, and was suddenly a London socialite, he maybe worked for or was part of the Society, too. Mr. Stewart did not know about the chalice. But he knew about Maximilion, and Africus and the Cavern of Lost Treasures.

"It is all coming together. Is Savannah working for her father? Does she really love me or is she a pawn in the search for some of the greatest Treasures in history!" He said out loud.

Soon he was looking over his shoulder at every passerby. He was now cut off from the world without his smart device. He could not go back to Boston. Everyone wanted to meet him. He felt alone. Suddenly, he did not even trust the grandmother.

He returned to the store, and saw it was closed. He knew the woman had taken his duffel bag to the ancient bed and breakfast. He walked the few blocks to the old colonial home. Its clapboards and windows were the originals. The roof had been redone with modern shingles, but the historic ambience still hovered around the house. He opened the door. She was not there. His bag was in plain sight.

He was exhausted. He took a gamble. He grabbed the bag, which he discerned had not been opened. He found one of the vacant rooms and crashed on the rickety old metal bed.

# 39.

H ALEY WAS CONCERNED about the message from Mika that Africus was having second thoughts about America. *I have not heard from Africus at all. I hope he still lands in Jefferson City today. What flight is he scheduled to take to Jefferson City? There are no direct flights to Jefferson City from Boston. With a connecting flight, I could hear from him at any time!* The news stations had sent reporters to the Jefferson City Airport awaiting his arrival. She knew local high school girls had planned rallies at the airport. A local chapter of the Africus fan club had already been formed by one high school girls' group with forty members already signed up. She knew people were not only awaiting his arrival in person, but also his Socialverse arrival. He did not have any accounts to follow. A few impersonations had burst forth, but she had publicly quickly dismissed them. The e-world already knew now that Africus was raised by Mika Williams and Haley Andrews as a foster child, and that he had grown up on his own in the savannahs and jungles of Africa. Haley's social media followers had boomed overnight. Her followers rested on every word she said. Gavin Blocker's followers had skyrocketed as well. His now famous quote that the "African Eagle, yes, the African Boy Legend, has landed!" was top on the list of topics mentioned in the e-world along with "Africus". *Nothing on the Cavern of Lost Treasures or the Waterfall.*

Haley ignored the repeated calls and texts from Shannon and Savannah. Savannah seemed star struck. Her focus seemed narrowly on her love for him, not what he was going through entering this fast-paced techno world of America. Haley had sophisticated tracking apps, which she had from the Preserve. She determined quickly that Africus had disabled his smart device and was in the shadows. She worried for him. *I should have just told him to stay safe in his home, the Preserve.* She had wanted to show him off to the world. But she was not so sure now.

A message from Mrs. Stewart came in as well.

"Where is Africus?"

Haley thought that odd. Why would she wonder where he was? The world still expected him to arrive today in Nebraska.

Her smart device rang again. It was from Massachusetts. She hoped it was Africus on another device.

"Haley, you answered. This is Africus," he spoke quietly.

"My dear Africus, are you ok? You are still in Boston, I see. Is your flight about to leave?" She asked desperately.

"I am not on a flight today. I am deciding what to do. I think there are bigger elements in play here, besides just me and football. I can't tell you now. I am just going to watch things play out for now. This is a new smart device I picked up today. Don't tell anyone the number. This is just for you. If people ask, just say I am delaying my arrival."

"Do you want me to fly to Boston. I can help you sort matters out. I can support you. If you want to fly back to

Africa, I will go with you," Haley felt eager to help her foster son, nervously wringing her hands.

"I am safe here. I will call you tomorrow. Let me know if you receive any calls from anyone you don't know," he warned.

"I received one from Mrs. Stewart wondering where you were. I thought that was odd," she told him.

"Ok," he said without any emotion.

Haley puzzled at the neutral response. Maybe she would be mindful of Savannah for now. She would not return Mrs. Stewart's call.

Africus hung up and turned off his device. He was not on any active accounts, and he had disabled all of his tracking devices. He felt mostly certain the new device could not be followed.

Haley texted Shannon and told her that Africus would not arrive for a few more days. She fully expected that a blog blast from Gavin Blocker would soon follow. A second later her screen lit up with the latest Blocker blog. Surely enough the world now knew of the delayed arrival.

Another message from Coach Smith, screaming for an arrival date.

"I thought he was going to redshirt, Coach Smith! Put the team first! You have a large buyout and only two losses, so RELAX!" she replied.

Savannah sent a flurry of desperate texts and emails to her.

"Savannah, he needs a few days to arrive. News that he was coming today is not in the cards. Just be patient. True Love is timeless, my dear!" she fired off another text to Savannah.

Haley did not bother to read Savannah's responses. No need for emotional roller coaster rides of the young in love.

"Now, I have some research to do," she thought.

# 40.

Wednesday, October 29, 2025
Gloucester, England

PROFESSOR DONOVAN LANCASTER looked across the wooden table. He was in the ancient study in the academic studies building housing the history department for Gloucester College. There sat the most powerful man in Africa, Sir Francis Stewart. Alongside him was an authoritative looking man with no name, a representative of an important group linked to the Crown. That is all they told him. Their eyes were wide, anxious for his opening words.

"I believe the photo is genuine. This is a picture of the ancient chalice of King Richard II. Legend is that it had healing powers. Researchers contend that the healing power came from the chemical makeup of the chalice," he opened, with his eyes steadfast and demeanor serious.

"But I know your interest is not in the chalice, as is mine, but rather where did it come from. Sir Stewart, you contend that John Maximilion is an alias for a young African male named Africus. You also contend that your daughter knows him, and that she has spoken of the Cavern of Lost Treasures. Your speculation is that this chalice is from the Cavern of Lost Treasures. You want me to confirm that, I suspect.

"The legend is that much of the treasury of English artifacts and memorabilia disappeared in the middle centuries. There is legend of a secret group, the Society, that sought to protect those precious items for posterity, and that Sir Marcus Aurelius VIII, took them around the world to a safe haven. He died, according to legend, without passing on the location of the safe haven. Now, the Society seeks its location and that the location is in Africa. Legend is that there is a Cavern of Lost Treasures, a legend passed on through the generations. The Society believes that the Cavern is the location of the lost English Treasures. Those with connections know that the Society has been searching for this Cavern for centuries. Legend is that there may be some magic, or mysticism, or scientific interdimensional time-space physics involved.

"I cannot add anything more for your hunt. Sir without a name, I presume you are a member of the Society. I have seen you in photos with members of the Crown. But I can say that the chalice of Richard II was held in an esteem just short of the memorabilia of King Arthur, and that the chalice was certainly an artifact that the Society would have protected. So, I do believe, that the young Africus, did in fact retrieve it from the Cavern of Lost Treasures," the professor concluded his remarks.

The two listeners said nothing.

"Keep this silent. Your life depends on it," the man with no name said, with steely cold eyes.

The two of them stepped away and convened outside under a nearby tree, as campus students strolled by, their eyes and minds locked in the 3-D images floating in front of their eyes projected from their smart devices.

"Your plan worked beautifully. We suspected that the Cavern was not traceable in the world as we know it. The lions have always been known to possess some type of super intelligence. Having a boy raised by the lions was risky, but it worked. The young English female sprint champion was unaware her egg had been compromised after her hernia surgery. And the Nobel Prize winning professor was unaware of the recipient of his genetic donation. Neither knew anything of your plot. After two years in the borough of Kensington and Chelsea as a foster child, you took the boy and placed the child in harm's way in the dense jungle of Kenya, where by good fortune, the lion named Maximilion and his father took the child under their wings. And it worked. Somehow the world of which we know so little opened up to Africus. Your daughter was the perfect unsuspecting agent here. She kissed him and was infected with some his magical powers. She too has mystical ties to this other world. She has told you of his magical places, including the Cavern of Lost Treasures, that she has seen in her visions and dreams in the Parallel Dream Universe, as she calls it. I believe the Parallel Dream Universe is a vision of a real universe, one in another dimension, or a time-space warped area. A Parallel Real Universe! There is likely a gateway or wormhole or specific Portal from our reality to the location of the Cavern, and all of our lost Treasures. How we find it and gain "Passage", I do not know. But Africus is the key. It appears he has gained Passage through the Portal to the Cavern. But we can't be certain. We must find out for sure. And if he has, then we know what we must do!" The man with no name spoke openly but firmly with Sir Francis Stewart, who had been knighted recently by the King.

"I have spent my whole life looking for the Cavern. I have made a fortune along the way, thanks in part to the Society.

We are so close. I don't know how we close the deal. If we capture Africus, he may rebel to protect his other world, his own kingdom. My daughter is unaware of her role here. She is hopelessly in love and loves America and Nebraska State. Africus is now an American sensation and obsession, and he hasn't even landed in Nebraska. We know he is in Massachusetts. We tracked his smart device. But he is crafty. He has abandoned or unhooked his device from the e-world. We believe his last location was in Ipswich or Gloucester, Massachusetts, two towns named for their English counterparts by the original colonialists. I think he will end up in Nebraska. We have time. We have waited for centuries. I think we avoid an international manhunt," Sir Francis Stewart responded, deep in thought.

"I think you are too close to the African Boy Legend. I think your daughter's relationship with him is tainting your vision. The Society will take the matter from here. The Treasures are most important here for the Crown and the world. The boy is only a pawn in a larger play. He may be athletic, as his mother was a gold medal Olympic sprint champion. But the Cavern of Lost Treasures is ours, and we wish to reclaim it," the no named man warned with a stern and dispassionate voice.

"I understand. But be careful. If he is your lone link to the Cavern, you must protect him."

"No one person is greater than the Society. Your role with the African Boy Legend is over. We appreciate all that you have done. We appreciate the use of your daughter to find the African Boy Legend and enrapture him, even though to her it is real. Your efforts have already been rewarded, as you know. We do not need you in London anymore. You should return to Africa. We will no longer support you, but we will not undermine or hurt you either, unless you interfere. Your role here with the Society is terminated. You have served us well, as did your father and ancestors, but you are too involved now. You and your ancestors have served the Society well, but none of you are or were members of the Society."

With that the man with no name left. A black smart luxury car pulled up and whisked him away.

Sir Francis Stewart knew all of his smart devices and computers would be bugged. They would use him and his family to help find the African Boy Legend.

*But I am crafty, too,* he thought. *I will make this work. I am the one who is responsible for the finding of the Cavern. I should be given my just rewards. And they will not use my daughter.*

He returned to see Professor Lancaster. He first changed all of his clothing and removed all of his jewelry and devices. Professor Lancaster took him to a room, that was not bugged, because no one knew it existed.

"So, Francis, I believe that man is the current head of the Society. He is ruthless. He will stop at nothing. The obsession with the Cavern, and in particular, King Arthur's memorabilia, is all consuming. It was their mission to preserve the Treasures, and they lost them. Now that seek to redress their monumental blunder. They sought you out. You are the son of a long line of African business tycoons, who were affiliated with the Society as consultants and advisors on African matters. Your family's role was always to assist them in finding the Cavern. It was your study of lion intelligence, that first captivated them. Then it was your idea to place a boy of extraordinary abilities and royal blood into the world of the lions, and into the magical world of their intelligence. And it worked. And now, I may have my chalice. I like you am an advisor to the Society, but not a member. I do not believe my life is in jeopardy. They need me to verify the Treasures.

"But I was skeptical that they can be retrieved from the Cavern without damage. But the chalice looks to be intact. I think the Treasures can be retrieved. This could be such a world changing event. The power of the original crown and the swords may be incredible!" The professor stated as he was giddy in his assessment.

"I know what you are saying. It has been my family's and my obsession forever to find the Cavern. But they have now cut me out of the picture. I feel my daughter and the African Boy Legend are in danger. And the Russians want to find the Cavern as well. They have sent emissaries in the name of poaching to find it. The Russian intelligence community is among the greatest in the world. I also believe they have known about the African Boy Legend for years. The poachers could have killed him but did not. They were watching him. They recently were sent to capture him, but ended up in a shootout, and wound up in a Ugandan prison. But we know they are free again. Russia was also behind the uprising, largely unnoticed and dismissed by the international press, where Uganda sought to take over the Preserve in West Kenya. That is where the Cavern is believed to be or near, because that is where the African Boy Legend lives. Insiders believe the General was after all of Kenya. Maybe so, but we believe the Cavern was his real goal. But the African Boy Legend defeated the uprising with extraordinary powers, powers that I believe he acquired from the lions and their relationship to the supernatural, or super realms of space and time," Sir Francis confessed his deepest secrets, most recently learned, his arms now hanging loosely at his sides.

"You know more than I on the matters of Africa and the Russians. I have been privy to much of the African Boy Legend experiment. I know the Society would send a scout on a safari to check on him from time to time. And you have had your eyes on him. But then the Society thought he had died. I thought it was a stupid endeavor, a waste of life. I surely expected the boy to be eaten by the lions. Maybe the lions were expecting him, like a prodigal son. I was skeptical of the intelligence of the lions. But no more. But what is it that I may do here. Why have you come back here? Do you trust me? I have no loyalty to you, the African Boy Legend or your daughter," the quizzical professor retorted, leaning back in his chair with his arms folded across his chest.

"Yes, I know. I thought he had died, too. But I know that you are a servant, or puppet, as am I. I have wealth and power, you have prestige and power, all bestowed upon us by the Society. Is there a broader theme here, that we need to protect? Should we protect the Cavern from the exploitation of the modern world? If it is discovered, would the fantasy and magic of the legends disappear? Is the dream of the Treasures greater than the Treasures themselves? Is there a risk of an interdimensional warping of time and space that could harm our reality and world?" Sir Francis ranted on, his face contorted and eyes roaming.

"Or is a scorned servant gone mad in pursuit on his own imaginations and quest for glory? Or gone mad in pursuit of the safety and well-being of his daughter and wife, and future son-in-law?" the cagey professor continued his attack.

"I have said enough, I shall depart."

The professor watched as the beaten man before him stood up with his shoulders hunched over to leave. The professor saw himself from a decade earlier.

"No, stay. I was abandoned by the Society a decade ago. I was banned from the great Universities and relegated to this tiny college in the rural hinterland. I thought you were a member of the Society. You are an advisor like me, serving solely at their whim and fancy. We are so close to the Treasures. I am not sure what to do," the professor backed down in his demeanor, now leaning forward in his chair and staring intently at Sir Francis.

Sir Francis returned to his seat, his shoulders now straightened, and a slight smile breaking across his mouth.

"I am sure the African Boy Legend will not give up his secrets. His connection to this other world, the Parallel Real Universe, likely provides him with protection, and he can return there as well, away from all of us. I am not sure why he wants to live in our world, anyway. But maybe the two of us can protect him and the Parallel Real Universe and the Treasures. And we can make sure that you obtain the chalice. The Society appears to have no interest in the chalice," Sir Francis gathered his emotions and returned to his scheming and creative ways.

"The Society is too powerful. I think you are on your own. But I will not sell you out. And if you think of anything that I can do, I can help, within reason and with precaution. I do want the chalice, for research, of course," the professor meekly replied.

"You think it is fountain of youth!"

"I do but have never published that view! The Society does not believe the chalice had any special powers. So, we shall see!" the professor now was giddy again, talking about his life-long obsession with King Richard II and the chalice.

"A deal it is. But keep me posted of anything you hear or know of. I am leaving for Africa in the morning," Sir Francis retorted.

"Have you seen Africus's photo on the internet?" Sir Francis asked as he was about to leave.

"Yes, I have," the Professor responded. "There is a resemblance to his mother and father. His father is the legendary physicist at one of our finest academic institutions.

He was the founder of the modern break-through discoveries in quantum physics, and space-time anomalies and multi-dimensional multiverses. His mathematical equations for portals into parallel universes and time travel garnered him the Noble Prize. He has passed away, unfortunately. Ha! Maybe his spirit is a guide to the young African Boy Legend!"

"Indeed!" Sir Francis laughed.

"The Crown also knows that there was no royal blood. Nothing against your daughter, who is quite extraordinary, but I would not be surprised if the lovely Princess Anne is sent to do the bidding of the Society and the Crown. I believe, as you, that Africus would be quite protective of his worlds, Treasures, and then two kingdoms!"

"That is most interesting. I need to give that some thought. She could give Savannah a run here. She is a princess. Hmm. So many irons in the fire. And for all these years I thought he had royal blood," replied Sir Francis, shaking his head.

With that the two men gave each other a hearty shake of the hands, and Sir Francis Stewart left the ancient study to gather his wife and belongings to depart for home.

# 41.

*Saturday, November 1, 2025*
*Nebraska Stadium*
*Jefferson City, Nebraska*

G AVIN BLOCKER SAT in the press box at Nebraska stadium. The team had not yet walked on to the field. The crowd suddenly roared loudly. It was not an earthquake roar, that the media liked to call it, but it was an immense roar. Blocker saw Princess Anne, daughter of the King of England, walking up the aisle in the student section. He immediately started typing one of his instant blogs.

*An international celebrity, Princess Anne, of London, has just arrived at the stadium. She is sitting in the student section. The students are going wild. The students have been on fire ever since the announcement of the coming of Africus, the African Boy Legend, from Africa. Everyone suspects the Princess is here to see Africus. Her recruitment and arrival seemed to have come out of nowhere. She is on an official school visit. She is being recruited for the Nebraskans national power soccer program. Officials even added that with her speed, she could walk-on the lacrosse program. Oh, a battle for the affections of Africus may be in store. Savannah Stewart, our own American Girl Superstar, is rumored to be in hot pursuit for the incoming Africus. Africus is scheduled to arrive any day now. No one is sure where he is. But he reportedly still has not missed an online lecture. She has just sat next to Savannah Stewart! Omigod! Let the games begin! More after the game. The Nebraskans will be favored today in a division game against Minnesota. But it will be tough, as both teams are still in contention and in pursuit of Oklahoma, and both teams have stout defenses. Nebraska will again rely on its power running game. Signing off.*

Savannah stared at the young Princess in awe. She was every bit as beautiful as she appeared in the E-magazine cover photos. She looked every bit as athletic as her recruitment warranted. She was highly suspicious about the visit, but not for the reasons the public suspected. Her Daddy had warned her about the rising tension around the African Boy Legend in certain circles. This was one of the circles. *A very powerful circle, indeed.*

The Princess had two body guards, who stayed below under the stands. She was well wired with buttons to push or words to say, to obtain help if she needed it. *But I am safe today.*

The two nodded to each other. Finally, the Princess smiled and spoke to Savannah.

"I am Anne Wellington, Hi! I know you are Savannah Stewart, best lacrosse player in America, and affectionately known as the American Girl Superstar!" she smiled broadly and extended her hand for a handshake.

Savannah checked out the Princess by searching her eyes. She seemed young and unexposed to the vagaries of life. She appeared honest and surprisingly nice. She shook her hand.

"I am Savannah. Hi! Thank you for the compliment, but I have done nothing on the field yet!" Savannah was soon drowned out by the second eruption from the crowd. The team ran on to the field. The two of them stood and cheered as well.

"Oh my, look, there we are on the big monitor!" The Princess beamed.

The crowd roared loudly again as the Princess waved in a regal manner to the cameras. Savannah waved, too, and much to her surprise the roar seemed a bit louder for her.

Soon the roar dimmed. The Nebraskans won the toss and elected to defer. Minnesota would receive the ball at the twenty-five-yard line.

"American football is so fun to watch. We love the London team that is part of the Professional Football Association. I even know the rules. And I watch VPR football, when I am at home. It is SO intense, you know."

"I love it, too, and I am a Baltimore fan, as that is where I am from," Savannah responded, relaxing a bit, but still waiting for suggestive questions.

The young women did not speak often, other than comments on the game and specific plays, particularly when the Nebraskans were on defense, when the volume of the crowd notched up considerably.

The crowd drew silent during a commercial break. Two eagles suddenly flew into the stadium and glided across the length of the field. The crowd gasped, more than roared. The eagles perched themselves atop the goalposts. The crowd then roared loudly again. The players and coaches gaped at the eagles. They were so regal.

Gavin Blocker could not help himself. He blogged again.

*It is a tight ball game. 10-10, with two minutes until the halftime. But if on cue, two bald eagles have royally flown across the field and perched themselves on the goalposts. The regal birds are here to honor Princess Anne, I am sure! Stay tuned. The two ladies appear to have hit if off in the stadium, too.*

Princess Anne smiled. Savannah noticed she did not seem surprised or in awe of the eagles. Then again, she self-observed that she was not surprised either, as she knew the connection of the eagles to the African Boy Legend.

When the crowd quieted down in the second half after a field goal by Minnesota, the Princess turned to Savannah.

"So, when is the African Boy Legend coming to Jefferson City?" She said with suddenly cooler eyes.

Savannah hesitated. *Does the Princess suspect my Daddy has told me about the Crown's quest for the Treasures? What does Princess Anne know?*

"I don't know. I have not spoken to him since he left Africa," she responded honestly, yet coyly, and then continued. "Are you here to meet him? That is what everyone thinks. Although I heard you are a tremendous soccer player. I am sure the University would love you here as an ambassador for the school, and to support the athletics here. I would like to play with you in lacrosse, too," Savannah opened up.

"Of course, I am here to meet him. I cannot disguise that. I hear that you and he may be romantic! I will certainly compete with you for his affections!" the Princess shot back, her mouth smiling, but her eyes casting a bedeviling and competitive look.

"I see. You are here to find a Legend! We shall see. There is more to reality, than reality!" Savannah rejoined, watching the Nebraskans line up for a game tying field goal.

"Yes, I heard about your Parallel Universes! We shall see about that. Shall we?"

Savannah felt that she had said too much. She did not want to put her Daddy in jeopardy, nor herself. But she felt it important to play this out and to stay with the Princess. Who knows when and if Africus would ever arrive.

Gavin Blocker sent out another blog, after the game ended.

*Another squeaker, Nebraska wins 16-13, with a stout defense and a good field goal kicker. Two late field goals sealed the game. They are now 6-2, and 4-1 in the conference. The crowd was raucous again, supporting the defense in incredible fashion. Another home sellout. The long streak continues. And royalty was here. It is amazing. But where is Africus? It is the most popular post in the E-world. We shall keep our eyes open. The invasion of eagles again. Surely a sign? World Series Game tonight. And its Halloween! What a day! Signoff.*

Savannah saw that the Princess had latched on to her. She did not need to worry about keeping tabs on her new friend and foe. Surely, the Princess only wanted to know about her Treasures and the Cavern. But how much did the Society and the King tell her. Maybe she was a pawn in the game, too. Or maybe, like most girls in America, the thought of dating the African Boy Legend, or Africus, was too much to ignore. After all, she was a Princess and had a lot to offer over most ladies. They walked back to Savannah's dorm room for a respite before returning to the coaches' offices.

"Anne, shoot straight with me. What are you doing here in Nebraska? You can play soccer in Oxford or Cambridge!" an exasperated Savannah finally yelled out, surprised at her own words.

"I suppose I could ask you the same question? Why are you here?" the Princess replied.

"I am sure you know, but if you don't, yes, I came here to find my childhood love and dream. He is not here yet, and he may not come. I will stay here for the year, even if he does not come. After that, I don't know, but my Daddy has suddenly moved from London back to Africa, therefore, I

won't be going to London. Or did you know that already?"
Savannah feigned strength as she spoke.

"I know some things, but not everything. Look, I dis-
armed my devices, no one is listening. Of course, Africus is
the most exciting boy to come around in years, yet I know
little about him. But my father wanted me to meet him and
get to know him. He even said a courtship would be highly
beneficial. He did not say why. But I am not uneducated. I
know of the legends. I know Africus is from East Africa. I
believe it all has to do with the legends surrounding his
name, the African Boy Legend. So, your suspicions are
right, but I am on a need to know basis. I personally am not
fond of being used as a pawn! I think the legends are bunk,
of course," The Princess pouted as she looked around the
sparse dorm room.

"Well, I certainly don't know if you are gaming me, and
likely will not know. I think Africus does love me. But I am
sure that you would be quite enticing to him. And if I lost
out to a Princess, that is not the worst defeat, I suppose. But
I am not sure if he will come here. He now surely knows he
is of importance to some. I have had visions in the Parallel
Dream Universe and believe I have been in the Parallel Real
Universe. Surely you heard this, for you referenced it at the
game?" Savannah asked, befuddled and confused.

"Yes, another man briefed me before my trip. He told me
to hang out with you, and find out what I could about the
Parallel Dream Universe and Parallel Real Universe, as they
seemed to be called now, and about the legends, what you
knew about the legends, and the Cavern of Lost Treasures?
Look, I know that is what they are looking for. My father
talked of the Cavern of Lost Treasures openly ever since I
was a child. It is an obsession of all English monarchs, and
their advisors. For some reason, they think a boy raised by
lions knows where it may be. So, I am the pawn! It is that

what you needed to hear?" the Princess said with exasperation and guilt for saying too much.

"I think we both have said too much!" Savannah suddenly laughed uncontrollably.

The Princess looked at her for a brief second and then laughed heartily with her. Soon the bodyguards were knocking at the door.

"Oh, I must have turned them off. Oops!" Anne winked to Savannah.

"Maybe Nebraska is a nice place to live after all," Anne added.

The body guards followed them to the coaches' offices.

# 42.

Ms. B, AS HE CALLED HER, had driven him to North Conway, New Hampshire. It was cold, and snow had fallen freshly the night before. The autumnal color of New Hampshire had turned to green, white and blue. The red, yellow and orange had turned to brown and then nothing, as the leaves all fell to the earth. The week in Ipswich had refreshed his spirit. The press and media had not found him. Ms. B, and her conspiring neighbors and friends had seen to that. Africus really loved Ipswich, with its rich history, and beautiful views, castles, islands, beaches and New England quaintness. He had even surreptitiously played nine holes of golf in Essex on a course overlooking Ipswich Bay.

Ms. B said good-bye to him. He had told her much, and she knew to keep it all secret, especially if there were visitors in dark suits. She hugged him, and they said good-bye.

Africus had perused the internet and E-world extensively. He saw that Princess Anne had attended the Nebraska State game on Saturday. He heard from Haley that Mr. and Mrs. Stewart had suddenly left London. He had not spoken to Savannah. He missed her terribly. He knew from Haley that Mika had returned to Africa to the Preserve. He went back from Paris. He pondered the meaning of Princess Anne's trip to Nebraska. It appeared that a softer approach was being taken. And Essence ultimately wanted the English Treasures returned to England. So why the worry. He had no assurance he could succeed in returning the Treasures. If he could return the Treasures they desired most, and preserve the Preserve, the Waterfall, and Cavern and the rest of the Treasures, that would work. He needed guidance from Essence. "*Where is she?*"

*And the eagles on the goalpost. How loud a statement was that? It is my destiny to go to Nebraska State! My eagles were there. Maybe Essence awaits. Can I get to Nebraska incognito? The express super trains can get me there. Should I play football in the year 2025? So many questions.*

Africus took a smart bus to Jackson, New Hampshire. There was a well-known cross-country ski center there. He did not know how to ski, Nordic or Alpine. He was in awe of the snow. *This is fun!* He rented some skis. The young woman at the desk sold him some skiwear, as well. They laughed at his naïveté about snow. She said she would serve as his trail guide. She was incredibly attractive and athletic. But he said he needed to be lost in his thoughts. "A cup of hot chocolate will await your return," she promised.

He skied clumsily at first at the trail headed up the Saco River. But he soon picked up the rhythm and cadence of the sport. He was skiing freely when he first spotted the river. *The stream is magnificent in its natural splendor.* The gently roar of the descending water, still not frozen, was invigorating and relaxing. He thought of the stream leading to the Waterfall. But it was colder here.

He headed north toward the end of the trail. He detoured onto some more difficult trails. He was climbing higher into the terrain. As he was lost in the quiescence and tranquility of the forest, a black bear started to follow him. The bear was female and not threatening him. It was not quite time to hibernate. This had been an early snow fall. One good for skiers, but not for bears trying to fatten up before their winter hibernation.

After a while he noticed the bear appeared to keep pace with him and follow him to different trail junctures. A few skiers would ski by at a faster pace. But the bear meandered along. Africus took off his skis and left them on the trail. He walked directly towards the bear. The bear did not seem to care. She kept eating berries. She did not look at him at all but expressed no concern at his approach. Africus had never seen or interacted with a bear. He did not know if his communicative abilities with animals extended to bears in North America. But they worked with the coy dogs. Finally, he was right next to the bear. He picked a handful of berries and extended his open hand to the bear. She ate the berries off of his hand.

He felt a powerful presence. He felt no fear.

"Is it you, Essence? I suppose there are no zebras in America!"

The bear turned slowly around, and she stared at Africus directly into his eyes. He instantly recognized the eyes of his long-time friend and guide.

"Oh, Africus, I have put you through so much. It was not intended to be this stressful," she said as she continued to eat berries.

"It is great to see you. I am glad you found me," he replied with relief.

"I am glad you are deep into the country. Cities do not work for me. But I know you have asked for my guidance. Are you not glad that you have the ability to communicate with your guides?

"You will find out about your past. Be prepared for these revelations. I cannot tell you this information now. But I can tell you some things. Mr. Stewart has the knowledge of your past, but I do not know if he will tell you. Savannah is in love with you, and not against you. She is not privy to the conspiracy that surrounds you. She is a part of it, but only as a pawn. And you are a pawn as well. The Princess Anne is of good heart and is a pawn as well. But the game of pawns is a good one.

"I will guide you on your decisions regarding the disposition of the English Treasures, but it your decision. I am not averse to the return of certain of the English Treasures. But that needs to be determined by you and those that you will meet. But the Treasures, if returned, must go to the King of England, not the Society that lurks in the background. The Treasures that abound in the Cavern other than those of King Arthur must stay there. The chalice may be returned to Gloucester. As the professor knows, Gloucester was the birthplace of King Richard II.

"Go Africus and enjoy Nebraska State and Savannah! You may like Anne, too, and certainly it is your choice, of whom to marry. That is up to you! I now have to get ready to hibernate!" Essence strolled away.

Africus followed her for a while. But dusk was arriving. He swung back to the trailhead and headed back to the lodge. The sweet New Hampshire girl was there with his hot chocolate by a warm fire.

"Hi, my name is Anne," she said, locks of curly light brown hair dangling across her forehead, the firelight twinkling in her green eyes.

Hmm, he thought.

# 43.

Tuesday, November 4, 2025
*Jefferson City, Nebraska*

SAVANNAH HEADED STRAIGHT to Coach Haley An-
drew's office. She was in tears and shaking uncontrollably. Haley met her at the doorway and sat her
down on the chair across from her desk. She
pulled up another chair next to her, closed the door, and
wrapped her arms around her like a mother would of her
child.

"I received a call from Africus. He said he is not coming
to Nebraska State. He is going to finish his semester as an
online student. He is in New Hampshire. I think he is with
another girl. I think it is Princess Anne! She said she was
going to stop in New England prior to returning to England. I suspected she meant to visit Harvard or Yale. But not
to see Africus!" She pouted more loudly.

"How could that be? I suppose I know, just as you may
know," Haley said glumly.

"My source is my Daddy. He has not told me everything,
I am sure. But I know that a secret Society is involved, and
that the English Crown is involved, and they want their
Treasures back, and I have seen the Treasures in my

dreams, my Parallel Dream Universe, and I believe in reality in the Parallel Real Universe, as Africus calls it, too. So, Africus is the key to unlocking the mysteries of the hidden Treasures. I think the Crown would love to have Africus in the royal family to secure his loyalty and cooperation! How can I compete with a Princess! She is just as good as an athlete as me! And just as pretty, if not more beautiful! She told me a lot. She knows what we know. She thinks she is a pawn. I trusted her. Maybe I was foolish. I feel betrayed. The guards whisked her away quickly. Maybe their intelligence found Africus in New Hampshire!" Savannah burst into tears and held her face in her hands.

"Africus sent me a text saying that he was fine. That he was in the mountains of Jackson, New Hampshire. There was a bear! It was a female bear. Maybe it is the bear you are thinking about? And she was a Special Being. Not sure what that is, but it sounds surreal," Haley tried to soothe her.

"The bear was likely Essence. I have seen Essence in my Parallel Universes, too. I saw her in Colorado, too, as a mountain lion. In Africa, she is the white zebra, or sometimes, Citra. I think she was a guide or more to Queen Guinevere and King Arthur!"

Savannah started to relax on news about Essence. "You know... Maybe, I was once Guinevere. I think Essence was suggesting that to me in my Parallel Universes!" Savannah suddenly looked up into the maternal eyes of Haley, wiping her tears away with her lacrosse jersey sleeve.

"Well, a Queen is certainly higher than a Princess! Particularly one that is a pawn!" Haley laughed with Savannah.

"I need to see Africus. I need to enter the Parallel Real Universe with Essence and Africus again. Maybe he and I should keep the English Treasures! Maybe they are his and mine!" Savannah started to talk quickly and excitedly. Haley wondered about the Parallel Universes and Savannah's fantasies about Africus.

"I think you are suggesting Africus is a King!"

"Well, I know that is a stretch, but he is the King of the Cavern of Lost Treasures!"

"Well, ok, let us not get too carried away, well, maybe, let's do just that!"

Haley started to gather increased excitement about all that seemed so fantastic, yet so real. *It would be nice to believe.* But in any event, she had to make sure Africus was all right. That the trap was not set for him. The thought of Society agents capturing him in New Hampshire suddenly alarmed her. She fired off a quick text to him.

"Be wary of Princess Anne of England!!!"

Savannah desperately tried to reach Africus as well, but to no avail. She made repeated warnings about Princess Anne.

# 44.

AFRICUS SAT ON THE CHAIR of his room. He had sat there most of the night. Lying on the bed was the cutest girl he had ever met other than Savannah. He did not know much about her. They were romantic for a while but stopped short of all out passion. He sensed she was someone other than a ski instructor. *Her name is Anne, but is it Princess Anne? Na, can't be her. She could not get here that quickly. But maybe. Let me play this out. It does look like her the more I look at her!* He felt some guilt not being with Savannah, and for not telling her in person that he was not going to attend the University. He still was uncertain as to his plans regarding the Treasures. He decided to open his smart device. He read the messages and texts. "Ah!" He said.

Anne awoke and stared enticingly at Africus. He suspected she may have known he was Africus, even if she was not the Princess. But now it was a new game. A chance to solve the mystery of the Treasures for the Crown and the Society, and move on with his life, maybe at the Preserve, maybe in

Nebraska, maybe even in London. *Or maybe I should protect the Treasures.*

"You look quite regal this morning. May I get you some tea?" Africus asked, with a twinkle in his eye, and a sly smile curling his lips.

Anne was silent.

"And how was Nebraska State? Are the guards outside ready to take me away? I hope they don't torture me! I may need to ask my friends in the animal kingdom to help me if they do that!" he threatened with a smile still on his face.

"Africus, I am Princess Anne. My devices are turned off. You are not being monitored. The guards are not going to capture you. We don't know if any of the legends are true. But this is the closest the Crown has been in years. And you don't have royal blood! So, you and I can marry!"

"Wait! What! You are going too fast. What does royal blood have to do with this? Are you saying I was not King Arthur? Marriage! We just met! What!" Africus was uneasy, his heart pounding. He feared this was the moment of truth, where information about his ancestry in the real world would be revealed. He waited with baited breath.

"Oh, I see you know little. I am not sure that I am the one to tell you. But we are not related. The Crown wants the Treasures back in London. They sent me to capture your heart and bring you and your Treasures to the Palace! After being with you for the night, I am sure we are meant for each other!" Anne desperately reached out, now willing to share herself with the man who might be the reincarnation of King Arthur himself.

"This is too wild for me. Tell me what you know about my bloodlines! NOW!" he screamed, trembling in fear and anxiety.

"I will but hold me in your arms when I tell you! I Love You!"

Africus lay next to her. He kept his clothes on, but held her and looked deeply into her eyes, waiting.

"I only know that you do not have royal blood. I heard that originally, you were supposed to have had royal blood, but you don't. You were a genetic match of two gifted people. One, I believe, your father, has passed. I don't know who they are, but my father does. It is a deep secret. But because the original plan of using royal heritage was abandoned, I am not related to you. So, the plan was for me to capture your heart and trust to lead us to the Treasures. But you have captured my heart! I will do what you want me to do. I don't care about the Treasures! I really like Savannah. I feel awful that I am doing this to her! But if you want her, I understand, too!" Anne started to cry sincerely and deeply. True Love she thought was so fleeting. Maybe the Parallel Real Universe was real? She wanted to go there in the worst way.

Africus was stunned. He was a pawn, too, not a King. He was sure his biological parents were extraordinary. The thought of the lion pride hit him hard. *Of course, the lions with their seemingly supernatural intelligence. They have access to the Parallel Dream Universe and their leader has the Knowledge to gain Passage through the Portal to the Parallel Real Universe, a Knowledge I now possess. I have always had access to the Parallel Dream Universe. Did that come from the lions. Does Essence guide me because of my relationship to the Cavern? She is the guardian of the Cavern.*

"This is crazy! My whole life, all a part of a scheme! I don't know. I don't know!" He shouted to Anne.

Africus left Anne's embrace. He crawled from the bed and returned to his chair facing her across the room.

"I have much to ponder. This is too large for me. I am just a ranger boy from Africa. Or maybe a farm boy in the future in Nebraska. We shall see," he stated, staring blankly out of the window at the snow-covered fields and gray sky.

"Let me be part of your journey. Take me to Africa. Take me to your Parallel Real Universe!" Anne now begged, mindless of her stature as a Princess.

"You sound sincere. But I do not trust you. But I need you to meet someone. Let us go skiing in Jackson. How did you become a ski guide at the center after arriving on Sunday?" He asked.

"Ms. B told us she would bring you there. She was promised a trip to the Palace in exchange. I was just a volunteer guide to help new skiers, that's all. I was not part of the resort at all. I was just there for you!" She admitted, now with a stealthy smile.

Well, do you even know how to ski?"

"I do. Let's ski Africus!"

Africus and Princess Anne skied deep into the woods, on the same river trail he had skied the day before. Africus was hopeful the bear would still be around, and not yet hibernated for the winter. He hoped Essence was still within the bear, too. A wild bear would not be a great encounter.

Princess Anne was now more interested in Africus than her task as a pawn of the Crown in securing the Treasures. She did her best to show off her athleticism, skiing faster than Africus on the trail, and taking the most difficult trail for him to follow. Soon she had sped ahead beyond a steep uphill turn. Africus was unsure of where she was.

Africus heard a hysterical scream. He sped forward as fast as he could. He turned around the turn where Anne had sped ahead. There was Anne surrounded by five wolves. Wolves had recently migrated east into the green and white mountains but had not attacked humans in any reported cases. Africus saw there was no bear around. He had no weapons. The wolves were howling. Africus kept skiing toward them. He would not let the Princess die alone.

Anne was stone cold in fear. She did not move. She heard Africus skiing closer. Soon he was next to her. She did not take her gaze off the alpha male, the leader of the wolves.

Africus was suddenly one in communication with the wolf pack. *Just like the coy dogs, the wolves are like the lions. They communicate with each other, mind to mind. I am in sync with them, and they know it.* The wolves closed their mouths, hiding their fangs, and sat on their haunches. It was if Africus and Anne were now part of the pack.

"Anne, you are safe, but do not take any aggressive actions. I think we can leave, and they will not follow us. Take my hand and turn your skis around to go back downhill. Can you downhill on Nordic skis! Ha!" he teased.

Anne suddenly felt warmth and safety. Her attraction to Africus intensified. *A knight has saved me from distress. How thoroughly romantic.*

"Anne, I was here to meet a special person, a guide, if you will, or Special Being from the Parallel Dream Universe, really, the Great Realm, with access to our world and the Parallel Universes. She was here yesterday as a bear. I fear she has left for the winter."

The wolves appeared to understand the conversation. Anne now was drawn into the circle of communication, as well. *The bear is still gathering berries over the ridge.* The skis would have to be removed. The wolves started hiking up the mountain. Africus and Anne removed their skis and followed the wolves.

"The legend is true! You are the African Boy Legend! The King of the Cavern of Lost Treasures! Once King Arthur! It is in this world, not just in the Parallel Universes!"

Anne cried out, holding Africus' arm tightly as they climbed the steep mountain.

The air grew colder, and the wolves marched on. Soon they were in the wolves' den. Some wolf pups ran to Africus and played with him. Anne petted one of them. It nuzzled into her lap and would not move.

Across the den entrance, a large female black bear ambled in. Normally, bears and wolves were enemies. But the wolves were in sync with Africus and the bear. They knew it was Essence, a leader from the Parallel Dream Universe and the Great Realm.

The bear looked at Anne. She was startled, but now believed everything, including that the Treasures were likely very real and attainable. She was on high alert, as her conscious mind started to gather strength, and her loyalty to her father, the King, was just as strong as her new attraction to the African Boy Legend. Her competing yearnings tugged and pulled at her soul. She just held on.

"Princess Anne, I am Essence. I am the spiritual guide to Africus. I was with him in a magical kingdom long ago. One where, I suppose you already know, he was King. You are to be part of our team. At some point in the future, maybe now or in decades or centuries, we need to bring certain English Treasures back to England, but we need to keep sacred and secret the Cavern of Lost Treasures. You will be instrumental here. We need you to talk to the King in a secure place. Tell him about the Treasures. Maybe he will want them to remain safe in the Cavern. The Society may have different plans. Can we trust you? If the King wants the English Treasures now, you will need to get them to England safely. Many people throughout the world will want to take the Treasures. I speak to you in your mind, as I suspect that not only the Society and King are listening in now, but also possibly the United State intelligence community, and Russians and Chinese government intelligence or secret societies. The power of the sword Excalibur is indeed extraordinary and of priceless value. As are the crowns of King Arthur and Queen Guinevere. Africus and I suspect that the Treasures should remain in safekeeping in the Cavern for now. The knowledge of the King of their existence should be cause for enormous jubilation in and of itself!"

Anne was stunned. But she understood the magnitude of bringing the sacred Treasures to the world. She spoke back in her mind, only.

"Shall I keep this all silent for now? Shall I reveal that Africus is only a ranger boy and dreamer! And return home! It can be just my secret. Someday, I shall be Queen, and then the secret shall be with the Crown! Or do I reveal the secret now to my father, the King. Should Africus and I meet my father in London, or even East Africa?"

Essence responded, again in her mind. "I have been the guardian of the Treasures for centuries. It has been my mission to return the Treasures to the Crown at some point, and Africus is now in charge of that process. But Africus and Anne, I think the time to inform the King about the English Treasures is now. Their disposition and return should be discussed now with the King. Africus believes it may not be possible to protect the Treasures once they have entered your Real Universe. An army may not be sufficient to protect them. Maybe the world is simply not ready for such a revelation of extraordinary magnitude and mystical proportions. But ultimately Anne, it is your decision with your father and Africus, the new King of the Cavern. The Society will want to control the process. But their role was to safeguard the Treasures and their location, and they failed. I have taken over their role! I do not believe they should have any role in the process.

"But, let us not just tell you of the Treasures. So, I have a plan. You shall enter the Parallel Dream Universe. I shall show you the Treasures with Africus," Essence exhaled.

Soon Anne was asleep, as was Africus. They all entered the Parallel Dream Universe and were soon traveling across space and time dimensions to the Cavern of Lost Treasures.

Anne rode atop a white zebra with Africus riding behind her with his arms around her waist. They rode deep into the Cavern. The sound of the water stream was calming and soothing. Anne dismounted in awe at the sight of the sword in the stone. Africus walked to the stone and pulled out the sword. Anne gasped in awe. He replaced the sword and took her to the boulders that held the two crowns.

"The last time I was here, in person, in the Parallel Real Universe, Providence, or Savannah, as you know her, was with me, and wore the crown. You see she was once Queen Guinevere! I wore the crown of King Arthur! It looks like I was him! Essence has stated that! And here is Excalibur, the most famous and magical sword of all time!" Africus told her, in a professorial tone.

Anne was amazed and in wonder. It was the happiest she had ever been.

"Was I a part of all of this? Or am I just a future admirer, afar in time and space?"

Essence grabber her and held her.

"Yes, you were part of the inner circle, as was your father. You were the maiden of honor for King Arthur and Guinevere, and your father was King Arthur's father. You loved King Arthur as you do now. To this day, you compete for his affections with Savannah. I think history may repeat itself. But these are our secrets, and certainly, we now put them in trust with you!" Essence forewarned Anne.

Soon the cycle of sleep driven dreams subsided, and they all returned to the wolf den. When Africus and Anne awoke, the bear and the wolves were gone. Nightfall was approaching. Over the silence, they heard the roar of snowmobiles.

"Anne, your guards are here to rescue you, and likely capture me. Go to them. I will hide. Recall the trust we have put in you. Let me know what your father says. I can meet him, too, maybe after the Thanksgiving holidays in the U.S. But don't tell the Society. And don't mention the Treasures that are not from England."

Africus gazed into her eyes again. He leaned over and softly kissed her on the lips.

"I will reach out to my father in person and in private, and only tell him, not the Society! But I will still try to win your heart next time around!" Anne smiled broadly.

Africus took off with great swiftness and agility. He easily found the well-hidden bear cave, where the bear had gone to hibernate. He would not be found there.

Anne left her skis and jumped on the back of the snowmobiles. Soon a helicopter picker her up.

She kept her secret for now and kept the dogs off the scent of the trail.

# 45.

COACH SMITH ADDRESSED his team at halftime. A forlorn quarterback Pierce held his head in his hands. He had nullified a tremendous defensive effort by the Nebraska State defense in shutting out the nation's leading offense. His pick six as Nebraska State was marching down the Oklahoma side of the field was devastating. His ensuing fumble on the twenty-five-yard line after the kickoff, was mind boggling. Oklahoma was up 10-0. RIP was steaming. His defense had performed so well.

"We get the ball back at the start of the half. I am going for it on every fourth down. We are going to run it down their throats! Offensive line, this is your time! This is the grandest tradition of the Nebraska State football! Pound it!"

Tamaric Jones sat next to Pierce. He put his arm around him.

"Just hand the ball off. You will be fine. We will try a play-action pass or two, short passes only. This game is not on your shoulders. Keep your head up," he tried to console his protégé.

The team sat silent. Smith left the room.

Shannon Garrison stood by the door way and grabbed the coach when he left the room. They spoke briefly. Tamaric Jones saw him. Coach Smith was frantic but said nothing. *He has a bounce to his step. Shannon just smiled at Coach Smith!*

The teams entered the field. Gavin Blocker sat up in the press box and prepared to flip his update to his followers.

*The defense was so good in the first half. But ineptitude at quarterback is finally catching up to us. A win and in, has been the motto. We are 7-1 in conference play, in second place. Oklahoma is 8-0. We win the tie-breaker if we win today. But Oklahoma's offense can't be stopped much longer. We shall see. It likely will take a miracle to win this game. Next year. Well, still no quarterback recruit. The Africus fantasy appears still to be the greatest hoax of all time. Even the Princess of England was fooled by all the excitement! The Crown issued a statement protecting her and denying any part of the hoax. I was fooled myself! Shannon Garrison was fired by Nebraska State for the hoax. She had even gone to Africa to perpetuate this fantasy. Haley Andrews will finish out the year. Savannah Stewart said she would stay for the spring. That saved Haley's job. Mika Williams is nowhere to be found. The ranger named Africus is a real person, but not the mythical, legendary superhero we all craved for. He is nowhere to be found either. It was all so crazy. But we all wanted to believe that a star from Africa could come to Nebraska State and lead the team to victory! I know I did. Shannon has gone to Spiritis. She makes so much money now, it is insane. They even have an Africus sneaker they are going to sell in the spring for lacrosse. Not sure there will be many sales if he stays AWOL. Shannon denies any wrongdoing. She still says he is a sensational athlete! But we have left that behind us now. We still have a good bowl game we will go to. We still have the American Girl Superstar. Well, let's see if Joseph can pound some yards for us. Signoff.*

# 46.

P RINCESS ANNE WAS AWAKENED by the buzzing
of her smart device. She opened the device. There
was a link. She opened it. She was stunned.

"Nebraska State beats Oklahoma! We love you
Africus! The roar of the African Boy Legend!"

The headlines kept pouring in. She opened a video link,
all 360 degrees of it. There was Africus flying down the
sideline for a touchdown. There was Africus flying through
the Oklahoma offensive line for a strip-sack. Then another
touchdown run for Africus. She did not know what to make
of it. She thought Africus was going back to the Preserve.
The video streams were so vivid. She played with her smart
device and watched the runs at every angle.

Soon her father and the man with no name summoned
her to the study in the Palace.

"We see that Africus is alive and well. You said that he
was going back to the Preserve. We wanted to meet him
there and retrieve our Treasures. We have been waiting patiently for him to return, and not to capture him. Now it
appears he may not be returning at all. Our Treasures are

more important than your crush on a fantastic boy. His celebrity will prevent us from kidnapping him. But there are others who may try to kidnap him. You say he would rather die, than give up his secrets. So, I think you need to talk to him. To save his life. We are putting heat on Sir Francis Stewart to have his daughter talk to him as well. Africus can return to the United States, once we have what is ours."

The man with no name stopped his conversation. Her father was the King, and he nodded in agreement. She was not sure who had the power here.

"Your father is King. I work for him. My Society is his protector. Do not fret, my dear."

Anne looked at him with disdain. She had lied to them. She had decided to keep the secret to herself and save it until she was Queen. She had told them there were no Treasures, and no lost Cavern. That they were the stuff of wild dreams of a boy raised in the wild. But now she knew they had never believed her. She also had lied and said Africus was returning to the Preserve to be a ranger, and that his only power was his great ability to work with animals. The press had not picked up on the Africus connection with the Cavern of Lost Treasures. It still had not, either.

"I do not control him. And how do you know he can lead you to the Treasures. It has been centuries."

"He sent a picture of a lost chalice from the time of King Richard II. It is authentic. He may have been lucky, and simply found it, as it has been rumored to have been stored in Africa. But the coincidence seems too much. Plus, this is all we have. We have not even sniffed the Treasures in centuries. And there is the legend of a boy with the medieval sword taking down the Ugandan army in Kenya. It is a legend, but how else could a single boy defeat such a large army. And our sources state that the army was after Africus and the Cavern of Lost Treasures. We also know that the bounty hunter and poacher Igor was sent from Russia to find him," the man with no name continued, in a more conciliatory manner.

"After his championship game next Saturday, we would like him to fly to the Preserve. We have Mika Williams in custody. We also have Minimilion, his lion friend," her father told her, not very happy about his doings.

"That is blackmail and wrong!" she shouted.

"We don't have much else."

"Look, Essence is not sure the Treasures will be safe in London at the Palace. Not even an army can protect the Treasures. Excalibur is priceless and all powerful!"

Anne gasped that she had broken the secret. She fell back trembling. The world was caving in.

The King and the man with no name said were wide eyed.

"Our plans need to be accelerated," the man with no name exclaimed, breathing heavily and sweating profusely.

"Excalibur!" the King roared.

"But it is not yours!" Anne shouted.

"Africus was King Arthur! Savannah was Queen Guinevere! The crowns are theirs!"

Anne fainted in the heat of the moment. She was depleted of all of her energy.

The King looked at the man with no name.

"Is that possible?"

"It may be why Africus has access to the Cavern. The elven-like monkeys know who he is or was. This is sounding more real by the moment. No mention of the sword in the stone, or any of Merlin's magical wands," he responded.

"We need to keep our timetable. And we need to find this Essence! Who is Essence?" the man with no name continued, in dire desperation. He combed his jet-black hair back with his right hand. His hair was wet from perspiration.

"Maybe this is all too much. Maybe the Treasures are safer in the Cavern. Even knowing they exist is a breakthrough for us. We have years to retrieve them. I think we keep the circle small. Shannon Garrison has some knowledge as does Haley Andrews and Mika Williams. And of course, the Stewart family. I think the Sir Francis Stewart will be cooperative. I do not think his wife knows any specifics. She has always thought of her daughter as a dreamer," the King ruminated, scratching his chin.

The King continued his rumination. "Let's plan a meeting next Tuesday in Nebraska after the championship game. It should be a fun game to watch. Nebraska State takes on the powerful school from Maryland. We will not attend the game, of course," the King said.

"That is the plan then. I will make sure it happens. We will make sure Igor is taken care of, too."

Off they left.

# 47.

Monday, December 1, 2025
Jefferson City, Nebraska

ALEXANDER HAMILTON HALL was the home of the American history department. Africus was late for class. He had not returned with the team. He had returned by a smart bus on his own. The campus was fearful he would not return. The campus had erupted in exuberance and hysteria over his entrance into the game and their lives. It was not often that dreams and fantasy became reality. It was not often that the real world exceeded the dream world. It was not often that reality exceeded dreams.

Africus entered the building. He tried to be inconspicuous. He slipped into the back row. There were many empty seats. Many students used the e-lecture technology for lecture courses. He went unnoticed. The professor was lost in her notes and did not look up either.

But Africus's heart was pumping furiously. The game was easy compared to this. But he saw her in the first row. Her blonde hair glistened in the overhead fluorescent light. She was tall and athletic. She was locked in attention to the lecture, so it seemed. He had not talked to her after the game.

They had texted, but he had gone offline. He was still nervous about the Treasure hunters. At least for now, Princess Anne had kept her secret. He had not heard from her, but he still had his smart device turned off.

She must have felt his presence. Whether it was their connection through the Parallel Universes, or just his overall aura, his presence seemed near.

Many in the press had said he was a one-shot wonder. Oklahoma was challenging his eligibility to play. The Conference of the North championship game to be held in Chicago was still up in the air.

But she felt his presence, if not his stare.

She knew if she turned and looked, the students around her would do the same. So, she held her poise. Slowly, she turned her head, as if pondering a large thought from the Professor. She had written one of the best papers for her class, so the professor seemed pleased that her prize student seemed to have grasped some deep meaning from her prior point of emphasis.

But Savannah had not heard the words at all. She strained to look through her peripheral vision. She knew what to look for. Not many boys had long hair these days. She thought there might even be a scent from the jungle, or the smell of wild animal.

Africus saw her head turn. He gathered she sensed his presence. He turned on his smart device. He was going to text her.

But to his alarm there were desperate messages from Princess Anne. A meeting was to be held on Tuesday after the championship game out in a farm in a rural town north west of Jefferson City. And if there was no game, then the meeting would be this Wednesday. There was a warning about Igor, too. He was deeply concerned. He wished he had nothing to do with the Treasures.

Soon his mind relaxed. He had faced many battles. He had defeated Igor twice. He could defeat him again. He would convince the King to preserve the Treasures in their safe haven. But now for more important matters. *True love. Will my love surpass my surprising feelings for Princess Anne? Is Essence right about my prior life. Are Essence and the Parallel Universes real at all? Yes, they are real!*

"I know you sense I am looking at you! Meet me after class. I will sneak out early not to cause a commotion. Meet me under the big maple tree behind the school library. Most students are at class. It should be quiet. Wow! You are so beautiful. You have a nice profile! Could you see me in your peripheral vision? Or were you not even thinking about me?" Africus sent the text.

Savannah's smart device was off. But her computer was open for taking notes and tracking the professors references real time online. A notification of a text popped up and made a slight buzz. Her heart pounded so loudly she thought the professor could hear it. She slowly turned her head back and looked at the professor, who oddly was looking at her. She feigned to take some serious notes and hoped this was not the time the professor would ask one of her famous thought-provoking questions, which Savannah was often the one who raised her hand first for an initial, usually perceptive response.

She opened the text, and flushed beat red. Her hands trembled, her breathing accelerated. She thought she would hyperventilate. Another text came in.

"Relax! It is me! Smile and exhale! My heart is pounding, too! But I am smiling and breathing!"

She followed his advice, and texted back.

"Leave now! I will follow shortly. I can't wait until the end of the lecture!"

"We can watch it online together later!"

Africus silently, like a jaguar, left the large room. The professor noticed him though, just as he left. She let out a gasp. The students turned, but he was gone. She gathered herself. She looked at Savannah and winked. *She knows,* Savannah thought. *So much for provocative statements,* the professor thought.

The class murmured and stared at Savannah. They sensed something was up. She retained her cool. She fired another text to Africus. "I will finish the class. Too much commotion."

Africus slithered quickly to the library and beyond. He dodged passersby quite well. He put a cap on his head and tucked his hair underneath. He was still tall. *But there are plenty of tall Nebraska boys here.* High above, he saw two eagles. He felt safe and protected. *Somewhere, Essence may be near. Maybe as cat or even a squirrel. Who knows.* Essence had put him together with Savannah, which is what he would call her in America, with the name Providence reserved for Africa and the Parallel Universes. He remembered his countless dreams of her in the Parallel Dream Universe. He recalled with happiness when he met her in person in Africa at the Waterfall and the Cavern. But now he was to meet her in the Real Universe for more than a glimpse of time and space. *Will the magic of seven years ago and the Waterfall and Cavern still be there? I can feel her spirit. I think the magic will always be there!*

Africus found the maple tree and sat up against it. He thought he felt its energy coursing through the trunk and the branches and leaves. He watched his smart device. No more messages. One alert. A man named Igor had been apprehended in London. Hmm. *The Crown is protecting me.* Another alert. He was fully eligible to play in the game. *Shannon has done her job! Somewhere she is smiling.* He had never met her, either, but thought he may have seen her in the chaos after the game in Oklahoma. *Someday, I will meet her.* And Haley. He had to see her after he met Savannah. She was a fine foster mother to him. She always meant well. It was cold in the Midwest, but he liked it so far.

Alas, the class was over. He knew Savannah would not arrive without a posse. So, it was possible he would have to wait to see her. *There will be chaos.* But eventually, he hoped he would mesh in, and be part of the whole, not a catalyst for hysteria and riots. Riots, good in nature, had overtaken the campus on Saturday night. *The victory must have been transcendental,* he speculated. *An historic rivalry renewed.*

A new text. "Meet me at the Barn on Pleasant farm, three miles north of the city. My friend's family owns the farm. No one is there right now. They are away for the winter."

Africus found directions to the farm. He grabbed a community bike and began his journey. He arrived there in fifteen minutes. He needed a place to stay, as well. In the commotion of the celebrations after the game, he had forgotten to secure living quarters. Shannon was not there to care for him. And Haley was not around yet, as she had gone home to Massachusetts for Thanksgiving with Lindsay.

He found the Barn. There was a horse in the Barn. He went to the horse and stroked its head. Essence winked at him.

"And of course, you would be here, when I meet her!" He laughed, with a beaming smile.

"I am already here, Africus! Up in the loft!" Savannah laughed, too.

Essence whinnied in approval.

Africus climbed the ladder up into the hayloft. It was a slight bit warmer, but not much. Savannah was underneath a horse blanket. He crawled underneath with her. All pretense fell away. Memories of their first meetings in Africa burst forth like a new flower in spring. *The Waterfall and Cavern. In the Parallel Real Universe!* They embraced in deep passion. They kissed again. It was still love, still powerful, still real, and still fantastic, they both thought. They stayed embraced and held each other for the next hour. Soon the horse down below started to neigh a little louder and longer.

They smiled and laughed and talked of their first meeting. Africus told her of his long journey from New Hampshire, and the fun he had traveling in the United States, somehow keeping a low profile. But the subject of Princess Anne soon came up.

"And did you see Princess Anne?" Savannah questioned him, nervous about the response.

Essence listened carefully. She was still confounded by what would happen with the Treasures.

"Essence is here. I think we have plenty to talk about. But after seeing you just now. I can tell you that my love for you is stronger. It is timeless I think! Is that not right Essence?"

Savannah was concerned about competing with a Princess. She just said nothing.

Essence spoke softly into their minds. A talking horse would freak out anyone nearby.

Savannah was soon up to speed again about the meeting for next week and happenings in New Hampshire. She was jealous that Anne had been to the Parallel Dream Universe but understood given her role in the original kingdom and the current kingdom in England.

"What are we to do. What will come from this meeting? The Society will be there. Did Anne break her secret? Or maybe it was the King who brought in the Society. It seems they may want the Treasures now. Even the Treasures from Atlantis! Will there be no discussion?" Africus asked, stumbling on what to do next.

Essence stayed silent. As did Savannah. Africus pondered his plan and then spoke again.

"I think it is up to me. I will meet with them, as they will track me down no matter what. You know that I believe that the Treasures are now safe from the greed of men and governments, and that they should stay safe in the Cavern. So, my plan is that we take the King to the Cavern in the Parallel Dream Universe in the dream state. Hopefully, that will quench his thirst. If he truly wishes to protect the Treasures of the Crown, he will leave the Treasures there. The secret will remain with the Crown and the Society until technology catches up with this fantasy. It will be passed on through the line of kings and queens, and heads of the Society. That is my plan for now."

"Well, that sounds good. But they know that a few of us know the secret. I fear for my Daddy. Even myself. And would it not be better for the one person on earth who has access to the Cavern to be married into royalty? Might they make that part of the bargain?" Savannah queried, sitting with her eyebrows deeply furrowed in worry.

"Your safety and that of others, like Shannon and my foster parents from the Preserve must be protected," Africus assured her.

"And?"

"Yes, of course. You are my true love!" Africus held her again in his arms.

Essence chirped in. "I would leave out the Society. They already failed. But you can see how that goes. I am leaving now. Be kind to this horse. I think she would like to take the two of you for a romantic ride around the farm!"

Essence appeared to exhume herself from the horse. Africus and Savannah were soon galloping around the farm in a joyous reunion.

# 48.

AFRICUS ENTERED THE COACHES' office of the Head Football Coach. Coach Smith, Coach Tamaric Jones and Haley Andrews were all there. He sat down at the table with the three coaches.

"So, you played three plays, and scored two touchdowns and caused a turnover. We won 14-10, and now are the Western division champions of the Conference of the North. We are now playing in the championship game for the conference in Chicago against the Eastern Division Champions from Maryland. Win and we receive an automatic bid to the College football tourney," Coach Smith said as a matter of fact.

There was silence. Then the three coaches broke out in laughter.

"Africus, I can't believe you decided to show up in the middle of the game. How did you pull that off?" Haley asked in disbelief.

"Well, I had called Shannon. She was always the one to work out the details. I had been traveling in the United States and had thought about watching this game in person.

I had gone to California and was heading back east, before I returned to Africa, or came to Nebraska State in the Spring. Shannon and I discussed this at length. We decided to keep it a secret. She had secured the uniform for me, and a pass into the game. Of course, Coach Jones was in on it, too, and somehow, kept it secret! Shannon had already cleared me to play weeks ago. And Coach Jones had put me on the roster. Everyone thought it was part of the hoax, and Coach Smith left my name on the roster to spook the Oklahomans. So, it all worked. I am glad you put me in the game. Coach Jones had drawn up those two plays for me. And you practiced them with one of the scout receivers. That was fun. I like football!" Africus smiled beaming with pride.

Haley smiled at Coach Smith with a mischievous smirk.

"You knew, too, I see."

"Of course, I did. Good to see you again Africus!" The coach bellowed.

"So, Jones, what do we do with Africus this week. Maryland will be all over him when he comes in the game next Saturday. He is too new to play quarterback; the plays are too involved and extensive. Maybe for the playoffs, if then. Of course, there is next year," Coach Smith interrogated his position coach, with a menacing look.

"I say we come up with four or five new plays. And we play him at defensive rush end on passing downs, if RIP is ok with that. I don't think he can be blocked. Maybe even play some outside linebacker as the game progresses. His instincts on hunting and tackling may be superhuman, so to speak," Jones offered.

"Ok, create the plays. Tell RIP to incorporate him into the game plan, too. Vegas is going nuts on how to handicap this game! Ha! The press is everywhere. Africus, how do you avoid them so well. I see your sweetheart is doing quite well with the press. And the reporters are now all over the

Princess Anne angle again. Seems her story about her interest in a football program, soccer, was really a ruse after all. Her interest was in a star from Africa! HA!"

"Yeah, Princess Anne. We shall see about her," Africus looked out into the distance to the track field below the coaches' windows.

"We offered Shannon her position back. But she declined, for now. I think now that you are really here, those Africus shoes will have to be renamed. I hope she changes her mind and comes back, even though it will be a pay cut," Coach Smith lamented.

"I miss Shannon, too," Haley added.

Africus thought about the meeting next week with English royalty. He thought about the safety of Shannon and Haley. His mind was calculating. Survival was always first. *A trip with the King to the Cavern in the Parallel Dream Universe might work. It worked with Anne.*

Africus entered the football facilities. They were state of the art, having been redone in 2024, and were the envy of programs nationwide. He passed by the staff studying their virtual computer programs and simulations and 3D imaging and holograms. He again walked by the nutrition center, tops in the country, where he had already enjoyed some sumptuous meals. And there were the health professionals, researching, monitoring and implementing the latest health and safety strategies and techniques. *No wonder so few players are banged up.* Africus's head was spinning. This virtual and modern world was amazing and confusing.

Africus was on his way to his third practice. *I already feel like a member of the pride. It is indeed a family atmosphere, even with the general-like Coach Smith. My teammates liked my stories about the jungle and Maximilion and even Minimilion My story about Savannah was the most captivating, as they all daydreamed of meeting a girl in such a storybook way. I won't tell them stories about the poachers and the army of Uganda or reveal the Water-fall, Paradise or the Cavern of Lost Treasures. Maybe later.*

Africus looked forward to practice. But thoughts of his escalating fame overwhelmed him. He still avoided the press. Wild stories and hyperbole that were filling the E-waves. "Africus Mania is Sweeping the Nation," he saw a few headlines read. He had watched the local kids from Jefferson City pack the campus quads and cheer wildly when he walked by. *A country in search of a real-time hero, not just the virtual heroes, is catching on.*

Africus walked on the practice field. Today they would practice his five plays. He knew the plays cold already. He had even tweaked them, to the dismay of Coach Jones. He had watched film with the other wide outs, and together they studied the defensive tendencies and formations of the Maryland team. Africus saw things they never would see.

Jones called Africus over to speak with him. "Look, there are too many folks here today. I am not going to run your plays. We will have you practice downfield blocking. And have you practice protecting Pierce. I would have you throw the football, but that would create a quarterback controversy. Next week, you throw the ball," Jones said as he left Africus to the graduate assistants, who demonstrated blocking techniques to Africus.

Africus's first block was a take-down of the all-conference rush end. The whistles blew. "No holding or tackling on offense, Africus!" the offensive line coach bellowed out from his two-hundred-fifty-pound frame.

Africus was a quick study. He held no more when blocking. He was steadfast, like the lion before the hunt, until the ball was snapped. No false starts for him, ever, he stated to himself. He learned each rule and play after one rendition.

Africus watched the defense on every play and quickly absorbed the play calls, formations and responsibilities of each player group. *The tendency to step out to be the lone hero does not work. It is the team effort that succeeds, just like in the jungle.* He noticed that if there was a breakdown, lightening quick decisions, rehearsed hundreds of times, took over to cover the breakdown, again based on group effort. *My years of hunting and watching hunting will yield high productivity and results on defense. But the coaches are more enamored by my world class speed and elusiveness.*

The whistle blew and there was a break. Players gravitated to him. They could not get enough of his stories of the wild. The Preserve seemed so magical. Some talked about holding one week of spring practice in the Preserve. Mika could arrange that, right? Africus laughed. He felt so welcomed. He was revered, yet still treated like a brother. He relished the comradery. He enjoyed the attention and sparring and combat. He enjoyed the competition that was fantasy to him. There was no life or death decisions. He knew from Haley and Mika the passion of the fans. But they still lived on and still came to the next game after a loss, even a disappointing loss. He did not like to lose, ever, but fear of death was not the driving force. He did not fear failure, he only yearned to survive. He knew more complicated emotions would arrive once he spent more time in such an advanced society. But now, his love for Savannah was paramount. His fondness of his new pride was immense. *Together we will win in battle!*

"Tell us how you outswam the crocodiles again. Tell us more about Maximilion. Why were the hyenas so nasty? Who was Citra?"

Africus laughed and told the story of how he ran from the hyenas only to find himself swimming in the river of crocodiles. He did not tell them the crocs were his friends.

"Citra was a cheetah. Citra saved me more than once, when I was so young. We became friends forever," he explained.

"But Maximilion was my closest friend. He endeared me to his father and his pride. I was part of their family for years. Later Maximilion was leader of the pride, and really the king of the animal kingdom in the Preserve. He and I worked together to keep the Preserve in natural order. Of course, the Kenyan government really allowed the Preserve to remain in its natural state. Animals cannot stop economic and urban expansion. And with land masses shrinking with the rising water levels, there is increasingly less land for the animals," Africus seemed to lecture somewhat as he drifted back to the Preserve from the bright lights of America.

"How can you talk to lions? Hard to believe," a skeptic fired in.

"I don't! It's all communication at a different level. Let's leave it at that."

"Reports of extreme lion intelligence have been around for a few years now. Obviously, you tapped into that intelligence. Maybe you can help humans find a more binding and meaningful relationship with the animals who share this world with us," Pierce piped in, jutting his chin out in defiance and pride for what he had researched since the game.

"Yes, they have extremely high intelligence, and superior communication abilities, as do the wolves in America and porpoises in the seas," Africus advised, beaming with a smile.

The skeptic sat back reflecting. Then the whistle blew. Practice started up in earnest. Africus switched to defense. On the first play, he held Pierce in his arms. The green jersey was on. Africus let him go.

"I can tell you much about the lions," he whispered.

Practice ended. The team headed to the team dining facilities. The food was plentiful, but carefully laid out for each position group to maximize their prescribed nutrient levels and caloric intake. The team members had almost perfect body fat percentages, and tremendous energy at each practice. Conversations were prolific. It was an excited team. The future seemed bright. A tall task was still ahead, but win or lose, the team felt excited to be playing for another conference title.

"Hey Africus, Haley said you can bust loose in song and dance, too," a big offensive tackle blurted out, laughing boisterously.

Africus laughed, and then looked around the room. Over in the corner was an old broom. He went to the corner and picked up the broom. So much music of the day was digital and computerized. Singers sang with the computerized back-up music of guitars, acoustics and drumbeats. But old movies of the 1960s with guitar playing band members and screaming, idolizing girls still were ever present in the minds of the youth adoring culture.

Africus picked up the broom and started playing a mock guitar. Soon he started singing some songs from the 1960s, not recognizable to most of his team members, but sounding so hip and fun. Haley had played these songs so often when he was at the Preserve that he knew them verbatim. Some of the players knew the songs and started singing along. Soon Africus showed some of his dance moves that he used to show to Haley to make her laugh so hard. The team was soon on its feet and dancing and singing in loud chorus. Laughter was everywhere. A new video would soon go viral.

News of the festivities spread quickly throughout the campus. The temperature was cold, so students headed into the basketball arena. Let's have a sock up, a cheerleader screamed out, and E-messaged to her long list of contacts. The sock-hop message lit up the E-world of the Jefferson City campus. Girls searched for white socks to wear and off-season sundresses. Guys had plenty of socks, but wore jeans and white tee shirts, but the modern ones, that tucked perfectly. The gymnasium was soon packed with students. Some neighboring high school students found their way in as well. There was no music yet, but plenty of singing.

Haley had heard of the commotion. She had the music for this event, she knew. She texted Africus with her plans. "Go for it," he responded heartily.

Africus ran to the dormitory where Savannah lived. She was immersed in studying for an Economics exam. He hugged her and told her about the singing and dancing he had done, and about the sock hop.

"Let's go have some fun!" he yelled. This type of fun was all new to him. Savannah sensed his extreme excitement and floundered for the appropriate attire.

"There, that sundress is perfect, white with sunflower patterns!

She agreed and found some athletic white socks to wear. No fifties bobby socks, they weren't made anymore. Together they ran to the gymnasium, half freezing. Africus had his ranger jeans on, blue denim, just like the old days.

Africus and Savannah entered the basketball arena to a deafening roar. Many faculty and coaches and administrators had arrived and sat up in the stands to watch and witness the frolic and simple fun. Haley right on cue, pumped in her "Haley music" over the loudspeakers. At once, hundreds of students started dancing with all their energy and hearts. Shrieking and shouting at the top of their lungs, the students sang out the words to the songs, or words that sounded close to the words.

Africus headed to a platform at the end of the gymnasium. He and Savannah were suddenly the lead vocalists in an imaginary band. The students roared in approval. Delirium was setting in. The energy level was so high, and decibel level so high, it rivaled an actual volleyball championship game. The whirlwind of old-fashioned fun, the kids called it, lasted for two hours. Haley's tapes ran out. Haley sounded the maternal alarm for everyone to go back to their studies and get a good night's sleep. The students were exhausted of energy and all headed back to their dormitories and apartments in good order. Smiles of exhaustion were everywhere.

Africus held Savannah tightly in his arms. He gave her a kiss, and the students cheered as they left.

*What a night!* Africus thought.

# 49.

*Saturday, December 6, 2025*
*Chicago Stadium*
*Chicago, Illinois*

AFRICUS STARED UP into the bright stadium lights overlooking the football field. There was a light snow falling, and the wind was howling. This was the coldest day he had ever been a part of. The cheerleaders were dressed in heavy pants and coats, but still looked great he thought. Steam blew from the mouths of the players on every breath. He had never seen that before. The stadium was packed, half red, and half black. Maryland ended up favored, as they were undefeated. Their fans thought a tourney berth was theirs even with a loss to the upstart Nebraskans, with their two pre-Africus losses. Oklahoma fans thought otherwise and were rooting for the Nebraskans. Nebraska State fans knew they needed to win to get in. Even with Africus, a win seemed daunting. Africus had read how Maryland had the speed on their defense to swarm tackle the speedster. And he was still light, part of the nutrition program for only one week, and inexperienced and with a limited playbook, the commentators all noted. And Maryland had a week to game plan with the nation's best coaches.

*Little do they know*, he thought pensively.

Africus walked to the sideline for a warm cup of coffee. All eyes and cameras were on him. He saw the stands and saw their eyes. A quick shimmy.

The crowd erupted. The Marylanders noted the frivolity, and their determination heightened. They banged their hands on their thigh pads in protest. The Maryland cheer-leaders did not join their protest but jumped in jubilation at the quick shimmy. It was Africus, larger than any football game, they intonated. The Maryland football players' intensity only grew larger. The Maryland head coach, on the job in his second year, after replacing yet another legendary Maryland coach, exhorted his team. They roared loudly.

Africus returned to the playing field. The roar brought back memories to him as well, including the fight between the hyenas and the lions that ended the life of Maximilion. Suddenly, this was the lions vs. the hyenas for him. The game of survival seemed all too real once again. His focus intensified as well. He held back his roar for now. The enemy was before him. His pride was with him. It was time to fight, not play. He sensed the Marylanders were of equal fight and intensity. He would need all of his instincts to survive.

Gavin Blocker sat up in the press box with the who's who of the sports entertainment world. He opened his blog.

*The E-ratings for this game are expected to smash records, other than the records still held every year for the Professional Football Association Championship Game. The E-cast behemoth, EBC, is E-casting the game over numerous platforms, including through its affiliate, the National Sports Network. The game is set up for VPR, like the Professional Football Association. Maneuverable 360-degree visual capability is available for all fans on their viewing* devices. *Fans everywhere clamor to follow Africus live during the game. He is hooked up for the Nebraskans. The All-American defensive back for the Marylanders is hooked up for Maryland, as are both of the quarterbacks. I think next year VPR will come to other college sports, including lacrosse. Yes, fans want to follow Savannah Stewart, the American Girl Superstar, too.*

*This is going to be an intense game. The Maryland team has been screaming all week about the attention the upstart Nebraska State team, with their new super hero from Africa, is adorned with. The African Boy Legend is a star from the savannahs and jungles in Africa, and such an amazing story. For so long he was all fantasy. Now he is here in the flesh. Nebraska State fans everywhere are thankful to Shannon Garrison for her work in making this happen. And of course, if two Nebraska State alums were not in the Preserve, he would not be here either. Thank you, Mika Williams, and wife, Haley Andrews. But here we are. Maryland is a touchdown favorite. The most predicted score is 21-14. Maryland has a fearsome defense, but Africus should be good for a couple of touchdowns, the prevailing talking heads have determined. I personally think it will be a fourth quarter game. I can't pick a winner. It's too close to call for me. How will the cold weather impact Africus?*

*The crowd is totally amped. Africus did a shimmy shiver of some type and fans went crazy. The fans are evenly split. It should be awesome! Signing off."*

Haley sat in the stands. Next to her was Mika Williams. He had made a point to finally come to America after hearing of Africus's return. *Thankfully, they let me go.* He thought about the armed men who had detained him briefly the week before. Shannon had given her ticket up for Mika. But Shannon was two rows behind them with another ticket. She was texting her new beau, Gavin Blocker repeatedly. She had an empty seat next to her. It was for Gavin to stop by during the game.

Africus sat on the sideline. Maryland won the toss and deferred. Maryland took the wind for the first quarter. The crown roared again as the kickoff sailed to the ten-yard line in the bitterly cold weather. The Nebraska State kick returner struggled to return to the twenty-yard line. The wind was howling directly into his face.

Pierce took his team to the field. Africus watched in an anticipation. The crowd screamed for "Africus". Pierce handed off to Joseph multiple times. Nebraska State picked up two first downs, but was stopped on the fifty-yard line, fourth and three. Coach Smith had won some field position, and pleased, elected to punt. The punt was successful, angling away from Maryland's star punt returner, the All-American defensive back, on the ten-yard line.

Maryland took the field with their All-American quarterback from western Pennsylvania. He was a throwback, with the best and most accurate arm in the game. He was fast and elusive, as well, but seldom ran, only scrambling to buy time to unleash the fury from his arm. The receivers were fleet, and rangy. They were hard to stop. *Nature is certainly helping the defense*, Africus thought. The Maryland running block backs, as they were called, as they blocked so well for their leader, the quarterback, were also able pass catchers. They ran hard but were not viewed as a threat up the middle. The Maryland run game was carefully crafted and orchestrated to complement the passing attack. It often was very effective.

"They think you ordered up the wind, Africus," Jones screamed to him above the howl of the wind and the roar of the crowd.

"Ha, let them believe. Birds of prey, maybe, but not the wind!"

Jones left. A little disheveled at the comment.

Maryland attempted a run play but was stuffed. The Nebraska State fans yearned for a third down, expecting Africus to arrive for a pouncing sack. The Maryland quarterback on the next play decided to play Africus himself. For the third time all season, he took off. He wasn't touched until the Nebraska State fifteen-yard line and fell forward for more yards. First and goal at the Nebraska State six. The Maryland partisans were frenzied. "Who wants Africus!" They jeered.

A play later one of the behemoth tight ends ripped the ball out of the frigid air for a touchdown. 7-0 Maryland.

Nebraska State went three and out. Nebraska State partisans wanted the quarter to end to get the wind behind them. The punt only sailed thirty yards. A fair catch at the Maryland forty-five-yard line.

Smith looked at RIP. RIP shook his head no. Africus watched the exchange and stayed on the sideline. On the first play the wind took the football and it sailed long on a deep post. The receiver was well-covered. *It would have been a close play,* Africus mused.

Second down, the running block back took a well-designed screen pass down to the Nebraska State thirty. The Maryland sideline shimmied in defiance. Africus could only chuckle to himself. Nebraska State fans booed the taunt.

Nebraska State's defense bowed. A wind aided field goal kick sailed through. 10-0 Maryland.

Nebraska State took the ball on the twenty-yard line after a poor return. Nebraska State managed two first downs with the rugged running of Joseph to end the first quarter. The Nebraska State crowd was anxious for more. Africus stared up into the crowd. He knew where Haley was seated. He found her. And there was Mika. He smiled broadly. *Mika is even here.* He swung his eyes to the student section. *There is Savannah in the first row with her lacrosse teammates. She is so pretty in her winter-parka, and red cheeks from the breeze. I wonder if Minimilion is following the game in the Parallel Dream Universe? Or Essence?* Then he thought of the meeting next week. Maybe Mika was here for the meeting. *A distraction for now. Focus.*

"Africus time!" Jones bellowed out. "Go!"

Africus ran to the field to start the second quarter with an extra hop in his step. He almost tripped in the excitement. His fierce determination at the beginning of the game was temporarily halted by the spectacle of the event. *It is just a game. Have fun.* He turned on his VPR devices. Around the country his fans erupted.

The Nebraskans huddled. A pass play was expected with Africus in the game. Pierce called out "Minimilion", one of the plays for Africus. Pierce could audible to run Joseph instead if Maryland went crazy in their coverage of Africus. Africus lined up wide right. Pierce was right handed. He liked throwing to the right side of the field. Maryland knew this, too. Maryland lined up their best cover corner on Africus-the All-American defensive back. He was six-foot three, just a shade shorter than Africus. Behind him was a cover three. But Maryland kept the line of scrimmage stacked, too. *The play should be a pass to the tight end to the left side of the field,* Pierce thought. But then an All-American linebacker lined up across from the tight end.

Pierce went to the line. He had no choice but to audible. The Maryland defense dropped out of cover three. It was too late for another audible. Joseph took the handoff and was stuffed for a loss of one yard.

Africus stayed in the game. The coaches called in the same play. No audible. Pierce took the snap, he faked a handoff to Joseph, and dropped back to pass. The blitzing All-American linebacker was on him in no time though. He flung the ball. It was tipped by the linebacker and intercepted by one of the defensive linemen back at the Nebraska State thirty-yard line. The Maryland partisans roared in relief and approval.

Smith and Jones huddled on the sideline. RIP was rallying his defense. The Nebraska State crowd was quieter.

The wind stiffened, and Maryland could only manage one yard, and with the win against them, they were out of field goal range. The Maryland punter stuck a perfectly angled punt down to the five-yard line.

Nebraska State took over. The Maryland coaches covered the edges and triple covered Africus. Jones and Smith saw the defensive alignment and called in a run.

Joseph plowed up the open middle to the twenty-yard line. He took the ball again to the twenty-eight. Maryland seemed content to let him run. Africus played the decoy multiple times. Nebraska State marched to the Maryland thirty-eight-yard line, with a crucial third and four. Joseph was tiring. Nine carries in a row. Smith expected an all-out blitz.

Pierce dropped back into the shotgun. He caught the snap and ran to his right. Africus had run down the left sideline with three defenders surrounding him. Pierce saw his other receiver open for the first down. He fired the ball. The wind lifted it long.

10-3 Nebraska State trailed after a long wind aided field goal. Nebraska State was on the board. Maryland ran out the clock to end the first half.

Gavin Blocker opened his blog.

*Grueling first half in these horrid winter conditions. This truly is the windy city. Neither team could defeat the wind. Maryland used the legs of their All-American quarterback to set up their only touchdown. The Nebraska State D stiffened after the Pierce interception, yielding only a field goal. The fans are still lively in the frig-*

*id cold. Africus has been mostly a decoy. They are triple and quad-ruple covering him, content to let Joseph pound away. Pierce has yet to complete a pass. He had a chance late in the quarter but over-threw his target. I see Mika Williams sitting with Haley Andrews, and Shannon Garrison is near them. Shout out to them. There are Africus signs everywhere. Many proposals for marriage! There were some crazy young women in sundresses and old-fashioned bobby socks dancing and singing to start the game. They are now in win-ter attire. Too cold! Expect more of the same in the second half. Sign off."*

Maryland elected to kick again in the second half and chose the wind. The Nebraska State offense was stifled to start the third quarter. On the ensuing drive, Maryland drove to the Nebraska State twenty-yard line. Two plays later it was third and eight. RIP nodded to Africus, his first defensive appearance. The Nebraska State fans exploded. Maryland lined up a tight end and a running block back across from Africus to help the left tackle. Surely, the quar-terback would roll to his right as well. Africus watched with intense focus. The sound of the crowd and the wind now only whispered. The bright lights dimmed. He was in the savannah again. The hyenas were at war. He was with his pride. He was the king.

The ball snapped. The great Maryland quarterback had looked at Africus before the snap. Their eyes had met. It was enough for Africus to read his fear. The quarterback raced to his right. Africus exploded off the line, pass the slower footed tight end and left tackle. He maneuvered across the running block back with strength and agility. He bore down on his prey. The stadium was at a fever pitch. He enveloped the quarterback before he could even take his throwing arm back to spiral a ball to his wide-open receiver in the end zone. The two crashed to the earth. The ball squirted free. The crowd roared. Africus had recovered the

fumble in one fell swoop. But to no avail. The whistle had
blown as the quarterback's elbow had touched the ground
first, as replay confirmed. Fourth down and fifteen. Maryland kicked the field goal. Maryland 13-3.

Nebraska State stalled again in the ferocious wind but
burned clock with three first downs. Joseph had eclipsed
the one-hundred-yard mark in rushing. Only the Michigan
running back had accomplished that feat against the rugged
Maryland defense.

Maryland took possession after the punt and drove to
the ten-yard-line, before stalling and kicking a field goal.
Maryland 16-3. The clock ran to 0:00; the fourth quarter was
about to begin.

Nebraska State started with good field position after the
ensuing kick reached only the twenty-yard line. The kick
returner took it to the Nebraska State thirty-five. Smith
stayed with Joseph until his team reached the fifty-yard
line.

Africus came into the game. The call was maximum protection, two tight ends, two blocking fullbacks. Africus was
the only receiver, back off the line in the slot to the right.
Maryland had plenty of back support with six defensive
backs. Two cover corners were on Africus at the line. Three
safeties were lying in wait. A third corner protected the
weak side. The crowd was restless and waiting. The ball was
snapped. The cover corners pushed Africus within the legal
bump area. One corner slipped, and Africus broke free with
his quick burst. The other corner followed in pursuit. Africus was the hunted, but he was the hunter, too. Africus
knew the play. It was the no play. Just get open. He saw one
of the safeties waiting for him down the right sideline. The
other safeties protected the middle of the field.

Africus broke diagonally across to the middle of the field
toward the two awaiting safeties. His blinding speed was

shortening the time frame for Pierce to unload. Pierce waited. Africus was soon on top of the back pedaling safeties. He juked to the right but bolted to the left. He blew pass the safeties. The cover corner chasing him had fallen three steps behind. But the other cover corner, the All-American, suddenly was doing an Olympic sprint down the left side towards the goal line. He did not even go after Africus. The corner had seen Pierce heave the football towards the left goal line. It was a race to the pylon. Africus watched his adversary. He cocked his head slightly to the left and saw the pigskin had been released. Pierce fired early right before the powerful rush end finally broke through to crush him to the frozen tundra. Pierce felt intense pain, as his shoulder crumpled underneath him. He listened for the crowd reaction. He counted to three slowly. That was the ball flight time.

Africus dialed in his angle of attack. He was a few paces behind. The Maryland All-American, with blazing speed and superior ball-hawking skills, had the lead. Africus knew an interception would be a fatal blow to his team. The crowd now roared in anticipation of the upcoming duel. Across America fans were witnessing the duel in VPR. But the noise quieted again for Africus. He heard the sound of the Waterfall. He saw the face of Maximilion. And in the corner of eyes, he saw two eagles soaring above the field, not noticed by the focused crowd. His gears shifted. He now was full throttle. He seldom ran full speed. There was the need for balance and change of direction, and 360-degree focus. But he had to close the gap. The Nebraska State fans saw the burst of speed and screamed even louder. The Maryland fans roared more loudly in defense and protest. Soon the two athletes were on a parallel track, the ball was sailing, but any more speed and both of them would overrun the ball. Africus followed the movements of his adversary. He had watched his ball hawking skills on tape. He anticipated the jump, and the quick hands to the ball. The defender turned at the five-yard line and started his ascent into the air. The ball was always his, and only his. He had so few chances to catch balls, as so few teams ever threw his way. *Close it down right here*, the defender thought.

But Africus now had the advantage. He was taller and stronger. He calculated his move based on instinct and preparation. He twisted and elevated higher into the air. He shielded the defender from the ball, and with his powerful paws swiped the ball into his chest. He kept turning in a complete turn and landed on his feet. He ran into the end zone and away from the defender. He handed the ball to the tired official, who finally made his way to the end zone. Half the stadium continued its roar; half was silent.

Savannah was thrilled. Her mind raced to what might happen next spring in lacrosse. Then she was back in the present.

The extra point made its way inside the left goal post. Maryland 16-10.

The Maryland coaches knew a long drive by them and a field goal would likely end the game in their favor. It appeared Pierce was done. The freshman back-up quarterback had not taken a snap all year. So, Maryland pulled pages from the Nebraska State playbook, and went on a time draining long march down the field with short passes and runs against a tiring Nebraska State defense. The Nebraska State crowd roared on third downs, but mostly just watched the relentless march. The Maryland crowd anxiously hung on and cheered for each first down. Africus came in on third downs, but Maryland never passed the ball, and ran away from his side of the ball. Finally, fourth down. It would be a thirty-five-yard field goal. Normally, this was an easy chip shot for the Maryland kicker. The crowd hung in the balance.

Nebraska State had a player back deep to field the kick if it was short.

The snap was made. The holder fumbled the ball and took off around the left end. He was uncovered and rumbled pass the first down marker. Nebraska State fans were stunned. The lone defender in the end zone ran to protect his turf. The holder cut sharply to his left, and the defender lost his balance. Touchdown! Maryland 22-10. The extra point was missed.

Africus entered the game as the kick returner. The Nebraska State crowd again geared up its cheers. Maryland purposely kicked the ball out of bounds. The ball was on the Nebraska State thirty-five. 0:45 left. All three timeouts were left. Two titanic scores and an onside kick in between were needed.

Africus came in at quarterback. He looked at the Maryland defense-nine in the box. *They are expecting me to run.* Africus called for the snap. He glanced at his slot receiver. There was no rush. He dropped back. His slot receiver was five feet eight inches but had the quickest feet. He had cut to the sideline, and with the defender's eyes locked in on Africus, he bolted down the field. He was open. The safeties were transfixed by Africus as well. Africus never looked down the field. He feigned to be looking for a running lane. The Marylanders were not going to lose their gaps.

Africus stopped and planted his right foot. He fired a strike to the slot receiver. Just like the countless strikes he had thrown to Mika. The ball entered the howling wind and floated. It was only a question of the speed of the slot receiver. The cover safeties frantically ran to catch up, hoping to stop a touchdown if the catch was made.

The ball floated softly into the awaiting hands of the slot receiver. He cradled it into his right arm, and then covered it with his left arm as he saw the fleet safeties descending upon him. There was a huge collision at the goal line. Africus watched the Nebraska State receiver fall into the end zone and hold onto the ball. Africus raised his hands above his head and then pointed to the sky. Yet another thunderous roar filled the night. But the kick sailed to the right. Maryland 22-16.

The all-important onside kick was next. Coach Smith sent Africus in next to the kicker. It was a play they practiced on Friday. Confidence was high on the Nebraska State sideline. The whistle blew, and the kicker hit a fifteen-yard pitch that was lifted up by the wind and over the first line of receivers. Africus darted by the Maryland players who were watching the ball but not him. He was first to the ball and plucked it out of the air. He cut quickly to the left and sprinted towards the sideline. The Maryland receiving team was now the hunter. He was the hunted. His vision was circular. The attackers were all around him. The wall of the sideline caged him in. He could not use the field behind him; he had to press forward. He cut back to the left, as a phalanx of Maryland soldiers were about to engulf him. Four defenders were now out of the hunt as they collided and fell.

He had already outrun the five receivers lined up to catch the onside kick when he captured the ball. Two defender/hunters left. Both ready with good angles for the kill. But Africus rushed right at them freezing them for the next move. He burst between them as they converged and easily broke their arm tackles. He danced towards the goal line but slowed to use of some clock. He finally stepped over, watching his coaches shouting and screaming for him to finish the job.

Pandemonium swept the entire state of Nebraska. The sideline was a sea of moving flesh, jumping and screaming. But the kick remained. As did 0:15 seconds.

The crowd was silent once more. This time the kick was good. One more play.

The kicker was jacked and pumped. Africus saw his breath firing from his nostrils. Africus watched the kick sail through the end zone.

Maryland's offense came on the field. Africus lined up as the ultimate cover safety. Nebraska State blitzed, and the Maryland quarterback was sacked. Timeout Maryland. 0:04 seconds left. One last play. The Maryland quarterback managed to heave the ball downfield. But the mighty wind slammed it down. Game over.

Nebraska State was the Conference of the North champions. The tourney awaited.

Africus watched the two eagles fly away from the stadium away from the city. *Good-bye, my friends. Somewhere, Minimilion is pleased. Hopefully, somewhere Maximilion is pleased. And where is Essence. Oh, and where is Savannah.* But he knew also the meeting was on Tuesday.

Gavin Blocker opened his blog. Short and sweet.

*NEBRASKA 2025! What a great year for the state and our conference champions! And for that matter, all of America. The rip-roaring of the twenties continues!*

Gavin headed for the empty seat next to Shannon. When he reached the seat, he embraced her.

*Oh, dreams do come true!* She thought with glee.

# 50.

Tuesday, December 6, 2025
*Farmhouse*
*North of Jefferson City, Nebraska*

T HREE BLACK LARGE SUVS were parked outside. Five U.S. secret service agents in black suits and armed were standing outside the Barn. It was the same Barn where he had met Savannah. Africus walked by them, nodding. He did not like their guns. But he understood. They were protecting the King. The King had secretly asked the President for their protection.

He entered the Barn. Savannah was there talking to Anne. To the side, was an elderly man with white hair and considerable girth. He recognized him. *The King of England.* Another man with lifeless dark eyes, stood next to the King. *Society man.* A third woman, adorned with a black trench coat, with her hair tied tightly under a cap, a scarf wrapped around her neck, and dark sunglasses covering her eyes, stood across the other side of the Barn. *Another secret service agent?*

Africus hugged both Savannah and Anne. Savannah hid her annoyance. Anne blushed.

Africus did not bow before the King. He approached him and shook his hand.

The man with no name stood silently in protest.

"He has no name," Anne explained.

"Yes, head of the Society," the King acknowledged.

"King George VII, it is an honor to be in your presence. But I have a question for you. If a boy shall have pulled the sword of King Arthur from the stone in the modern day, shall he not inherit the Kingdom of England?" Africus toyed with the King and man with no name.

The man with no name was stunned. He looked at the King. The King said nothing.

"I have pulled the sword from the stone! I have held Excalibur in my hand and held it up into the sky to defeat a mighty enemy. I have worn the crown of King Arthur. Savannah, or Providence, when she is in Africa, has worn the crown of Queen Guinevere," Africus finished, his eyes firm and steady.

A defiant man with no name glared at Africus and spoke to him in a condescending voice.

"We have already been informed of your discovery. At least most of it. The Treasures belong to the Crown. You must return the Treasures to us immediately. You would not exist, but for our experiment and genetic engineering. You were born to a surrogate mother and were the genetic combination of a great English athlete and an extraordinary scientist. Both have passed. We owe you nothing, and the Kingdom of England is not yours. Only the first to pull the sword and his ancestors are in the true line of Kings and Queens. Whether past lives are real, or the Parallel Universes are real, is not relevant. You must turn over all of the Treasures back to their rightful owner, the English Crown. Your life means nothing to me. I created you!" The man with no name angrily finished his theme, breathing heavily, as perspiration moistened his brow.

"I had not heard my biological mother had passed. Is that true, Anne?" Africus asked, watching Anne's reactions carefully, but not intimidated by the demeanor of the man with no name.

"It is not true. I know she is still alive. But she does not know her genes were ever used to create such a special life!" Anne rebelled and blurted out.

The man with no name was caught in a lie. But he did not care.

"I do not fear the Society. And you are powerless to access the Cavern in person in the Parallel Real Universe or the Real Universe," Africus baited the man with no name.

"You do not know who you are dealing with! We will bring you to Kenya, and you shall deliver us the Treasures. We know you have that power! You retrieved the Chalice. Maybe you live, maybe you don't. We will not protect you either. You know too much," the man with no name had lost his composure.

"I think not," said the American in a tone of authority and confidence, as she removed her sunglasses, scarf and trench coat. "Africus will be under the protection of the U.S. government, as will Savannah Providence Stewart. And I am the President of the United States, so you have my word on that!"

Africus and Savannah were stunned. The King knew it was the President. He embraced the President in a warm greeting. President Parsons continued.

"Africus, U.S. intelligence has tracked you for years. We heard about this meeting. I am a highly interested in the Cavern, but more so in the Parallel Universes, wormholes, Portals, and alternate realities. The technology in those space and time dimensions could launch our space program and world society to unknown heights! When the King asked for protection and told me he was meeting with you, I demanded to attend the meeting. The King had no choice," the President stated again with authority.

Africus looked at the President and nodded. She smiled broadly, and he returned the smile. He then returned his gaze to the man with no name.

"Man with no name, your bark is louder than your bite. You are nothing more than a hyena. The ancient days of the power of the Society are not the same. The Society lost the Treasures and has been struggling ever since. And the Crown, not the Society, has proprietary rights to the English Treasures. Princess Anne has disclosed this to me. So, I shall not take orders from you!" Africus reprimanded the man with no name, with a quick nod to Anne.

He walked over to Anne and grabbed her hand. They walked to the King.

"King George, I can indeed retrieve the English Treasures for the Crown. But Essence, Savannah, Anne and I would like to take you to the Cavern of Lost Treasures in the dream state, by way the Parallel Dream Universe. You will then have your confirmation of their existence. When we return, we can discuss what to do with the English Treasures. It is my view that they should stay in safekeeping in the Cavern. The other Treasures, including the Treasures from Atlantis, must stay. I do not wish to be King of England, so fear not. But let us see if you can pull the sword from the stone!" Africus took control, with some levity at the end.

The King was dumbfounded. *They are real. The Treasures are real! King Arthur was real. After all these centuries, we are so close! They are within our grasp. The experiment worked. The lions are intelligent. The Cavern is real. But wait. I still am only relying* on the word of this African Boy Legend. And he must still lead us there.

"Where is Essence? the King queried, breathing heavily. Savannah handled the question.

"Essence is here. She is our spiritual guide and guardian of the Cavern. She is one of the Special Beings from the Great Realm, heaven to you, that can access the Cavern through the Passage through the Portal. You, of course, have heard the legend of the elven-like monkeys. They are Special Beings, as well," Savannah explained. "If you listen, you can hear her. She is the spirit of the horse, over there, and has listened to all of this!"

Soon Essence spoke. Even the President and the man with no name could hear her thoughts.

The man with no name finally had heard enough. He buckled and wept. His ornery demeanor melted away. His life-long pursuit was so near in hand. He had to hope and believe it was finally true. *I am at the precipice of my dream. My dream is folding into reality. I like these Parallel Universes. I am a believer. I believe. I am no longer in servitude to the mistakes of my predecessors in losing the secret location of the Treasures!*

"Your grace, our mission has been accomplished. We have protected the sword for centuries, and now it is back at your doorstep. It was always safe. There is no more need for the Society. The sword and other Treasures are yours to dispose of or use as you wish. I, for one, agree with the young Africus that safe keeping in the Cavern is likely the best place for them. It has been an honor serving you, My Grace!"

Africus placed his hands on the man with no names shoulder, as the man knelt before his King.

"You have been a loyal servant. The King shall certainly reward you. You may come to the Parallel Dream Universe with us."

"Thank you, my African Boy Legend!"

"And am I to stay here alone? The leader of the free world?" The President beckoned, hoping for an invitation, but still trembling at the words of Africus and Savannah and the thoughts of Essence.

"Yes, join us," Essence soothingly cajoled her.

Essence lead the convoy into their dream state and on to the Parallel Dream Universe. The King, the President and man with no name were anxious at first but were calmed by the spirit of Essence. Soon they entered the Cavern. The King was in total awe at all of the Treasures. There were more Treasures than either he or the Society had accounted for. There were Treasures from other time periods on earth and other dynasties and cultures. The President gasped at the Treasures from Atlantis. Essence gave her a brief history and tutorial about Atlantis. Princess Anne held her father's hand and brought him to the sword in the stone.

"I shall not take it out of its rightful place," he whispered to her.

Anne then took the sword from the stone, to her father's astonishment.

"I shall one day be Queen. I have no brothers, so I am the rightful heir. And I have pulled the sword from the stone!" Anne proudly announced.

Anne gazed at Providence, thinking of her African name.

"But I will never wear your crown, Queen Guinevere! I know that is you. And King Arthur, welcome back to your Kingdom! Your crown shall always remain safe in this Cavern!" Anne exhorted.

"And what of Excalibur?" the man with no name asked the King, while looking at Africus.

Africus looked at the King.

"I have decided. I would like to keep the Treasures here, including Excalibur," the King said solemnly.

"King George, Essence says it is your and my joint decision, you as the rightful owner and I as the trustee. I agree with your decision. The English Treasures stay in the Cavern for now, for their safe keeping. But I believe that going forward, the Crown and I shall jointly undertake the stewardship and custody of the English Treasures," Africus further advised, his shoulders held back and head high.

"I agree. How shall that be done? The Crown has no power to enter the Parallel Dream Universe or to gain Passage through the Portal to the Parallel Real Universe," the King humbly asked.

Africus looked at Essence and heard her thoughts. He then gazed at Anne. "Essence shall grant your daughter, Princess Anne, full access to the Cavern through her dreams in the Parallel Dream Universe. And more importantly, Anne shall be permitted to enter the Cavern in the Parallel Real Universe by Passage through the Portal with me or with the assistance of Essence, at her request. She shall be your agent to fulfill the Crown's custody obligations of Excalibur and the other English Treasures. Anne, I trust that you will leave Excalibur in its safe haven here. She will be permitted to return the English Treasures to England, at her discretion, but subject to my consent, and while you are alive, your consent. At her death, Anne's rights shall be passed on to the next monarch of England, and such person shall be contacted immediately by Essence. This right shall pass for centuries, or until all the English Treasures have returned. On my death, Essence shall take my spot as joint trustee and custodian and must consent to the return of the English Treasures. But Excalibur! It should stay for a while. It is powerful. Merlin made sure of that! Is not that right Essence!" Africus gazed at Essence.

"Yes, I was the guide to Merlin, indeed, as I am to you now. I was once the queen of Atlantis, too, the wife of King

Atlas V, when Atlantis met its doom. And Maximilion, the king of the lions and the savannah, and long-time friend and guide to Africus, was once King Atlas V! Yes, Excalibur has great power. It is now under your stewardship, Princess Anne. Protect it safely," Essence admonished, proud that her true identity was now revealed.

"I accept that plan," the King said excitedly. "But I would like access to the Cavern via the Parallel Dream Universe, too!" He exclaimed in excitement.

"Yes, that will be fine," Essence agreed.

Princess Anne was overwhelmed with excitement, but also with the impending enormous responsibility. "I accept this duty with great honor. Father, I will protect the Treasures."

"Man with no name, you shall continue to serve the Crown. Father, he shall be knighted, Sir Man with No Name!" Princess Anne requested of her father.

"Indeed, so it shall be said, so it shall be done," the King agreed.

"Should I return the chalice to the Cavern, Africus asked the King.

"No, let the conspiracy crowd have some bait. I think the Cavern is safe. And Providence, we have made peace with your father. He after all, was working for the Society, and has withdrawn from his duties, with an oath of silence. We hope that you will take that oath as well," the King directed his question to Providence.

"The secrets have always been safe with me. No one believes my fairy tales anyway. Who would have thought that dreams do come true!"

Princess Anne saw the love in Providence's eyes and turned to speak to Africus. "I love you, Africus, but you shall be betrothed to your one true love, Providence! I am fine with that, but if you do marry, I want to be maid of honor!" Princess Anne concluded with a flair and smile.

The President had remained silent, but piped in. "And what of the Atlantean Treasures. The knowledge and crystals and history could be of such momentous importance to the world!"

Essence spoke to her mind only. *Let it be. For now, they are under the control and ownership of Africus and shall stay in the Cavern.*

*All right. But not forever!*

They all returned to reality.

# 51.

*Sunday, May 24, 2026*
*Foxboro, Massachusetts*

AFRICUS MADE HIS WAY to the front row of seats at a jam-packed stadium. As he strolled down the aisle, dozens of young boys and girls screamed and took selfies with him. It took a while, but he finally got to his seat on the center line of the field. Chants of we love you Africus filled the air. His blonde hair was still long, and tied into a pony tail, with a head band wrapped around his forehead. But now his focus was on Savannah. He sat next to Haley Andrews and Mika Williams. They were back together, living in Nebraska on a recently purchased farm north of Jefferson City, the one with the Barn.

The crowd roared as the lady Nebraskans made their way on the field. Africus heard his hit song "Hey Safari Girl!" blaring over the loudspeakers. He recorded it shortly after the National Title Game for football. The lady Nebraskans seem to swing and sway with the African rock beat, as the commentators called it. Savannah's blonde ponytail was wrapped in a red and white ribbon, as were the ponytails of all of her teammates. The name Africus was spelled out on each white twist of the ribbon. Africus began to gyrate to the beat of the sound. His image was cast onto the big screen, and screams erupted. Africus smiled an even bigger smile. He was relaxed. He had brought home his national championship! Now, it was time for the player of the year, Savannah Stewart, now known to everyone as the American Girl Superstar, to do the same. She had broken the national scoring record for points, with an equal number of goals and assists. Her first-year teammate, Clay, had scored almost as many goals, and was playing in front of her adoring New England fan base. Africus watched them pass it quickly back and forth to each other, as if they knew exactly when the pass was coming before it was fired. *What a tag team.*

The North Carolina team was ready in their light blue and white uniforms, made by Spiritis, as were the Nebraska State uniforms. They were undefeated and had the nation's best goalie. Africus watched them play smothering defense in warmups on their own prolific attackers. They were tall, strong, and fast. They had long wingspans, and covered wide swaths of ground, he noticed. But he saw some of the attackers staring at him and snickering. Some smiles were directed his way. Over on the other side, he saw Savannah take notice of the snickering and his gaze at the pretty Carolinians. He saw Savannah hug her friend, Bethany, too. She was on the Carolina roster, but had been sidelined with a hamstring pull the entire tournament. Bethany had still made all conference as a freshman defender. *Savannah was so proud of her. And Becca was an all-conference attacker at Stanford!* He mused.

The teams took to the sidelines. The rosters were announced. The crowd was giddy. The stadium was full to capacity. The men's national title game was on Memorial Day at 2:00 P.M. It was sold out as well. Lacrosse, with its speed and high scoring, had captivated the otherwise virtual world adoring fans. It was a break from virtual reality, as so many professors dreamed about these days. The day was fair, with 74 degrees' temperature, Fahrenheit, and a light easterly breeze from Massachusetts Bay. A few white cumulus clouds drifted by. A dozen drones whirled above, eyeing the festivities below. Included among the drones and camouflaged magnificently were two eagles. Africus saw them and waved. Dozens of fans looked skyward, as if on command when he looked up. The eagles blended in too well. But a couple of young boys saw the eagles and hooted loudly at them. More and more people noticed the eagles. Soon a rumble reverberated across the stadium. The eagles were spotted. The memory of the eagles landing on the goalposts at the National Title Game for Men's football was deeply ingrained in the sports minds of American fans. The eagles opened their wings just after the winning field goal for Nebraska State sailed through the uprights as time expired, with Nebraska State winning 38-35 over the powerhouse champion from the Conference of the East. As if on cue, the two eagles landed on the football goal posts which still stood on the end zones and out of play for the lacrosse game. The North Carolina coach hung his head momentarily. The goalie swung her stick loudly against the goalposts of her lacrosse goal with a ferocity and intensity that garnered the attention of the gazing eagles. Africus watched her continue her drumbeat. Even the lady Nebraskans heard the steady pounding of the drums. The Greek and Trojan armies appeared ready to battle, Africus thought, in his ever-present Parallel Dream Universe. He had been called Hercules, in the National Title Game, by the announcers for the National Sports Network, known as NSN, based on his physique and looks. And his leadership and athletic skills were deemed just as legendary. Africus led his army into battle against the fierce opponent and won. He had five sacks, and ten tackles for loss. He scored three rushing touchdowns and threw for two more. He outplayed the National Player of the year, the opposing quarterback, a consensus Number One pick in the upcoming Professional Football Association draft.

The NSN team was on hand to E-cast this game as well. Africus saw an attractive sideline reporter heading his way.

"Africus! Africus! How is it to watch a National Title Game that you are not the main attraction!" She yelled above the din.

"I am a Nebraskan! And a fan of the American Girl Superstar!" he yelled back, smiling broadly, as usual these days.

"Did you invite the two great eagles?" She yelled even louder as the fans around the camera screamed at her presence.

"They are invited, of course! To bring good spirit to the game!" He responded, laughing.

"Will you return to Nebraska State in the fall? Will you travel to London to find the Princess Anne? Will you return to your Parallel Dream Universe? To the Preserve in Africa?" She battered him with questions, as she swung her long dark hair across her shoulders.

Haley turned to the reporter and grabbed her mike.

"Mika and I are here in the States. The Preserve is in good hands with a new Preserve team of rangers and guards. And Minimilion has moved to a new Preserve in Northern East Africa. So, I think Africus will return to the States with us. Time to watch WLAX!" Haley yelled while pushing the reporter away.

Soon the game began and the reporter headed up the aisle, staying within striking distance. The network had a special camera trained on Africus for the game as well. Ratings were important, and Africus drove ratings, like no one had before.

Africus watched as North Carolina won the draw. Their midfielder flew down the field but was matched stride for stride by Savannah. Savannah veered her away from the goal, preventing a shot on net. North Carolina went into a play. They passed the ball around the circle four times. The play clock was winding down, and the star midfielder on the opposite side of Savannah found a crease and exploded into the scoring zone and blasted a shot into the back of the net. Twice more, the same midfielder won the draw and scored, to give the Carolinians a 3-0 lead.

Timeout Nebraska State.

Nebraska State had fallen behind 10-3 in the National semi-final game to Florida. A furious comeback to tie the game resulted in overtime, at 10-10. The New England crowd had gone into a frenzy over the pace of play and scoring barrage late in the game. Nebraska State won 12-11 in the second overtime, on a snarling whizzing shot by Savannah into the top right corner of the net as time expired. North Carolina watched in anticipation, as they had knocked off Nebraska State's fellow Conference of the North foe and champion, Maryland: 10-9. Nebraska State's only loss of the season was in the semi-finals of the conference tournament to Pennsylvania 7-6, and its smothering defense. Maryland took down Pennsylvania in the finals of the conference tournament, 6-5. In the regular season, Nebraska State had upended then Number 1 Maryland, 12-11, in double overtime, in Jefferson City, Nebraska, at its state-of-the-art lacrosse stadium, in front of 20,000 adoring fans. But the anticipated rematch had not occurred. North Carolina had taken care of that.

Africus saw the anxiety in Savannah's face. He was seated behind the bench of the lady Nebraskans. He searched for her gaze. But she was locked into Lindsay's words. Haley Andrews had stepped down from coaching to focus on recruiting and WLAX administration, so was not down there to help her sister coach. Lindsay had hired two coaches from Trinity and Bates, from the New England Small College Athletic Association, as her new highly paid assistants.

Savannah drew a deep breath after the words of her coach. Clay smacked her on the back. Savannah stepped into the draw circle, as Clay stepped away for the first time. The whistle blew and the two top midfielders in the nation battled for control of the ball. Savannah snatched it out of the air away from her taller opponent and fired a freeing pass to Clay streaking down the sideline on the left side away from the benches. Clay was soon upon the awaiting All-American goalie. Before the goalie could flip her stick in defense, Clay whirled a behind the back-blind pass to Savannah who found pay dirt at the bottom right corner of the net, as the goalie missed the ball for a kick save by less than an inch. The goalie slammed her stick in disgust, and screamed at the Nebraskans, "no more!"

Africus watched in awe. He stood and roared with the young Nebraska State students sitting in the first row in front of him. Members of the soccer, volleyball and track women's teams all had the pristine tickets for the front row.

The teams then traded multiple goals to end the first half 7-5, North Carolina.

The reporter returned to see Africus.

"We have a live feed from London. Princess Anne is watching the game at the palace! We are told she is with a new boyfriend, a prince and billionaire from a neighboring Eurozone state! What do you say about that? She is likely listening live!" The reporter was excited at her breaking story.

"Hi, Princess Anne! I hope you are enjoying this marvelous American game! Maybe, I will see you in the Parallel Dream Universe! Ha!" Africus laughed again.

"Are you not jealous! She is a Princess! In the latest E-Love magazine poll, the world favors the Princess as you paramour, 54-46 percent! What do you say to that?" She conspired to knock him off kilter with the new late breaking poll results.

"Love is a splendid matter. It finds itself. Savannah is sensational today! She is the American Girl Superstar!" Africus smiled broadly again and did a little shimmy shake. The fans screamed and drowned out the reporter.

The reporter then blurted out that she was free to see Africus, too. He kissed her hand, and she left shaking and smiling.

The game started up. One of the soccer girls sent a written note to Savannah. It informed her about the conversation about the Princess. Savannah looked back, glaring at Africus. Her eyes turned steely, and more competitive.

By the time the final whistle blew the game was knotted at 10. Another overtime thriller. The eyes of a nation were on the game, and the games new number one fan, Africus.

The first overtime was a stalemate at zero goals. Twice, the All-American goalie had stymied hard shots from Clay after deft passes from Savannah.

Soon the clock was winding down, with North Carolina holding on for the final shot in the second overtime. The North Carolina bench and partisans rang out the countdown of the clock. The All-American midfielder for North Carolina, had six of her team's ten goals, and had matched Savannah's goal total of six. Savannah guarded her with a ferocious intensity.

Africus looked on with equal intensity. He recalled the intensity of Maximilion in the fight with the hyenas. He hoped for a better result. "Ten, nine, eight..."

With a flash of super human speed Savannah broke free down the sideline. The North Carolina midfielder was momentarily stunned by the departure of her rival. She wanted to beat Savannah Stewart for the winning goal. *Where is she going!?* The Carolinian was runner up for the National Player of the Year award, and as a Senior, would not have a chance to win it next year.

In her hesitation, Clay burst forth, and swiped the ball away. She lofted a pass over a tall North Carolina defender, that landed softly in the streaking Savannah's stretched out stick. Two other North Carolina defenders raced to protect their goalie. They had a head start and a better angle. The Nebraska State attackers were flying down the field as well. The crowd was hysterical and frenzied. Africus watched with a calmness. The players seemed to slow down. Reality slowed down. He thought he was entering the Parallel Dream Universe but wanted to see the real-world results. He saw the eagles take off and soar. He saw Savannah double nod to the eagles, as did the crowd. The eagles soared high above the stadium above the drones.

Savannah had run past the two streaking defenders and her own attackers. There were only four seconds left. But there was a remaining defender near the net who came out at her with a vengeance. A powerful body check was coming to push her wide.

Savannah's mind flashed back to the National Title game for men's football. Africus was flying down the field with a powerful and swift safety about to launch at him at the thirty-yard line. Africus had appeared to momentarily float into the air, and then dramatically swivel cut to the right down the sideline for a touchdown. The safety had grasped at air and fell harmlessly to the ground.

Savannah reenacted the famous move but cut left into the center of the field. She was past the defender. Only the clock and the All-American goalie stood between her and a National Title.

The clock struck one second. Savannah ripped off a shot. The ball was in the net. The game was over. The red light went on. The crowd rocked the stadium in a mass rhythmic motion, other than the fans of North Carolina. Soon the crowd hushed. The referees had to review if the goal was timely scored.

Africus waited anxiously. The replay was on the big screen. He saw the ball was securely in the net, before the clock expired. The referees soon agreed. Pandemonium hit the field as the lady Nebraskans rushed their goalie. Africus sighed in relief. He watched in admiration as the Nebraskans soon lined up and shook hands with the Carolinians.

The trophy was presented. Lindsay Andrews hoisted the trophy high above her head. Next the All-Tournament teams were announced. Only Savannah and Clay made it from Nebraska State, but Savannah was tournament Most Valuable Player. Finally, rings were given to the champions. Spiritis had donated the rings, and had sets made for each team. The final inscription of Champion was added to the Nebraska State rings, and runner-up to the North Carolina rings, immediately after the game. Mika and Haley smiled at each other as Shannon Garrison presented the rings on behalf of Spiritis.

Savannah hugged her counterpart at North Carolina. Africus watched, as the two had a lengthy conversation. They hugged again on departing. The goalie also congratulated Savannah. They hugged as well. *Good sportsmanship by all,* Africus thought.

Africus and Haley walked on the field. The crowd went silent. Savannah stood in the center of the field. She was exhausted. Her goggles were off, and she took off her head band and ribbon, letting her hair flow freely in the now stronger easterly breeze. Her legs ached, and her upper arms stung with bruises. But she felt little pain in her joy of victory. And there walking towards her was Africus. She had not seen him since he won the National Title in football for Nebraska State. He had gone back to Africa to secure the Preserve under its new leadership and administration. He trained the new rangers and guides and relocated Minimilion to another preserve in northern East Africa. Mika had helped in the transition. Mika departed back to Nebraska in April. No one knew for sure if Africus would return. And then there was the visit by Princess Anne. She was still perplexed and unsure about that visit. But now, here he was at the game. Here he was walking towards her. The crowd hushed even more.

He approached her more slowly. Haley stopped, and let him advance without her. Time seemed to slow again for Africus, and Savannah felt the same. The crowd noise had fallen silent in the real world, and the Parallel Dream Universe they appeared to be heading for.

Finally, Africus reached her and grabbed both of her hands. He looked deeply into her eyes in the flesh, not on a smart device, and not in a dream. The crowd now started to murmur, then rumble. He leaned over, and together they pushed forward for yet another totally magical kiss. The crowd now roared in delight. As their lips departed, they hugged each other ever so tightly. They clicked their National Championship rings together. They looked up into the sky and watched the two eagles look down at them and then soar off into the sky towards the north. They held hands and departed the field, as the crowd continued its crescendo.

When they were alone under the stands, Africus reached into his pocket and pulled out an ancient antique ring. He put it on her right ring finger.

"The ring of the Queen!"

Savannah cried in joy and remembered her daydream of the summer before. *"Dreams do come true!"*

# 52.

*Saturday, June 27, 2026*
*West Kenya National Wildlife Preserve*

AFRICUS LOOKED AT PROVIDENCE sitting in his range vehicle. They laughed for the hundredth time together that day. They both were in ranger gear. The weather was hot, but not humid. A breeze made it somewhat blustery.

Africus whispered to Providence. She understood. He found the tracking device on her shoe. He turned off the one inside her smart device. He found one on the range vehicle. He had already found one on his shoe. They each had to have a tracking device surgically removed by one of the guards from the back of their neck. A secret nighttime strike had been made without their knowledge. But they each felt itchy and sore in the same spot and suspected it may have been a planting of a tracking device. The guards took out Africus's first. *Surely enough*, Africus had thought.

"Now we are free. The listening devices are turned off or removed. The tracking devices are removed. I will place them on some wild animals. There, those two zebras. They appear to be mated. They will run together. If we split up the devices, the followers would be suspicious," Africus pointed to the two zebras.

He walked over and put a tracking device safely into one of each of their ears. Off they ran together toward the northern part of the Preserve.

Providence spoke openly. "It must be the President trying to track us. The President called me this morning!"

Africus gazed at her lovingly. "The President is obsessed with Atlantis. She desperately wants to lead the world to colonize Mars and Europa and beyond. She is surreptitiously trying to find the Portal by following me. The President called me, too. She wants to start a commission on parallel universes! She wants me to be on the commission. Top scientists from around the world are clamoring to be on the commission. She is extraordinarily smart. She thinks the recent breakthroughs in quantum computing are a start. She thinks the Atlantean crystals utilize quantum theory and time crystals. She said that she has been to the Parallel Dream Universe on her own! She wants me to take her to the Cavern, too, by Passage through the Portal into the Parallel Real Universe. She is obsessed with Atlantis! She did not add Atlantis to the charter of the commission, though. That is her secret. She is on fire now! Whoa!"

Providence walked from the range vehicle.

"I think I may see it," she whispered again, straining forward.

"Yes, your mind is rapidly catching up to mine! It is a mile from here. Let's go," Africus said, happy at her rapid ascent into the intelligent mindset of the Parallel Dream Universe.

They walked hand in hand for a mile. Soon they were at the edge of the Deep Jungle. They saw an opening, clearly marked with a trail. Neither had seen it before.

The Great Ape soon appeared. Providence looked at Africus in amazement.

"We can hear you, Great Ape!" She exclaimed.

The Great Ape looked at each of them. He waved them to follow him.

Africus was pleased. It appeared Providence had gained the Knowledge, too, of the Passage through the Portals. He saw the deep green of the forested jungle, and strong smell of the jungle floor. They entered the Deep Jungle on their own. And they were fully conscious. Then a white zebra appeared. It was Essence.

"Providence, you have advanced so far spiritually and mentally, that you now have access to the Waterfall and Paradise. You came here on your own. The Great Ape was here to greet you, not take you here. You now see the entrance, just as Africus and I do. You have the Knowledge to gain Passage through the Portals to the Parallel Real Universe. The entrance through the Deep Jungle you walked through is indeed a second Portal, but to Paradise and the Waterfall. The Waterfall is also the rear entrance to the Cavern. Africus knows that. Up the Waterfall and you reach the Cavern!

"And there is one more secret for you to know. Africus, you were the unborn son of King Atlas V and me, his Queen in Atlantis at the time of its fall. You were to become Atlas VI. Maximilion, the lion, as I told you before, was once King Atlas V in Atlantis. Providence, you had just been born in Atlantis. You and Africus were supposed to meet.... But we all perished in the fall of Atlantis! Your mission was unfulfilled. Then you met in England and built a new kingdom. Now, you meet again! You now have a chance to fulfill your true destiny! But for now, I think you both should enjoy the Waterfall and its splendid beauty for a few days!" Essence laughed.

Providence and Africus reached the Waterfall. Providence scaled the rock pillars up the rear cavern behind the falling waters. She wanted to dive in but waited. She saw the two eagles on their perches on the rock formation high above the landing she was on. *Amazing and wonderful.* Soon Africus joined her with Essence.

"This is truly Paradise. Enjoy its beauty and wonder! And I have a special guest for you, Africus!" Essence stated.

Minimilion walked from the other side of the landing and raised up and placed his large paws on the shoulders of Africus. Their eyes met in gleeful recognition.

"The northern Preserve in East Africa is good. There are no poachers and no hyenas! The animal kingdom is good now. You can return to America. But please come back once a year. We may need you again," Minimilion reported.

"Hello, Providence! Nice to see you again!" Minimilion roared lightly.

"Yes, I am so happy to be here again, in the Parallel Real Universe. I am so happy to be here at the Waterfall and Paradise!" Providence smiled in joy.

Soon Essence, the eagles and Minimilion retired to other parts of the Paradise. Africus took the hands of Providence, and then embraced her tightly. He turned towards the Waterfall, and dove a wonderful dive deep in the awaiting lake below. Providence followed suit. They swam for hours, and fell ever more deeply in love.

Finally, they slept. They entered the Parallel Dream Universe and traversed to the Cavern of Lost Treasures. They played King and Queen with their crowns. Africus again drew the sword from the stone and held it high. They kissed passionately. Africus thought of Atlantis, and Healica and Exotica. Soon slumber took over.

The next morning, they were fully refreshed. Providence leaned over to Africus.

"It is time to take our next journey!"

Together they looked at a trail of steps climbing the walls next to the Waterfall above.

"Indeed, the yellow-brick road!"

And off they went in search of Treasures and their next destiny.

# Postscript

The author's pen name is King Atlas V. King Atlas V was once an Olympic hero in Atlantis. He later became King of Atlantis in its final months to save the continent from destruction. He did not succeed. Atlantis was a highly developed and technologically sophisticated society. In the 2020s and beyond mankind will match that success in technology. Hopefully, mankind will not make the same mistakes as the people of Atlantis did. This was a tale of the early lives of two remarkable individuals, once destined for life on Atlantis, whose true destiny now lies in the future beyond 2025 and their early fantastic lives!

# ABOUT THE AUTHOR

The author now lives in Florida with his wife of over thirty years. He has keen interests in the future, legends and myths, the dream world, alternate realities, healers and, sports. He plans on writing of the dreams of the fantastic and the mythical, so that others can enjoy those dreams. Check out other books written by the author at: https://www.amazon.com/author/kingatlasv.

www.ingramcontent.com/pod-product-compliance
Lightning Source LLC
Chambersburg PA
CBHW031031030726
47497CB00004B/1087